A Moment In Time

Lyn Marill

A MOMENT IN TIME

iUniverse books may be ordered through booksellers or by contacting:

iUniverse
1663 Liberty Drive
Bloomington, IN 47403
www.iuniverse.com
1-800-Authors (1-800-288-4677)

Because of the dynamic nature of the Internet, any web addresses or links contained in this book may have changed since publication and may no longer be valid. The views expressed in this work are solely those of the author and do not necessarily reflect the views of the publisher, and the publisher hereby disclaims any responsibility for them.

Any people depicted in stock imagery provided by Getty Images are models, and such images are being used for illustrative purposes only. Certain stock imagery © Getty Images.

ISBN: 978-1-5320-6926-0 (sc)
ISBN: 978-1-5320-6924-6 (hc)
ISBN: 978-1-5320-6925-3 (e)

Library of Congress Control Number: 2019902141

Print information available on the last page.

iUniverse rev. date: 04/04/2019

To Kathleen and Reileigh Doweck, with love,

and to Micaela Tyson, for inspiring me to write this story

You were the one
I wanted most to stay
but time could not be kept at bay.

—Lang Leav, *Lullabies*

PROLOGUE

There is a strange duality to time. The moments you wish could linger seem to accelerate, while those that bring pain and anguish move slowly, creating a feeling of timelessness. Then there is that one moment when your life is completely changed.

I could not alter events, only accept their existence. Connor was gone, and he'd taken all my tomorrows with him. How was I supposed to continue to live? Was it possible for a person to die from a broken heart? If so, I would welcome it. Despair gripped me in a cloud of disbelief.

Why did you leave me? You told me you'd love me forever. Why did you lie to me? Why? The words screamed through my mind until the excruciating reality of loss slipped into a place beyond thought.

Staring into the space that had been my bedroom these past two years, I noticed the suitcases, packed days before in preparation for my flight to New York. I recalled the exhilaration, tinged with uncertainty and apprehension, that I'd felt about my future at the time—a future I would share with Connor. It didn't matter anymore. I'd promised Dad I would be okay, but I knew it was no longer possible; I would never be okay. He'd sacrificed so much to put me through college. My determination to be a Broadway actress hadn't diminished, but the passion I once felt had faded. Connor wasn't going to be with me.

Dad had tried his best to comfort me. "The heartbreak will pass," he'd said. "Broken hearts mend, and life goes on. Memories fade and wither in time." I didn't think he believed it any more than I did.

The sound of children giggling in the play yard echoed through my open window. Their laughter stung my soul. It was doubtful I would ever laugh again.

Willing my arms and legs to move, I went through the ritual of brushing my teeth, washing my face, and pulling my mass of hair into a ponytail. I dressed in jeans and a sweatshirt. It didn't matter what I looked like anymore. I called a cab to take me to the airport. Dad wanted to drive me, but I refused his offer. At nineteen, I could find my own way. We'd said our goodbyes in the morning before he went to work.

Dad had fought back tears. "I'm sorry, Micaela, for what you've been through. I wish I could make it all go away."

"I know, Dad," was all I could say. There was nothing he or anyone else could do to change what was stolen from me.

Dad was leaving our home in Florida as well. He was moving back to Toronto and taking a position at the university. Toronto was a lot closer to New York than Florida, which meant we could be together on holidays. It was some comfort knowing that I wasn't leaving him behind, but it didn't even begin to ease my sense of desolation.

I gazed around the apartment. Everything looked the same, but it wasn't the same. The images of Connor sitting on the couch, laughing, kissing me by the front door, and sneaking into my bedroom when Dad worked late slipped away like ghosts in the morning sun. I was glad to be leaving all the reminders of what once were the happiest moments of my life. Connor and Micaela didn't exist anymore.

The buzzer announcing the cab startled me. One last glance, a deep breath—then I left. I would do my best to move on but never forget the past year and the amazing man who had filled every day with more joy and love than I could ever possibly conceive.

I did move on, and, in time, I did forget—almost.

CHAPTER 1

Now

There were moments in my life, usually before I fell asleep, when memories came unbidden into my mind. Often just bits and pieces but sometimes entire segments. If I tried to link the segments together, the images blurred and huge chunks of darkness filled the spaces in between. Those were the parts that created the most anxiety, and I learned that if I wanted to completely forget and get on with my life, I needed to convince myself that Connor never existed and that it had all been a dream. In time, I'd gotten pretty good at it. Thirty years had made me an expert in avoiding the memories.

Sleep was impossible. My mind filled with images faster than I could deal with them. Every attempt to replace them with thoughts of my daughter, Jess, or my granddaughters failed. I was anxious, and I knew why. I had a doctor's appointment in the morning, and I wasn't feeling positive about it. I listened as a branch, blown by the wind, knocked against my bedroom window. The constant tapping only increased my anxiety. I gave up trying to sleep, turned on the light, and reached for the magazine from my bedside table I had been looking at earlier.

Normally, I didn't read magazines about famous people, but the daughter of an actress I had worked with was on the cover, and I couldn't resist the gossip, even though I knew most of it was complete garbage. It didn't help sidetrack me from my memories; it only allowed them full access to my mind. I stopped trying to fight them.

I recalled the years I'd spent in New York, struggling with acting lessons and auditions. I still felt it had been an endurance test. I'd been trapped in a spiral of grief. My greatest difficulty had been hiding my secret. That was something I would never forget, no matter how hard I tried. I still felt the overwhelming guilt. Aunt Florence, who I lived with for nearly a year, figured out what was wrong and provided a solution—one I didn't want, but it offered the only possibility of ensuring my future as a singer and Broadway actress, at least in my immediate future. When I thought about it now, I was grateful, but the guilt would never go away.

The story about the actress didn't hold my interest, but it did mention her once-famous mother. I remembered her fondly. We worked together on my first movie. I couldn't recall why I'd accepted the part. I'd always preferred the continuity of live theater, and it took me a while to get used to working out of sequence. Broadway had been my dream since I was twelve years old, after my parents took me to see the stage production of *My Fair Lady*. The recollection of my singing songs from the musical to my parents and their clapping made me smile. I was so lucky that they encouraged my dream. Telling your parents you wanted to be a Broadway actress back then was like stating you wanted to be the first woman astronaut or the first female president. The response would simply be an indulgent smile or maybe all-out laughter, but you would be told that it was almost impossible to make a reality. I realized now how fortunate I had been when my mom told me that I could be anything I wanted; all I had to do was want it badly enough and keep focused on my dream. My dad agreed.

I knew it had been my performance in the Broadway hit *West Side Story* that caught the attention of the movie's producers. I remembered being flattered but couldn't recall exactly why I'd agreed to take the part. My best guess was that I was attracted to the role of a woman with a dual personality; it felt like my own life at the time. I'd changed my name to Michelle Lewis in an effort to reinvent myself, but when I visited my dad, I was still his Micaela; those were my favorite moments. He had been my oasis from my grueling schedule and the demands of fame.

I glanced at other articles in the magazine. Not much had changed over the years, just the names of those involved. The first time I'd seen an article about myself and a picture with my leading man, who was supposed to be my new love interest, I was appalled. I had been asked to have my picture taken with him for a publicity photo. I loathed the guy. I soon learned not to read—or even look at—those magazines, and I hoped Dad hadn't seen any of the trash headlines that lined the shelves of the local convenience store and supermarket he went to. If he did, he never mentioned it. The disturbing part to me was that, although grossly exaggerated, some of them were partly true.

I would like to think I handled success well, but I didn't. I surrounded myself with industry friends who drank too much, smoked too much, and traded relationships like children traded toys. I succumbed to their influence, living each day in a state of semiconsciousness, rationalizing my newfound demons by pretending it was all temporary. I'd tell myself that once the movie was completed, I would return to Broadway. Instead, I accepted other movies. I was addicted, not only to the numbing effects of alcohol but to living my life in a fog, blinded by fame.

The wind had picked up more momentum, and rain drumming against the window now accompanied the tapping of the branch.

Like my memories, it persisted until I gave in and allowed the sound to lull me into a hypnotic-like trance. The magazine fell to the floor, and I switched off the light, pulling the covers up over my head. Tomorrow I would face whatever fate had in store for me. The last thought I had before sleep claimed me was of Jack. I saw his face clearly. It was the face I remembered from our wedding day. Even though we were now divorced, and my feelings were anything but kind, I was grateful he had offered me what I thought of as a normal existence as a wife and mother. I remembered how charismatic he was, a pleasant change from all the superficial, self-absorbed men I'd been dating. His charm and persistence had won me over, but what really sealed our relationship was a positive pregnancy test. That thought led me to my beautiful daughter, Jessie Katrina Webster, and I knew it was because of her that I'd made the doctor's appointment, but I was afraid I'd be faced with another moment that would change my life forever.

CHAPTER 2

Dr. Elizabeth Marshall, my family physician, sat at her desk, her face expressionless as she spoke the words that suspended time again. "Mrs. Webster, I'm sorry, but the tests confirmed the tumor is malignant."

I'd hoped for a different outcome. I thought I was prepared for the worst, but the reality of cancer left me numb and paralyzed. I was only forty-nine. Cancer isn't selective. It didn't care how old I was.

I sat motionless, staring out the window at a slate-gray sky, and watched in stunned silence as raindrops slithered down the glass, forming small pools on the window ledge. They reminded me of tears. I closed my eyes as my own tears welled up and spilled like the raindrops down my face. The intensity of my breathing filled the air around me. Then I heard a string of words, a litany of sound. I opened my eyes to see Dr. Marshall was speaking. I tried to focus on what she was saying.

"Are you all right?" she asked.

Her question seemed ridiculous. How could anyone be all right after hearing they had cancer? I didn't answer. My lack of response was ignored as she continued outlining the different options I might consider. She informed me her office would make an appointment with an oncologist to discuss a plan of approach; then she wrote something on a notepad.

She handed me the note. "In the meantime, here's a prescription for painkillers, if you need them."

Her matter-of-fact tone annoyed me. What if the situation were reversed and *she* had just learned her life was threatened? It seemed that professional detachment replaced compassion. I asked the obvious question. "How long?"

She explained the complexities of bladder cancer. It sounded straight from a textbook. "It's difficult to predict an outcome," she said. "You will have to discuss this with the oncologist."

"And without treatment?" The idea of chemotherapy repulsed me.

Her facial expression said more than words. I detected disbelief. Pushing her chair back, she came around to stand beside me. "The sooner you get treatment, the better your odds." She left without any expectation of a response.

I retrieved my raincoat and umbrella from the reception area and headed for the coffee shop next to the clinic. I did not want to go home.

The cafe was crowded with people taking shelter from the rain, which was coming down in sheets. Spotting a vacant booth in the corner by the front window, I quickly claimed it. While waiting for the server, I watched people texting or talking on their cell phones. It was a common scene, but it felt somehow wrong. I recalled my teenage years when we spoke face-to-face. If we were lucky enough to have mobile phones, they were the size of shoeboxes and not easy to transport. Perhaps if teenagers had had cell phones in the eighties, they would have done the same. I was glad we didn't. A memory of a similar coffee shop in Florida invaded my mind. I pushed it back, where it took its place among the many other memories I avoided. I checked my own phone and found two messages—one from my daughter, Jessie, and the other from the college where I taught the History of Theater. Both could wait. I knew why Jess was calling. The thought of telling her the results of my tests was overwhelming. She was only twenty-four, old enough to comprehend how devastating cancer could be but not mature enough to handle it. I was fifteen when my mother was diagnosed with ovarian cancer— another one of those moments that altered my life. Watching how sick she'd been after the chemotherapy and radiation treatments was instrumental in my decision to forgo that form of treatment. There was a naturopath not far from my home outside Toronto. I would make an appointment with her, and Jess would just have to accept my decision.

The rain stopped, and people left to go about their days. I watched as they hurried past the window, still clinging to their phones. The server took my order: a coffee and a cheese sandwich. Probably not a wise choice, considering the cancer. A woman who looked to be in her late sixties approached my table.

"Excuse me. I'm sorry to bother you, but my husband and I"— she paused to indicate a man of about the same age sitting across from her—"were wondering if you're Michelle Lewis. If you're not, you sure do look like her."

There was no point denying it. Over the past twenty years, since I'd retired, if anyone requested my autograph, I would simply tell them they were mistaken. It got easier as I got older, but in the beginning, when I returned to Toronto, I was forced to wear disguises in public. I didn't care anymore. Perhaps having cancer and sensing the fallibility of my life changed my outlook.

As far as I was aware, no pictures had been taken of me since I was thirty. I was still slim and wore my hair shoulder length, but the once-blonde curls were now a sandy brown; my nose, which I'd always felt was too long, seemed more prominent; and small lines had formed around my eyes. Although the changes weren't drastic, I'd aged significantly enough to deny any resemblance to the person

I'd been so many years ago … but I didn't. I simply answered, "Yes. I'm Michelle Lewis."

The woman was ecstatic. She waved her husband over. "It is her, Tom." She fumbled through her large handbag.

Tom joined us and held out his hand in greeting. "It certainly is a pleasure, Miss Lewis. We've seen all your movies. You sure were great."

The woman who identified herself as Wendy Fowler, a devoted fan, provided me a pen and the back of a sheet of paper that had a list of food items on the opposite side.

I signed the paper but not with my usual scrawl. I took the time to write their names and clearly wrote *Michelle Lewis* in my best handwriting. On impulse, I wrote, *Thank you.*

After reading it, Wendy appeared puzzled. "What you thankin' us for?"

I thought about it a second. "For caring. It's been a long time."

"Of course we care. We were sad when you didn't make movies anymore," Wendy explained. "We read that interview you did for *People* magazine, sayin' you wanted a private life."

Tom interrupted her. "Wendy, she saw *The Streets Have Eyes* probably five times. No kiddin'. And that movie about the woman pilot at least three."

"Amelia Earhart," Wendy told him. "You were good. Damn good! You should have won the Academy Award and not that kid."

"Thank you, but it was nice just being nominated, and that young girl did deserve it." The memory flashed across the screen of my mind. The nomination was more than I could have dreamed of, and losing to a teenager who had since become a phenomenal actress had felt right.

"Just out of curiosity," Tom said, "is there some other reason you stopped actin'? I got the feelin' there was more to it."

"Tom!" Wendy interjected. "That's none of our business. Maybe she really did want a normal life. All those Hollywood people changin' partners and takin' drugs. It's no wonder she'd want to give it up."

"It's okay. I don't mind talking about it." I had no objection to disclosing my reasons, up to a point. Perhaps another result of my cancer diagnosis. "It's true. I did want a normal life ... the husband, kids, and a home in the suburbs. I was tired of being in the limelight. It wasn't what I wanted originally. It just happened. I wanted to find myself again." I was amazed at how forthcoming I was. "I have a daughter and twin granddaughters."

Wendy looked surprised. "You don't look old enough to have grandkids."

It was not necessary to inform them of Jess's teenage pregnancy, nor my cancer diagnosis. I also didn't add that my husband left me for a younger woman.

"It's nice you got the life you wanted. I'm glad it worked out for you." Wendy folded the notepaper and tucked it into her purse. "We gotta be goin'. Tom has an appointment with a heart specialist. Thanks for takin' the time to talk with us. I can't wait to tell my sister. She's a huge fan too."

Tom held out his hand, and again, I offered mine. He startled me by lightly kissing it. "It was a real pleasure, Miss Lewis. Take care of yourself."

"I'll do my best." I watched them leave and waved goodbye as they passed the window. It felt strange writing *Michelle Lewis* again. I believed by changing my name, I could wipe out my past. I wanted to be an entirely different person, so I invented a personality to go with it. I hadn't been completely honest with Tom and Wendy. The real reason behind my retirement was discovering I didn't like Michelle very much. It had been time to stop and create a new person I liked better.

CHAPTER 3

The first week after my diagnosis, I'd thrown myself into work. The harder I worked, the less I thought about it; the less I thought about it, the more I remained in a state of denial. It was telling Jess that haunted me, so I put it off. I purchased a book online about each stage of the acceptance process. Apparently, I was moving through the first stage—anger! Asking *Why me?* was useless. Who was going to answer? I did what I always did. I vented the anger on myself.

I held the scissors, ready to cut the mane of curls that had been my trademark since I was fourteen. It took only seconds to make the decision and start cutting off large pieces at a time, as if by doing so I might disassociate myself from the woman who had cancer. Anger distorted my ability to reason. Hair fell in chunks to the bathroom floor. I stared at my reflection. The anger had been satiated, but shock and remorse took its place. There was barely enough left to tuck behind my ears. The satisfaction I'd hoped for never happened. I threw the scissors at my image in the glass shower door. They landed next to my foot without even a mark on the door. It did nothing to subdue my despair. I tried the breathing exercises suggested in the book. By the time I'd done ten deep breaths, I felt more resolved. I couldn't change what was happening to my body, but I definitely had to do something about the mess I'd made of my hair. I called a local salon, and the stylist was able to salvage it. A few gray hairs, once hinted at, were now more noticeable. The short style made my cheekbones more pronounced and my already long neck appear longer. I'd lost several pounds and was beginning to look anorexic. I barely had anything resembling breasts. I never had much to begin with, and no amount of bust exercises worked as promised. It was unlikely anyone would be asking for my autograph now.

Jess loved my new look. She arrived unannounced, minus the kids, and insisted on taking me to lunch. She thought I looked like a "sexy mama", which I interpreted as a reference to my age. It seemed like a back-handed compliment. I let her choose the restaurant. It seemed the perfect time to tell her of my diagnosis, as being in public assured no melodramatic outburst, but I was wrong. I should have been more considerate. Her first response was normal—shock! The book explained I was to acknowledge her feelings, but all the suggestions as to how seemed superficial, and I wasn't capable of acknowledging my own, let alone hers. We cried together, and she went straight into her fix-it mode.

"Cancer is not a death sentence anymore. You're going to see the oncologist, right?"

"I'm not sure. I need more time to think about it."

My response only annoyed her. She looked incredulous. Being in a public place didn't seem to make a difference. Oblivious to her surroundings, she yelled at me, "What's there to think about?"

I suggested the discussion be at a more appropriate time and apologized for telling her such horrible news in the restaurant. I begged off with a headache, which wasn't far from the truth. She agreed to leave it until I felt better but couldn't resist calling after dinner and lecturing me on what she thought was my procrastination. It was her belief that I was deliberately putting off going to the oncologist because I was frightened. I didn't tell her I was considering other options, as I suspected she'd disapprove. We argued, and she abruptly hung up.

It was almost a week before I heard from Jess, and I hadn't called her either. When it came to handling anger and frustration, Jess was like me. We both chose the silent treatment. She was the first to give in. She called and informed me she would be coming over on the weekend, and as much as I wanted to see her and get this cold-shoulder attitude behind us, I dreaded more lectures.

I preferred to spend my Saturday morning reading, but Jess wanted to arrive early, as she had swimming lessons for the girls after lunch. It required a great deal of motivation to leave the comfort of my bed and at least try to look presentable. My reflection in the bathroom mirror told me it would take a lot more than foundation and lipstick to improve my appearance. I wasn't sleeping well, and the dark circles required two applications of concealer. It helped a bit. I wouldn't win any beauty contest, but God bless makeup! I was sure I saw new lines forming around my eyes. I once spent a fortune on creams labeled "anti-aging" when I was married to Jack, who was five years younger; whether they worked or not, I didn't know. I might look worse if I hadn't used them.

I heard the front door open. Jess still had her own key. I took one last glance in the mirror and figured I didn't look half bad for a woman my age with cancer, but I was a far cry from a "sexy mama." I'd chosen a soft, bulky-knit blue sweater with faded jeans to hide the fact I was losing weight.

Jess was grinding coffee beans and removing mugs from the cupboard when I entered the kitchen. She looked nothing like me. Her looks had come from Jack's gene pool: straight, dark brown hair, falling halfway down her back; heart-shaped face; green eyes; and a fuller figure—definitely more endowed than me. Probably the result of an estrogen overload that seemed to be the affliction of most young girls these days, a nice side effect of hormone-laden meat.

"Hey, Mom! Have you eaten?" Her previous anger and frustration appeared to have passed.

"Not really. I didn't feel like it."

Opening the fridge, she located a carton of eggs and removed four. The crisper yielded a few edible items. There wouldn't be much to choose from, as I hadn't the energy to shop in over two weeks. She did manage, however, to find a tangerine and a still-recognizable tomato.

I settled on the stool at the kitchen island and watched as she created her breakfast masterpiece. Not only did she not look like me, but our talents were vastly different. Cooking wasn't something I was very good at.

"How are the girls?" I figured this was a fairly neutral question. Jess's twin six-year-old daughters were neither identical in looks nor disposition. Nora, who was technically the older by ten minutes, looked more like me: the golden curls, fine features, and blue eyes. Jess described her as a girly-girl, all princesses, fairies, and pink frilly dresses. Her sister, Tina, was her opposite: dark-brown hair like her mother's and the same green eyes. Tina hated dresses and loved to draw, do puzzles, and hang upside down on the monkey bars in the park, which did not lend itself well to dresses.

"Nora has a bit of a cold. Tina is fine for now, but if one gets something, you know the other isn't far behind. How you doin'? And don't lie to me."

I nibbled at the scrambled eggs. "No new symptoms. I still have to pee all the time, and I have a lot less energy. Other than that, I'm okay." There was no point in disclosing the pain in my lower back and the nausea that sometimes accompanied eating. She would try even harder to sway me to her point of view. She tried anyway.

"So have you thought any more about what we talked about?" She poured the coffee into mugs and added a small amount of cream to hers but kept mine black.

I hated this subject, but there wasn't much I could do to avoid it. "A little." It wasn't a total lie but having to explain continuously that I had no intention of taking rounds of chemotherapy or radiation treatments was becoming tedious and only added to my stress. I knew her intentions were good, but what about what I wanted? I recalled the feelings I'd experienced when Mom had ovarian cancer. I remembered how sick she'd been from the chemotherapy, how her hair had fallen out, and how frail and weak she'd become. She couldn't even get out of bed and go to the bathroom. It was hearing her constantly throwing up that bothered me the most. I had felt helpless. And after all the suffering from her treatment, she died anyway. Jess had never seen someone she loved in that state, and I didn't want her to. I couldn't stand the thought of her seeing me frail, skin pulled across protruding bones, eyes sunken into my skull, staring blankly, while she wiped vomit from my lips. The cancer would take its own toll; it didn't need to be hastened.

I wanted Jess to respect my decision to try alternative therapies, ones that didn't tear and burn their way through my body. If there was a chance to slow it down, I wanted to take it, and maybe, if I was fortunate, I might be one of those lucky few who actually was cured. I told her what I wanted to do. It didn't go well. She insisted I was making a mistake and tried another tactic.

"Think of the girls, Mom. They want you around a long time. They love you so much. You have to at least try." She was fighting back tears.

A phrase from a *Star Wars* movie popped into my head, and I blurted it out. "There is no try; only do, or do not!" I realized it sounded stupid the moment I'd said it.

"That was lame. This isn't a joke."

"I don't think it's a joke, but a little humor isn't a bad thing. I am trying, Jess, just not the way you want me to."

"God damn it, Mom!" The anger and frustration returned. She looked over at the assortment of vitamins and herbal remedies on the kitchen shelf. "Whatever quack you're seeing is probably filling your head with all kinds of stupid promises about how you can be cured. I'll bet you're spending a fortune on all that useless stuff." She motioned to the array of bottles. "Like, really?"

"Yes, really! She's not a quack. Naturopathic medicine is a legitimate form of health care. I'm kind of surprised at you. You weren't so against it as a teenager. In fact, you were the one who started me thinking about organic food, vitamins, and even herbs. Where did that go?"

Judging by her facial expression, I obviously had touched a nerve. "That was different."

I knew I was only adding to her frustration but had to ask, "What's so different about it?"

"You didn't have cancer then. I think it's important to take vitamins, but this is something a lot more serious than just staying healthy. You need to explore other options. Think of me and the girls. It's not fair, Mom. You're just thinking of yourself. It's simply not fair!"

"Of course I'm thinking of myself. It's my life and my body, and this isn't about what's fair." She'd pushed my buttons. "Was it fair when your father walked out on us for another woman? Was it fair when your loser boyfriend headed for the hills when he found out you were having twins? How do you think I feel, finding out I have cancer at forty-nine years old? Nothing too fair in that!" I took a breath to center myself. "No, Jess, life is never fair." I hadn't included the most unfair thing of all in my list, but it was a deliberate omission. Jess didn't know about Connor.

She slammed her fist on the counter. "It's not the same. You're my mom. I love you very much. What do I tell Nora and Tina? That Nana's refusing to try to get better and probably won't be at their seventh birthday party?"

I touched her arm. She pulled away. "I'm sorry you feel this way. There's no need to tell the girls anything at this point. Sweetheart, life doesn't offer guarantees. You know that. You've had your share of challenges and disappointments, but you've always done things your way, no matter what your dad or I said. Please try to understand how I feel."

Pushing off the stool, she grabbed her purse from the counter and headed for the front door. "I can't take this anymore, Mom. Please, please reconsider."

I decided to pacify her. "I will consider it. Thank you for making breakfast."

She didn't answer. She simply left. I could hear her sobbing as the front door closed. I wanted to run and hug her the way I did when her pet bunny died or when she'd been teased by kids at school, but she wasn't a little girl anymore. Hugs didn't help when the hurt was tainted with anger and frustration. I knew that well.

I gazed around the kitchen. She'd left a mess, a reminder that life kept going, chores needed to be done, and I had papers to grade. My students were still important. I'd decide when the year was finished if I was able to continue. Teaching had been an alternative to my forsaken career, but it never filled the gap left behind.

I cleaned up, watered the plants, and spent the next two hours in my office, focusing on essays. Some were good, some were bad, and some were downright ridiculous, with more grammatical and spelling errors than I dared to count. I had a mixed group. The problem was, my course was mandatory. It was a pleasant surprise when I did find a good essay. That particular student had chosen the evolution of theater from the Middle Ages to modern times—well researched and articulate. She got an A.

I was almost halfway finished with the essays when a wave of exhaustion ebbed through my body. At school, I would drink energy shakes and push through the day until I got home. Exhaustion was part of my new situation. That was how I referred to the cancer, just a new situation.

I opened the containers of supplements and took them according to the chart I'd posted on the fridge. My naturopathic appointment was scheduled for next week, and I wanted to tell her I was following the plan—if not exactly then close to it. Would it work? Maybe … maybe not.

I'd tell myself, "If you are truly serious about getting better, you'll do this." In that moment, I would be motivated. It was better than succumbing to the chemo.

I lay down on the living room sofa in front of the bay window overlooking the front patio and walkway. Two large cedar trees stood majestically beside the front porch, as if guarding the occupants. I loved those trees. I knew I would miss looking at them if I had to be hospitalized. The ping of my cell phone startled me and stopped my pessimistic thinking. I resisted looking at it but reconsidered. It might be Jess, texting to apologize for her behavior. If I didn't respond quickly, she'd be worried. It wasn't Jess. It took a second to register. It was Vini, my dear, outrageous, unpredictable friend. It had been months since we'd last spoken and years since we'd actually seen each other. Life went by so quickly, and time got longer between visits, but true friends don't notice the spaces in between.

I read her message. *Call me when you get a chance. Miss you!* It ended with two large red hearts. I missed her too. She had been a dear friend my last year of college in Florida. We had sworn to meet at least once a year, but circumstances, more than distance, kept us apart. I had no intention of returning to Florida, and she was never financially able to visit me. Even after she relocated to New York fifteen years ago, we rarely saw each other; my fault, not hers. It was difficult being with Vini. It brought back too many memories—the dark ones. On rare occasions when Jack went on business trips to New York, I accompanied him. It had been five years since our last visit. We'd met Vini for dinner. When the conversation hinted at those forbidden memories or they crawled to the surface accidentally, Vini would say something funny to make me laugh. We talked mostly about her new profession. Her transition from hair salon manager to a prosecuting attorney was startling. She'd shared her aspiration of becoming a Supreme Court justice—a pretty lofty goal, but Vini would probably do it. Jack, as usual, monopolized the conversation. He had a colossal ego. We talked about Jess, my job, and her brother, Jason, although conversations involving him would be kept to his interior design business. We would cry and hug and promise to keep in touch. We'd email from time to time but more Vini than me. I felt her love and caring. I hoped she felt mine.

I resolved to call her later when I felt stronger. It didn't take a college degree to figure out why Vini wanted to speak with me. I suspected Jess, who knew Vini's number, had called her with the intention of forming an alliance in support of my taking chemo. I dearly hoped Vini wasn't going to persuade me in that direction. She might try, but I doubted she would press me when she heard my point of view. Vini respected my opinion, even if she didn't always agree.

My gaze returned to my trees, but my focus shifted. Memories of Vini paraded across my mind. I let them flow, knowing other memories would follow. This time I gave in. I was too exhausted to fight them off. And the dreams started ...

CHAPTER 4

Then

I was thrilled when the letter arrived confirming my acceptance into the Dramatic Arts and Music program at a college in St. Petersburg, Florida. I deliberately chose it so I could be with Dad. An opportunity at an engineering firm in Tampa tempted him into accepting a position as head of their Human Resources Department. He wanted a change from being an engineering professor. We both had dual citizenship, so there was no problem making the transition from Canada to the United States. My career choice had been decided when I was twelve, and now at seventeen, it was a driving ambition. I was going to be a Broadway actress.

I understood why Dad wanted to make a life change. Our house in Toronto was too big for him to maintain, and with Mom gone, it felt cold and lonely. It had been a year since she died, and Dad decided it would be better for both of us to start a new life. We would still be together, at least until I graduated in two years. I hoped to move to New York, continue with acting lessons, and try out for small parts in off-Broadway musicals. Dad had contacted his sister in Queens, who agreed to allow me to stay with her until I got on my feet. It would be difficult for both of us when that moment finally arrived, but a lot could happen in two years.

Leaving Toronto didn't bother me. I didn't have close friends, as I spent my summers and weekends taking dance and singing lessons. There had been one girl, Veronica Stanford, who I called a friend for a short time. We spent hours on the phone and going to movies together, but her family moved to California just after my sixteenth birthday, and I hadn't heard from or seen her since. Closing that chapter of my life made me feel like a caterpillar emerging from its cocoon and learning to become a butterfly.

We sold the house and packed our things, and a moving company took our furniture all the way to Clearwater. We drove down; it was kind of a road trip. Dad wanted to make it an adventure, and we stopped at several tourist attractions, played the same silly word games that amused me as a child, and sang along to all our favorite songs that Dad had taped. It was an experience I would remember the rest of my life. Dad had a friend who found us a two-bedroom apartment near St. Pete's Beach. When we arrived, the humidity was so intense not even a cold shower helped for more than five minutes. The air conditioner broke, and it was three days before it was fixed. I practically melted into the carpet. We'd sold or given away a lot of our furniture, but I made our new home look cozy with the remaining possessions. For a month, I was free and looked forward to spending my days helping Dad get settled and attempting to change my very pale complexion to a light bronze. School didn't commence until the second week of August, and we arrived there in mid-July. Unfortunately, Dad had to start his new job sooner than expected. Any plans to familiarize ourselves with the area would have to wait until the weekends. I was okay with it. As an only child, I was used to being by myself.

The month flew by. Dad bought me a secondhand Volkswagen. The color was a cross between pistachio and lime green. It was my first car, and I wasn't going to be picky. He taught me to drive, and within a few weeks, I had my license. I was nervous at first, but it wasn't long before I mastered the streets of Clearwater and the surrounding area. It was the late eighties and not many teenage girls had cars, at least not the ones I'd known.

My first day at college was scary and exciting at the same time. I was grateful for my car, as buses would have been complicated and time-consuming. The first term was fairly easy, and I did well on my finals. My determination to excel was not just for my own satisfaction but for Dad, who was helping me financially. I didn't go to parties, although I had plenty of offers. Dating and romance wasn't important. Any of my free time was spent with Dad. We were both still healing from mom's death. I knew he wanted me to have a social life, but I didn't need anything distracting me from my goal. It wasn't that I couldn't make friends; I just didn't want to … at least not until I met Vini.

CHAPTER 5

It was April. Final second-term exams were coming up. All my evenings were spent immersed in notebooks and writing my term essay. I auditioned for the school musical, *The Sound of Music*, and was chosen from six other candidates to play the lead. I was excited and scared at the same time. I'd always been nervous before my high school plays, but the enormity of this production was different— kind of like going from primary school into high school. I was determined to make an impression. My perfectionism drove me to work harder. Rehearsals were after class and I used my lunch hours to focus on my lines. Vini came into my life on one of those rare hot spring days when I chose to sit outside and eat lunch. I settled on a table near the parking lot and was going over my lines for the fiftieth time when I sensed someone standing near me.

"Do you mind if I join you?"

Startled, I looked up. A very attractive girl about my own age, with skin the color of milk chocolate, placed her tray on the table while taking a seat on the bench across from me. Her long, curly black hair was tucked behind her ears, exposing huge silver hoop earnings that hung almost to her shoulders. Her bright purple blouse with orange detailing along the collar made me appear drab in my practical gray sweater. Full lips lined with bubblegum pink, accentuated with pink lip gloss, gave her a sensual look. Black liner extended out from the corner of her almond-shaped eyes. A little too dramatic for my taste, but it suited her. What really caught my attention were her eyelashes. I envied her those lashes. I had to use at least three coats to achieve a similar effect.

Miss Dark Lashes continued speaking. "My name is Lavinia DeMille. I know it's rather dramatic, but my mom decided to change our last name. Not that Miller was so bad, but she didn't want any association with my father. He was sent to prison for robbing a bank. I think secretly she wanted a fancy name. She took it from one of her stupid romance novels. But you can call me Vini; everybody does."

I wasn't sure what I was expected to say. I opened with, "I'm sorry about your dad." It was all I could think of. Her forward manner was unnerving.

"No problem. It was a long time ago. I don't really remember him. I was two." She unwrapped the paper from what looked like a cheeseburger and took a bite. She continued speaking, even while chewing on the burger, which was, for me, a bit of a turn-off. "What's your handle?"

I wasn't sure what she meant and didn't respond.

"Your name! What's your name?"

"Oh ... Micaela Lewiski."

"You Polish or something?"

I enlightened her. "It's Ukrainian."

"Were you born there?"

"No, but my dad was. I was born in New York, but we moved to Toronto, Canada, when I was two." I knew I had to include Canada, as people here looked at me blankly when I simply said Toronto.

"Wow! That's cool. So you're an American turned Canuck."

I found that term offensive, so I ignored it.

"A lot of Canadians move to Florida. It's become like a retirement community." She took another bite of her cheeseburger. "Do you live off campus?"

"I live with my dad in an apartment near here." I closed my script, sensing I would not be getting back to it before my lunch hour was over. I tried to finish my tuna salad.

"I live just outside of St. Petersburg with my mom, so we're practically neighbors. Your parents divorced?"

"My mom died two years ago." It sounded blunt, but her questions started feeling like an interrogation. I stabbed at a tomato, which insisted on moving every time I tried. I finally nailed it.

"Now, it's my turn to say sorry." She seemed to sense my discomfort and quickly changed the subject. "What are you taking?"

"I'm studying Theater and Vocal."

"That's exciting. Are you going to be a famous actress?"

I wanted to tell her it was none of her business but decided it might seem rude. "I'm planning on going to New York when I graduate. With any luck, I might get a part in something. I prefer musicals, but I guess it's whatever I'm offered. As for being famous, I don't think so."

"My brother, Jason, goes here too. He wants to be a set decorator, but who knows. He changes his mind like I change outfits. In fact, that's why I'm here." She checked her watch—a Mickey Mouse one. "He was supposed to meet me ten minutes ago. That guy couldn't be on time if his life depended on it." She took a huge bite of her burger. "I don't go to this college. I'm taking a beautician course in Tampa. I've always liked doing makeup and hair, so I might as well get paid for it."

Suddenly, Lavinia—or Vini, as she wanted me to call her— stood and waved frantically at someone coming out the side door of the school. He noticed and waved back. There was absolutely no mistaking it was her brother. The resemblance was striking. They both had the same long black curls and facial features.

Vini saw me staring. "A lot of people think we're twins, but we're not. Jason is almost four years older."

They hugged. "Sorry I'm late. Had to call Owen," Jason explained. "He was in a panic about some leak in the living room. You know how he is. It couldn't wait until I got home. Hey, who's this pretty lady?"

"This is Micaela Lewiski. She's taking Drama."

"You in first or second?" Jason asked.

"This is my first year."

"How long have you known my little sis?"

"About a half an hour."

Jason laughed. "That's my sis. You gotta love her. She's always doing that. She brought home stray animals until we had three dogs and four cats. She even brought home some chick she'd met at the mall and wanted her to live with us. Hope she wasn't bothering you."

"No, I was open to company," I lied. "She's actually quite entertaining and delightful." That part was true. I did actually find her entertaining. Although I didn't care for being compared to stray animals or some girl she'd picked up in a mall, I got what he meant. Vini had a big heart.

"I like your name. It's pretty, like you are," Jason commented.

"Thank you." I was usually uncomfortable with compliments but accepted his.

"Don't worry, Micaela," Vini jumped in quickly. "He's not flirting with you. Jason is gay."

"Thanks a bunch, Sis, for letting *that* cat out of the bag."

I wasn't put off, just surprised Vini would be so forthcoming with her brother's sexuality. I'd never known a gay man personally but suspected there were a few in my classes. It was no big deal.

"Discretion isn't my sister's strong suit," Jason explained.

I wanted to put him at ease. "It doesn't matter." I was sure it sounded lame, but I had no idea of the appropriate response.

"Try being a gay man in this day and age, especially a gay black man. Just to let you know, I don't wear makeup or dresses. Drag isn't my thing, but it's not something I shout from the rooftops. People get nervous around gay people. Maybe someday it will change." He checked his watch. "If you want to go shopping, Vin, we'd better get going. I skipped class, but I have to be back in an hour."

"Hey, I've got an idea," Vini interjected as she gathered up her garbage. "Why not ask Micaela to your twenty-first birthday party?"

"You just met her, Vin. She might have plans, and besides, she barely knows us."

Vini didn't give me a chance to decline. She kept insisting. "I know we just met her and all, but I'm super-good at judging people, kind of a sixth sense, and I think, Micaela—if you don't mind my saying so—you seem like someone who needs to put more fun in your life." She nudged Jason's arm. "I'm just sayin' 'cause I really believe it's true, and besides, I really like her. Convince her, Jase."

"I think you're making her uncomfortable. Let her be, and let's get going before we have no time left."

"Come on, Micaela, please think about it? It will be fun. It's at Jason's friend's house on the beach. There will be a bonfire, dancing, and singing. Jason and his boyfriend, Owen, play guitar, and Owen's loads of fun."

I had no intention of going to a party with people I'd just met. "Thanks for the invite, but I have something planned." Then I actually volunteered more information, which was unusual for me. "It's my eighteenth birthday on Saturday, and my dad is taking me out for dinner." Our plans were for Sunday, the actual day of my birthday, but Vini didn't have to know that. I crossed my fingers in the hope my slight alteration of the truth would be forgiven by any power in the universe paying attention.

"Can't you change it? We can celebrate your birthday too. I bet your dad would understand."

Vini's enthusiasm and presumptive nature was difficult to comprehend. How could she know what my dad would understand?

"I'd really love it if you would come. Please?" She was practically begging.

Jason grabbed her. "Come on!"

"Hold on, I'm going to give Micaela my number in case she changes her mind." She rummaged in her purse and found a lipstick. Grabbing a napkin still laying on the table, she wrote down her telephone number and handed it to me. "Gotta go." She waved goodbye. "See you Saturday."

I shook my head at her assumption that I would go, gathered my books, placed the napkin carefully in my purse, as I couldn't just leave it on the table, and watched them as they crossed the parking lot. Jason gave Vini a gentle cuff to the head, and she playfully pushed him back. I'd never experienced brother-and-sister interaction before, and it made me smile.

The rehearsal hadn't gone as well as I'd hoped. The male lead kept forgetting his lines, and one of the actors didn't show up. My frustration interfered with my performance, and I fumbled my lines—something I never did. I vowed to never again let my fellow actors affect my work. It was a learning experience.

While driving home, I thought about Vini. She had a certain charm that made me overlook her forwardness. Her brother had that same charm but wasn't so outspoken. I thought about the party. "What the heck? Maybe she's right. Maybe I do need a little fun in my life." I said it out loud to convince myself. I decided to call her when I got home before I changed my mind.

She was, as she described it, "over the moon with delight" when I told her I would go. Her excitement seemed somewhat odd, considering we barely knew each other, but it was if we'd been friends for years; there was a comfortable kind of acceptance. I may not have had Vini's sixth sense, but I wasn't a bad judge of people. She seemed nice enough, and so did her brother. Dad was thrilled when I informed him I was going to a party. "Finally!" was his response.

Vini provided directions. She'd added, "Wear something sexy. You might meet that special guy." She'd stopped speaking suddenly, as if a thought had popped into her head. "You don't have a guy, do you?"

"Nope. I'm guy-less."

"Good! We'll have to remedy that."

Her desire to find me a guy was ridiculous, as I wasn't interested in any relationship, but fate had other plans for me.

CHAPTER 6

Now

The setting sun cast shadows across the living room wall. I must have slept most of the afternoon. The memory of my first meeting with Vini was fading with the sunlight, but it left a wistful nostalgia. She was quite a brash, outspoken woman. I imagined she was a force to be reckoned with in a courtroom. Jason used to tease her. "Look out world; my sister is coming." There was no stopping the Vini train when it got started. I remembered her text. Searching for my phone, I located it on the rug beside the sofa, where it must have fallen when I drifted off to sleep. I checked the time. It was ten past six, and if I didn't miss my guess, she would probably be in her office, poring through legal documents and files. She wasn't a workaholic like Jack, just totally dedicated to being the best prosecuting attorney on the planet. As far as I knew, she had only lost one case in all of the fifteen years she'd been practicing. Vini was the second name in my contact list. It took only two rings before she answered.

"Hey, lady! I was wondering when I was going to hear from you. How are you doing?"

It was great hearing her voice again. "I'm good."

"You're lying." There was no fooling Vini, no matter how upbeat I tried to sound. I'd been an actress for over ten years, but my skills seemed to have declined in direct proportion to my exhaustion.

I decided to get straight to the point. "Did Jess call you?"

"Yeah, she did. Don't get pissed at her. She loves you so much, and she's worried."

I was suddenly more annoyed at my daughter.

"Micki, I can't believe it. Is it true? Do you really have cancer? I know Jessie wouldn't make something like that up, but is there a chance it's a misdiagnosis?"

"Yes, it's true. Apparently, it hasn't spread."

"That means there's a chance, right? You've got time to do something about it."

"I'd like you to know I am being treated."

"Jessie told me. She's crazy pissed off at you for going to a naturopath, but I understand, so I won't press you. I believe in a more natural approach too. So I'll ask you again: how are you doing?"

I decided to be truthful. "I'm feeling more tired than usual, which makes teaching a full day difficult, and my appetite is nonexistent."

"You always ate like a bird anyway, but you have to eat to keep your strength up."

"Thanks, Mom. The worst part is that I have to pee all the time. My students must wonder why I keep excusing myself."

"Is there any pain?"

"A bit, especially if I don't go to the bathroom when my bladder says it's time, but I'm coping."

"It sucks! It really sucks." I detected a sob. She paused, and I heard her blow her nose. I waited until she composed herself. "It's so shitty. You've been through so much in your life. Damn it! It's not fair!"

I wasn't about to give Vini the same lecture on fairness I'd given Jess. I felt tears stinging my eyelids and wiped them away. "No, it's not fair."

Suddenly, her mood changed. "I've got an idea, girlfriend. The case I'm working on is a shoo-in. This guy is going to prison for a very long time. He's lucky this isn't Florida, or he'd be bacon. I should be free before the end of the week."

She didn't have to elaborate on the charge. I guessed it was a murder trial. "So what's your idea?"

"How about we have a real girl weekend like we used to when we were young. You and me and a bottle of that Italian red wine you like so much. I'll fly up next Friday night and stay until Monday morning. You don't have plans, do you?"

"You know me—a real social butterfly!"

She laughed. "Then it's a go?"

"I'd love it, Vini."

"It's settled. I'm going to book the flight right now. I promise I won't pressure you like Jessie. You have to do whatever feels right for you. I have to go. I have a date."

"A date! Is this the same man you were seeing last year?"

"Are you kidding? That jerk couldn't handle a woman making more money than him. It was sayonara, baby. This new one runs a huge ad agency so no intimidation. He probably makes more money than I do—not that it matters. Can you believe this! I put his brother-in-law in prison for a few years, and he still wants to date me. Must be my irresistible charm. His sister hates my guts, but I guess that's to be expected. I'll see you next Friday night. I'll text you when my flight gets in. I'm really looking forward to seeing you. Love ya lots."

"Love you too." Vini may have changed her career and become a more dynamic version of herself, if such a thing was possible, but regardless, she was still the Vini I'd met so many years ago.

The dark enveloped me like a cozy warm blanket. With the darkness came a sense of peace. The house was quiet. I didn't want to break the spell by turning on lights. I switched off the ringer on my phone and placed it on the coffee table. Jess would probably call and check to see if I had eaten dinner. I didn't want to talk to her or anyone else. I just wanted to lie still, and instead of resisting, let memories of Vini drift through my mind. They didn't feel as threatening, now that I'd spoken to her. I felt comforted by her caring, loving nature. I grabbed the afghan from the back of the couch and wrapped it around my shoulders, closed my eyes, and drifted back in time.

CHAPTER 7

Then

I had forgotten to ask Vini what the dress code was for the party but assumed casual. I tried on four outfits before settling on my favorite acid-washed jeans with a silver rope leather belt and my bright-red halter top. I chose the silver chain with the small silver musical note that my mom had given me on my sixteenth birthday, just two months before she died. I washed my hair and let it air dry, which made it curlier and fuller. Bright-red lipstick complemented my top and blonde hair. Then the eyeliner. I tried duplicating Vini's winged look but a little more understated. I selected light-blue eyeshadow, which made my eyes look even bluer, and applied the usual three coats of black mascara, which added some years to my youthful appearance. Checking my chosen look in the full-length mirror on the back of the bathroom door, I was pleased with the results. Dad wasn't home, so I wasn't subjected to any disapproval. He wasn't used to seeing me in makeup. The shoes were black flats; at five feet seven inches tall, I didn't need to add any height.

The directions Vini provided were spot-on. I had no problem finding the house. It was set back from the road with a circular driveway—a two-story stucco with a huge expanse of windows across the front that reminded me of the homes in the *House and Garden* magazines Mom loved to drool over. Jason's friend was well off, or at least his parents were. It occurred to me that I didn't know Vini's or Jason's social status. I assumed they were like Dad and me, constantly pinching pennies and living in middle-class suburbia. So much for stereotyping!

Vini was waiting at the end of the driveway, as arranged. I parked my green Volkswagen beside a red Corvette—a Christmas theme! She ran to meet me as I locked the car door and put the keys in my purse.

"Am I early?" I looked around. Other than a jeep parked in front of the Corvette, there were very few vehicles. I was beyond nervous and still questioning my sanity for accepting an invitation to a party from someone who was almost a stranger.

"Not really. There are quite a few already here." She locked her arm through mine and steered me toward the side of the house. "Hey, girl! I practically peed my pants when you called, but I knew you would." She tapped her head. "That sixth sense, remember? Jason said you wouldn't. He loses."

"You made a bet?"

"Yup, and now I'm five dollars richer than I was yesterday." She looked me up and down. "Love your outfit. Great choice." She let go of my arm and twirled in front of me. "What do you think of my new purchase? Jason doesn't like it, but who gives a crap? He's practically color blind anyway."

I checked out her mini dress—deep purple, with a gold band trimming the edge of a scooped top, which displayed a hint of cleavage. It wasn't my taste, but it definitely suited her. The gold hoop earrings were a nice touch.

"It's very nice. Are you here with anyone?" I'd forgotten to ask if she had a boyfriend. I hoped she didn't. I would be more comfortable knowing I wasn't the only one minus a date.

"Nope! Mr. Right hasn't shown up yet, and I don't want to waste time with creeps just to fit in, if you know what I mean."

I sort of did. I certainly wasn't looking for Mr. Right either.

Vini led me down a walkway that curved around the side of the house. Small white lights illuminated the path, which opened to a large terrace filled with tables loaded down with a variety of snack foods and vegetable trays. In the middle of the largest table, a punch bowl containing a pink liquid with assorted pieces of fruit floating on the surface was surrounded by glasses and paper cups. A pool and hot tub cast a bluish glow, blending with the light from colored lanterns strung on a wire and stretching across the entire area. A huge "Happy birthday, Jason" sign decorated the top of a bar situated in a corner between two palm trees, their trunks encircled like candy canes with the same small glowing white lights. A man wearing a brown corduroy jacket and beige pants was chatting with Jason at the bar. Jason was taller by a least a head. The man's hair was pulled back into a ponytail, if that's what you called it when guys did it. His pale skin resembled mine. Vini and I joined them.

"Hey, girl, good to see you." Jason put his glass on the bar and gave me a hug. "Glad you could make it."

"I hear you lost the bet," I said.

Jason looked annoyed. "Vin shouldn't have told you that, but I'm glad I lost. Was your dad upset?"

"No. He has a date, so it worked out great." It seemed strange, saying Dad had a date. I was not entirely comfortable with the idea. He'd met a woman on the elevator who, he told me, lived upstairs from us, and apparently, they'd hit it off immediately.

"Aren't you going to introduce me to this lovely lady?" said the man with the ponytail. Jason didn't have time to respond. "I'm Owen, the better and prettier one." He put his hand out in greeting. I recalled Vini saying Jason's boyfriend was named Owen. His handshake was firm. I wasn't expecting it—another stereotype I needed to change.

"I'm the smarter one," Jason said, countering Owen's description. "Can I get you two a drink? I can mix up anything you want."

"Jason works as a bartender at a club in downtown Clearwater on the weekends," Vini explained. "I'll have my usual. What do you want, Micaela?"

"Aren't you sick of piña coladas, Vini?" Owen said. He gestured to his own drink. "Why don't you try something more daring?"

"She's only seventeen, Owen. I think her usual is a better idea, and that's pushing it," Jason said. "But I guess it will be all right since she's not driving, and I don't think Mom will notice if she keeps it to one. So, Micaela, what will it be?"

I wasn't a drinker, except for the occasional glass of red wine with Sunday dinner, so I requested a cola.

"One piña colada and one cola, coming up." Jason went behind the bar and proceeded to make Vini's drink and take the soda from a bar fridge.

"What are you drinking?" I asked Owen. It was probably a dumb question, but I was curious, and I couldn't think of anything else to say.

"It's a concoction of the gods. Want to try?" He tipped his glass in my direction.

"I wouldn't if I were you," Vini warned. "Jason created it, and there's four different types of alcohol and a liqueur. You wouldn't be sober for at least twenty-four hours, and you'd have a hangover that would last a week. I have no idea how Owen can tolerate it."

"I can hold my liquor better than most. Years of experimenting."

"You're not that much older than us," Vini announced.

"I'm the old man of the group," Owen told me. "I'm twenty-five, so that gives me a head start." He didn't look more than twenty, but I was not a good judge of age.

Jason put our drinks on the bar. Vini's had a cherry and a tiny umbrella. Before she had even taken a sip, she was distracted by a couple walking hand in hand along the pathway to the terrace.

"Jase, there's Terry and Connie. Let's go say hi. We haven't seen them in ages."

They left me alone with Owen. I felt stranded. Vini had invited me, and now she was ditching me.

"So how do you know the dynamic duo?" Owen asked.

"Excuse me?" I wasn't sure to what he was referring.

"Vini and Jason," he explained.

"It's rather odd, but I don't really know either of them. I met Vini on Thursday afternoon at lunch. She was waiting for Jason, and I met him when he came to get his sister."

"That's our Vini. She assumes everyone is her friend."

"Is this your home?"

"Good god, no! I can't afford a pot to piss in." He must have noticed my startled expression. "Oops, sorry. Vini swears like a trouper. I forget not all her friends are like her. The house belongs to Dr. Jonathan McKenzie and his socialite wife, Corina. The yacht club crowd—very posh. Their son Connor is nothing like them, which is a good thing. Connor and Jason have been friends since they were five years old. A very unlikely pairing. The rich white kid with the poor little black kid."

Now that I knew Vini's social standing, I felt relief. I was not used to hanging out with wealthy people.

"Jason being gay did nothing to endear him to the McKenzies," Owen said. "He came out when he was sixteen, and, as I understand it, Connor's parents went ballistic and even doubted *his* sexuality. I think they believed being gay was somehow contagious. They put up with the friendship only because Connor threatened to leave home, but Jason was no longer allowed to come to their house. They'd freak if they knew who this party was for—especially bringing his gay Jewish boyfriend." What could have been a slight smile played on Owen's lips, but it seemed almost a smirk to me.

"Are they not at home?" I couldn't imagine parents allowing a bunch of teenagers the run of their house without some kind of supervision.

"Nope! They're away on one of their trips with Connor's brother. What is it they say? 'When the cat's away, the mice will play.' Besides, they trust Connor to take care of the house, even if they aren't too thrilled with his choice of friends."

Jason returned minus Vini and started making drinks for a couple standing near us. Owen had already finished his drink and placed the glass on the bar motioning to Jason for a refill. A look passed across Jason's face that I interpreted as disapproval as he began taking different bottles and pouring shots into the glass. Owen appeared pleased in spite of the look Jason sent him.

"Is Connor here?" I was curious to know what he looked like.

"He's down at the beach. What do you say we go find our host?" Owen grabbed his drink, offered me his arm, and led the way down the path to the beach area. While walking, he continued his narrative. "Things changed when Connor moved out. His parents wanted him to be a doctor, but that didn't happen, and that's a story better saved for another time."

As we got closer to the beach, I saw a group huddled together around a large fire, where flames danced almost in time to the rhythm of the music coming from a boom box on a blanket. I looked in the direction Owen was leading me. A few people were standing and laughing. I spotted a good-looking guy in the center of the group.

"Is that Connor?"

"You mean the fabulous-looking one with the beer and very tight jeans? If so, that would be a good guess. It's a shame he isn't gay. He's gorgeous."

His comment startled me, but I tried not to show it. Owen picked up on my discomfort. I would have to practice my facial expressions if I wanted to be an actress.

"Oh, don't get so rattled. You're not used to being around gay men, are you?"

"No, I never met anyone who is gay before; at least not to my knowledge."

"Well, we're not much different from you. We love; we hate; we eat; we drink" He lifted his glass in the air as if toasting.

As Owen and I approached, I took in Connor's thick brown hair, which instead of being slicked back like most of the guys in school, looked as if he had just gotten out of bed. One piece fell carelessly across his forehead. Like Owen, I noticed the tight blue jeans. His jean jacket was open, exposing a white T-shirt that contrasted against the tan of his neck. He was staring right at me. I smiled. He smiled back.

A girl in leopard-patterned tights, blazing red hair, and tons of makeup was snuggled against him, and judging by the way his arm was draped over her shoulder, I assumed they were more than friends.

"Hey, Owen! Where's our birthday boy?" Connor asked. He continued to stare at me.

"Still working the bar," Owen responded. "I think he's forgotten it's *his* party."

"Who is this beautiful creature you have on your arm?" Connor looked me up and down as if I was something to be assessed.

I hated it when boys did that. It made me uncomfortable. I was also being referred to as some kind of *creature*. He reminded me of the arrogant guys at school who thought they were God's gift to the female population. I decided I didn't like Connor McKenzie, regardless of how good-looking he was.

"This is Micaela, friend of Vini's," Owen announced. "Micaela, this is Connor McKenzie, our host."

I nodded and returned his stare. I was struck by the color of his eyes. They appeared amber in the light from the fire. The girl clinging to him noticed us staring at each other. She didn't look happy. Connor didn't introduce her. Not only did I think he was arrogant, but he was rude as well. She placed her hand on his chest as if asserting possession of him.

"I'm Bonnie," she announced. "I think we go to the same school. I've seen you around the campus."

I had no recollection of seeing her at school, but for the sake of polite conversation asked what she was taking.

"Same as Jason—set design, but I'm in first year." She nuzzled closer to Connor. She didn't ask what I was taking and made it obvious she didn't care.

Connor noticed my cola. "I see Owen has taken care of the beverage department. Sure you don't want something stronger?"

I said I was fine. I didn't feel any necessity to disclose my age.

"How about we introduce you around?" He pulled away from Bonnie, but she refused to be stranded and followed as he approached me. I moved aside to let them pass. It was apparent I was to accompany them to the fire pit.

"Hey, everyone! This is Micaela," Connor yelled. "Friend of Vini's."

They all shouted back in unison, "Hi, Micaela!" Then their attention immediately returned to whatever conversations they were involved in before we approached.

I felt awkward and embarrassed. I wanted to retreat to the terrace and find Vini. Owen took a seat on a bench in front of the fire pit, while Connor arranged a blanket on the sand. Bonnie was the blanket's first occupant. Instead of sitting with her, Connor sat at one end of the bench, which meant I could sit beside Bonnie or with Connor and Owen. Neither option appealed to me. The glare Bonnie shot me only added to my discomfort. It was apparent she didn't want me anywhere near Connor. I made a decision to invent a reason to leave. Even though I disliked lying, sometimes it was just necessary.

"I completely forgot I have an assignment due on Monday, and I haven't even started it yet. I'm really sorry, but I think I should go home. I'll make my apologies to Jason and Vini." I didn't bother to wait for a response.

"That's a shame. You just got here. Hope we'll see you again," Owen said as I turned to walk back up the path.

I heard Connor say, "Methinks fair maiden has been offended."

I did not look behind me but sensed someone approaching. I picked up my pace, hoping it wasn't Connor.

"Leave her alone, baby. She's a big girl. Come here and keep me company." It sounded like Bonnie. She must have been successful in stopping him, as I no longer heard anyone behind me.

By the time I reached the terrace and looked down toward the beach, I noticed she was standing with her arms curled around his neck.

I just wanted to get away. It was stupid of me to have come in the first place. This was not how I wanted to end my months of antisocial behavior. Old movies or a good book seemed a better alternative. I placed my half-finished can of pop on one of the tables and made my way around the side of the house. Vini must have spotted me.

"Hey, girl, where you goin'?" she shouted from wherever she was.

By the time she'd caught up with me, I was already at my car, searching through my purse for my keys. "Home," was all I answered. I didn't owe her—or anyone else—an explanation.

"How come?"

I knew she wouldn't let up until I provided some kind of answer. "I've got a ton of homework, and I'm not feeling all that well."

"Do you want to use the bathroom? I can show you where it is."

"No, I'll be fine. Probably too much studying and not enough sleep. Thanks for the invite."

"Come on, Micki. Please stay."

Startled, I turned to face her. "What did you call me?"

"Micki. It's sort of cute."

It felt offensive. She had no right to call me that. It was my parents' nickname for me. I chose to ignore it. "Say goodbye to Jason for me. Tell him I'm sorry I couldn't stay for his birthday, but I'm exhausted, and I really have to get my project done. How about I call you tomorrow?" I probably wouldn't, but it seemed to help her accept my leaving.

She hugged me. It still amazed me how open and affectionate she was.

"Okay, I guess, but promise you'll call me, and I can tell you all the juicy stuff you missed." She didn't wait for my answer. "Be careful driving home," she called out as she ran back to the house to join her friends.

I'd located my keys and was about to open my car door when I felt a presence behind me. I turned abruptly.

"Holy shit!" I rarely, if ever, used swear words and didn't even realize I was capable of saying something that vulgar, although I'd heard Dad curse often. My heart was beating fast. I could barely catch my breath.

"Is that the way for someone who looks like an angel to talk?"

"You startled me." The last person I expected to see was Connor. I had no idea what his intentions were, so I did not turn my back to open my car door. I prayed they were purely innocent, as I wasn't sure anyone would hear me yell over the loud music drifting up from the beach.

He raised his arms in a submissive gesture. "Not going to hurt you. Promise!"

I wasn't totally reassured, so I remained still and waited.

"I want to apologize for embarrassing you, and I'm not drunk. Not even a wee bit. I was just being a jerk."

"I wasn't embarrassed. I'm not feeling well, and I have to start an assignment that's due on Monday," I lied.

"I was a jerk, and you know it. I could have introduced you properly, and as for Bonnie … well, she isn't known for being too fond of girls prettier than her."

I shrugged. Having decided I was safe, I turned to insert the key in the lock. I felt his hand on my arm.

"Okay, so you won't accept my apology. Maybe you might accept my offer. Will you be my date for this evening?"

"Excuse me? What?"

"You heard me. Will you be my date for tonight?"

"What on earth is wrong with you people? I just met Vini the other day, and now she is acting like I'm her best friend. I met you twenty minutes ago, and you want me to be your date. Are you crazy?"

"Maybe we're just needy people." He smiled. "I'm serious. I don't want you to leave."

"Why? Because you want another female to conquer? Isn't Bonnie enough?"

Connor laughed. "You've known me twenty minutes, and you think you've got me figured out. Don't concern yourself with Bonnie. I know it looks as if we're a couple, but we're not. Although she'd like to be. Up until twenty minutes ago, I didn't care. I've known her since I was eighteen, and yes, we dated a few times but nothing serious."

"It looked pretty serious to me."

"Okay, I'm a guy. What can I say? I'm guilty. Bonnie never leaves me alone, and she's like comfort food."

"I don't think she'd appreciate being compared to food." There was an arrogance about him I found unnerving but compelling as well. I couldn't deny he was good-looking and understood why Bonnie wanted to be near him. He was not pretty-boy handsome like the actors I'd watched in teen movies, but there was strength in his features. His wide forehead and jawline actually complemented his longer nose; unlike mine, which I felt dominated my face. His eyes actually were a soft amber, and when he smiled, his entire face lit up.

"I think I'll pass on your offer, but I will accept your apology." I opened my car door and realized he still had his hand on my arm. "I don't date men I don't know."

"Well, give me a few minutes, and I'll take care of that."

I shrugged my shoulders. The information Owen provided was enough, and I didn't want to hear more. I tried releasing my arm, but his grip was firm. I resigned myself to listening.

"I'll give you a brief rundown, and then you can decide if I'm date material." He paused for a moment and ran his hand through his hair. "Okay, here goes … First of all, I'm twenty-two, and no, I didn't go to college, but I did spend a year at university. I quit and opened my own charter company."

I was tempted to ask why he quit but decided it was none of my business.

A smile touched his lips, and he continued as if he'd read my mind. "I quit because I prefer the freedom of having my own business, and I love being out on the ocean. I answer to no one but myself, and that's how I like it. Not a huge fan of other people's expectations."

I suspected he was referring to someone specific, but again I kept my mouth shut. I was anxious for him to finish so I could leave.

He gestured toward the house. "You probably guessed my family has money, but I don't. I make a living, but it's pretty basic. My father isn't too thrilled with my life choice."

I suspected it was his dad he was referring to whose expectations he didn't like. I smiled politely and tried pulling my arm from his grasp. "I'm glad you like what you do, but I really do have to go."

He let go of my arm, and as I went to close my car door, he grabbed it before it shut. I sighed and rolled my eyes. "Okay, just a few more minutes, but then will you let me go?"

"I know I'm probably boring you, but I'm actually a great guy, once you get to know me."

I rolled my eyes again. "You have a rather high opinion of yourself."

"I have to; my family doesn't." I sensed annoyance in his tone. "That's not totally true. My little brother seems to think I'm pretty special. He's fourteen and loves spending time with me on my boat. He's got some challenges, but he's pretty cool."

Connor didn't elaborate on what those challenges were. I was sure I would never meet his brother, so it really didn't matter. "Are you finished?"

"Are you warming up to me yet?"

"Maybe a bit, but unless there is more to add, could you please let go of my door?"

"Not much more, except I like baseball and football and watching movies. My musical taste varies—I kind of like the early seventies and eighties; not a big fan of heavy metal—and I love photography. So there you have it—the condensed version of my life. You don't want to know all the goofy kid stuff. Rich kid turned poor who probably can't afford a fancy girl like you, but I had to try."

"I'm not fancy! My parents weren't rich. I'm lucky to have a father who used most of his savings to pay for my college tuition."

"Okay then! Now that we've established we're both penniless and struggling, what do you think? Do I stand here all night sharing my life stories and trying to convince you to stay, or do I walk away and let you slip out of my life? Can't say that idea appeals to me. Who knows? You might even like me if you give me a chance."

At this point, I was weakening. The annoyance and dislike I'd felt only moments before hadn't totally disappeared, but it was dissolving into a passable acceptance. His smile was winning me over, but I had no desire to return to the beach, especially with Connor, while Bonnie had her claws out.

"Thanks for the offer. I'm sure you'll survive when I leave. I probably shouldn't have come in the first place, but I didn't want to disappoint Vini." I tried again to close the car door, but his grip was strong, and he still wouldn't release it.

"Let's call it a draw. You give me your phone number, and I'll back off, and you can go home and do all the studying you want. I can stand here all night if I have to."

I tried tugging on the door, but I couldn't budge it, so I gave in. "Okay. My dad is listed in the phone book under A. Lewiski. It's the only one."

"Guess that will have to do." He let go of the door. "Be safe driving home."

I closed the door, switched on the engine, and carefully backed out of the driveway. Connor stood watching me until I could no longer see him in my rearview mirror. I had a strange feeling I'd be seeing him again.

CHAPTER 8

On the drive home, I kept seeing Connor's face in my mind. Replacing the visuals with visions of puppies and kittens didn't work. He dominated my thoughts. It was like trying not to think about a pink elephant. Even my heart betrayed me and insisted on sending strange electrical impulses with each mental image.

Get a grip, you idiot, I thought while trying to concentrate on my driving. *You just met him, and if first impressions mean anything, this guy is trouble.* I recited "Forget him" over and over, attempting to wipe my brain clean.

I was no sooner through the door when the phone rang. It wouldn't be dad, as he thought I was with my friends. We didn't get many calls, but when we did, they were usually important ... so I answered it.

"I wasn't sure whether you'd be home yet. Just checking to see if you're okay." He didn't have to identify himself. I knew immediately it was Connor. That strange electrical impulse shot through my heart again, and my gut did somersaults. Definitely a new experience for me, one I found disturbing but pleasant in an odd sort of way.

"Shouldn't you be partying with your friends?" I asked, trying to sound composed.

"Jason is entertaining them with his version of "Is It Love?" He thinks he's Bob Marley. Heard it a thousand times, so the opportunity to call you was handed to me. Couldn't pass it up."

"And Bonnie is okay with it?" I had to ask.

"Forget Bonnie. I told you; we're just friends. It's not a thing. Her parents are friends with mine, so it's hard to avoid her. She tends to be a bit possessive and has difficulty accepting I'm not interested in her."

"It didn't look that way to me."

"You're right. I probably shouldn't encourage it, but like I said, it was simply a thing when I was younger. I'm not out to score with you, if that's what you think. I want to get to know who Micaela Lewiski is."

"Why? She's nothing special, I can assure you."

"Don't agree. Vini told me you want to be a Broadway actress. Sorry, but I had to ask her about you. She tells me you're sweet."

"How would she know? We just met."

"It's in your eyes. When I saw you with Owen, the light from the terrace was behind you, creating a glow around your hair. To me, you looked like an angel. When I looked into your eyes, I knew I had to get to know you. I realize it sounds corny, but it's not a line. It's the truth."

His disclosure created more tingling sensations throughout my body. It felt strange. Whether he was telling the truth, I wasn't sure, and I remained quiet.

"I'm sensing by your lack of response I've made you uncomfortable again. Sorry, but I wanted you to know. I'd also like to apologize for coming on so strong earlier. I just couldn't let you walk away. It's kind of a bad habit I have. When I see something I want, I have to have it. I'm not implying you're a thing … it's just … well, it's … I'm not doing a good job at this, am I?"

I laughed. Now it was his turn to feel uncomfortable. I had to admit I was flattered. I wasn't used to guys telling me they wanted me. In a way, I liked it. I thought I'd help him out and change the subject. "How was Jason's party?"

"Judging by the noise, they are still going at it. Oh, before I forget, Vini told me it's your birthday. Happy birthday!"

I didn't correct him, as it meant explaining that I had misled Vini. I simply thanked him.

"I wasn't supposed to tell you this, but she got you a cake. I think on Monday you're going to have to blow out some candles. Act surprised, and don't let on that I told you."

That sealed it. I had to call Vini to make up for spoiling her surprise.

"I'll let you get back to your studying. But first, I think I'm going to stick my neck out and take a chance on asking you out. Here goes … are you busy next Sunday?"

"Not to my knowledge."

"Will you go out with me? Please say yes."

"I guess … Okay, I will." There was something about him that made me agree, although I hoped I wouldn't regret it.

"Good! You made my day, Micaela Lewiski. I'll call you next week to let you know what the plans are for Sunday. Don't get second thoughts. Good night!"

He hung up, and I stood holding the phone, wondering what just had happened. My decision not to get involved with anyone melted like a snowman in July.

Dad and I celebrated my birthday by watching two romantic movies—my choice, not his, but he endured them. He gave me eighteen red roses and a book on the history of theater I'd wanted. We ate dinner at an Italian restaurant, and while enjoying my favorite pasta dish, he asked about the party. I replied that it had been great but avoided disclosing my early departure. He inquired about my new friends. I provided a colorful description of Vini that made him laugh and said her brother was attending St. Pete's as well, but I omitted that Jason was gay. I wasn't sure of Dad's stand on the subject. My other omission was my encounter with Connor. The reason being that Dad was old-fashioned, and I knew he would insist on meeting him.

There had been one boy who interested me enough to go out with him when we lived in Toronto: Allen Townsend, the captain of my high school football team. He'd been my date for the prom. Dad insisted he pick me up at our house, and after ten minutes of Dad's not-so-subtle interrogation, there was never a second date. Dad said it was because his intentions weren't honorable. I figured Dad intimidated the poor guy. It wasn't something I wanted to repeat. And I didn't want him to get all hopeful about his eighteen-year-old daughter finally having a relationship with a boy when I wasn't sure if the date with Connor would go anywhere. It just wasn't on my comfort radar at the moment.

Dad did a lot of reminiscing about my childhood, shaking his head and saying, "How did my little girl grow up so fast?" He would have a lot of adjustments to make when I graduated and left for New York. We both would.

I called Vini as soon as I got home. She inquired about my day and how I was feeling. After assuring her I was fine, she described all the party details. I got the impression she was more interested in gossip than my well-being. Apparently, Jason did his "usual songs," as if I would know what they were. She added it was boring and moved on to Owen, who got plastered and made an idiot of himself doing head-banging dances until he fell over and passed out. A few couples retired to private areas. She named them—again, as if I should know these people. I got the drift. Her ramblings were just a lead-up to what she really wanted to know. What did I think of Connor?

"I think he's got the hots for you, Micki."

I still had trouble with her calling me that but let it pass.

"He asked me all about you. I told him we'd just met, but I liked you a lot and hoped we could be friends. He said he hoped you and he could be friends too. He pretty much disappeared until I found him in the living room on the phone."

I didn't disclose that he'd been speaking with me. I still wanted my privacy and didn't feel the need to gossip about Connor.

"Bonnie—you met her, right? Well, she was thrilled when you left. Too much competition for her. When Connor came back down to the beach, she was all over him, but he pushed her away. He stayed long enough to watch Jason blow out the candles on his cake. After that, he went back to the house. Speaking of birthday cake, be at our table for lunch tomorrow. Gotta go. My mom's yelling at me for something, and she'll keep it up if I don't answer her. See ya tomorrow."

My birthday cake was double-chocolate with a thick layer of fudge icing. Not my favorite, but Vini wouldn't know that. It wasn't easy blowing out eighteen candles, but with a little help from a breeze, I accomplished it. I made the obligatory wish. I wished for a great performance with more to come. Asking for two things might have canceled them both out, so I crossed my fingers and feet to be on the safe side. I still didn't share my upcoming date with Connor.

Tons of homework and rehearsals made the rest of the week fly by. I felt more nervous for Sunday than I did for my performance. I finally gave in and told Dad I had a date. His first reaction was as expected. He wanted to meet him. I said no, not yet. It was just a date, not a proposal. Dad trusted my good sense but added that the young man had better have good intentions.

Connor called on Saturday, as promised, and inquired about my week and if I liked my birthday cake. He wasn't forthcoming on what we would be doing but told me to dress casually and bring a sweater. He said he was looking forward to our date. He teased me about getting cold feet. I assured him my feet never got cold. He liked my answer.

Sleep was impossible. There was no denying how excited I was in anticipation of our first date. It just happened. I felt like a thirteen-year-old girl with a crush, even though all my crushes were on actors and singers rather than regular boys. I liked the feeling. I suspected something new was happening to me, something a lot bigger than any crush.

CHAPTER 9

Sunday afternoon finally arrived. I couldn't decide what to wear. It wasn't like my closet was filled with a great selection of clothes. I rarely wore dresses and preferred jeans with oversized shirts for slopping around the apartment, but I did find a pair of beige slacks and a navy-blue jersey with a matching sweater. The blue made my eyes more vivid. Connor had said casual, but I still didn't know what he was planning. I hoped my choice was appropriate and not too understated. I checked my eyes for dark circles; I didn't notice any but opted for some concealer anyway. I used mascara but passed on eyeliner. Pink lip gloss was perfect. My hair I kept loose and natural. A ponytail seemed a little too casual.

Connor arrived promptly before lunch. I was impressed. I hated it when people left you waiting. He was leaning against his jeep and smiled as I approached. He was wearing black pants and a tan dress shirt, open at the collar, with the sleeves rolled up to his elbows. His hair hadn't changed. It kind of curled behind his ears, while one strand hung carelessly to the side of his forehead, which, instead of appearing messy, seemed artfully placed. I felt a fluttering sensation in my chest when I looked at him.

"I was scared you wouldn't show, considering your first impression of me." He grinned, creating deep lines around his mouth, adding to his charm rather than distracting from it.

"I'm a person of my word," I said. "Could be I misjudged you. We'll see."

"That sounds like a challenge, and I'm always up for a good challenge."

He opened the passenger door of his jeep, and I could almost hear my mom saying, "A man should always open doors for a woman. It shows respect and consideration. All this women's lib stuff will only lead to men disrespecting women more in the long run." I wasn't sure if she was right, but I appreciated the courtesy.

Before Connor put the key in the ignition, he turned to look at me. He said nothing, just stared.

"Do I have something on my face?"

"No, you're perfect. I'm just absorbing the moment." He started the jeep. "First, I'd like to take you to my favorite restaurant by the marina. It's seafood. You don't have any allergies, do you?"

"Allergy-free." Breakfast had been a piece of toast and a cup of tea, and I could sense my stomach was ready for something more substantial.

The restaurant was small, with a few tables outside under a red-striped awning. We chose one close to the front window rather than by the sidewalk. After checking the menus, I settled on a shrimp pasta dish, and Connor went straight to the lobster. I never mastered how to eat lobster without making a mess, and I wasn't about to try.

He asked me all kinds of questions. Where did I grow up? Did I have any brother or sisters? What were my favorite movies, and what kind of music did I prefer? He was a great listener. I felt myself relaxing and opening up. I told him about Mom and how I missed her, and how great Dad was at being a single parent, and that I had no brothers or sisters and very little family to speak of. I even told him about my first puppy, a terrier named Chippy who was run over by a car, and how dad buried him in our backyard and put up a stone marker—I had cried for weeks. I shared my dream of being a Broadway actress and my love of musicals. He laughed when I told him I could sing every song from *West Side Story*, and I adored the Beatles, but only some of the Rolling Stones, and I didn't really like synthesized music, and hated heavy metal. I was getting tired of talking about myself.

"Okay, now you."

"I'm a Beatles fan too, and I do like the Stones. I agree some of the current music is a bit hard to take. I also like Stevie Nicks."

That surprised me.

"Why are you surprised? You think a guy can't like female artists?"

"Most of the guys at school are into Metallica or Iron Maiden. I think it's great that you like female artists."

"Looks like I scored a point." Connor continued to tell me about his brother Ricky, who, it turned out, was afflicted with a mild form of autism. He explained that helping Ricky overcome some of his behavioral problems was instrumental in his decision to become a doctor and focus on special-needs children. He added, and quite emphatically, that it was not because of his father, who was a doctor, a plastic surgeon. Connor didn't appear to have much respect for altering women's breasts and faces. He wanted to specialize in learning disabilities and help children. It was an impressive goal.

"Why didn't you do it?" I was unsure whether I'd trespassed on something private.

"Changed my mind."

He didn't provide an explanation as to why, and I didn't press him for one. He passed me the dessert menu. I loved cheesecake, so decided on the New York version, and Connor did the same.

"I like a girl who isn't afraid of dessert."

That made me laugh. "I'm not afraid to eat sweets. I just have a healthy respect for them. I've always been slim. I don't gain weight easily."

"There are a lot of girls who'd like to trade places with you. My mother's always following some new diet craze."

"Do you spend a lot of time on your boat?" I wanted to change the subject.

"I live on my boat. I enjoy being out on the ocean. Ricky spends weekends with me, and he loves it. The boat should be paid for in another year, and if—and that's a big *if*—I should decide to go back to university, I can start putting money away to pay my tuition."

I sensed that even though Connor came from an affluent family, being financially independent was important to him.

"There you have it—an extended version of my life."

The server brought our desserts, and we continued talking about the kinds of movies and music that interested us. I was surprised how much we had in common.

When Connor got his wallet to pay the bill, I took money from my purse and handed it to him. I wanted to pay some of it.

"What do you think you're doing?" He pushed the money away. "I know women want to be more independent, but I asked you out, and you don't want to bruise my ego, do you? I'm a very sensitive guy."

"I'm not a total women's lib type, but I think the women's movement makes some interesting points. Women have been suppressed for too long. Change is coming, although it's slow." The subject was one I could talk about for hours, and I couldn't subdue my passion. "Take movies, for example. Women are portrayed as clinging vines who can't seem to make a decision without the aid of a man. There aren't many good parts for women. Hopefully, that will change."

"Whoa! I get it. You're not for burning your bra, but you might carry a protest sign."

"Do you even know what the women's movement stands for?"

"Nope, but how about you enlighten me while we take a walk on the beach." He paid the bill, and we left the restaurant. "I'd like to get my camera from the jeep, if you don't mind. I'll be two minutes. Don't go anywhere."

While waiting, I discreetly glanced in the mirror I kept in my purse. I wouldn't say I was vain, probably more self-conscious. There was nothing between my teeth, but my lipstick had faded. I returned the mirror quickly when I saw Connor running toward me, camera in hand.

"I must be doing okay. You didn't run away." He strung the camera strap around his neck and pushed back the hair that had fallen across his forehead.

The sand was still cool enough to walk barefoot. In the middle of summer, it was impossible to walk on the beach, even with sandals. Spring was my preferred time of year. Connor asked me what living in Canada was like. I laughed at his perceptions. He knew Toronto was a city, but beyond that, he had no idea we enjoyed long, hot summer days and that our beaches were always packed with families having picnics. He was under the impression that Canada was cold year-round and that was the reason why so many Canadians retired to Florida. When I teased him and said I didn't own a parka, had never seen a dogsled, and never used snowshoes, he gave me a gentle nudge on my arm.

"What about those igloos you live in?" he said, teasing me back.

"They melted."

We both laughed.

As we walked toward the pier, Connor stopped every so often to take pictures of sandpipers scampering along the sand. A majestic heron, standing quietly on one leg, looking out at the ocean as if posing, was the subject of several shots. After the birds, Connor took pictures of me. I finally just went with it, although every once in a while, I made a silly expression that had him laughing. At one point, he even approached an elderly couple strolling along the beach and asked if they would take our picture. After a few instructions on camera usage with the man, Connor was beside me with his arm around my waist. I wasn't sure whether I was supposed to duplicate the gesture. I did, but without actually making full contact with his body. My arm just lightly brushed his shirt. He pulled me closer. I smiled, hoping my discomfort didn't show. The strange thing was, it felt sort of natural. Connor retrieved his camera and thanked the man for his kindness. The couple introduced themselves as Ed and Isabel from Wisconsin and explained they were on vacation but were seriously thinking of retiring here. Connor told them to enjoy their trip.

I heard Isabel remark, "You two make the cutest couple."

We waved goodbye. "Hear that? She thinks we make a cute couple." Connor winked.

No comment from me.

The wind blowing across the pier whipped hair across my face until I could barely see, and wisps kept sticking to my cheekbones. I tried to push them away, but it didn't work. Connor's thick mane created the same problem. Gulls taunted us, swooping lower, looking for food scraps. Between the gusts playing with our hair and the shrill cries of the birds, conversation was nearly impossible. We returned to the beach.

"You up to going to the marina?" he asked.

"As long as we don't have to walk there."

The marina was closer to St. Pete Beach. I noticed row after row of small fishing boats and several bigger cruisers sitting alongside, overpowering them. Connor parked near a building where a sign indicated Boat Owners Only. I guessed what he wanted me to see.

At the end of the main dock, Connor stopped to indicate a small boat, where a young man covered in blue paint was focused on the task of painting what I presumed was the hull. I knew very little boat terminology, but *hull* came to mind. The young man was so dedicated to his work he didn't look up when we approached.

"Hey, buddy! You're doing a fine job." Connor placed his hand on the boy's shoulder.

The boy, who I guessed was his brother Ricky, jumped, almost spilling the can of paint. "Where have you been? You said you would help me."

"Don't you remember? I told you I had a date."

"Oh yeah! Is this her?" Connor introduced us. Ricky stared at me intently. "Yup, you are pretty, like Connor said."

"It's nice to meet you, Ricky." I held out my hand in greeting, unsure whether he would take it. I knew children with autism didn't like to be touched. He switched the paintbrush to his other hand and grabbed mine, shaking it up and down vigorously. Touch wasn't an issue. Blue paint transferred from his hand to mine.

"Oh, sorry!" He removed a clean rag from a box and handed it to me. His curly brown hair and huge grin gave him the appearance of being very young, but I recalled Connor saying he was fourteen. "Do you wanna see the boat?"

"I'd be honored."

While Ricky closed his paint can, Connor explained that usually Ricky didn't like being touched, especially by people he didn't know, and this was the first time he'd reached out to someone. Connor looked pleased. He jumped in the boat and offered his hand to help me. At the same time, Ricky leaped from the wharf to the deck, landing so hard the boat rocked back and forth, causing me to lose my balance. I tried to steady myself, and Connor's arms encircled me. They remained around me a lot longer than necessary.

Ricky did the tour guide thing. "The boat can hold fourteen people and maybe sixteen if they squish in. We've never had that many, but it could." He indicated padded benches on either side. He explained that one was the starboard side and the other was the port side. We were in the stern.

This was the start of my nautical education. Connor went to the front, which Ricky informed me was called the bow. I was sure I would never remember these terms.

I ducked my head when entering a tiny area that looked like it might be a kitchen. Ricky provided the terminology. "It's the galley," he explained. "Connor's going to kill me if I don't clean up this mess." He quickly wiped the peanut butter from the counter, screwed the lid back on the jar, and placed it in the cupboard. He swiped vagrant crumbs into the sink and ran water to get rid of them. He rinsed a glass and deposited it on a rack. "There—clean as a whistle." The expression seemed odd for a teenager, more something Mom would say after spending hours cleaning our kitchen.

"I'll show you where Connor and I sleep." He opened a door where steps led to a sleeping cabin. Against one wall, I noticed a twin-sized bed and a sleeping bag on the floor. Across from the bed, cupboards lined the wall, holding a lamp on one end and a small television on the other. "I sleep in the sleeping bag." Ricky sounded proud of the fact.

"Isn't it rather hard on the floor?" It didn't seem comfortable to me.

"It's cool. At night the boat will rock back and forth, and I sleep good."

"It's not the Ritz, but Ricky's got a point. Sleeping on a boat is soothing." Connor stood in the door well with his hands grasping the top of the frame. I noticed he'd changed his dress shirt for a white Tshirt that lifted slightly exposing the muscles of his abdomen. I tried not to notice.

"Micaela will have to try it," Ricky stated enthusiastically. "Do you have a sleeping bag?"

He waited for my answer. Another awkward moment.

"I don't think her dad would be too thrilled, buddy, but maybe we can take Micaela out one weekend when I don't have a booking. How's that?"

"Cool!" Ricky grinned.

"Don't you have some painting to finish?" Connor shot Ricky a glance, one I'd seen Dad give me when he wanted to talk privately to Mom.

"I get it; you wanna be alone with Micaela, but I haven't shown her the head yet."

The look of surprise on my face made Ricky laugh. "That's the bathroom," he explained. "You thought I had a severed head or something?" He found it quite amusing.

"Do you have to use the bathroom?" Connor asked me.

"No, I'm fine." I wasn't totally, but I felt too self-conscious to admit it, and I didn't like using strange washrooms.

Ricky returned to his painting assignment, and Connor showed me the front of the boat, where numerous gauges and instruments were set in a panel under an expanse of window.

"Probably doesn't seem very exciting doing the same excursions day after day, but now and then, we see whales and dolphins. People love that. One lady almost fell out of the boat last week when she spotted a whale."

The image made me laugh. "Do you get a lot of people wanting tours?"

"There's a lot of competition now, but I get enough to pay the bills. On weekends, I work with Jason at the Blue Lagoon. It gets me a few extra bucks. It's a karaoke bar on the strip. He's the bartender. I'm just the announcer."

I didn't recall him mentioning his other job. "That sounds interesting."

"Not so much, but the pay is good. I don't get too many night excursions. The club pays well, and it gives me extra money. The faster I get this boat paid off, the closer I get to accomplishing my dream."

"Do you mean going back to university?" I wasn't sure if I was treading on sacred ground, but my curiosity won out.

Connor glanced at his watch. "We'll have to save that for another time. That is, if there is another time. Right now, I need to get you home. I don't want your dad thinking I'm irresponsible."

I'd told Dad I would be home between five and five thirty, and it was now five fifteen. The marina was about ten minutes from the apartment building, so there was no risk of Connor's looking irresponsible. Ricky was cleaning up when we returned to the dock. I thanked him for the tour.

"Promise you will come back?" he said.

"I promise." I wondered how many other girls had been given the same tour.

"I think you won him over." As if he'd read my thoughts, he added, "Oh, and if you think I've brought other girls on the boat, you would be mistaken."

"How did you know I was thinking that?"

"Micaela, you are transparent, and considering your first impression of me, it only figures it would be something you were wondering."

I really had to work on my acting skills.

He walked me to the elevator. I wasn't a kiss-on-the-first-date kind of girl. Although I appreciated his not trying, I was a little disappointed. I thanked him for the fun day and for introducing me to Ricky.

"Well?" He cocked his eyebrow and tilted his head. "Do I get a second date?"

"Let me sleep on that." I pushed the up button on the elevator, and the doors opened immediately.

"I think I'm going to take that as a yes. Have a great evening, and thank you for today."

The elevator doors closed. I couldn't remember ever feeling so light-headed and happy. That was the beginning of Connor and Micaela.

CHAPTER 10

Now

A sound like bees buzzing in my brain startled me from my dream. Images of Connor still floated amid scattered pieces of reality that tried to find their way to the surface of my consciousness. I sat up and looked around, trying to fight the feeling of disorientation. The buzzing continued. It was my phone, vibrating on the coffee table. I answered it.

"Mom, what the hell! I've been trying to get you for the past two hours. Are you okay?" Jess sounded frantic.

"I'm sorry. I had the ringer on my phone turned off, and I fell asleep."

"It's eight o'clock. Have you had dinner?"

I wasn't going to tell Jess I hadn't eaten. She was already treating me like an invalid, and I didn't like her fussing. "I had some soup and left-over lasagna," I lied.

She changed the subject. "I'm taking the girls to see Grandpa on Thursday, and I was wondering if you want to join us? They have a PA day at school, and, as usual, I can't find a sitter, so I'm calling in sick."

It had been over a month since I'd visited Dad. He would be eighty-five his next birthday. Placing him in the nursing home had broken my heart, but there had been no other choice. The Alzheimer's had taken most of his memory and his vitality. My once strong, amazing father was confined to a wheelchair, staring into space. He remembered me, not as the woman I was today but as a young girl. He still thought Mom was alive. He would ask when she would be coming. In the beginning, I'd tell him the truth. He would accuse me of being crazy, making it up to hurt him.

"Why would you tell me something like that?" he'd scream at me. I learned quickly that lying was my best option. I'd tell him she would be coming soon. He would relax and seem satisfied, at least for the moment. Then he would ask again, and I would tell him the same thing, until I found a subject to distract him. He didn't remember Jess or even acknowledge the twins. He never asked about Jack. The peculiar thing was, he wanted to play Scrabble with me. I purchased the game, and we'd play until he was too sleepy to continue. I was amazed how he remembered difficult words but could barely recall his own life.

I agreed to go with Jess, as long as she didn't get upset if he didn't remember her. I think she hoped he would get a flicker of remembrance. She and Dad had been close when she was little. She was a stranger now.

"When is your last class?" Jess asked.

"I'll be finished about two, if you want to pick me up at school. It's probably closer for you."

She shared some funny stories about the girls, making me laugh, and then said good night. She seemed reassured I was fine.

I managed to pull myself from the couch, turn on some lights, and head for the kitchen. I heated up the soup but passed on the lasagna. The house felt like a tomb. Jess had been gone for just over a year, and the sounds of the children that once annoyed me now echoed in my mind, and I actually missed them. No matter how hard I tried to subdue the memories of Connor, they remained on the fringe of my awareness. I hadn't thought about him in years, and any time I did, I simply pushed the memory back into the dark bowels of my mind, where I stored all my forbidden thoughts. It wasn't as easy as it once was.

I decided to distract myself by working. I still had papers to grade. I disciplined myself to check emails. Nothing noteworthy there. I sorted the rest of the essays by what I believed their grades would be—good ones on the top and the failures at the bottom. It was a game I liked to play once in a while. I was always about 95 percent correct. I didn't know why I even bothered to read them. This time, though, I got a surprise. Two students who had been average last semester got A's, and one who had failed got a B. Maybe I wasn't that bad a teacher after all.

By the time I turned off my bedroom light and cuddled under my comforter, I had moved from exhaustion into a state of tossing and turning. I hated taking sleeping pills but gave in and fell into a dreamless sleep. I paid the price for the pills the next morning. My head felt like it was filled with cotton candy. Two coffees and an energy drink got me through three lectures and a staff meeting and, finally, home. I rarely drank coffee and was totally against using stimulants, but what the heck; I wasn't exactly an advertisement for glowing health. I already had cancer. I knew my bladder wouldn't be happy with my caffeine boost.

No sooner had I arrived home, taken off my jacket, and set my briefcase on the dining room table than the doorbell rang. A glimpse through the dining room window indicated a man standing on my porch. I recognized the profile. It was Jack. He was the last person on the planet I wanted to see, but I opened the door anyway.

"Hi" was the extent of his greeting.

We stood staring at each other for what felt like a minute. I hadn't seen him in over a year. He was still Jack—no significant changes; not particularly handsome but attractive in his own way. His age was starting to creep up on him. A few silver hairs in his beard and the sides of his hairline actually gave him some character, which the man sadly lacked.

"Aren't you going to invite me in?"

I stepped aside without comment.

He clearly assumed I would let him stay, as he removed his coat and hung it on the coat tree in the hall. "You're looking good."

I was sure he was lying, but it helped fill the awkwardness between us. He didn't acknowledge my short hair. "Why are you here?" I chose the direct approach, which was always best with Jack. I wanted to add *Does your girlfriend know?* but censored myself.

He walked straight into the kitchen as if he still lived in the house. "Got anything cold to drink?" He sat in the chair that was once designated as his.

"Just water or iced tea." There was no longer any reason to stock beer. I strongly disliked the taste, and pop and alcohol were on my forbidden list. His choice was limited.

"Iced tea will be fine."

I poured the beverage and added ice, as Jack always wanted lots of ice, even if he drank beer from a glass, which Jess felt was stupid—a complete waste of beer, she thought. Placing the drink on the table, I repeated my original question. "So why are you here?" I chose to lean against the kitchen counter rather than sit with him at the table.

According to Jess, she had informed her dad of my new "situation." I wasn't happy she'd taken it upon herself to disclose my cancer diagnosis, but I supposed it really didn't matter anyway. I didn't care what Jack thought one way or the other. I figured it was the inspiration for his visit. There was no other reason I could think of, short of some financial problems that kept him from paying alimony, that would make him bother to take time from his girlfriend and busy life to see me. I decided to be direct. The sooner he told me, the sooner he would leave.

"Did Jess send you over to talk me into being 'reasonable,' as she puts it? She seems to be doing that a lot lately."

"Yes, but I told her it would probably be a waste of time, knowing how stubborn you can be."

"Why is it when I defend my own needs and feelings, I'm considered stubborn, and when the two of you want to defend your opinions and feelings, you're just being reasonable and logical?" I didn't bother to mask the annoyance in my voice.

"I'm not trying to start an argument, Micaela. I actually came here to tell you how sorry I am for everything."

Jack was never sorry. This was something new. "Define *everything*." I had to admit I was curious.

"You know … the divorce … Lisa … not communicating my feelings as well as I should have, but you weren't that forthcoming either. I always felt as if you were keeping things from me. You rarely talked about your past and why you went through bouts of depression."

He was right. I didn't talk about my past. "So why now? It's a little late, don't you think? Oh, I get it. Now that you think I'm dying, you want to ease your guilt. I'm surprised you could even feel guilty."

He ignored my sarcasm. "I guess you have a right to be angry."

"I'm not angry. I'm way past that."

"Lisa left me."

"So that's it. You've lost your playmate."

"You were right all along. She was too young. She's taking me for a royal ride. What the hell? We weren't even married. I offered her a decent settlement, but she refused. She wants half of everything."

"You lived together for three years, Jack; that makes it common law, and guess what? She's entitled." There was a certain satisfaction in knowing karma might actually exist.

"I was an idiot. She reminded me of you in some ways—at least the you I met and married—and when our marriage started to fall apart, I needed the distraction to help me get over losing you."

"Short memory! You left me, remember?"

"Technically speaking, yes, but you had already left our relationship almost from the time Jess was born. Probably even before that. Jess became your world, and then it was your teaching. You thought I spent so much time at work, but I felt more wanted and needed there. Some nights I didn't even want to come home."

This revelation didn't surprise me.

"I sensed something was wrong," he said.

I must have made a disagreeable face, as he qualified his comment.

"It's true. You would spend time with your dad on weekends and use Jess as an excuse to avoid sex, and even when we did make love, you seemed detached. I used to make excuses for you when you were still acting, thinking you were stressed or wrapped up in whatever project you were involved with, but it didn't change when you gave up your career. Then I thought it was because you'd left the theater, and you were depressed. You were different when I first met you, at least you seemed different. Maybe I just didn't notice. I was crazy about you."

"I was seeing a shrink then."

He looked startled. "Well, this is news! Why didn't you tell me?"

"Because it was none of your business. We weren't married, and I stopped going when we got engaged."

"Don't you think it might have been important to me? Why were you seeing a psychiatrist?"

"It's not important. It was a long time ago, and it's still none of your business."

He appeared surprised but backed off. "It has to do with that Connor guy, doesn't it?"

It was my turn to be surprised. I'd never told Jack about Connor. I'd spent three-quarters of my life not thinking about him, let alone speaking his name. I knew there was only one person who could have informed him. I felt betrayed by my closest friend. She'd agreed that never—not under any circumstances—would Connor be mentioned.

Jack confirmed my suspicions. "Don't get mad at Vini. I manipulated her into telling me."

"When?"

"Last time we were in New York. I would never have asked her if you hadn't said the guy's name in your sleep. Not once but several times. Don't you recall? I asked you who Connor was. You got pissed and told me I imagined it."

I vaguely remembered but didn't let on that I did. "What did Vini tell you?"

"She said there was a guy, a friend of her brother Jason, who hung out with you and your *crowd*, as she called it, when you lived in Florida."

"And ..." I prompted.

"Only that you two had the hots for each other when you were at school, but the relationship died, and you went off to New York, and that was the end of it."

At least Vini hadn't totally betrayed me.

"Was that really the end of it, Micaela?"

"Yes" was all I volunteered. "Please let's drop it. It was a very long time ago. I was young and vulnerable. Mom had died, and I was still mourning her. Connor was just there."

"You obviously didn't get over him if you were dreaming about him."

"Enough, Jack! Look, I'm tired, and I have papers to mark." I didn't, but it was a great excuse. "You said you were sorry. I accept your apology. I'm sorry if I was responsible in any way for your thinking you had to find a twenty-year-old waitress to make yourself feel better. Oh, and I'm sorry it didn't work out." I wasn't the least bit sorry but said it anyway. "Let's call it a night, okay?" I faked a yawn.

Jack didn't take the hint. "Micaela, I think you still love the guy, and maybe you never did love me."

Any patience I felt was dissolving. I wanted Jack to leave. "Leave it alone, Jack. Will you just go?"

"Okay, I get it. I'm leaving."

I followed him to the door. He touched my arm, but I pulled away. After putting on his coat, he stood looking at me. He had more to say.

"Micaela, I have always loved you, despite what you think. I wasn't a great husband. I was an okay father, at least Jess says I was. I loved you and still do, although it probably doesn't count for much. Please call if you need anything."

I couldn't imagine what I might need that Jack could provide but agreed, just for the sake of ending any further disclosures. He turned to go, and before closing the door, he asked how Dad was doing, as if it was an afterthought. They got along but were never close. Dad didn't let on, but I guessed Jack Webster wasn't one of his favorite people.

"As well as can be expected." There was no use describing Dad's condition, as Jack would probably not be interested.

"Say hi to Art for me," he called as he got into his BMW sports car.

I closed the door and secured the latch. Despite any bad feelings I had toward Jack, I could understand why he felt the way he did. I'd never been transparent with him about my past. I knew there were doors I didn't want to open, and Jack would have asked questions … questions I didn't want to answer or probably couldn't. I'd locked those doors a long time ago and wanted them to stay locked. Tears rolled down my cheeks. They weren't for Jack. He was right about my still loving Connor. I knew that would never change.

I struggled upstairs. I didn't want anything to eat. The conversation with Jack had left me even more exhausted and completely drained. Just the mention of Connor's name created waves of anxiety and stirred long-forgotten memories. I collapsed on my bed in tears and cried until sleep returned me to the past.

CHAPTER 11

Then

The week following my date with Connor was hectic. I barely had time to think about him, and when I did, I would distract myself with studying my lines or practicing my vocal exercises. He called every night but kept our conversations short out of respect for my time constraints. He made me laugh with Ricky stories, sharing all his hilarious antics. Ricky, apparently, hadn't stopped talking about me since we'd met. Connor was sure he had a crush.

The night before my performance, I did not take his call. I already felt butterflies forming in my stomach and needed no distractions. Dad told me later they'd had a nice chat, as he referred to their conversation. He informed me that Connor would be attending my performance with friends, which I assumed meant Vini, Jason, and Owen. Dad passed along Connor's well wishes, using the expression "break a leg," which I thought made no sense at all. I knew it meant good luck but never quite understood why people said it.

Vini was a different story; she wasn't thrilled at being put off. She'd learned from Jason that Connor and I had dated and was dying to find out any juicy details, and when I wasn't forthcoming on providing a play-by-play, I could almost sense her pouting. I disliked gossip, especially when the subject was my private life.

I was already nervous about performing my first major part in front of a group of people, and knowing Connor would be in the audience sent the butterflies into even more of a frenzy.

When it was time for the curtain call, my heart was racing. It was like an electric shock passing through me—total elation! The audience wouldn't stop clapping and stood, requesting more. One of my fellow actors nudged me forward and whispered in my ear, "They want *you*." It was too surreal to believe. The clapping got louder when I moved to the front of the stage. I heard hooting and whistling. I knew then, beyond a shadow of a doubt, that the theater was where I wanted to be.

The head of our Theater Arts Department crossed the stage with two dozen red roses and placed them in my arms. The lights were blinding, and I could only make out the front row but hoped Connor was out there somewhere. Backstage was filled with friends and parents, all hugging and congratulating my fellow performers. I stopped and spoke with a few. One grabbed my arm and pulled me aside. It was Kevin Marshall, who played my leading man.

"You were fantastic, Micaela. I'm chopped liver next to you."

I assured him he was great and that he only enhanced my performance. We hugged. More hugs were waiting for me in the dressing room.

Dad stood by the dressing room door with a dozen of my favorite ivory roses, waiting patiently until all the excitement died down. He looked as if he'd been crying. I placed the other flowers I'd been given on the dressing table and took his.

His voice was husky with emotion. "My little girl is all grown up. I am so proud of you, Micaela."

"I wouldn't be here, Dad, if it wasn't for you. I can't tell you how grateful I am for your support and all the sacrifices you make financially to send me to college. I couldn't ask for a better father."

A woman standing to the right of him placed her hand on dad's arm.

Dad introduced her. "Micaela, this is Gloria, the lady who lives in our building." He didn't add to his introduction. This had to be the woman he'd met in the elevator.

"Hello," she said, offering her hand. Her handshake was like brushing against a warm blanket. "It's nice to finally meet you, Micaela. Your dad never stops talking about you. I certainly enjoyed your performance."

"Thank you."

Dad hadn't informed me he was bringing her. It was the second date, at least that I knew of. I decided mentioning Mom might not be a good idea, but Dad did anyway.

"Your mom would be so proud of you."

Gloria hooked her arm around Dad's. "Art, we have reservations at the Captain's Feast for eight, and Saturday night is very busy. We might not get a parking space. I think we should go before it gets too crowded. Doesn't Micaela have her evening performance to get ready for?"

I noted what I interpreted as a hint of possession in her tone and flinched.

Another hug from Dad with a reminder that he would pick me up later. I hadn't driven my car, knowing I would be unable to drive in the state I was in. Before I even had a chance to say goodbye, Vini rushed at me, practically knocking me over.

"Wow, wow, and wow! Micki, I can't believe how good you were." Her excitement was almost childlike.

"Why do you think she goes to college? Certainly not to find a man, at least one who isn't gay."

I shot Owen a look, registering my annoyance at his comment.

"Sweetie, my gaydar is lighting up in a huge way," he said. "Sorry if I offended." He hugged me, something I didn't expect. "You have star quality written all over you. I hope you remember us little people when you have your name in lights on Broadway."

Jason took his turn at hugging and apologized for Owen's outspokenness. "Your voice is amazing. We will have to make a demo tape together. I have a few songs we can try out."

I laughed, and Vini punched him. "Don't be ridiculous. Micaela wouldn't be interested in your stupid songs. She's more cultured."

"My songs *are* cultured, and they are not stupid. You never listen, so how would you know?"

"Hey, you two! Stop bickering! This is Micaela's time to shine." Connor's voice sent an unexpected sensation of pleasure throughout my body. He handed me one beautiful long-stemmed red rosebud, which had more significance than the dozens I'd already received. "You have a beautiful voice, and I forgot you were Micaela for a few moments. You were a perfect Maria."

"I'm no Julie Andrews."

"I wouldn't say that. You're certainly going to give her a run for her money. Is your dad around? I'd like to meet him." Connor glanced over my shoulder.

"He has a date and apparently is taking her to dinner, so they left," I said.

"You sound pissed, Micki. You don't like her, do you," Vini stated. I guessed she was using her sixth sense again.

"I don't even know her. Why would I be pissed?" I thought about it for a second. "Yeah, I guess I am a little. I'm not used to seeing him with anyone but Mom."

"Well," Connor said, "I'll just have to meet him another time. I hope your second performance is as great. I have to pick up Ricky at the boat. Some of my father's friends are visiting, and my parents insisted we join them for dinner. Will you be up to taking a phone call later, or do you have plans after the performance?"

"There's a cast party, but I'm passing on it. Dad is picking me up. I'm not much on parties, as you already know." Trading off the party for a phone call from Connor was a no-brainer.

A caterer with a platter of sandwiches shoved his way through the dressing room. Vini swiped one from the tray.

"You're disgusting, Vin," Jason said. "That's not for you. Put it back." He looked embarrassed, and Owen did an eye roll.

"Too late," she said as she popped the sandwich in her mouth.

"Guys!" Connor said," We need to let Micaela get something to eat and relax before she has to go on again. If you want a ride back into Clearwater, we have to leave now. You know how my parents get if I'm late for one of their dinners."

"I'm stayin'," Vini declared between bites of her egg salad sandwich. "I want to see it again." She looked at Jason. "You guys can go with Connor. I can get the bus back. No problemo."

"We'd stay too, but I have to work tonight," Jason explained. "And Owen is dog-sitting for a friend. He's such a pushover for anything involving animals."

"Are you coming, or do I leave without you?" Connor seemed to be losing patience.

Owen kissed my cheek. "Break a leg, sweetie." It was the second time that expression had come up, but it worked for my first performance.

After the guys left, Vini stuck around, eating more sandwiches, while I nibbled on some cheese and crackers. "So tell me what's up, girl," she said between bites.

"Nothing to tell," I replied.

"Bullshit! I have eyes, you know. I saw the way you looked at each other, all starry-eyed, like there was only the two of you in the room."

"It was just one date, and no, he didn't kiss me." I'd anticipated her next question.

"I'm sure there will be more. I know Connor. He doesn't look like that around other girls."

"How many other girls are there?" I couldn't help it; I had to ask.

"None that I know of. Not now, at least. There was a girl when he was in university. She was all fluff and dumb as a pig."

"Pigs aren't dumb, Vini." It was a strange expression.

"Anyway, you know what I mean. She made Bonnie look smart, and that's saying a lot. Jase and I tried to be nice to her, but it was hard. I can't tell you how boring she was. I don't know what Connor saw in her. I admit she had a great body. Guys can be so dumb. She actually had the nerve to tell Connor she didn't want him hanging out with me and my 'fairy' brother. That was their first argument. They broke up later."

"What happened?"

"She walked out. Bonnie pulled a stunt and convinced Alicia—that was her name—that she was sleeping with Connor. When Connor denied it, Alicia didn't believe him. Bonnie can be pretty convincing when she puts that stupid brain of hers into action." Vini finished the rest of her sandwich and took a cola from the tub of ice sitting on the floor. She popped the tab and guzzled down half of it. She burped. "Sorry."

I sipped at the water I'd chosen. I wanted to know more about Connor's relationships with Alicia and Bonnie. "So what happened after that?"

"He quit university. Boy, were his parents pissed off. That's when he moved out and—what is it they say?—the rest is history."

My curiosity at what she referred to as Connor's history had been piqued, but the stage manager popped his head through the door and asked friends and family to leave. The next performance was in a half hour.

Vini finished her pop and burped again. No apology this time. "Guess that's my cue to move my ass. If I don't see you after, I'll see you Monday for lunch, same time, same place."

The evening performance went well, almost better than the first. Same curtain calls, and the initial excitement still lingered. I was floating on cloud nine when Dad picked me up. Vini was nowhere to be seen. I felt I was letting my coactors and teachers down by not attending the afterparty, although I didn't think they would be too disappointed, given the buzz of excitement in the air. They were all on their own clouds. Dad asked how it went. I told him great. I asked him about his dinner. He said okay, but there was no mention of Gloria, and I didn't ask.

When we arrived home, I found two empty jars in the cupboard and placed my roses in water, clipping the ends off as Mom used to do. My single bud rose I placed in a glass and carried it to my room. I heard the phone ring and ran to get it before Dad picked it up.

"It's not too late to be calling, is it?" I felt that familiar warm feeling in my chest as soon as I heard Connor's voice.

The clock on the kitchen stove said ten minutes past eleven. I didn't feel the least bit tired, still riding on the adrenaline of the evening. "No, it's fine."

Dad shot me one of his all-knowing looks, gave me a thumbs up sign as if he knew who I was talking to; then went to his room.

We talked about the play. Again, Connor launched into compliments about how great I'd been. I didn't think I was as great as he thought, but I was happy with my work and loved hearing it from him. He told me dinner with his parents was awful. I felt sad that he and his family did not get along. I was fortunate to have great parents I loved being with, even though I no longer had my mom.

"How do you think you're going to feel tomorrow?"

"Not sure at this point. Why?"

"I was wondering if you would like to go to lunch again."

I jumped on the invitation. I had planned on sleeping until noon but didn't care how tired I'd be. My desire to be with Connor was greater than my need for rest. "Sure."

"Good! I'll pick you up around noon. You get some sleep, and I'll see you tomorrow."

I couldn't sleep. I tossed and turned most of the night. I relived the excitement of the play, but the real reason was probably my anticipation of seeing Connor again.

Lunch was short but fun. We talked more about our lives and my ambition. Connor said he fully understood why I wanted to pursue the stage. A serious look crossed his handsome face when he suggested he would probably lose me to the bright lights and glamor of stardom. The implication we were an established couple and the extent of his feelings thrilled me, but a new awareness set in. I was suddenly sad. Leaving was going to be more difficult now. I knew myself well enough to know he wasn't just some passing interest. I could feel the stirrings of love bubbling up in my heart. I still had another year of college and lots could happen in a year.

I simply said, "No chance you will lose me." I wasn't sure I convinced him.

He again walked me to the elevator. This time, he took my hand and kissed it; not what I expected, but I wasn't totally disappointed. My vision of our first kiss was not in the middle of my apartment lobby. I pictured moonlight and a stroll along the beach. I hoped with all my heart that it would happen as I pictured it and that it would happen the next time we were together. I just didn't realize how little time we had.

CHAPTER 12

My first year was almost complete, and I was looking forward to spending a few weeks with Connor before my second year started. Unlike high school, there was no summer vacation. Shorter holidays meant courses could be completed in two years, not three. It took a little getting used to, but I didn't mind. Jason wouldn't stop talking about how glad he was to be finished and to start looking for work. He was graduating in two weeks and already applying for jobs in Los Angeles. I tried convincing him that set decorator positions would more likely be available in New York, but he hated winter, even though he'd never actually experienced it. And if Owen was relocating with him, which of course he was, then no snow! Owen claimed he was allergic, much the same as some people suffered from hay fever. He called it winter fever. I thought he was kidding, but he insisted it was a real issue. Jason was grateful to have a partner who would give up his job and go with him. I agreed and wondered if Connor would do the same for me. Doubtful, but a girl could dream.

Exams were over. A break, even a short one, before the next year sounded heavenly. Dad was preoccupied with Gloria, and I was trying to get used to that. I didn't have a choice. He sensed my discomfort and reassured me that no one would ever take Mom's place in his heart, but there was room for someone else.

"See, right here," he'd said, indicating a spot somewhere around the top right side of his heart. "This little corner is empty. You and your mom have the rest."

I realized Dad deserved to be happy, and after I left, maybe having Gloria in his life would ease the loneliness, so I made an effort to accept her. She would visit during the week, bringing casseroles and baked goods and, on occasion, stay for dinner. I didn't get the vibe he wanted much more than a friendship, but I could have been wrong. Maybe, out of respect for my feelings, he didn't show affection in front of me. She, on the other hand, was sending out huge messages of wanting more. She would lean over him when serving his plate, reach out and touch his hand, and giggle like a schoolgirl at his jokes. I felt sorry for her if dad didn't intend creating a deeper relationship but also relieved.

The week before school ended, Jason joined Vini and me for lunch at what we now thought of as our table. Vini decided we should celebrate Jason's graduation. Vini loved parties. She suggested the Blue Lagoon, where Jason and Connor worked, and asked if I minded her choice. I didn't know much about the bar scene, but I thought it would be okay. I figured if Connor worked there, it had to be somewhat decent, so I agreed.

"You sure? It's a gay nightclub," Jason explained.

I tried not to look shocked. Connor had not been forthcoming on what kind of a bar it was. I prided myself on my open mind, but it would certainly test my comfort zones. "Are regular people allowed to go?" I knew it sounded awkward the moment it was out of my mouth. "I mean non-gay people." I was embarrassed.

Jason laughed. "Yes, non-gay people—or you *regular* folk—can go if you're cool with it. Connor pays no attention, but you should see the number of times he gets hit on. I've got it covered, though. I put the word out that Connor's straighter than an arrow, and anyone who touches him will have to answer to our bouncer."

"You should see that guy. He's built like a brick shit house." Vini and her colorful language again, but it made me laugh.

"Will you please stop swearing, Vin? It makes you sound trashy. Mom taught you better than that."

"Gee! She has a trashy daughter and a gay son. Aren't we making her proud?"

I ignored the brother and sister banter and asked if Connor would be joining us or if he'd be working.

"Yeah, he has to work," Jason replied. "But that's okay. He works for an hour for two sets, and I think I can probably get the night off."

"He's going to be blown away if you come." Vini sounded excited. "Not even Bonnie has been there. Of course, she wouldn't be caught dead going into a gay bar. Be funny if she did, though. Bonnie dead sounds like a plan to me."

Vini's dislike of Bonnie was more intense than simple annoyance. There was something more to it. "You really don't like her." I didn't ask why, hoping she would tell me.

Jason offered an explanation. "For starters, Bonnie doesn't like black people, and she's made that very apparent. Her family is middle-class pro-white and wouldn't miss Sunday lunches at the yacht club for anything. She tries to make Vin and me feel like outsiders. Then there's the fact that in high school, Bonnie was the prom queen and was past obnoxious. She tripped Vin in the hall once, and she and her stupid friends wrote on Vin's locker in red lipstick something I won't even repeat."

"Nigger, go back to where you came from," Vini interjected. "Didn't bother me. I had some friends of my own, and we put 'Clearwater slut' on hers. Thing is, she didn't get caught. We did. Got suspended. That bothered me more than what she put on my locker."

Jason continued his explanation as if Vini wasn't present. "When Connor was dating Bonnie in high school, it drove Vin nuts."

I couldn't help reacting to what I'd just heard. "Were they going steady?" Connor had made it sound like it wasn't serious, and I was just insecure enough about our relationship to inquire. I wanted to believe him, but he might have left out some information in an effort to convince me he wasn't a player.

"No, nothing like that," Jason said. "You couldn't call them boyfriend and girlfriend. They dated a few times, but Connor was never serious about her. When he was eighteen, he might have been attracted to her, but he got over it fast. He tried to ditch her, but she couldn't take a hint. She followed him around until he went to university. He had a girlfriend, and Bonnie tried to break them up."

"I told Micaela about Alicia. Bonnie is such a bitch. Her little scheme worked." Vini practically spat the words out.

"I think Vin was glad when it happened because she was hoping that maybe Connor would finally deal with Bonnie and see what she was really like. She went after her. There was one hell of a cat fight."

"Yeah, you should have seen it." There was a look of satisfaction on Vini's face.

"We should have sold tickets," Jason added. "We would have made a few bucks. Vin got in trouble when Bonnie's parents pressed charges, but they didn't stick. Connor intervened, and the charges were dropped. It was too bad because Connor quit university after Alicia walked and never said anything to us about Bonnie, but we're pretty sure he gets it."

Vini jumped in. "I probably shouldn't have gone after her, but shit, it felt good. I broke her nose. She better not even think about trying to break up Connor and Micaela, or I'll rip her throat out."

"You're lucky the charges got dropped," Jason said.

"You're talking like we're a couple. We're just dating," I explained. But I liked the thought.

"Get with the program, girlfriend. You're a couple. You probably haven't done the deed yet, but it's gonna happen soon."

Jason nudged Vini's arm. "You can be so crass."

"First, I'm trash. Now I'm crass. I love you too!"

"So when will this party be?" I asked, attempting to change the subject.

"How about Friday night?" Jason replied.

I wasn't able to discuss weekend plans with Connor, as he and Ricky had gone with his parents to Seattle for his paternal grandfather's funeral. I had extended my condolences, but Connor said he barely knew him. He'd seen him once when he was ten. The more I heard about his family, the more grateful I was for mine.

Suddenly, Vini grabbed her brother's arm. She looked as if she was going to jump out of her skin with excitement. "I've got an idea!"

"What now, Vin? Do I dare ask? If it's something crazy, forget it."

Vini ignored her brother. "How about we don't tell Connor that Micaela is coming. He has to work Friday and Saturday night anyway, so chances are he won't be asking her out. We can surprise him."

"How do you think you're going to pull that off?" Jason questioned.

"Not sure yet, but I'll figure it out."

"Of course you will." Jason's sarcasm was apparent.

"Do you think he'll mind my showing up at his work?" I still didn't know Connor well enough to be sure he'd be okay with it.

"What? Are you nuts?" Vini said. "Of course he won't mind. He'll love it. Let's do it!"

And so we did.

CHAPTER 13

Asking Dad for money to buy a new dress for the party wasn't easy. It felt like a frivolous expense, and I was positive he would turn me down. He surprised me and agreed, but he made me promise it wouldn't be too sexy. I wasn't sure what he thought was too sexy but suspected it was anything that suggested I was no longer ten years old.

Having Vini accompany me on a shopping trip was a bad idea. Our tastes were vastly different. She wanted me to try on brightly colored shiny dresses and matching tops with glitter and flowers on the front. To make her happy, I tried on a lime-green satin skirt with a similar-colored beaded top. I laughed when I saw my image in the mirror. I'd blend in with my car.

I finally settled on a very simple red-crepe cocktail dress. I suspected Dad would not approve of the strapless bodice that exposed cleavage, wrapped around my bust, hugged my torso, and outlined the curve of my hips before it fell gently to my knees. I decided to risk his disaproval and purchase it. I loved it and so did Vini. My flats would look ridiculous, so shoes were the next purchase. My height was no longer a concern. Connor's six foot two inches would still surpass me in three-inch heels. Vini chose a pale-gold strappy sandal with a high back. They were a little more than I intended to spend, which meant dipping into my gas money for the month. I wouldn't tell Dad.

Connor called as soon as he arrived back in Clearwater. I told him I didn't find my exams too difficult but didn't mention Jason's party idea. I could hear Ricky begging to speak with me. Connor passed the phone to him with the stipulation he couldn't keep me too long. He was shy at first but got over it quickly. I heard about his exams, which were coming up the following week, and how he'd won his baseball tournament. He didn't like Seattle because it rained all the time, but he loved seeing his grandmother. Before giving the phone back to Connor, he asked if I could come Sunday on the boat.

I heard Connor, in the background, quickly interject, "Whoa, guy! Before you get too excited, I don't know if I'm booked for Sunday yet."

Ricky pleaded for him to check, and when Connor came back on the line, he apologized for Ricky's impulsiveness and added, "The funny thing is, I was going to check anyway. I have to work Friday and Saturday night at the club, and I have three trips around Clearwater most of the day Saturday, so ..." He stretched out the *so* and paused. "What do you say the three of us go to Indian Shores on Sunday? There's an ice cream shop Ricky really likes, and maybe we can manage a run along the coast. We'll have all day. What do you think?"

"I think that sounds great." I hoped Vini was right about his loving my going to the club, or Sunday might be a whole lot different than expected.

I was still in my room, deciding what necklace to wear, when Owen announced his arrival Friday night. He was instructed to drive me, as Vini didn't want Connor seeing my car and spoiling the surprise. Dad's eyes practically popped out of his skull when he saw my dress.

"I said a little sexy. That's way beyond what I meant." He shook his head and smiled. "I guess I just have to face the fact you're a woman now. It's a tough one, though."

Before he could say anything more, I grabbed my purse, gave him a kiss, and headed for the elevator. Owen was waiting for me beside his blue Honda and opened the passenger door—another gentleman!

"Darling, you look absolutely stunning. If I weren't gay, I would fall madly in love with you. Connor will be blown away, and speaking of his royal goodness, he'll be at the club in an hour. Vini wants us to meet Jason at the back entrance near the kitchen. She didn't think it was enough just having me drive you and leaving that repulsive car of yours at home. I'll explain on the way."

Vini hadn't told me her plan. Whether she actually hadn't formulated it at the time I asked or wanted to keep me in suspense, I didn't know. "So what does Vini have planned?" I asked as we pulled on to the highway. I wasn't sure I would comply but was interested enough to consider it.

"That girl loves drama. She wants you and Jason to sing a duet. I think it's that Sonny and Cher song. You know the one—'I Got You Babe.' Personally, I think that delicious creature is far too good for Sonny."

"She wants me to sing?" I didn't like the idea already.

"With your voice, doll, it will be sensational. Jason isn't as bad as Vini makes out. He just likes music he can play on his guitar. She wants you and Jason to hide backstage. She's going to slip the announcement card to Connor, and he'll have to introduce you. She brought her camera to catch the look on his face. Told you she likes drama."

Having never done karaoke before, I was more nervous about singing an unrehearsed song than Connor's reaction. "I'm not sure I want to do that."

"I think it might be fun. You'll be fine. You just have to follow the prompter, and he can carry it off. The hardest part will be keeping a straight face with all the gestures he makes. It's quite hilarious."

"I'll think about it."

"You have about fifteen minutes, so you better think fast."

Owen pulled around the back of the club. He'd made the decision for me. Jason met us at the back door and escorted us through the kitchen, where Vini was waiting. I followed, so my fate was sealed. Jason said I looked fabulous. Vini agreed. I got a few stares from the waiters, but for the most part, we were ignored. I obviously wasn't their type. Vini glanced at her watch, the Mickey Mouse one. It clashed with her orange-and-black flowered dress. A red-and-blue hair ribbon only added to the mismatched color scheme.

"Connor's not here yet, but he shouldn't be too much longer. Jason says the deejay goes for his break in twenty minutes. You're going to have to hide out in the back room. Jason will get you when it's time. Do you want a drink or something while you're waiting?" Vini acted as if she ran the place.

"No alcohol, Vin. You know the rules. I don't want to lose my job," Jason said as he led the way to the back office. "I cleared it with my boss. He's a pretty cool guy. I'll be back in about fifteen minutes."

"I'll keep her company." Owen's offer was appreciated. "If Connor asks where I am, tell him I'm in the little boys' room."

Jason left and closed the door. I was feeling extremely nervous and stupid. "I wish I hadn't agreed to this."

"It'll be over before you know it, and Vini will have something to talk about for weeks." Owen planted himself in the leather chair behind a very messy desk. I sat in a rather beat-up version in front of him.

"Did Vini tell you Jason and I are going to Cancun for a week at Christmas? It's my gift to him for all the hard work he's put in over the past two years."

"No, she didn't. That will be nice."

"Do you like to travel?" Owen's attempt at small talk was helping me with my nerves.

"I never really thought about it much. Other than Toronto and New York to visit my aunt, I haven't been many places. When Dad and I drove here, I saw a few interesting cities. My parents didn't have a lot of money, and whatever they had, they spent on my singing and dance lessons."

"Your parents sound like they love you a lot."

"Yeah, I'm pretty lucky. My mom passed away when I was sixteen, and it's just Dad and me now. How about yours?"

"They were killed in a car accident when I was four. My sister and I were raised by my grandmother. She's still alive and going strong. Quite the character."

"I'm sorry about your parents."

"Don't be. They were both alcoholics who enabled each other. My father was drunk at the time of the accident. I don't remember much about them. My sister's in rehab. She fell in love with the bottle too."

Jason peeked around the door. "Connor's here, and Vin's about to give him his intro cards. Let's get this show on the road." I was relieved I didn't have to respond to Owen's sad story.

Jason and I remained at the side of the stage. From where we stood, I could see a deejay sitting in a glass booth above the dance floor, where two heavily made-up women were gyrating to Madonna's "Like a Virgin," their undulating bodies suggesting they were more than mere acquaintances. A mirror ball flashed dozens of colored lights on and off in time with the music. I had a basic idea what clubs looked like, but this was my first real encounter. I hadn't shared that information with Vini, as I didn't want to appear unenlightened. At eighteen, I wasn't even legal drinking age. Dad would probably hemorrhage if he found out I was in a bar, let alone a gay bar.

I could see Connor clearly. He was dressed in a pair of tight jeans, white T-shirt, and jean jacket. I think I expected him to be in a suit, but this was a gay bar, not Carnegie Hall. I felt overdressed, which only added to my discomfort. Jason and Owen were wearing jeans with corduroy jackets, a little more formal but still casual. Connor bantered with the audience for a few minutes. Several guys, wearing only black leather pants and gold chains and medallions against their bare chests, hooted at him; some whistled. There didn't seem to be a dress code. Connor looked quite comfortable in this environment. He knew how to handle it. Vini approached the stage. He stared at her, put his hand over the microphone, and leaned down to speak with her. She just handed him the card. He read it. The look on his face was difficult to interpret. He paused and reread it. Vini took his picture as he broke out in a huge grin.

"Guys and gals, we are in for a treat tonight. The Blue Lagoon's own bartender, Mr. Jason DeMille, and the amazing and beautiful Miss Micaela Lewiski, Clearwater's promising Broadway actress, will be performing Sonny and Cher's 'I Got You Babe.' Let's give them a big welcome." Connor's introduction was overwhelming. The crowd hooted again. I suspected it wasn't for me. They were most likely regulars and knew Jason.

Jason and I came out from behind the curtains to join Connor, and Vini took his picture again. I smiled. He looked as if he'd been hit by a stun gun. Jason leaned over and whispered in his ear, loud enough that I heard it.

"Hey man, close your mouth; you're drooling."

Connor winked at me and touched my arm as he left to stand at the side of the stage. The music started, and Jason pointed to the monitor above us. The words scrolled across the screen. I sang the first line, and Jason followed. By the time we were halfway through the song, I was totally comfortable. Owen was right; Jason's attempt at duplicating Sonny was funny. The crowd responded by cheering and shouting; some even blew kisses, more at Jason than at me. Vini kept taking pictures. We teamed up on the last line, and when the music stopped, Jason gave me a kiss on the cheek. The audience clapped and yelled for an encore.

Jason took the mic. "Sorry, folks, you know what they say—always leave them wanting more."

Connor returned to the stage and took the mic from Jason. "Weren't they great! Let's hear it for Jason and Micaela." More clapping and hooting. Conner leaned into me. "Don't you dare go anywhere. I will be about an hour. Tell Jason to look after you. It can get pretty rough in here."

Jason, Vini, and I joined Owen in a corner booth and ordered ginger ales. Owen ordered a double martini; judging by the empty glass in front of him, it was his second. Two men in leather pants approached and hugged Jason. I guessed by the look on Owen's face he wasn't thrilled.

Vini was acting smug. "Told you Connor would be over the moon. I can't wait till I get these pictures developed. You two were amazing. I take it back. Maybe you and Jason should cut a demo record."

The next hour was fun. Two men singing "Big Yellow Taxi" sent us into gales of laughter. They were drunk and kept stumbling over the words. Three women chose Laura Branigan's "Gloria" and weren't half bad, but I couldn't help thinking it was a bit ironic, considering that was the name of Dad's girlfriend, and I still wasn't sure whether I liked her. I didn't want to think about Gloria, so focused mainly on Connor. He seemed different, very professional, and his sense of humor surprised me.

The lights on the stage went out, and the deejay returned to his cubicle. Connor joined us and slipped into the booth beside me.

"You guys got me good." He leaned over and gave me a gentle kiss.

"You're not mad, are you?" I needed to know. If he was, he'd done a good job of hiding it.

"Are you kidding? That was great. I couldn't believe it when Vini handed me that card. I had to read it twice in case I was hallucinating. By the way, you two make a great team." He turned to me. "That dress is something else." He didn't stop staring. It was becoming a habit. "You look amazing, but you always do, only now even more amazing."

"Thank you."

The look in Connor's eyes made me glad I'd chosen the dress. He took my hand and held it gently, rubbing his finger across my knuckles.

"Break it up, you two," Vini said. "The waiter's going to bring Jason a cake, and we have some presents for him." I got the impression that Vini's answer to everything was cake.

"I'm still digesting the one from Jason's birthday, but bring it on." Owen reached into the side pocket of his jacket and took out an envelope.

I felt guilty. I hadn't given Jason anything for his birthday, and now, nothing for his graduation. I apologized for my thoughtlessness.

"No problem," Jason said. "I don't expect gifts, but you actually did give me one. I loved singing with you. Thanks for doing that. I was positive you wouldn't, but I was wrong again, and Vin was right."

Vini interrupted him. "Told you."

"We didn't make a bet this time. Good thing, or I would have been out another five dollars." Jason opened his card and almost squealed when he saw the tickets to Cancun. He and Owen kissed. Vini and Connor didn't react, but it was not something I was used to.

Vini handed Jason a small package wrapped in silver foil with enough tape on it to fill a tape dispenser. "You might not want to open it here."

He ignored her warning and opened it anyway. Fumbling with the wrapping, he tried to break through the mass of tape. He looked at his sister. "You sure you're not secretly working as a security guard at Fort Knox?" Connor handed him his penknife. Jason opened the box, only to discover another well-taped one inside. He laughed. "You really didn't make it easy, Sis." More tape removal, and then he pulled out a black velvet case. Carefully, he opened the lid to view the contents. He gasped. "Vin, my God; how did you afford this?"

"I'll take it back if you don't want it."

"Not a chance." Jason turned the case so we could all see what lay in the velvet interior. It was a gold link bracelet with a gold band in the middle. He read the inscription out loud: "To the World's Best Brother. 1988." Jason cried.

"Told you not to open it here," Vini reminded him as he grabbed his sister and held her in a huge embrace.

"I think you topped me, Vini," Owen said, wiping the tears forming in his eyes.

The waiter brought the cake covered with sparklers. Written in white icing across the chocolate was "Congrats on graduating. Best wishes, with love, from all your friends." Jason remarked on the sparklers. "At least I don't have to blow out candles."

"That's only for birthdays." Vini passed Jason a knife. The first piece went to Owen. Connor and I refused our portions, telling Vini it was a lovely cake, but we would pass. Three floor staff and a few male patrons came by our table and sang "For He's a Jolly Good Fellow." Vini offered our pieces to the men who squeezed into the booth beside Jason. They lit cigarettes without even asking if we minded. The smoke swirled in the air around me. I was practically choking.

"I think Micaela and I will take a walk on the beach; that is, if she wants to."

"I'd like that." I was grateful for Connor's intervention.

No one minded. Jason and Owen were conversing with two of the guys and Vini with the other. She didn't seem to care in the least about being in the company of gay men. She was laughing while practically inhaling her second piece of cake. They barely noticed our leaving.

The night air felt good after the smoke-filled bar. I inhaled deeply, hoping to clear my lungs. After crossing the street, we followed the path to the beach. My feet hurt, and it was impossible to walk in my new shoes, so I removed them—instant relief! Losing the three inches put me just above Connor's shoulders.

The beach was deserted. A full moon cast a glow on the ocean, sending a ghostly light across a sky sprinkled with stars. Waves gently brushing the shoreline blended with the sound of traffic and late-night partygoers along the strip. As we continued walking, the sounds of humanity faded, leaving just the swish of the rolling waves. We stood together, gazing out at the ocean. At least I did. I could feel Connor looking at me.

"You're staring again."

"Sorry, can't help it. I really can't get enough of looking at you. You are so beautiful."

"I'm not beautiful."

"Yes, you are. The best part is you don't know it. When I saw you walking across the stage tonight, you took my breath away. It's not just the dress. It looks great on you, by the way. There's something about you. I knew from the moment I first saw you." He took my free hand. "You had an effect on me. ... Still do." He lifted my hand to his lips and kissed it. "You are my earth angel."

The feel of his lips sent warm tingles down my spine, sidetracking me from the chill of the night air.

"You're a brave girl, coming into a gay bar. Vini's used to it. Everyone knows her, and because she's Jason's sister, she gets a little respect. You're even braver, taking on that crowd from center stage, but it looked like they loved you."

"It wasn't me they loved."

"Give yourself some credit. You were great."

I wanted to change the subject. "How was your time in Seattle?"

"I guess okay. It was a funeral. I didn't do much sightseeing. It was raining most of the time. My grandmother came, so I got to spend some time with her. She and Grandpa divorced when I was about eight. She moved to California two years ago. Grams is very different from the rest of my family."

"Sounds like you really love her."

"I do. She took care of my brother and me when my parents were too busy or away on business. If it hadn't been for her, Ricky wouldn't be the person he is today. She helped him overcome his fear of people and homeschooled him until he was mainstreamed into high school. She was there for us when our parents weren't." A smile changed his features. There was a warmth to it, and it was obvious Connor had fond feelings for his grandmother and his brother. "It made Ricky happy to spend time with her again. And he told Grams about you. All good things, of course. She was thrilled I finally met someone and says she wants to meet you. We have a standing invitation if we ever go to California."

"I hope you explained we've only known each other for a short time, and it's unlikely we will be traveling to California together." I didn't intend for it to sound so abrupt. "I mean, that ... well, I am leaving next year and—"

"I know what you mean. I let Grams think what she wanted. I'm very much aware you'll be leaving. A lot can happen in a year. Let's just enjoy the time we have."

An awkward silence filled the air between us. We continued walking. The sand was cooling down, and the warmth of the day was passing.

"You're shivering." Connor removed his jean jacket and placed it around my shoulders. Still holding the collar, he pulled me closer until our bodies touched. I looked up into his eyes. My heart raced, and I could feel his heart beating rapidly. He lowered his head, and his lips touched mine, softly at first; then a passion I'd never experienced melded our bodies together and deepened the kiss until I could barely breathe. His jacket fell from my shoulders, and my shoes dropped to the sand as my arms wrapped around him. I felt his hands stroking my back and down my spine as we clung to each other. The heat of desire sparked flames within me, and I pressed my hips against him. Finally, he took my shoulders and gently pushed me from him. His finger traced the line of my jaw, and he tipped my face to meet his. I could see the moonlight reflected in his eyes.

"Micaela, I think I'm falling in love with you." His finger traced my lips, and he pressed it against them. "Don't say anything right now. I realize you have your dreams, and God knows, I would never want you to change them because of me. I want to make the next year special for you. I've decided to quit the club."

I went to speak, but his finger again pressed against my lips.

"I probably only worked there to piss off my parents. Yeah, I needed the extra money, but there were other part-time jobs I could have taken. I can get by, now that my business has picked up. I've given it a lot of thought. It's not an impulse decision. I want to spend as much time with you as I can before you go running off to the big-city lights and break my heart." He kissed me again, leaving me unable to comment.

A couple walking their golden lab skirted around us. We pulled apart.

"Don't stop on our account," said the man, dragging the dog away from greeting us. They continued on, and Connor retrieved his jacket, shook out the sand, and placed it around my shoulders. I grabbed my shoes, and we walked hand in hand back to the club. Neither of us spoke until we reached the front of the nightclub.

"Did you bring your car, or do I have the good fortune of driving you home?"

"Owen drove me. Vini didn't want you to see my car."

"She really thought it out, didn't she? Guess I'm your chauffeur this evening."

"Shouldn't we say good night to them?" It didn't seem right to leave so abruptly on Jason's big night.

"Do you really want to go back in there? They won't mind. Owen is probably too loaded to notice, and Vini will be dancing her heart out. Don't concern yourself with them. I'm finished for the night anyway."

He took my hand, and we walked to where Connor's jeep was parked beside Owen's Honda. Before opening the car door, he pushed me against it, pressed his body to mine, and kissed me even harder than before. My lips felt bruised, but it was a nice kind of feeling.

"Get a room, you two," a male voice shouted from the back of the parking lot. We could almost taste the intoxicating smell of marijuana and noticed a group in a circle, passing a joint.

"Great idea!" Connor shouted back and opened the car door for me.

The drive home was quiet, each of us still held captive by the magic of our kiss. He parked the jeep in the front of my building, leaned over, and kissed me lightly. "We still on for Sunday?"

"Of course. We wouldn't want to disappoint Ricky."

"Not a chance." He smiled and went to open his door.

"I can see myself in."

He waited until I was in the elevator before leaving. My thoughts turned to our first kiss. It was everything I had wanted it to be, right down to the moonlight. I would hold that magical moment in my heart forever, but there were never any guarantees of forever. I just didn't know that then.

CHAPTER 14

It felt like an eternity before Sunday arrived. My body ached in anticipation of seeing Connor. I drove Dad nuts, asking him if my outfit looked okay. Did it make me look childish? Should I wear my hair down or in a ponytail? I opted for jeans and a candy-pink long-sleeved shirt with a brown leather belt. My sneakers seemed to be the most practical, and Dad preferred the ponytail—more appropriate for being on a boat out on the ocean. I went minimalist on the makeup. I had Dad's approval. By the look on Connor's face, I had his as well. When Ricky saw me, he catapulted from the front seat and grabbed me in a huge bear hug. Connor just shook his head in bewilderment. I had done some research on autistic children and knew it was not a common occurrence. Ricky was different. Connor had told me that his autism wasn't as severe as most, but he was still selective when it came to touch. It needed to be his choice and his comfort zone. I requested release from his grip.

"Come on, buddy! You're going to crack her ribs." Conner's comment succeeded where mine didn't.

Ricky's enthusiasm subsided, and he jumped into the back seat, forfeiting his usual place beside Connor, and proceeded to share all his activities since we'd last spoken.

"Connor took me to a baseball game. Did you know that the Tarpons got sold? They are the Sarasota White Sox now. They won't be playing here anymore. I saw their last game. It was cool. Connor bought me this hat." Ricky shoved the hat between the front seats to display it.

"Tell Micaela who you got to meet at the game."

"Oh yeah! This is super cool. I saw Michael Jordan, and he shook my hand and gave me his autograph."

My knowledge of sports was limited to what I'd overheard when Dad watched baseball or basketball. Michael Jordan was a name I recognized but couldn't attach to a particular sport. I pretended to be surprised and thrilled. I had no intention of acknowledging my ignorance. "Wow, Ricky, that's great. Where did you see him?" I asked, hoping it might provide a clue to the sport.

"He was at the game, watching just like us. He was sitting two rows in front of us. Can you believe it? I got him on the way out. Look inside the hat."

He handed it back, and I saw a blurred ink scrawl across the white band but could only make out an M and maybe a J. Staying with awestruck, I told him it was super-cool.

The marina was crowded with people waiting for designated tours. It was almost an hour before we arrived at Indian Shores and found a slip to dock the boat. I took in the surroundings, and judging from the construction that seemed to be everywhere, it wouldn't be long before tourists swamped the area and made this an alternative destination to the beaches of Clearwater.

Ricky led the way from the Intracoastal Waterway to the street. A few restaurants, some in the middle of restoration, and outdoor cafes hinted at the tourist attraction this would become. Ricky headed straight for Ben's Ice Cream. He had obviously been there before. He selected a triple-scoop surprise and took so long deciding which three flavors he wanted that Connor had to step in and help. I went with a banana split with two spoons. We chose an outdoor table under a huge red-and-white striped awning. Ricky continued telling me about the baseball game and his unexpected encounter with the sports icon. After about ten minutes, I figured out Michael Jordan was a famous basketball player and was often referred to as MJ. I had furthered my education of sports.

Connor was quiet, allowing his brother center stage. He sat back, arms folded, staring at me, as usual. He smiled. I smiled back between spoonfuls of whipped cream, which apparently strayed to a vagrant strand of my hair that had come loose in the wind. Connor leaned over and removed the cream and then licked it off his finger.

Ricky scrunched up his face in disgust. "That's gross." He was practically wearing mint chocolate chip and butterscotch ripple. He hadn't yet reached the double-chocolate fudge when Connor handed him a napkin. I loved Ricky's childlike energy. "Hey, Connor! I guess you forgot. Weren't you going to give Micaela her present?" Ricky wiped ice cream from his chin with the sleeve of his jersey.

"No, I didn't forget, and thanks guy for spoiling the surprise."

I detected a look of hurt on Ricky's face. It seemed Connor had spotted it too and assured him it was okay. He was just teasing him.

"Why do you have a present for me?"

"Considering I didn't get you a birthday present, I decided better late than never." He reached into his jean jacket pocket and removed a small blue box and placed it in front of me. "I'm not much on wrapping—sorry."

It took a few moments to get used to the idea of receiving a present from him. We hadn't known each other very long. Vini had purchased a present for me too, and it had been difficult accepting hers as well. I always felt awkward with getting gifts. I liked giving more than getting.

"Aren't you going to open it?" Ricky was twitching with excitement and the anticipation of my response.

"You really didn't have to do this." I removed the lid. A small gold chain lay in a cloud of cotton. Carefully taking it in my hand, I watched as sunlight sparkled across the surface of a gold angel charm dangling from the bracelet. "Connor, it's beautiful. I love it. I don't know what to say." The awkwardness was setting in.

"You said you loved it. That's enough for me."

Pulling up the sleeve of my shirt, I offered my wrist for him to put it on. I decided I would never remove it.

Connor clasped it to my wrist and held my hand while staring at the angel. "When I saw it, I knew it was perfect. You're my earth angel. I'm glad you like it." He kissed my hand.

Ricky had devoured his three scoops, while I still had some ice cream left. Connor helped me finish it.

Walking back to the boat, Connor took my hand, and Ricky took the other one. Perhaps he did have a crush on me, as Connor suggested. Rather than being embarrassed by his display of affection, I welcomed it. I'd always thought I wouldn't mind a little brother, although it would have been competition for Dad's attention. Knowing I had a tendency toward jealousy, it was probably better I didn't have a sibling, although a brother might have been cool.

Connor took his place at the front of the boat, while Ricky and I sat on the bench watching Indian Shores recede into the distance.

"You really like the bracelet?" Ricky asked.

I reassured him. "I love it."

"Connor let me come with him and pick it out."

"That was thoughtful. I will treasure it always."

Ricky's attention was caught by something in the water. He jumped up and pointed. "Look! Look, Micaela! It's a school of dolphins."

I glanced in the direction he indicated. Three dolphins were swimming toward the boat. We both watched as they glided beside us, each poking their noses above water as if in greeting.

"I love dolphins," Ricky explained. "When I was little, my Grams took me to the marina. They had two of them. Their names were Donner and Blitzen, which I think is stupid because that's reindeer names. Grams and I named them Patience and Virtue, at least Grams did. She said those names were important because people needed to have more of those things."

"Your grandmother sounds very wise."

"Yeah, she's great. I don't get to see her as much now. She lives in California. My mom is going to take me next year." He continued with his story about the dolphins. "Patience died, and we didn't go anymore, and they sent Virtue to another marina in Miami so he could have a new friend. That was sad."

"I'm sorry, but at least you got to spend some time with them."

"Yeah, but I kinda miss them."

We watched the dolphins until they disappeared. We no longer held their interest. We joined Connor up front.

"He's not overwhelming you, is he?"

"No, not at all. We were watching dolphins."

"There's a number of them out here. We have time, if you'd like to go out further and see if you can spot a whale. Keep your eyes peeled." Connor smiled, and it lit up my world.

Ricky and I stayed with him staring out at the mass of blue in front of us. It was mesmerizing. Every so often, I could sense Connor looking at me.

"You ever been out in the ocean?" Ricky asked.

"I've never had the chance. Where I live, there's a big lake, but I didn't know anyone with a boat."

"It's pretty cool, isn't it?"

"Your odds of seeing a whale are better if you go on deck." Connor reached under the wheel and found a pair of binoculars that he handed to me. He turned to Ricky. "Yours are in the cabinet next to the sink."

Ricky located his and joined me, staring out into the endless blue water. We kept our eyes glued to the binoculars as we waited. I thought of patience and virtue—the values, not the dolphins. Ricky was the first to spot one. It took a second, but I located the

101

black hump. My first whale! Suddenly, it breached. Its huge body propelled into the air and landed with a magnificent splash; then it disappeared in the wake of its own making. I was thrilled.

Connor yelled from the cabin. "Did you guys see that?"

Ricky yelled back. "Yeah! Wow, that was cool."

I agreed. Hoping to get another glimpse, we continued to stare through the binoculars. We waited and tracked what we thought would be its path. I spotted a geyser of watery mist in the distance and pointed so Ricky could see it. I couldn't wait to tell Dad. Still watching, I noticed dark clouds forming in the distance. They were moving quickly.

Ricky spotted them too and reacted. "Looks like a storm is coming. I better let Connor know." He went to tell him.

I wasn't nervous, just a little edgy. I had no idea what being caught in a storm was like, and I didn't want to find out. We were a considerable distance from shore. I hoped we could make it to the marina before the storm hit us. Ricky returned, informing me Connor was heading back, and there was a strong possibility we could outrun it. I felt relief.

The brewing storm hinted at its arrival as thick, voluminous clouds smothered the afternoon sun, creating an eerie gray stillness. The only sound was the boat engine. I watched as the horizon gave way to the sea, blending together in a blue-gray mass. Ricky knew what was expected of him. Like a soldier preparing for combat, trained for the inevitable, he slowly and meticulously placed anything that might become a projectile into cupboards—heavier items on the bottom, and lighter, less-threatening objects at the top. He latched all the doors. I offered my help, but he was so focused on the task he didn't appear to hear me.

It was too late to outrun it. It came suddenly, like a tiger pouncing on its prey. Connor yelled over the ever-increasing gusts of wind for Ricky and me to find something to hold that felt secure. He was concentrating on keeping the boat steady, dealing with waves that were becoming mountains edged in white froth, each swell moving us up and down and tossing the boat like a child's toy.

The air became thick with a salty mist as waves crashed against the side of the boat and washed over the railing. I trusted Connor, but fear was stalking me. Knowing we were within range of the Clearwater shoreline provided some comfort, but the uncertainty of our outcome grew as more waves splashed across the front deck.

Ricky and I chose to sit on the bottom step of the stairs leading to the sleeping cabin. He latched the door. The wind howled in angry protest. We wedged our bodies tightly together, with one hand holding the door frame, the other holding each other, but it seemed futile. Ricky was yelling at me. I could barely hear him over the raging gale surrounding us.

"Don't be scared, Micaela" and something about Connor handling the boat were the only words I could make out. Whatever else he was saying was cut short by a sudden tilt sideways, sending him sprawling across the floor like a rag doll. Before I could react, the lamp fell and dangled from the cord, swinging back and forth until it smashed against the cupboard door. I watched helplessly as the television came crashing down, just missing Ricky's head but landing directly on my leg. A stabbing pain shot from my leg to my brain.

Another sideways tilt and the television slid across the room, hitting the bed. My leg was free. Ricky rolled on top of me. I held him tightly through more swaying and rocking. Gritting my teeth, I tried to endure the throbbing pain while concentrating on keeping Ricky safe in my grasp.

I desperately wanted to know how Connor was. Did he still have control of the boat, or did something terrible happen to knock him unconscious? Were we now helpless victims of the sea's wrath? I knew I would have to trust whatever fate had in store for us. Attempting to move and check on Connor would seal my own fate, and I could not leave Ricky.

I willed the storm to pass as quickly as it had come. Fear now latched on to every nerve and spread throughout my body. All my senses were saturated with it. I could taste its acrid flavor.

The boat tilted so far over that Ricky and I slid against the bed. We clung to each other as if we were one. I could feel his rapid heartbeat keeping time with mine. We were going to sink. I was sure of it.

A sudden low, moaning howl, and the door to the cabin came loose and flew open. The wind became a cyclone, trying to pull us into its vortex. Water splashing through the open door well created a waterfall on the steps. I felt the icy wetness through my shirt and pants, and watched as it pooled around our bodies. I'd always wondered what drowning would be like. I imagined a slow, helpless, agonizing torment. How long would it be before we were pulled under? I thought of my father. He would fall apart. Connor's parents would probably wish they had treated him better, and then Connor … He would die alone. I ached to be with him.

As I prepared for the worst, the rocking stopped, the wind subsided, and a calm, eerie quiet took its place. Nothing, not a single sound. It was as if the storm had simply been a nightmare, leaving a residue of unsettling fear, catching me between the safety of reality and the lingering horror of an imagined experience, taunting my senses.

Ricky moved away and cautiously stood while holding the edge of the bed. I tried sitting up. Water dripping from my hair blurred my vision and stung my eyes. I wiped them with my wet sleeve, but it didn't help much. I could barely make out Ricky staring at me, his jeans soaked in something darker than water. It was blood.

"Ricky, you're hurt."

He was sobbing uncontrollably and pointing at my leg. I looked—the blood was mine. My pants were torn, and blood was seeping from a gash. Rivulets of red dripped into the water, creating small swirls and fanning out into weird shapes.

Ricky insisted on going to Connor and letting him know I was hurt. Unsure as to whether we were safe, I still felt protective and grabbed his arm to stop him, but he pushed free and sloshed his way to the stairs.

I heard it before I felt it. A slow roll of thunder, a crack of lightning—then the jolt. More waves pounded relentlessly against the boat. The silence had been a teaser between nightmares.

"Ricky!" I yelled, but my words were gobbled up in the wind. Grabbing the side of the bed, I pushed up with my right leg while trying to maintain my balance. It made the pain worse, and waves of nausea matched the rolling waves rocking the boat. I swallowed, hoping to stifle the feeling and summoned the strength to push through the agony consuming me. I had to get Ricky. Connor would never forgive me if something happened to him.

Struggling to the stairs, I managed to steady myself and lean against the wall. Placing all my weight on my right foot, I dragged my left foot behind until I was able to grasp the door frame. An upward movement knocked me off balance. I tried desperately to remain standing. Throwing myself forward, I grabbed the edge of the small kitchen counter with both hands. I took a second to breathe through the pain.

I glanced frantically through the gusts of rain whipping my body and blinding my vision. Carefully I inched forward almost tripping over Ricky, huddled between the galley and the front deck, his feet pressed up against the wall for support. The waves washing the deck had made it almost impossible for me to see him. I struggled to get to him. I noticed Ricky still had his hat. How did it stay on with all the lurching and tumbling? From the way he was clutching it, he seemed to be more afraid of losing his ball cap than his own life.

The deck tilted back. We were ascending. I was sent backward and grabbed the edge of the table that was secured to the wall. I tried standing. Gusts of wind tore the ribbon holding my ponytail, and wet strands of hair whipped across my face. Then, as the boat descended the wave, we were both propelled forward. My feet flew from under me, and fiery bursts of pain shot up my spine into my brain. As I fell, I saw Ricky thrown toward the railing. He managed to catch hold of the bottom rung and wrap his arms around the top one. Instinctively, I let go of the table and lunged out in an effort to take hold of his leg. I connected with his ankle. Lightning lit up the darkness. I saw, rather than heard, him screaming. He was no longer wearing his hat. The deck leveled out, and I tried desperately to pull him to me, but he wouldn't let go of the railing.

It dipped again. My body was pulled down. I could no longer maintain my grip on Ricky's ankle. The unyielding rain and wind snatched at my body like icy tentacles, hurtling me against one of the side benches. I tried keeping my eyes on Ricky, praying he would not lose his grip. I saw the torment of fear in his expression.

"Please, God, don't let us die. Not like this," I pleaded out loud. "Please save us."

Saltwater engulfed me. My mouth filled with the briny taste. My eyes were unable to open. My body slid sideways. I felt something hard against my back, and then a shock wave of pain tore through my head. Then only darkness.

CHAPTER 15

My eyelids felt as if they were weighted down. Slowly, I attempted opening them. I blinked several times trying to adjust to the light. A figure stood in front of me—a man, holding something. Bursts of reality flooded my brain—the storm … being swept across the deck … hitting something. My thoughts were fuzzy but were taking form. I was alive. This revelation sent a pulse wave of gratitude into my consciousness, disrupting my recollection of events. Suddenly, I panicked.

"Connor, Ricky …" I blurted out. I did not want my gratitude to be just for my own survival.

"We're safe. It's okay." I recognized Connor's voice. I felt his arms around me, holding me close. More prayers of gratitude.

Blankets were being pulled over my shoulders. I couldn't stop chattering. The cold … I remembered the icy water. The man standing in front of me was offering me a drink, encouraging me to take it. The strong and familiar smell teased my nostrils. I didn't drink coffee but took it anyway. Grasping the cup with both hands, I held the steaming brew next to my chest appreciating any heat it provided. Sipping it slowly, I felt the warmth radiate outward into every cell of my body. The man who had given me the coffee wore a uniform. The words *Coast Guard* were written across his bright yellow jacket. He identified himself as Steve.

"You're going to be okay, but we have to get you to the hospital." Steve's voice sounded muffled, as if it was far away.

There was still water in my ears. Tilting my head to the side, I tried clearing it.

"You probably need a few stitches in your leg," he said. "And you hit your head pretty hard."

Connor pulled me closer. "Micaela, I'm so sorry. My God, I thought I'd lost you. I was crazy with worry for you and Ricky and prayed you would be safe." He kissed my forehead.

I spotted Ricky's running shoes and glanced across Connor to see him sitting in blankets also. We were on a different boat—a bigger boat—sitting in a cabin, and finally, the storm had passed. Mother Nature was finished reminding us of her fickle temperament. The sun was setting. Wisps of pink clouds painted the skyline of Clearwater as we approached the dock. I looked at Connor. There were dark circles under his eyes, and I could see only sadness reflected in them. There was a small cut on his cheek.

As the numbness in my brain subsided, I became aware of the burning sensation in my leg and the throbbing in my head. Moving the blanket away to check, I saw a small white strap just below my knee. Steve explained it was a tourniquet to stop the bleeding. It had worked. The bleeding had stopped, but the pain now increased its intensity. I heard him tell Connor what a good job he'd done in controlling the boat and keeping it from sinking.

"I wouldn't have given anyone a snowball's chance in hell out there today," Steve said. "You're very lucky. We got your distress call after the storm was in full force. These coastal storm surges are buggers. They come out of nowhere, but I'd suggest you check in with us in the future. Then at least we'll know you're out there and can get to you faster."

Connor agreed, adding how stupid he was, especially since he ran a charter service.

I glanced over at Ricky. Connor explained that he didn't have any broken bones or major cuts, but he was sure there would be dozens of bruises. He said he was more concerned with his state of mind, as Ricky wouldn't speak.

The late afternoon sun still warmed the cabin, and I welcomed the feeling as the chill subsided. It was hard to believe that what seemed to have been only moments before had been filled with darkness and fear. Seagulls returned to flying above us, squawking as if nothing had happened.

"Is the boat gone?" I was afraid to ask but needed to know.

"It doesn't matter, Micaela. You're alive! Ricky's alive! Nothing else matters."

Steve supplied my answer. "It didn't sink, as far as we know. When we airlifted you off, it was still bobbing around out there. If you're lucky, it might wash into shore near the Keys. I figure if that happens, though, you have horseshoes up your ass."

Ricky spoke, but it was more a plaintive cry. "It's all my fault! It's all my fault!" He repeated it continuously while Connor kept insisting it wasn't. When he finally stopped ranting, he looked at Connor. "I hurt Micaela. I didn't look after her like you asked me to. I was afraid." He was crying and repeatedly touching his head. "I didn't want to lose my baseball hat because of my autograph. I'm stupid … I'm stupid!" He continued this litany, rocking back and forth.

My heart ached for him. I recalled the week after Mom died. I'd felt, for some dumb reason, it had been my fault. In Dad's effort to comfort me, he took me to a friend's farm. He knew how much I loved animals. I recalled sitting by a fence, watching a lamb jumping around, while its mother, oblivious of her baby, ate grass nearby. The lamb made me laugh, and I hadn't laughed in such a long time. I wrote a song that day. It wasn't very good, but it made me feel better at the time. The melody was simple, almost like a lullaby. I began to sing to it …

> Oh, little lamb; oh, little lamb
> with fleece as white as snow.
> I wish that I could stay with you
> and watch you as you grow.
> You frolic and you jump around;
> your innocence is pure.
> I wish that I could stay and play;
> you've touched my heart for sure.
> Oh, little lamb; oh, little lamb,
> you do not understand
> that someday when you're all grown up
> you'll feel the hand of man.
> The joy I feel when watching you
> takes all the pain away.
> How sweet to be a child again;
> I'd really like to stay.
> Oh, little lamb; oh, little lamb,
> it's time for me to go,
> for I must leave my childhood
> and learn how I must grow.

It took three rounds of the song before Ricky stopped rocking. He turned to face me.

"I love you, Micaela."

"I love you too, Ricky."

He reached his arm across Connor's lap, and we held hands. His fingers were icy. We sat like that until the Coast Guard's boat docked in Clearwater Harbor.

While helping me off, Steve said to me, "Little lady, you have a nice voice. You in all that pain, and you're singin' to the boy. Pretty impressive."

There was an ambulance waiting by the dock. I turned to Connor. "My dad ... I told him I'd be back at six. I was supposed to pick up some groceries for dinner. He knew I was on the boat. He must be sick with worry."

Two medics arrived with stretchers, and I was put on the first one. Connor took my hand.

"I'll call him as soon as we get to the hospital."

Steve explained he would contact Dad, but Connor interrupted. "No disrespect, sir, but it would be better if I called him. You'll scare the hell out of the man, and he'll assume it's far worse."

I didn't think it would make any difference who contacted him. He'd be relieved I was alive but seriously worried about my well-being.

Connor and Ricky had to be examined in case of serious injuries. They were released quickly, but I was to remain overnight under observation. I had a concussion and a slight fracture on my lower leg bone; the doctor referred to it as my tibia. Fortunately, no cast; for that, I was grateful, but I would require the use of crutches for a few weeks, and life would be a whole lot more challenging. The gash required twenty-six stitches, and I would probably have a scar the rest of my life. I was prescribed antibiotics and painkillers and taken to a room. Connor explained how my head hit the steel post supporting the bench, and fortunately, I had been wedged under it. Otherwise, I would have been washed overboard.

Connor tried contacting Dad but only got our answering machine. He left a brief message, assuring him my injuries were minor and I was fine, but I'd have to remain the night in the hospital just to be on the safe side. It seemed odd that Dad wasn't home, as he'd been expecting me at six. It was now approximately seven fifteen, and I was worried.

It was after seven thirty when Dad unexpectedly arrived at the hospital. Connor was sitting beside the bed and Ricky in a chair. Connor stood as soon as Dad entered the room. Dad looked more furious than relieved. I rarely saw that look but recognized it and felt suddenly apprehensive. He nudged Connor aside.

"Son, I know what happened." I detected tension in his voice. "I knew something was wrong when Micaela didn't come home and didn't call. I saw the storm report on the local news, so I drove over to the marina. Her car was still there, but your boat wasn't. Do you know what that felt like?" He wagged his finger in Connor's face. Connor backed away and wasn't given a chance to explain. "All I could think about was that she was out there somewhere, maybe even drowned. I called the Harbor Coast Guard. They explained everything and told me which hospital she'd been taken to. I'm asking you to leave." He glanced over at Ricky. "And him too."

Sensing my father's anger was directed at Connor, Ricky came to his brother's defense. "Connor didn't do anything wrong."

"I'm not talking to you, young man."

I'd never seen my dad this angry. It was completely out of character. He would get annoyed when I did something he didn't approve of, but then again, I couldn't recall anything that I might have done to trigger this degree of anger.

"Dad, you're being unreasonable." He was upsetting me.

"Unreasonable! I let you go out in that boat with him." He motioned his head toward Connor. "You told me he was responsible. You think it's unreasonable for me to be angry? You said you were just going along the coast, but you went a lot farther, didn't you? And as far as I'm concerned, anyone who runs his own charter business should have more sense than going out that far without checking in with the authorities. Maybe the storm did come out of nowhere, but if you'd been near the shore, you could have made it back safely, or the Coast Guard could have helped you sooner, before you got hurt."

Conner took Dad's tongue-lashing well. He responded with, "You're right."

"You bet I'm right. Now leave, and let me have time with my girl."

Connor glanced at me, and I saw the sadness in his face. He motioned for Ricky to follow.

"Bye, Micaela," Ricky said, and as he passed Dad, he looked up at him. "Please don't get mad at my brother or Micaela."

Dad ignored him. He leaned over and kissed my forehead. "The doctor explained you have a concussion and required a lot of stitches in your leg. Looks like you're going to need crutches." His initial anger had passed, now we were alone.

"I'll be fine, Dad. You weren't being fair to Connor. Even the Coast Guard said he was amazed at how well Connor handled the boat."

"You told me he was taking you to Indian Shores and along the coast. I don't expect you knew how far out you got, but he did. You can't trust someone who's irresponsible and breaks his word."

"The storm came up really fast." I continued trying to support Connor. "I'm sure he would have checked the weather report. We wouldn't have gone if he'd known."

"Enough said. You are alive, and I'm grateful for that. From now on, I want you to stay away from him."

I was shocked at Dad's hasty decision. "No, you can't mean that. I'm eighteen years old. I'm not a kid. I'll see him if I want to."

"Not while I pay all the bills." This wasn't the dad I knew. The kind, loving, generous man I so dearly loved had been taken over by some self-righteous monster, but his threat hit home. I knew that while I depended on him, I had no choice but to respect his wishes. He was distraught at the thought of possibly losing me, and his protective instinct was strong. I gave him the benefit of the doubt and hoped he would come to his senses when he realized how much he was hurting me. For now, I didn't want to talk to him.

CHAPTER 16

The worst part of the next two weeks wasn't the crutches or Dad and me not speaking; it was not hearing from Connor. It was unbearable. Obviously, Dad totally had intimidated him. I didn't understand why Connor couldn't at least make an effort to contact me. He would have no idea that Dad issued the directive not to see him again. Unless Vini told him.

A part of me—the part that held all my insecurities and doubts—whispered things like, *"If he really loves you, then he wouldn't let Dad intimidate him."* It would shout at me, *"He's a coward! Is that what you want, Micaela? How could you love a man who won't stand up for you?"* My feelings contradicted my thoughts. My heart would scream back at my mind. *"But he seems so genuine, and I love him so much. Something must have happened."* I had to find out why I was getting the silent treatment.

Vini was sure Dad would change his mind, once he realized how upset I was, but as the days turned into weeks, it became increasingly obvious it might not happen for a very long time, if at all. Dad seemed oblivious to my personal torture. I broke my vow of silence and tried speaking with him. It was a useless endeavor. He was adamant that I stay away from Connor, which meant not calling him as well.

"A clean break is the best way. You'll get over him in time," he'd said. "Just focus on your schoolwork." (Another reminder of my financial obligation to him). Dad and I rarely argued, more like mini-disagreements that would end in one of us apologizing. This time, I yelled things I knew I might regret later.

"Stop trying to control me. I'm not Mom. You convinced her that she was totally dependent on you. You wouldn't let her work or even have an opinion of her own." It was a huge exaggeration, but my intent was to hurt him, and I did. I didn't do myself any favors. My comment only infuriated him. He went silent and took several very deep breaths. When he did speak, I knew I'd gone too far.

"If I find out you have gone behind my back to see him or have anything to do with him at all, that will be the end of your schooling. I don't care how much money I've spent so far. You'll just have to get a job and pay for it yourself."

His ultimatum crushed me. This was a side of Dad I'd never experienced. I spent the rest of the day crying in my room. Dad left without saying where he was going. Probably to see Gloria.

I told Vini about the argument. She was my best friend, and talking to her made me feel better. She had a suggestion. Vini was good at coming up with ideas, so I listened.

"It's a bit complicated," she said, "but try to follow my thinking. First, Jason could call Connor. That way, you wouldn't be going against your dad."

I couldn't see any harm in it and agreed. Anything to find out why he wasn't contacting me. She said she'd call me back with the results and explain her plan.

She called within an hour and shared what Jason had found out. I was shocked to discover that Dad had gone behind my back and spoken with Connor, and he'd made it clear that there would be no contact between us. I guessed Dad was covering his bases on the chance I might try to call Connor. He had made it clear to him that my financial assistance depended entirely on his staying away from me. Now I understood why he hadn't contacted me. Jason reported that Connor felt responsible for my brush with death and could not forgive himself. He'd declared I was probably better off without him.

How could he believe such a stupid thing? He had inquired about my leg and informed Jason his boat had been located. That was great news. He had been lucky. Very lucky! Losing the boat would have ruined him, even if it was insured. Apparently, it was pretty banged up and needed a lot of work, and Connor was doing all the repairs himself. I wanted desperately to tell him how happy and relieved I was, but I decided even using the school phone might have repercussions.

Vini shared the rest of her plan. The objective was to put Connor in the same room with me without his knowing I was there. Some place Dad wouldn't suspect or find out—the Blue Lagoon. She would have Jason tell Connor that he was needed to fill in at the club. She figured he would jump at the chance to make money since he was losing his charter income while his boat was being repaired. Jason had added to her idea by suggesting that he tell Connor to arrive early because the manager needed him to sign some form before working. It seemed Jason was just as good at deception as his sister.

I hoped Connor would comply. It was worth a shot. Vini felt it was better to try and fail than not try at all. She continued with her plan. I was to tell Dad I was having dinner with her and her mom. Mrs. DeMille, being an advocate of true love and who liked Connor, went along with it, although she was worried my dad would call. Vini took care of that too. She convinced her mom to say we had gone to the movies and a little white lie was okay. The next part of her deception involved my hiding behind the office door, and I would just pop out. Jason would close the door, and then the rest was up to me. Vini, ever the mastermind, was convinced it would work. There was no guarantee, but I was hopeful.

My crutches were now a thing of the past, and my leg was healing well, so driving wasn't a challenge. Dad was at Gloria's, and he'd left a note, telling me not to wait up. It seemed their relationship had proceeded to the next level. Just in case he came back early for some reason, I left a note of my own. My nervousness at confronting Connor surpassed my caring about Dad's spending the night with Gloria.

When I arrived at Vini's, it was just before dinner. Her mom, who insisted I call her Lydia, was like her daughter—a hugger! I liked her immediately. She'd prepared fried chicken and potato salad, the best I'd ever had. While eating, she shared stories about Jason and Vini when they were little. I laughed so hard I almost forgot how nervous I was. She adored her kids. When we left, she kissed me on the cheek and wished me good luck. Vini had insisted on being present, just in case her plan failed and she had to resort to forcing Connor to listen to me—by what means, she didn't say.

Vini wanted me to park my car down the street from the club, as she was concerned Connor would see it and get suspicious. There was no denying it was easy to spot.

Just as instructed, I hid in the manager's office. Standing behind the door, like a child playing hide-and-seek, made me feel a bit foolish. I heard Connor's voice.

"Why does Joe want me to sign something?" he asked, presumably of Jason.

My heart pounded, and I could feel perspiration on my neck.

"A new rule, just a formality; no big deal," Jason responded.

I wasn't sure what I was supposed to do. Jump out like an idiot and scare him to death, or simply stand there until he turned around. I opted for just standing. He turned when Jason closed the door. I couldn't read his expression. It was somewhere between startled and thrilled, with a little annoyance thrown in. I let him speak first.

"Micaela, what are you doing here?" This seemed like a logical question.

"I wanted to see you and hoped we could talk." My voice trembled. I was nervous he would leave. Now that the opportunity was right in front of me, I wasn't feeling very confident.

"Looks like I was tricked. This isn't a good idea, Micaela. Does your dad know where you are?"

"He's spending the night with Gloria." I was hoping my answer would suffice. It didn't.

"That's not what I asked you."

"Okay! No, he doesn't, but I'm eighteen years old and sick of being treated like a child."

"Okay! I get the picture. I'll bet Vini cooked this up, and it seems Jason helped."

I decided to get to the point. "Why haven't you tried to contact me? I know my dad called you, but couldn't you have at least tried?"

His next expression was one I recognized. Sadness.

"Don't you think I'm torn up about this? I couldn't risk calling you and have your dad stop helping you financially. What would happen to your dream of being an actress? Believe me, I picked up the phone at least one hundred times—no exaggeration—but stopped when I realized your dad wasn't just making an empty threat. He sounded pretty serious, and he's right. I acted irresponsibly. I almost killed you. I shouldn't have taken you out so far, and I should have notified the Coast Guard. No amount of apologizing to your dad can change that. And don't say it wasn't my fault. It was! I've had time to think about what he said. You need to be focused on your schoolwork. Maybe he'll change his mind, but what he said hit home with me. He told me that if I love you, I'll let you go."

"You can't believe that."

He ran his hand through his hair and sighed deeply. "I know how much you love your dad, and I know how honest you are. I don't want to put you in the position of lying to him, and I don't want you to lose your opportunity. You're better off without me."

"That's just stupid. I am not better off without you; in fact, I can't focus on school or anything else right now. What happened was terrifying. Not just for him but for me, you, and Ricky. Maybe Dad should stop thinking about himself. Can't I be in control of my own life? I feel like I'm ten years old. This is more than his anger at you for acting negligently. I have a theory." I paused, waiting for Connor's reaction.

"And ..." He seemed interested.

"And ... I think it's about Mom ... her cancer. Dad did everything he could to help her. He even took a leave of absence from work to be with her. When she had to go to the hospital, it tore him apart. Dad is a bit of a control freak, and cancer wasn't something he could control. He couldn't make it go away."

"So how do you relate that to this situation?"

"Just listen ... I know I'm no psychologist, but I've given this some thought, and I think there might be some truth to my conclusion. When Dad thought he'd almost lost me, it brought back those helpless feelings, and by telling us we couldn't see each other again, he probably figured he could at least control something. It sounds far-fetched, but I understand that helpless feeling."

"Have you discussed your theory with him?"

"Haven't had much of a chance. It's been difficult. He's barely ever home. I admit I treated him badly at first. I wouldn't talk to him, and we argued. I said something I regret, but I feel like he's punishing me for that too."

"Even if what you're telling me has merit, it doesn't change what happened or his feelings about me."

"He doesn't know you, Connor. Probably my fault, as I haven't provided an opportunity for the two of you to get acquainted."

Connor sighed again. He stood staring at me, and I stared back, hoping my words had made a difference. He moved toward me and took me in his arms.

"Micaela, let's give him some time."

It felt like heaven reached down and encircled me.

"I love you, and nothing and no one can change that. I want him to know how sorry I am and that I would never deliberately hurt you. Your life is precious to me. He'll come around, but until then, I won't let you lie to him or put you in a situation that compromises you. Do you understand?"

I nodded as I placed my head against his chest, savoring the moment. "I'm happy your boat was found. Vini told me."

"You have no idea how relieved I was when the Coast Guard called. Same guy, by the way. He's now convinced I have those horseshoes up my ass. It would have put me back at least a year before I could have purchased a new one and got up and running again. It would have meant finding a full-time job. She needs work, but it has kept me busy. How's the leg?"

"It's good. I hated the crutches. Very inconvenient."

He bent his head and kissed me. I understood the word *bittersweet*—love and sorrow combined. I had no idea how long we would have to wait until Dad came around. Time wasn't on our side. I was leaving next year. I would have to apologize for my outburst and try again to convince him that Connor was as important to me as my career and him—only this time without losing my temper. The good thing was that Connor still loved me. I remembered the dolphins, Patience and Virtue, and realized his grandmother was right. These were two very difficult traits to master.

The door opened. "Everything good in here?" Jason saw us embracing. "Guess so. Vin's champing at the bit to find out if you two lovebirds have come to a resolution. Can I tell her yes?"

"Tell her it's all good." Connor shook his head in a kind of disbelief. "Vini is something else. Guess I owe her one."

"Yeah, you do." Vini shot through the door and grabbed Connor and me in a hug. She could barely wrap her arms around both of us, but we felt the love.

She wasn't thrilled when she discovered the only thing we'd accomplished was waiting until I could convince Dad his decision was wrong. She was, however, happy to know we were still a couple.

Connor walked Vini and me to my car, and he kissed me again. I didn't want to let him go. Our goodbye felt as if I'd been swallowed up in a fog. The loss and sadness overwhelmed me. I made a mental promise to speak to Dad as soon as possible. I glanced in the rearview mirror before pulling on to the highway and saw Connor turn and walk back to the club. I tried not to cry.

Vini knew better than to speak. She stifled her usual babble, knowing I was lost in mixed emotions. When I dropped her off, she said good night, blew me a kiss, and waved goodbye.

The apartment was dark. My note still lay on the kitchen table where I'd left it. I felt a horrible loneliness. Maybe I wasn't as grown up as I thought.

The next morning, when Dad wasn't in the kitchen making our Sunday breakfast, I felt disappointed. We rarely missed Sunday mornings together. *Things change; people change.* I kept busy cleaning the apartment and filing my past assignments in a box. It was well past noon when I began feeling worried. It occurred to me that Dad might be trying to show me what it felt like when I didn't come home the day of the storm, or maybe he'd decided to spend his Sundays with Gloria from now on. That thought hurt me. I was making tea when the phone rang. Dad's voice was barely recognizable. It sounded as if he'd been crying.

"Dad, what's the matter?" My fear barometer skyrocketed.

"It's Gloria." Then he did cry.

"What, Dad? What about Gloria?"

"She died!" His cry became a sob.

I couldn't speak. I wasn't sure I'd heard him correctly. It didn't seem real. I waited for his sobbing to subside. "Dad, how? What happened? Where are you?"

"At the hospital. She had a massive heart attack last night. ... We were watching a movie. ... I called the ambulance. ... She was alive ... then she wasn't. She died in my arms. God, I can't believe this." His words came in broken sentences. Suddenly, all the anger I felt toward him and my previous dislike of Gloria created massive feelings of guilt, along with a hurt I was familiar with. His pain was my pain.

"I don't know what to do." He choked back another sob. "I tried calling her son … left a message … horrible having to tell him his mom passed away on a goddamn answering machine."

"Do you need me to come and get you? What hospital?"

"No, I'm just going to stick around here for a while. Maybe her son will call."

"Will you be okay?" It was a ridiculous question. How could he be okay? I didn't know whether he loved her, but I knew he cared a great deal and had to be in shock.

"Yeah. I'll be home later." He hung up.

I sat at the kitchen table, digesting what I'd just heard. My mind filled with images of Gloria. I wished I'd been nicer to her. I thought about how Dad must feel … how I would feel if I lost Connor. The thought overpowered me, and I cried.

The day of the funeral was overcast and drizzling on and off. It was as if the universe was shedding its own tears for Gloria. I met her son and his wife. They seemed nice and were very considerate of Dad, especially when they had no idea the extent of his and Gloria's relationship. I didn't say much to Dad, other than how sorry I was, not because of our argument but out of respect for his mourning.

While having dinner, Dad finally spoke. "Micaela, if you want to see Connor, I won't stop you." Nothing more, just a simple statement.

I said thank you and went around the table to put my arms around his neck. He cried.

The sad thing was, it took a tragedy to change his mind. We never spoke of it again.

CHAPTER 17

Now

Jess picked me up at the college on the day we'd decided to visit Dad. The kids were excited to see me. They'd drawn pictures. Tina created a very good butterfly and had taken a page from her Disney princesses book and colored a mermaid named Ariel. The butterfly was impressive. The mermaid picture was almost perfect. Nora, in an attempt not to be outdone by her sister, chose the same mermaid in her book, but her picture displayed her free-spirited nature. No staying within the lines for her. She'd chosen some interesting colors I was sure were different from what Disney intended. She even added her version of a butterfly. Her competitive spirit was showing. I did my usual oohing and aahing and told them I would post the pictures on the fridge, along with the gallery of other pictures they'd created over the past few years. After lots of kisses and hugs, I joined Jess in the front seat of her minivan. The girls were in the back, playing with dolls they said were monsters who went to high school. With their attention solely on the dolls, I felt freer to talk with Jess.

"I know what this is all about, Jess. This is more about my spending time with the girls than you visiting your grandfather. You're hoping it will make me change my mind."

She gave me her cat-that-swallowed-the-canary look. "So is it working?"

"Maybe." There was no use in arguing, especially with the kids in the car. They were adorable children, and my heart ached at the possibility of not seeing them grow up.

"Oh, and just so you don't think I'm a totally devious bitch—"

"Watch your language." I hated it when she swore around the girls.

"I do want to see Grandpa. I chose today because ... you know ... two-birds-with-one-stone kind of thing."

I just shook my head. "Your dad paid me a visit, and no, he didn't change my mind, as you hoped, but he did ask me to forgive him for walking out with that bimbo. Apparently, they've split up."

"Wow! I'm glad. I didn't like Lisa, and she didn't like me, so we didn't spend much time together. Did you accept Dad's apology?"

"Yes."

"Are we there yet? I have to pee." Nora's outburst was echoed by her sister.

"Hold on. We'll be there soon," Jess assured them.

We arrived within ten minutes, and Jess swiftly escorted the girls to the washroom. I took the elevator to the fourth floor. Dad's door was open. He was sitting in his wheelchair by the window, staring out at an oak tree that practically covered the entire view—what there was of it. I didn't want to startle him, so I announced my arrival.

"Hi, Dad. It's Micaela." I wasn't sure he'd heard me. He seemed so frail and sad. It was difficult to accept. I stood beside him and gently touched his hand. It felt cold and skeletal. He turned his head to look at me. The blue eyes I remembered were rimmed in red and had faded to a milky gray. He smiled.

"Hey, sweetie!" He glanced around me. "Where's your mom?"

"She'll be by this evening when she gets a chance." Better to lie than risk upsetting him.

"You good?"

"Yes, Dad, I'm good. How about you?"

"Guess I'm okay for an old fart."

Jess entered, holding the girls' hands. They were quiet, almost apprehensive.

Dad spun around in his wheelchair. "And who are these sweet little cherubs?"

Jess's face registered disappointment. "They're your great-granddaughters, Grandpa."

Dad made a huffing sound. "If you say so. And who are you, young lady?"

"Your granddaughter Jessie." Her expression went from hopeful to sad in a second. They had been close when she was little, and she adored him. It hurt me to see how disappointed she was.

"You're Jessie. Of course! Come closer and let me look at you."

I could see tears forming in her eyes. We were both startled and pleased at this sudden revelation. Jess let go of the girls, who immediately came and held my hands. They had no memory of Dad. They were three when he was admitted to the nursing home. Jess knelt beside Dad's wheelchair and took his hand. He didn't flinch as he had done on previous visits. "It's good to see you, Grandpa."

"You grew up so fast. Your grandmother will be so happy to see you." The fact that Jess had been born long after Mom died didn't register with him. I gestured with a slight shake of my head for Jess to say nothing. Dad patted her hand and then wheeled himself over to a small cupboard and opened it. Jess and I just looked at each other, somewhat bewildered. He searched through the pocket of his overcoat, found his wallet, took out a ten-dollar bill, and offered it to her.

"How about you take those cuties and buy them an ice cream. I think, if I remember right, there's a store in the lobby."

This seemed a rather odd request, but rather than refuse, Jess accepted the money and thanked him. She kissed the top of his head, and he smiled at her. We were both taken aback by this sudden gesture. It was if he wanted to be alone with me. I saw relief on the girls' faces when their mother told them they would get ice cream and wait downstairs for Nana.

Once they'd left, Dad wheeled himself over to his bed. "I'd like to rest now. Can you help me, Micki?" He hadn't referred to me as Micki since I was twelve. "I don't want one of those damned nurses. They treat me like a complete invalid."

He was able to heave himself from the chair to the bed but struggled with the blankets. I pulled them up and grabbed the pillow from the floor, where it must have fallen, and placed it behind his head. Dad reached for my hand and held it. "Micaela, I want to tell you something."

I was no longer Micki. I sat on the edge of the bed, still holding his hand. "Okay, I'm listening."

"I may forget a lot of things, but I haven't forgotten what I did to you. I'm sorry for forbidding you to see Connor. I know it hurt you. I was so scared when I nearly lost you, I took it out on him. He acted foolishly, but he also saved you."

How could Dad even remember this? It must have stuck in whatever was left of his memory, and he felt he needed to purge it. I brought his hand to my lips and kissed it.

"It was like when I lost your mom."

This startled me. Now he remembered Mom was gone. I didn't want to break the thread of his thoughts, so said nothing.

"I was angry for a long time," he said. "Angry I couldn't make her well again. Angry at the doctors. No matter how much I prayed, God still took her. I was angry at him too. The day of the storm, when I figured you'd drowned, I thought God had taken you as well. I couldn't handle the anger. I just transferred it to Connor. I'm sorry. It wasn't fair." No mention of Gloria or the fact he finally did allow me to see Connor again.

"It's okay, Dad. I forgive you." I thought this was what he needed to hear. It surprised me to know the theory I'd speculated to Connor so long ago was close to being correct. It just took thirty years to surface. I thought of my cancer. As much as I didn't want to take ownership of it, the reality sat like stale garbage, waiting to be dealt with, but it wasn't Dad's reality. I hated wishing he would lose more of his memory, but in the event I passed before him, it seemed like a good thing. Parents shouldn't bury their children. It would be better if he had no knowledge of it.

Dad smiled and closed his eyes. He'd made his peace with me, himself, and God, if he thought it actually mattered.

I kissed him on the cheek. "I love you, Dad."

"I love you too, Micaela." His hand went limp as sleep claimed him.

I tiptoed to the door and then turned around to look at him. I felt the weight of immense sadness. Time seemed like a cruel joke.

I found Jess sitting in the lobby with the girls, eating ice cream from plastic containers.

"Can you believe that, Mom? He remembered me."

I hugged her. I realized it was one of those rare moments the doctors had told me about. There would be times when Dad would appear quite coherent, but it would pass as quickly as it came. I was grateful—and thankful—it had happened now, and I got to experience what I had waited so long for. It brought me a sense of peace as well, knowing that after such a long time, Dad finally talked to me about it. How much time either of us had was questionable.

CHAPTER 18

Then

The weekend before my next school year, I was busy sorting texts and school supplies when Vini called and asked if I wanted to join her and Owen at the arcade. Jason had taken his first design job, and Owen was feeling abandoned. As great as it was to be able to see Connor again, he was super-busy, trying to make up for all the lost income, and he didn't have a lot of free time. Our relationship had been reduced to late-night phone calls and the occasional lunch during the week. I was grateful I could now see him, so didn't complain. I agreed to Vini's suggestion that the three of us get together, but my expertise at video games was nonexistent.

The August heat was stifling, just as I recalled from the previous summer. No walking on the beach, except for the brave tourists wearing flip-flops, who lasted about five minutes before retreating to the walkway. My fair skin practically sizzled, so sunscreen became a necessity.

Vini laughed, mocking the tourists trying to get the perfect tan—anywhere between her beautiful mocha skin or dark chocolate.

"You know what really gets me?" she said, looking out at all the sunbaked bodies lying on towels, lined up like soldiers on the beach. "They waste time cooking to become my color and then snub me. Most of them probably wouldn't sit beside me on the bus." Vini sounded disgusted.

"That's a little harsh," Owen commented. He also had fair skin and smelled like Vini's piña coladas.

"Not!" Vini stated emphatically. "How would you know anyway?"

He looked down his nose at her while changing dollar bills to quarters in the machine outside the arcade. "You're kidding, right? Earth to Vini. I'm living with your brother, remember? You should see the looks we get when we go shopping, and even our landlord gives Jason and me the evil eye."

We went from the stifling heat pounding the sidewalk into the icy air-conditioned arcade. Owen chose a game I'd never heard of and placed a quarter in the slot. Lights flashed, and the screen came to life. Dragons fired flame balls at characters who looked distinctly Japanese. Owen dodged them. Double Dragon was a little too aggressive for my skill set. I played it safe with Pac-Man. I could master the funny little yellow character munching his way through ghosts.

Owen made it through six rounds and handed Vini a quarter. She had to beat his score. "How's your dad doing?" he asked me.

"He's okay." I continued playing but was defeated after four tries. "He's pretty quiet. He watches reruns of old movies, mostly. Thanks for asking."

"Pretty sad about his girlfriend, or was she his girlfriend?"

Vini distracted Owen momentarily with her resounding exclamations. She had just beaten his score.

"I think she was," I replied. "I was never sure exactly. He's pretty heartbroken but not nearly to the same degree he was when

129

Mom died. I think Gloria helped him get past the loneliness, and she definitely helped him through my silent treatment. I'm worried about him. He seems to have regressed. The funny thing is, he doesn't even talk about Gloria, and he barely speaks to me."

"Give him time, Micaela."

"I guess." I shrugged. Everyone always said the same thing, as if time was some magic potion you could drink that made everything all right again. They never mentioned just how much you had to drink.

Owen went another round with the dragons while Vini watched. They played until they ran out of quarters. I found watching a lot more fun than playing. Vini, being highly competitive, looked like she was competing for an Olympic event. It paid off. She won.

"Whooped your ass," she gloated to Owen.

Owen checked his watch. "Gotta go, girlfriends. Jason needs me to pick him up. His car is at the shop. Some kind of gear problem. I have no idea. Don't know diddly about cars. He's at some rich woman's house, choosing paint for her living room. Not exactly a job from *Better Homes and Gardens*, but he's being paid." He planted a kiss on our cheeks and sauntered off. I was growing quite fond of him.

I drove Vini home and stayed just long enough to get a hug from her mom. Dad made dinner but ate alone in front of the television set, as usual. I retired to my room and looked at magazines, waiting for Connor to call. Hearing the phone ring, I ran to answer. Dad was still lying on the couch watching television. He grunted something, turned off the TV, and trudged into his bedroom.

"Hey, you!" This had become Connor's normal greeting.

"Hey, you back," I said. "How was your day?"

"Same old, same old. I did manage to get the boat seaworthy and took out a charter. A guy vomited over the side of the railing, and the wind caught it and flung chunks in a kid's face. It was actually quite funny, but the boy's mom didn't think so. How was yours?"

I told him Vini had wiped Owen off the map in a video game. I, on the other hand, was a complete failure. Connor asked about Dad. I provided the same explanation I'd given Owen.

"So what are you up to tomorrow?"

"Same old, same old"—I borrowed his phrase—"unless you have something in mind." I hoped he did.

"How about a movie with Ricky? The kid has been so sad these past few weeks, wondering if he's ever going to see you again. When I told him I was going to take him to a movie and ask you, he practically jumped out of his skin."

"Sounds like a plan." I really wanted to see Ricky again. I kept remembering him rocking back and forth on the boat and how he had reached out to me and held my hand.

"He's got something for you."

"He does? What is it?"

"I'm not supposed to tell you. It's a surprise."

I glanced at my bracelet and the little angel resting against my wrist. "What's up with you McKenzie brothers and surprises?"

"We're in love. What can I say?"

"How about good night? I'm exhausted from watching Vini and Owen compete. It was very hard work."

He laughed, noting my sarcasm. I loved the sound of his laughter. "Okay, fair maiden. I'll let you get your beauty sleep. Pick you up after lunch tomorrow."

I slept like a baby. Whether it added to my beauty was questionable.

CHAPTER 19

When Connor buzzed the intercom to announce his arrival. I called out to Dad requesting that he answer the door as I was still getting ready. I wanted them to face each other, especially after their last encounter at the hospital, so I deliberately took longer with my make-up. I waited for what I thought was a reasonable amount of time and then made my grand entrance. Dad and Connor were shaking hands. It looked like a truce. Grabbing my purse, I kissed Dad goodbye, with a promise to call him as soon as the movie was over. It still made me feel as if I was ten, but if Dad felt better, it was no big deal.

"Your dad is actually a pretty nice guy," Connor commented on our way down in the elevator.

"Yeah, he is, usually."

Ricky was ecstatic when he saw me. It was as if the experience of the storm had never happened. He was his usual happy, talkative self.

The movie was *Big*. I liked the theme of a twelve-year-old boy who makes a wish to be grown up and turns into a thirty-year-old man. Ricky thought it was cool, especially when the boy meets a woman who has romantic feelings for him, although Ricky was disappointed in the ending, when the young man finds living as an adult too overwhelming and longs to return to his former boy self. It was humorous and heartwarming. Ricky loved it.

As we were exiting the front lobby, a skinny girl with long, platinum-blonde hair, wearing a black spandex body suit, and another girl, who looked like the actress in *Dirty Dancing*, my all-time favorite movie, waved in our direction.

"Hey, Connor! Great to see you," the blonde said as she approached him. She didn't even glance my way. "Funny movie. Bonnie's in the can. She'll be out in a minute."

The other girl took off in the direction of the washroom.

"I heard you guys were at the Parkers for dinner last week," Blondie said. "Bonnie told me it was a complete bore, but she enjoyed being with you. Hey, why don't the two of you join us at Sonny's next Saturday? Should be a blast!"

It was evident she meant Bonnie, not me. I simply wasn't on her radar.

I stiffened, waiting for Connor's reaction. We'd been separated for nearly a month. It never occurred to me he might have seen someone else, especially Bonnie. Ricky had no idea what was going on and was anxious to leave. So was I.

Connor excused himself, explaining he was with his brother and had to get him home. No mention of me. I stiffened some more.

"Aren't you going to wait for Bonnie?" Blondie asked.

"Just tell her I said hi."

I quickly went from stiff to seething. Ricky and I left together, and after saying goodbye to the blonde girl, Connor caught up with us outside.

While walking to the jeep, Connor and Ricky exchanged their impressions of the movie. I offered nothing. We passed a store selling ice cream cones, and Ricky asked if he could have one. The bucket of popcorn and licorice he'd wolfed down hadn't made a dent in his sweet tooth. Connor asked if I wanted one. I shook my head.

Ricky was happy with his double-chocolate mint cone and tried licking quickly around the edges, as the summer heat was melting it faster than he could keep up. Chocolate was dribbling on his hands. I gave him some tissues from my purse.

I still hadn't spoken. We walked along the sidewalk until we spotted a bench facing the beach.

"You stay here, guy. I want to talk to Micaela."

Ricky complied. I thought my silence had gone unnoticed. I was wrong. When we were far enough away from Ricky that he couldn't hear, Connor said, "Okay, what's with the silent treatment? Is this about Joanne? She was the blonde girl."

Now Blondie had a name. "Not exactly." I knew I had to answer.

"So it's about Bonnie?"

"You could say that. What did this Joanne mean about you and Bonnie being at some dinner?"

"It's nothing, Micaela."

Connor's answer did not provide the satisfaction I was looking for. "Didn't sound like nothing."

Connor sighed deeply. "My parents dragged me to one of their friends dinner parties. I was feeling pretty down, so I went, mostly to get my mind off you. I had no idea Bonnie would be there with her parents. She doesn't usually go anywhere with them, but I guess my mother told her mother I was coming, and that's all it took for her to show up. I think I might have said two words to her the entire evening."

"I'll bet she said more than two words to you." I sounded like a jealous shrew—something I hated—but I was unable to control my feelings.

"So what you're saying is that you don't trust me?" Connor's annoyance was obvious.

"I want to trust you."

"But you don't?"

I detected a hint of disappointment accompanying the annoyance. "No … I mean, yes, I trust you." I was trapping myself with my own insecurities. "Why didn't you introduce me?"

"Because I think you're a hell of lot better than those two, and I didn't even want to place you in the same ballpark as Joanne. I'm sorry. I guess I should have."

I sensed his irritation, and it scared me. "I guess I'm just being a possessive bitch."

Connor laughed, making me feel far less threatened by any impending breakup—on his part, not mine.

"You're not a bitch, but you can possess me any time." He took my hand. "I'll tell you again: Bonnie means nothing to me. She's just someone I've known for several years. Our mothers are friends. I didn't spend any time with her at all."

I accepted his explanation, but I still had my doubts about Bonnie.

"Now can we get back to Ricky? I'll bet he's covered in ice cream and itching to give you your surprise."

Connor was right. Ricky was a mess. We got him cleaned up and returned to the jeep. He took my hand again. Connor just smiled and winked. "I think I have competition," he said. I smiled back.

As soon as we were settled in our seats, Ricky leaned forward and shoved a little blue box between Connor and me. It looked identical to the one my bracelet came in. The same store, "Jenn's Fine Jewelry," was etched in silver letters across the top. I took it and carefully opened the lid. In a similar bed of cotton was a tiny gold dolphin.

"It's a charm for your bracelet. It's probably Patience 'cause we all need more of that. Virtue was smaller anyway," Ricky explained.

"It's beautiful. Thank you." I didn't ask why he wanted me to have it. I sort of knew. I felt tears forming and tried to wipe them away.

He noticed. "See? I told you she was going to cry."

"She didn't cry when I gave her the angel." I knew Connor was teasing. "Guess you're her favorite guy."

I took the little dolphin from the box and attached it to my bracelet, where it hung beside the angel. "I will always treasure it, and I'll never take it off. I really, really love my angel and dolphin. Thank you both so very much."

Ricky was beaming. Then his voice took on a more serious tone. "Do you really have to go to New York, Micaela?"

Connor must have told him. This was a subject Connor and I avoided, and I let him provide an answer, saving me the difficulty of dealing with it.

"A lot can happen in a year, buddy. Maybe she might change her mind."

Ricky seemed satisfied with the answer. I just looked at Connor, and he looked at me. My leaving hung between us like a hovering ghost. We couldn't see it, but we could feel it.

CHAPTER 20

We had to take Ricky home. His mother felt he was spending too much time with Connor on the boat and wasn't attending to his hygiene. Connor said there was no point in arguing with her. He was sure it was more about his father's believing he was a bad influence on Ricky than the number of showers or manicures Ricky got. When we arrived, Connor reminded me of my promise to call Dad. He'd left his mobile on the boat, so I was escorted into the living room to use the phone on a table beside an enormous white couch. I glanced out at the pool area, which was already familiar but looked bigger in daylight. A woman sunbathing by the pool looked up. I assumed it was Connor's mom.

"Thanks for coming with us today. I have to go to the bathroom," Ricky informed me. "See ya." We hugged, and he headed upstairs.

Mrs. McKenzie opened the sliding glass door. She removed her oversized sunglasses and hat. Connor had her hair—thick, brown, and wavy. Other than that, they didn't look alike. She was petite and rather plain with a round face. Ricky resembled his mom.

"Well, hello! You must be Michelle."

"Micaela!" Connor corrected her, seemingly annoyed.

"That's okay," I replied. "A lot of people call me Michelle. It sounds similar." It did bother me, but we had never met, so I gave her the benefit of the doubt.

"Ricky's gone to his room, and Micaela and I are in a bit of hurry. She has to call her dad."

I could tell Connor was trying to escape as quickly as possible.

"That's nice that you're calling your dad." She directed her comment to me. "I never know where Connor is, and he never calls."

"I'm twenty-two, and if you recall, I don't live here anymore." Connor sounded even more annoyed.

I felt the tension between them. There had been a disdain in his voice and an awkward silence from his mother. She left the room; on her way upstairs, she called out, "It was nice to meet you, Michelle."

Connor shook his head, rolled his eyes, and handed me the phone.

I dialed our number and waited. Dad answered after two rings, and I told him we were on our way. Connor waved his hand back and forth, trying to get my attention.

"Ask your dad if I can have you for a few more hours." He checked his watch. "Say, until after eight or nine."

Asking Dad if it was okay made me feel childish. His overprotective nature still bothered me. He agreed, as long as I didn't go out on the boat. I promised we'd remain on land. Connor took my hand and pulled me toward the front door.

I was happy when we were in the jeep, headed back to Clearwater. I wasn't sure what to make of his mom. Connor kept apologizing. If first impressions counted for anything, I found her to be somewhat shallow, but I probably wasn't being fair. I was comparing her to my mom. I was curious what Connor was planning and glad to have more time with him.

"What's up?" I asked.

"You hungry?" He didn't wait for my reply. "How about pizza? Not fancy but filling."

"I love pizza. I haven't had pizza in forever. Dad isn't a fan of take-out, and I have no idea how to make it."

"Can't say the same. It's become a staple … all the food groups."

"Where are we going?"

"Well …" Connor paused. "I kinda had this idea I could order one, and we could watch the sunset from my boat. A sort of picnic."

I reminded him of my promise to Dad. No boat, at least until he felt more comfortable with Connor.

"No problem. I won't take it out. We can just stay dockside, and you won't compromise your integrity."

It seemed like half a compromise, but it sounded nice, and it didn't threaten my life, so Dad couldn't possibly be upset. He'd never know anyway.

The marina was filled with tourists, some leaving and a few lined up for sunset cruises. Connor told me most would be gone after six o'clock. The boat still looked worn at the front but nothing a little paint couldn't fix. Ricky would have more work. I noticed a small table set up on the deck, complete with tablecloth, napkins, and two wine glasses.

I glared at Connor. "You planned this, Connor McKenzie."

He winked and gave me a very sheepish grin. "Cannot tell a lie."

"How did you know Dad would be okay with my staying out later?"

"Got lucky!" He helped me into the boat. "What do you like on your pizza?"

"I'm not fussy. Whatever you like."

He disappeared into the galley to find his mobile. I shook my head in amazement. A few lingering tourists glanced in my direction. They smiled. One gave me an A-okay sign. What did they know that I didn't know?

Connor appeared, holding a bottle of red wine and a corkscrew. "Not sure what you preferred, red or white, but if we follow Italian tradition, it has to be red." He placed the bottle on the table and began uncorking it.

I gave him my dubious face.

"What?" He gave me his innocent little-boy face.

"If I don't miss my guess, you're trying to seduce me."

"Me? I wouldn't think of it. But on the other hand, it's worth a try." He poured the wine into glasses he said were borrowed from his mom's china cabinet.

The only thing in my stomach was a piece of toast, half a bag of popcorn, and three licorice sticks I was sure were congealing into a gelatinous mass. The pizza I could handle, but the wine might not be a good idea, considering the condition of my digestive system, but I accepted the glass and held it while Connor made a toast.

"Here's to the most beautiful girl in the universe, and may all her dreams come true."

It seemed odd making a toast to myself, especially for such an exaggerated claim.

"Oh, and I'd like to add … may her dreams always include me."

That one I could toast to.

"Hey, Connor! Got your order!" A kid about sixteen stood on the dock, holding a pizza box. "Heard about you getting caught in that freak storm. Glad you got your boat back. You're pretty lucky."

"Thanks, Todd." Connor handed him cash; judging by the kid's expression, it was a lot more than the pizza was worth.

"Thanks, man!" Todd shoved the money in his pocket and waved goodbye.

"You two seem to know each other."

"Todd's been delivering pizzas here pretty regularly for over a year. Hate to admit it. Guess I should learn to cook."

"Well, it won't be me who teaches you. My culinary skills are pretty sad. Dad does most of the cooking, and I attempt a few things. I'm pretty good with spaghetti."

"That's a start," Connor said as he separated the pizza slices and offered one to me.

"Are you suggesting I learn to cook? 'Cause that's probably not going to happen any time soon."

"Wouldn't think of it. My mother can't even make spaghetti, so you're one up on her."

"Doesn't she have a housekeeper?"

"Yeah, but Grams did most of the cooking when I was younger." He quickly changed the subject. "How do you like the pizza?"

I nodded my approval while pulling a string of cheese away from my mouth. The pepperoni, sausage, and anchovies were an interesting combination. Connor refilled his wine glass and topped up mine.

The effect of the sun's heat, the gentle rocking of the boat, and the wine lulled me into a groggy stupor. I was halfway to inebriated. I could feel my inhibitions slipping away. If Connor's intention was to seduce me, his plan could work. My body tingled in anticipation.

While I finished my second slice of pizza, Connor placed a tape in his cassette player and pushed the play button.

"May I have this dance?"

He took my hand. I stood, and he pulled my body close. Both his arms encircled my waist as my arms wrapped around his neck. The song's rhythm was slow and the melody unfamiliar. I'd been so busy with schoolwork and consumed with my feelings for Connor that I'd missed most of the current popular music. We stood swaying together, staring into each other's eyes, oblivious to our surroundings. Connor sang the lyrics, his voice a perfect match to the artist's rich baritone voice. It was obvious he'd chosen this song for a reason. I closed my eyes and absorbed the sound of his voice.

> Nothing's going to change my love for you.
> You ought to know by now how much I love you.
> My world may change my whole life through, but
> Nothing's gonna change my love for you …

As the singer declared how lonely he'd be without the woman he loved in his life, Connor repeated the lyrics in my ear. Shivers of passion flowed like silk down my spine. I didn't wait for the song to end. I lifted my face and pulled his head down to meet my lips. He held me tighter and returned the kiss. Our bodies locked in passion. We broke apart at the sound of someone whistling. An old man on a fishing trawler stood watching us.

"I think we've become the local entertainment," Connor said as he picked me up and carried me through the galley and down the stairs to his room, kicking the door shut behind him.

The last stanza of the song trailed off. My heart raced. There was enough of my inhibitions left to feel apprehensive. I was eighteen years old, still a virgin, and very nervous. Passion and instinct won out over my apprehension. He caressed me softly at first, as if sensing my nervousness. All I wanted was to let him love me and love him back. Touching him and feeling his body next to mine was ecstasy. My awkwardness passed, and I was swallowed up in passion. His pleasure was my pleasure. The gentle rocking of the boat blended with our own rhythm.

The setting sun and the swell of the waves created by incoming boats sent shadows dancing across the small room. I lay quietly, locked in Connor's embrace, savoring the remnants of our passion. I couldn't recall ever feeling this content or happy.

I was the first to speak. "You have an amazing singing voice."

"I can carry a tune."

"I think it would be fun to sing together."

"I wouldn't count on that." Connor pulled me closer.

"Looks like it worked," I teased, referring to the dinner, wine, and music.

Connor laughed and kissed the top of my head. "I really don't want you thinking I set you up, Micaela. Yeah, I wanted this more than you know, but it had to be your choice. Let's say I encouraged it. I love you so much. Do you believe in divine intervention?"

"You mean like angels and a God who gets involved in our lives?"

"Something like that. I was your age when I started to feel there had to be more to life than chasing the almighty dollar like my parents. After I bought the boat, I would take it out by myself and watch the sun set. I felt there was something a lot bigger that I was missing. I began reading a few books, and yeah, I actually read the Bible. Don't laugh."

"I'm not laughing, Connor. We didn't go to church. Dad was raised a Catholic, but he didn't have much use for all the 'holier-than-thou stuff,' as he called it. Mom liked to read from Psalms. I liked the one—*The Lord is my Shepherd, I shall not want.* I don't remember the entire verse, but that always stuck in my head. I think my mom wanted to teach me gratitude and forgiveness." Thoughts of my mom made me sigh.

"You miss her a lot, don't you?"

"Yes, I do. I have to admit when she died my belief in God went from a child's naive faith to downright hatred and then faded to nothing. I haven't thought about it in a long time."

"You know what's great?"

"What?" I snuggled closer to him.

"I can talk to you about my feelings. Believe me, it's not a subject I can discuss with my friends or family. Sometimes I try with Ricky, but I don't think he understands. He asks too many questions I can't answer."

He gently pushed a strand of hair off my face and traced my cheek with his finger.

"The reason I asked you about divine intervention is that before Jason's party, I was pretty bummed. My life was stagnant. I almost believed my parents when they told me I would amount to nothing if I didn't finish university. Then there you were, my beautiful angel. I knew beyond a shadow of a doubt I had to have you in my life, and the next reason is a bit weird. You'll think I've lost my mind."

"No, I won't." I loved his sharing his thoughts and feelings with me.

"The night of the storm I was crazy with fear. I had no idea what was happening with you and Ricky. I really thought the boat was going to capsize, and we would drown. I tried desperately to focus on beating out those waves. There was a moment when I was going to give up and just go to both of you and hold you until it was over, whatever the outcome. That was when I heard a voice—in my head, of course—and there was this amazing aura of light all around me. At first I thought I was imagining it, but it seemed so real."

"What did the voice say?" I wanted to believe him, so I tried not to sound skeptical.

"It told me everything was going to be all right. I felt this warmth, and I found the strength to keep fighting through it. Sounds crazy, right?"

He was right; it did sound crazy, but I accepted that Connor believed it. "Considering we made it okay, in spite of my leg and concussion, I'd say we were amazingly lucky, and whatever that was, I am grateful it happened."

The setting sun cast orange light across the bed sheets. In our haste to satisfy our passion, we had forgotten to shut the drapes. Connor reached up and closed them.

He checked his watch. "I'd better get you back before your dad sends out a search party. My ass would definitely be grass!"

I grabbed my bra and T-shirt from the floor and searched through the sheets for my jeans. Connor found his, and I admired the view as he pulled them up over his hips. I took in the tanned muscles of his back, his narrow waist, and amazing butt.

"I think I have to use the 'head,' or whatever Ricky called it."

Connor laughed and directed me to a small space containing a shower stall, sink, and toilet. I gasped at my reflection in the mirror. My mascara had created raccoon-like smudges under my eyes and my hair … well, that was a lost cause. I was a far cry from beautiful. After relieving my bladder, washing my hands, and wiping the black smears as best I could with wet toilet paper, I tried fixing my hair—not much improvement.

When I joined Connor on the deck, he'd already removed the pizza box, which still contained several pieces, and was putting the wine in the small bar fridge.

"Think we'll keep this magic potion for another time." He winked and grinned at me. Then, pulling me closer, he kissed me, and I felt his hands moving across my lower back. He had now gained the privileges of intimacy, and so had I. I grabbed his butt and squeezed.

"We'd better get going before I forget about your dad and kidnap you for the night."

We held hands the entire trip home, making his driving more challenging. He walked me to the elevator, as usual, and kissed me until I finally broke free for air.

"Are you okay with this?"

I knew what he meant. "More than okay," I reassured him. "I won't ask how a condom just happened to be so handy."

"Old Boy Scout motto: Be Prepared."

"Were you a Boy Scout?"

"Nope, but it's a great motto."

One more kiss and I entered the elevator. He stood and watched until the doors closed.

As usual, Dad was asleep on the couch with the television blaring. I tiptoed to my room without acknowledging him. If he woke up, he'd know just by looking at me that his little girl was now a woman in every sense of the word. I washed my face, brushed my hair, and changed into my pajamas. I tiptoed back to the living room, turned off the television, and kissed him on the forehead. It woke him.

"Have a good day, Micaela?"

"Yeah, Dad, I did. I'll tell you about the movie in the morning."

He grunted and fell back to sleep. I took the blanket from the chair beside the couch, covered him, and went to bed with memories of Connor still lingering. I wasn't sure I had the right to be this happy while Dad was suffering; I hoped someday he would find happiness again. I wanted this feeling to last forever, but forever was a long time.

CHAPTER 21

Midterms were over. I hadn't seen Conner in almost two weeks. To say I was walking on air sounded incredibly cliché, but Vini used the phrase to describe my obvious detachment from reality. She figured out why. She wanted details. She wasn't getting any. Studying and exams provided some grounding, but every so often, my mind would slip back to Connor and our beautiful moment together on the boat. I ached to see him. Phone calls were just teasers. Connor's birthday was in three days, and I had no idea what to get him. Vini, as usual, suggested a surprise party, complete with cake. I knew Connor wanted to spend as much time alone together as we could get, and I wanted that too. Vini sounded disappointed when I told her.

"I get it. You guys want to get jiggy with it." Her vocabulary needed some adjustments.

No matter how crudely she described our desire to be together, the fact was, she was right. Two weeks without Connor felt like an eternity.

He agreed to take Saturday off. I would drive to the marina and make him a birthday lunch—my infamous spaghetti, accompanied by the wine we hadn't finished. He said it sounded great. As for a present, I had an idea. I wanted to give him something to remember me when our relationship was challenged by distance and time.

Lunch went well. I didn't burn anything. Connor said it was the best spaghetti he'd ever eaten, which was probably not true, but I accepted the compliment. We danced to our favorite songs and made love. The day was perfect.

The gentle rocking of the boat and the warmth of Connor's embrace lulled me into a state of bliss. Two glasses of wine added to my euphoria. I cuddled closer, pressing my body into his.

"You're determined to wear me out," Connor said as his hand moved across my bare thigh. I felt his desire match mine. The world around us disappeared. Only our passion and love mattered.

I kept thinking how elusive happiness could be. *It comes, and it goes.* The happiness I was feeling now I would store in my heart and remember when we were separated. We lay together quietly, our bodies covered in sweat, exhausted and satisfied.

"I love you, Connor." Finally, I said it out loud. I'd come close many times but was afraid that by admitting it, I would only add to the burden of pain that my departure would have for us.

"I know you love me. It's in your smile and your eyes when you look at me. It's in your touch, and you would never give yourself so passionately if you didn't love me." He turned my head and looked directly into my eyes. "I want you to know the time we have spent together means everything to me. You are my precious earth angel. I love you more than words can express. I know you feared saying it out loud, as if not declaring it would somehow make your leaving easier. Words are irrelevant."

I couldn't contain the tears. Feelings I'd never felt before overwhelmed me.

"Why all the tears?" He wiped them away with the tips of his fingers and put his arms around me.

"I'm happy … very happy. It's a girl thing."

He smiled. "That was an amazing birthday present."

I was suddenly reminded of the gift I'd made. Connor's shirt was entangled in the sheets. Leaving the comfort of his arms, I retrieved it. He watched me as I put it on.

"You have a beautiful body."

"You're kidding, right?" Being on the thin side with small breasts was not my idea of beautiful.

"I know what you're thinking. For your information, I'm not a boob man, not that there's anything wrong with yours. More of an ass kind of guy, and you have an amazing one."

"Yours isn't bad either."

"That sounds somewhat average." He made a sad face.

"It's amazing." I leaned down and kissed him.

"That's better."

I found my purse in the kitchen and took out the card. It was almost dark. Connor turned on his new lamp. I sat cross-legged at the bottom of the bed while he propped himself against the wall behind.

"What do you have there?"

"I didn't know what to buy you, so I made you a card." I handed it to him.

"You didn't have to buy me anything." He opened it. "Did you draw this? It's beautiful."

I nodded. My musical talent far outweighed my artistic ability, but I had attempted to draw his boat from a picture I'd taken. My sunset needed improvement. I created an image of a man and woman holding hands on the deck. It was simply an impression, any likeness was merely coincidental, although I tried my best to make it took like us.

He opened the card. I'd written a poem. He handed it back to me. "You read it."

A sudden shyness made me hesitate. I took a deep breath and started.

You touch me,
and my heart takes flight.
I feel the wings of angels
brush my soul.
You smile, and my world stands still.
You laugh,
and I feel the joy of heaven's light
cast beams across my heart.
Your love,
the precious gift you give.
Each moment
leaving footprints time cannot erase.
For me,
there is no time.
There is only you.

Connor sat very still. I waited. He reached across the bed and pulled me into his arms. I saw tears in his eyes. "It's a girl thing," he explained, teasing me. His voice cracked with emotion. "You are not only beautiful, you are a goddess."

He rolled on top of me and pulled my leg up, our bodies entwined, and the card fell to the floor. I was again lost in his love and his passion.

"Knock, knock. Are you guys decent?" It was Vini. The door to the cabin was open. I'd forgotten to close it, but thankfully, she remained on deck.

"What the hell is she doing here?" Connor jumped from the bed, grabbed his jeans, and wiggled into them. I gave him his shirt. "Depends on what you think is decent," he yelled.

Searching for my clothes, I found them in various places. I dressed quickly. I heard Jason's voice.

"Sorry, guy. Vin insisted we drop by."

I hoped she hadn't brought a cake. Emerging from the cabin, I tried not to appear annoyed by their sudden appearance.

"Good God, girl! Your hair looks like you took an eggbeater to it," Vini announced.

"That's subtle." Owen appeared, holding two bottles of wine—one white, one red.

I found my brush in my purse and tried to remove the tangles. *Too difficult!*

"Tried to tell her we'd be an imposition, but you know Vin." Jason took his sister's arm. "We should go."

"Not before I give Connor his birthday present." Vini ignored Jason and removed a card from her purse. Connor accepted it and gave her a hug.

"What are you hugging me for? You don't know what it is yet," she said.

"It's the thought that counts, Vini," Owen said as he put the wine on the counter. He had brought along some paper cups. "So what will it be?"

The thought of more wine made my stomach do somersaults, but I indicated the red. Connor did the same. While Owen poured, Connor opened his card. His laugh was contagious. Owen and Jason joined in. The card depicted a man with his pants around his ankles, sitting on a toilet. It read "Just wanted to let you know I give a crap." It was so Vini! All three of them had signed it. Two tickets were tucked inside.

"Hey guys, this is great." Connor showed me the tickets to the Monsters of Rock tour, featuring Van Halen. The seats were near the front. It was almost a year away, but acquiring them now was a good idea. July 30, the date of the concert, was one week before I would be leaving. I gathered the second ticket was for me. It would probably be our last date before I left.

"We got tickets for ourselves too." Vini was pleased that Connor liked his gift. "Let's have a toast."

We all waited, paper cups in hand.

"Give me a minute. I want to make it a good one." She paused. "Okay, I've got it." She raised her cup, and we all did the same.

"Here's to love. May it flourish always, and may Connor find the happiness he deserves."

Connor placed his arm around my waist and drew me to him. "I've got all the happiness I need right here."

He kissed the top of my head, and Vini added to her toast. "May our lives always be entwined, and no matter where our journeys take us, may we all find our way back to each other."

We tipped our cups again. "Very poetic," Jason added.

"Speaking of poetry ..." Connor said and then turned to enter his bedroom. I knew immediately what he intended to do and was surprised he would share something so personal, even if it was with our friends.

When he returned, he handed the card to Vini.

"Micki, wow! You are so talented. I want to be you when I grow up." Vini passed it along to Jason and Owen, who declined reading the poetry. At least *they* respected my privacy. I knew Connor wasn't perfect, but I was disappointed at his lack of respect for my feelings.

Connor looked at my face. I sent him a look I hoped conveyed my annoyance.

He must have picked up on it. "I'm sorry, but it was so good. Please don't be mad."

A voice from the deck, rather slurred and horribly familiar, called out, "Let's get this party started." I recognized Bonnie's voice. "Where's the birthday boy?" she yelled.

"Shit on a stick! How did she know we were here?" Vini looked as if she was gearing up for something.

Jason was quick to grab his sister's arm in an effort to stop her from making any unexpected movements in Bonnie's direction. "She must have seen the light on in the boat. There's no way Connor would have invited her," he said, still holding firm to Vini's arm.

"Someone help me? I can't get into the boat," Bonnie called out. She definitely sounded drunk.

No one moved. I looked at Connor.

He shrugged. "Looks like I'm elected. In the state she's in, she could fall between the boat and the dock and hit her head. I have to get her."

"No, you don't. Let her fall in." Vini seemed to like that idea.

Bonnie wasn't alone. We heard another female voice say, "Come on, Bonnie. I haven't got time for this. I have to meet Marcus in twenty minutes."

Bonnie paid no attention, and I saw her reach out for Connor's hand. She struggled over the side, and her body swayed. Then she collapsed in Connor's arms. Vini saw it as well.

"That calculating bitch." Vini looked as if she was about to carry out her threat of slitting Bonnie's throat. Her glance fell on a bread knife sitting on the counter. Jason quickly pushed it away. He saw the look in her eyes too. I might not have chosen such a violent reaction, but I seconded Vini's feelings.

"You can go, Joanne. Say hi to Marcus for me." Bonnie still held tightly to Connor.

He pushed her away. "What are you doing here? You're drunk."

"It's your birthday, baby. Remember on your nineteenth birthday we went skinny dipping in your mom and dad's pool. They're not home. I know 'cause I was at your house. How 'bout we do a replay?"

Jason was holding Vini in a viselike grip. Any moment he'd have to contain me as well.

"Not gonna happen." Connor kept trying to distance himself from Bonnie, but she kept grabbing him. "Will you stop it? I'm with Micaela now."

I was grateful Connor at least reminded her of that fact.

Bonnie glanced toward the kitchen where the four of us stood taking in the scene. "That scrawny thing. What could you possibly see in her?" She stumbled toward me. "You think Connor loves you. Well, he said the same thing to me."

"That's enough, Bonnie," Connor said. "How about I call a cab, and you go sleep it off."

She paid no attention to him. "Well, what do we have here?" She shot a glance at Owen and Jason. "The two fairies!"

It was Owen's turn to grab Jason. I wasn't sure if Jason released his grip on Vini, or she managed to free herself, but before he could stop her, she punched Bonnie square in the face. Bonnie fell back and screamed. "You bitch. You black bitch!" A steady stream of blood was running from her nose.

Connor grabbed Vini. "Please, just go, guys. Thanks for the tickets. Sorry it had to end like this."

"No problem, but I think you might just have your hands full," Owen said as he stepped around Bonnie, who was sitting at the bottom of the stairs with her back against the wall, holding her nose.

Vini couldn't resist spitting on her as she passed. Jason shoved his sister forward, just as Bonnie reached out to grasp her ankle. Bonnie missed.

"You'll pay for this, you black bitch!" she yelled at her.

Vini yelled back, "Just bring it on, you white whore!"

Owen and Jason must have subdued her. The only sound I heard was them walking down the pier. I looked at Connor. He was kneeling beside Bonnie, offering her a wet towel. I grabbed my purse and ran to the deck, avoiding Bonnie. Connor followed. I stopped thinking and simply reacted. I had just enough space to jump to the deck. Miraculously, I didn't fall in.

"Where are you going? Don't leave. I'll call a cab and get rid of her. I don't want you to go."

The frustration in Connor's voice almost swayed me, but I kept running until I reached my car. My beautiful day had been ruined. I didn't want to spend two seconds in the same room with Bonnie, and I was angry at Connor for allowing her to infringe on our happiness.

Dad was sleeping when I arrived home. The phone was ringing. I knew it was Connor. I didn't answer it. It rang a second time, and I removed it from the hook. My anger had taken over, and all thoughts of how precious our relationship was—and the short time we had left—were obliterated.

CHAPTER 22

The school was humming with gossip. Bonnie offered a creative explanation for her broken nose, making sure her version slandered Vini, Jason, and Owen and placed me in the category of super-bitch. I tried ignoring it. One of my classmates filled me in on the story, whether for verification or simply to let me know she was well informed, I wasn't sure. Apparently, I was the intruder, and Bonnie was with Connor, celebrating his birthday. The fact her friend Joanne knew the truth didn't seem to matter. My guess was, Joanne had been manipulated into supporting Bonnie's lie. I was supposed to have pushed her when she asked me to leave, and when she tried to defend herself, Vini punched her. She included Owen and Jason by saying they kept Connor from protecting her, although by what means hadn't been elaborated. She added that if we tried to deny it, we were lying. I didn't feel the need to counter her story. If people wanted to believe her, they certainly wouldn't accept the truth. She made sure everyone was aware of how upset Connor was and that he had taken her to the hospital. That part was probably true.

Three nights of crying hadn't put a dent in my anger. I avoided Dad, who kept asking me why I was in such a foul mood. I would say it was nothing. I let him answer the phone when it rang, in case it was Connor. I gave Dad strict instructions to tell Connor I was busy, which confused Dad even more. I was sitting on my bed, doing homework, when he knocked on my door. Jason was on the phone. Jason never called. My curiosity made me answer.

"You up to meeting me for lunch?" Jason was difficult to ignore, and he didn't deserve the cold shoulder from me. He was just an innocent bystander. I had the distinct feeling he was calling on Connor's behalf.

"This isn't one of Vini's plans, is it?" I wouldn't put it past her to talk Jason into something.

"Totally my idea. I really want to talk with you. We all love you Micaela, and Vin's hurt she hasn't heard from you. She thinks you're mad at her for spoiling Connor's birthday. She's called you a few times and left messages, but you don't return her calls. What do you say I meet you for lunch tomorrow at the same place you and Vin meet?"

I agreed. Part of me was beginning to think I might have overreacted, and losing Connor because of it would create an unbearable guilt. I wanted to hear what Jason had to say.

The table where Vini and I usually met was taken, so we had to find one closer to the school grounds. I tried avoiding the whispers of those who believed I was ruining Bonnie's life. Jason sat across from me, which inspired more whispering and glares from students who believed Bonnie's lies.

"Thanks for coming. I kinda miss school." Jason had purchased a cheeseburger and fries from Carley's Burgers, his sister's favorite fast-food establishment. "I usually eat alone, so it's nice to have the company."

I had my usual tuna salad and tea from the cafeteria. "How's the job search coming along?" I thought I would open the conversation by focusing on him.

"Not so good, unfortunately. Owen's encouraging me to open my own interior design business in Clearwater and forget going to California. He said it was better being a big fish in a small pond than a small fish in a huge pond."

That made me laugh. It sounded like Owen. "Is that what *you* want?" Having my own dream, I preferred the small-fish idea, with the hope of becoming the big fish.

"I'm not sure. I'm not against it, but I need to think about it a little more." Jason took a bite of his burger and, unlike his sister, waited until he finished chewing before he spoke. "Owen wouldn't have to look for something, and my family is here. That's a big consideration."

I poked at my salad. I wasn't sure what to say next.

Jason decided to get to the point. "Are you angry at Vin? You don't return her calls. She's sorry about spoiling Connor's birthday, but this time, I'm not the least bit sorry she took a second shot at Bonnie's nose. Have to admit I was with her on that one."

"I've been busy, but no, I'm not angry at Vini. I just don't feel like talking about it."

"Okay, so what then? Is it Connor? You seem to be avoiding him too."

I said nothing.

Jason took another bite of his cheeseburger and washed it down with a cola. He ignored my lack of comment. "Maybe it's none of my business, but I'm going to stick my neck out anyway. Vin loves you, Connor adores you, and … well, Owen and I love you too—not in a romantic way, of course."

I smiled. Jason's sincerity was having an effect.

"So I think you're mad at Connor for two reasons." He put his index finger up to indicate his first point. "He showed Vin the card you made. I get that. It was not meant for anyone else to see. A bit thoughtless, if you ask me, but he loved it, and I think he was proud of you. Just so you know, he hasn't come off that boat of his in three days."

Jason had my attention. I stopped eating. "What's your second reason?"

He held up another finger to match the first. "Two, he allowed Bonnie on the boat. I understand why you're pissed off about that, but I think he was caught between—what is it they say?—a rock and a hard place?"

"How do you figure that?" I asked.

"Connor is a caring kind of guy. I think it's a bit misplaced when it comes to Bonnie, but you saw what happened. She would have taken a nosedive into the water; might have gotten hurt pretty bad. Who knows? She's super-determined when it comes to Connor. What did you expect him to do?"

I hadn't given an alternative situation much thought. "I guess you're right. It's just that seeing her in his arms was too much."

"You have to admit it happened pretty fast. Vin called him to apologize. He told her he understands why you're upset. He has tried calling you too, but he says you're not taking his calls either. Do you think you could cut the guy some slack? He's nuts about you."

"Jason, you're pretty good at this."

"At what?" He looked puzzled.

I smiled. "At fixing stuff … just like your sister."

"Maybe. Owen doesn't like talking things out until he's had some thinking time. I wait it out because it works better. He's good at the communication stuff, but it just takes a while." He gathered up his garbage and stood to leave. "Call Connor, okay?"

"Thanks for putting it into perspective for me. I promise I'll call."

"You're welcome. Any time." He turned and left.

Jason was a great guy. I had to admit his intervention released my pent-up anger.

CHAPTER 23

Mom once told me, "If you look hard enough, you'll find good in everything, even the bad stuff." I wasn't sure I agreed, as anger usually clouded my judgment. Now that my anger at Connor had passed, the opportunity to experience the good part presented itself. My vision wasn't blocked anymore.

Before I had a chance to call Connor, Dad asked if he could speak with me. He'd made tea, and two cups sat on the kitchen table, waiting. It looked like it was going to be a serious conversation. He wanted to know what was wrong and wasn't accepting *nothing* as an answer. So I told him but omitted the more intimate details. I expected him to see my point of view. He didn't; he sided with Connor, which surprised me, as two months ago he didn't want me anywhere near him. He expressed the same sentiment as Jason.

"I think you're being too hard on the guy. This Bonnie girl is a problem, for sure, but your friend—"

"Vini."

"Right … Vini. She shouldn't have hit her, but that wasn't Connor's fault. You just told me he didn't invite her and asked her to leave. Maybe the problem is that you don't trust him."

I was beginning to suspect someone had influenced Dad.

"Other than the boat incident, has Connor given you any reason not to trust him to be faithful?"

"No. Not really … but …"

"No buts! You either trust him, or you don't."

Dad had a point. I knew in my heart I trusted Connor, but for some reason I didn't understand, I let my insecurities take over. I'd have to work on that.

"And," he added, "you have a bad habit of shutting down when you're hurt. I guess you get that from your old man. Your mom liked to talk things out. Sometimes too much. I suppose that's better than holding it all in." He reached across the table and took my hand. "You and Connor don't have a lot of time left to be together. Before you know it, you'll be flyin' off to New York. Do you really want to waste time being angry?"

I squeezed Dad's hand. "How did you get so smart?"

"Being around you and your mom. You know Micaela, time is so precious. You just don't know how much of it you have. Losing your mom and Gloria taught me that."

I decided not to share the conversation with Jason and my intention of calling Connor. I thanked Dad for his advice.

"Say, how about you and your old man go out for dinner? We haven't done that in a long time."

Calling Connor would have to wait. Since Dad and I hadn't spent much quality time together in months, I accepted his invitation. He chose a restaurant a couple of blocks from our apartment building. It was a beautiful evening, and being with Dad was one of those precious moments. He was his old self again. He laughed at my Vini stories, although some were censored where necessary. It was the first time in months I'd heard him laugh, and it made me happy. We were just finishing dessert when I felt a hand on my shoulder. I jumped, practically spilling half a piece of cheesecake on my lap.

"Mind if I join you?" It was Connor. "Sorry if I startled you."

I looked at Dad. He took a sip of his coffee and pretended not to notice. My conspiracy feeling was obviously correct. Someone had planned this. I was speechless.

Connor grabbed a chair from another table and sat beside Dad. I stared at my two men. It was my turn to laugh. "I don't believe it. How on earth did you manage this? Let me guess … Vini?" It didn't take much to figure it out.

Connor smiled, confirming my suspicion, and Dad kept drinking his coffee.

"Are you cool with it?" Connor asked.

"Yeah, I'm cool." There was no point rehashing what had happened. Sometimes you just have to move on. It no longer seemed important. All that mattered was I had my dad back, and Connor and I loved each other. Dad was right. We had so little time left; I shouldn't waste one moment.

Dad and Connor were bonding. They shared two loves: me and boats, hopefully in that order. As their relationship grew, so did Dad's trust. I was now allowed to go out on the boat. He was thrilled when Connor invited him to share the ocean sunsets. I couldn't have been happier. He was even becoming comfortable with what he referred to as my "overnights," although he was quick to ask if we were taking precautions. I could tell he was embarrassed. Sex wasn't a subject you talked about with your dad. Connor and I avoided discussing the incident with Bonnie, as I just didn't want anything to spoil the time we had together. I hoped I had learned a lesson.

The week of midterm exams was tough. Connor was a distraction, so I decided it would be best to wait until exams were over to be with him. Seeing him again was like finally eating sugar after one week of abstinence.

Ricky was waiting for me in the parking lot of the marina. He was either excited to see me, or something was up. After a huge hug, he placed a black scarf in my hand and instructed me to put it around my eyes.

I hesitated. "What's up?" I asked.

"Trust me, okay?" Ricky said. "It's a blindfold. Connor and I have a surprise."

I went along with it.

"No peeking." Ricky offered me his hand. "Are you sure you can't see?"

"Blind as a bat." I took his hand, and he carefully guided me down the pier. We stopped.

"Okay, you can take it off now." He sounded excited.

Connor stood on the deck with his camera pointed at me. I wasn't sure what I was supposed to see. Then I noticed it. *The Sea Witch* was now *The Micaela*, written in bright blue letters. Connor took a picture.

"So what do you think?" He took another picture. "I probably should have asked your permission, but Ricky really wanted to surprise you."

"I'm not sure. It feels weird having a boat named after me."

Ricky looked disappointed. "Don't you like it?"

"Of course I like it. It will just take a little getting used to."

"I hated the name Sea Witch," Ricky explained. "I asked Connor if we could change it, and I wanted your name."

"Thank you. I'm honored." We exchanged another hug.

The afternoon was spent eating hamburgers and sharing fries at the restaurant near the marina. Connor had an evening charter, and Ricky had to be home by four, so we were land bound. Ricky dominated the conversation, as usual. He wanted to know what I was going to be on Halloween. I hadn't thought about it.

"You're coming to the party, right?" he asked while wiping ketchup off his chin.

"What party?" I had no idea what he was referring to.

Connor looked startled. "Vini didn't tell you? That's surprising."

"Not so surprising. We haven't talked in days." I didn't add *since the Bonnie incident.* It wasn't that I'd deliberately avoided Vini. I'd been too wrapped up in exams and being with Connor. She had given up calling me. Our friendship had changed, most likely my fault. I'd ignored my friend, and I felt guilty.

"We always have a Halloween party at our house," Ricky said. "I'm going to be Luke Skywalker, and Connor is going to be Han Solo.

"I'll think about it," Connor said as he stole a french fry from my plate. "Sorry I didn't mention it, but I figured you knew. It's become a tradition over the past couple of years, combining Vini's birthday with a Halloween celebration."

I had completely forgotten Vini was a Halloween baby. It wasn't like she'd never told me. She loved telling people. She even made up a joke about it: *"When my mother asked what sex her baby was, the doctor said it was a little ghoul."* Vini would kill herself laughing. She always laughed at her own jokes. How could I have forgotten? I was a lousy friend.

The first thing I did when I got home was call her. She accepted my apology, and I hers. I didn't let on I'd forgotten her birthday and asked if she had made plans to celebrate the event. She jumped on my question with her usual enthusiasm.

"Guess Connor forgot to tell you … you two being so busy and all." Her sarcasm was obvious, but I ignored it. "I'm planning a combination Halloween and birthday party. It will be a blast. We usually have it at Connor's. His parents always go on holidays at this time of year. I swear those people are never home. Good for us, 'cause we get to use their house. They'd have a shit-fit if they knew it was for me and that Jason would be there, but until then …we have a party house."

I had the feeling the McKenzie residence was party central. "So have you decided what your costume is going to be?" I asked.

"Not sure yet. I'm still thinking about it. Connor has to be there, so I guess you're coming."

I spotted another dig. I wasn't sure she'd actually forgiven me for abandoning our friendship.

"Of course," I replied. "I have no idea what costume to choose."

"Well, if it helps any, the guys have chosen a *Star Wars* theme. Jason has decided on Lando Calrissian. Not sure if it's because he's black or if he really likes the character, but who cares? Owen is going to be Darth Vader. They wanted me to be Princess Leia, but it's not my style. How about you be Princess Leia? My mom can make the costume, and I have a black wig. I think I can make those stupid bun things. I'm pretty creative with hair."

"You're sure your mom won't mind?"

"You kidding? She'll love doing it. Why don't you come over tomorrow and we'll work on it? I'm sure you and Connor can be separated for a day."

This time I responded to the sarcasm. "Vini, you are just as important to me, and I want to thank you for bringing Connor and me back together. You're the best, and I love you lots."

"I love you too. See ya tomorrow."

It felt good to have our friendship back. I vowed to never ignore her again.

CHAPTER 24

There was no denying that Vini loved parties. Judging from the number of cars parked in the driveway and on the street, she must have told half of Clearwater. I noticed a space just big enough for my small car behind Connor's jeep. A large sign with bold red lettering was posted in his rear window it read: ***Anyone Who Dares Park Behind Me Will Be Towed Away***. I laughed and mentally thanked him.

Jason had been chosen to provide decorations. I took the time to admire his creation. Authentic-looking bats hung from trees, numerous pumpkins with devil faces were placed strategically around the front porch, and fake mutilated body parts were strewn on the walkway. I loved a skeleton sitting on a lawn chair, with a beer in one bony hand and a sign reading, "Happy Birthday, Vini" in the other. It was more funny than scary. Cobwebs laced the front door, where a large hairy black spider sat directly over the doorbell. I avoided it, knocked, and waited, but the music was too loud for anyone to hear. Reluctantly, I pushed the spider. Its legs moved. I jumped back, stifling a scream. The door opened, and Luke Skywalker, complete with light saber, was laughing. He must have noticed my reaction through the window beside the door.

"You wanted me to do that, didn't you?" I was embarrassed and glad it was just Ricky who'd seen me.

"Yup." He still hadn't stopped laughing. "You should have seen your face." He pointed to a bowl of candy. "I'm the door monitor."

I assumed he meant he was handing it out to children brave enough to get past the body parts and spider. "That's a pretty cool costume. You look just like Luke."

"And you look like Princess Leia."

The wig was uncomfortable. Securing it with dozens of bobby pins helped, but I could feel one poking my ear. Vini and her mother had done a great job of making the dress with white fabric we'd found in a thrift shop.

Connor barely gave me time to get past the front entrance. He pulled me into his arms and kissed me.

"If I didn't know it was you, I wouldn't have recognized you." He kissed me again.

"I knew it was Micaela," Ricky interrupted.

If I didn't miss my guess, there was a hint of jealousy in Ricky's voice. I was an expert in jealous reactions.

"Where did you get those costumes?" I asked. "They are so realistic." In my opinion, Connor was even better looking than Han Solo.

"Owen found a rental place in Tampa." Connor led me into the living room, leaving Ricky to tend the door.

Michael Jackson's "Thriller" was pumping from the stereo while couples danced or sat in groups, talking. I had no idea who these people were, with or without costumes. Orange and black balloons were everywhere, attached to similarly colored streamers. The sofas were pushed aside and covered with black sheets, which I figured was a clever idea, considering the sofas were white—less likely to get stained. It was very generous of Connor's parents to hand over their house to a swarm of teenagers; that is, if they were aware of it. My guess was they weren't. Clusters of people were in the dining room, and Connor introduced me to those he knew and recognized. We found Jason and Owen entertaining Mickey and Minnie Mouse in the kitchen. It was amusing to see Lando and Darth with cartoon characters. Owen removed the Vadar headpiece, stating it was a bitch and restricted his breathing, and he didn't have to try very hard to sound like Darth with it on.

"Where's Vini?" I was curious what she'd chosen as a costume, as she had kept it a secret.

Spiderman walked into the kitchen and pulled a beer from the fridge. "If you're looking for Vini, she's outside on the terrace with some of her smoking friends."

I thanked him, and Connor and I headed for the terrace. Four girls stood by the pool, two holding cigarettes. I didn't immediately recognize Vini in the red wig.

"Bet you thought you'd never see a black Cindy Lauper." She introduced me to her friends, three girls from her hairdressing class who were supposed to be the singing group the Supremes.

Vini's decision to be the pop star was perfect. They both dressed in outrageous clothes, and she probably didn't have to go much farther than her own closet for the purple taffeta skirt and red polka dot blouse. I expected her to break out singing "Girls Just Want to Have Fun" at any moment.

When Connor and I returned to the living room, Ricky was dancing with a young girl in a skintight black cat suit. She had her arms around his neck. His were encircling her waist. They were rocking back and forth to a ballad I didn't recognize. Connor had his serious face on. Ricky's fun was about to end. Catgirl took one glance at Connor and ran off, leaving Ricky looking like a puppy whose favorite toy had been taken away.

"Weren't you supposed to be watching the door?" Connor's tone matched the look on his face.

"I got bored, and besides, I want to have fun too."

Connor checked his watch. "You've got twenty minutes. We agreed that if you wanted to dress up and be included, you would go upstairs at nine o'clock. It's almost nine thirty. You have a movie, remember?"

"Why do I always have to be treated like a kid?"

"Because you are a kid. Don't push me."

I could relate to Ricky's feelings.

He took off to the kitchen, probably in search of Catgirl.

"You'd be an awesome dad," I commented as we danced to another slow song.

Connor gave me a quizzical stare. "Wow, that came out of nowhere. Are you thinking about getting pregnant? Wouldn't that mess up your plans?"

I jabbed him in the ribs. "Don't be stupid."

"I wasn't thinking about now. Maybe sometime in the future. Can't say I'm opposed to the idea."

I didn't get the chance to comment. Vini, as anticipated, took the floor and sang along with "Girls Just Want to Have Fun." Her dance moves were hilarious. People joined in, even Jason and Owen. I preferred to watch. Ricky's time was up, and Connor had to practically drag him upstairs.

They say—whoever *they* are—that lightning doesn't strike the same place twice. *They* are wrong. I could barely believe what I was seeing. Bonnie was walking through the open terrace doors, wearing a harem outfit that left nothing to the imagination. Owen noticed my reaction and was quick to divert me.

"Ever dance with a gay guy?" He took my hand and swirled me around, holding me tightly before my actions caught up with my emotions. He whispered in my ear, "Vini's in the bathroom. Looks like Jason's gone to head her off."

Whether he found Vini in time, we didn't know. If he did, it didn't matter. She had a one-track mind when it came to Bonnie. Owen and I watched as Vini charged into the living room and headed straight for her.

"What the hell are you doing here?" Vini snapped, sending Bonnie a look of pure hatred.

"Keep that bitch away from me," Bonnie instructed Jason, who was now holding Vini in a viselike grip. Someone turned the music up.

"I have a right to be here. Connor invited me," Bonnie yelled over the music.

"I don't think so. Not on *my* birthday," Vini yelled back. "You're a liar."

Connor entered the room and stopped suddenly, as if someone had thrown ice water in his face. "Vini, please, no more scenes." He didn't deny Bonnie's claim.

"See!" Bonnie shot Vini a self-satisfied look.

Vini stormed off. I couldn't believe Connor would have invited Bonnie to Vini's party, especially after what happened on his birthday. I stared at him. He stared back. It was a standoff.

Owen whispered in my ear. "I think you need a drink and something stronger than pop."

He was right.

Connor moved toward me; I hoped it was to provide an explanation for Bonnie's sudden arrival, one I could accept. Bonnie shoved me aside and took hold of Connor's arm, pressing it against the swell of her almost-exposed breasts.

"I love your costume, baby," she purred at Connor. "But I think you made a better Zorro. We looked so good together. I was a Spanish senorita, remember?" Her glance fell on me. "Did you ever tell Micaela about the time you got so drunk and we got caught making out in your car? I was grounded for a week."

Connor hadn't removed his arm from Bonnie's grasp. "That wasn't one of my finest moments."

Owen handed me the drink and whispered, "I took the liberty of adding another shot of tequila."

"Good!" I drank it in two gulps.

"Be careful, Micaela. You're driving," Connor warned. He finally wrenched free of Bonnie's grasp, but she pulled his arm back.

"She's a big girl, Connor. Come on; let's dance. You love this song," Bonnie said as she rotated her hips in time with the music. It was the Rolling Stones hit "Let's Spend the Night Together."

"Yes, Connor, why don't you dance with her?" I made no attempt at hiding the anger that was bubbling up inside me.

I handed my glass to Owen and went to find the bathroom. I located it across from the kitchen. It felt like dozens of wasps had taken residence in my head, and my stomach churned. I took five deep breaths. Dad's speech about trusting Connor passed through my mind. Why was it so difficult? But I knew why! Even though Connor denied any current relationship with Bonnie, he'd done nothing so far to get her to back off and get out of his life. It was time for us to have a serious talk, and I didn't want to wait for a more appropriate time. It had to be now!

I passed the kitchen on my way back to the living room. What I saw stopped my heart. Bonnie had her back pressed against the counter with her arms wrapped around Connor's neck. His arms were on her shoulders. They both looked at me. I ran, found my purse, and headed for my car. When I got to the front door, I was grabbed from behind and swung around.

"Wait, Micaela! I know that looked bad, but believe me—I was trying to push her away. She followed me to the kitchen and was coming on to me."

"Right!" I tried twisting away, but he held me tighter.

"I've told you numerous times Bonnie means nothing to me."

"Yeah, you have. You've told me a lot of things. Did you dance with her?"

"No, I didn't. It's pretty obvious you don't trust me."

Our voices were getting louder. Vini was standing in the hallway, listening.

"Is that bitch at it again? Sorry, Connor, but she's going down." Vini flew into the living room before Connor could stop her. Within moments, we heard a scream.

"What the hell!" Connor took off in the direction of the sound. I followed. He pushed through a crowd gathered on the terrace, but he wasn't fast enough. Vini had Bonnie by the hair and was dragging her to the pool. Bonnie squirmed and kicked but wasn't able to free herself. Vini shoved her in.

Ricky must have heard the scream and joined the crowd by the pool. He kept laughing while Bonnie thrashed and kicked, making her way to the side of the pool, where Connor pulled her out.

"Ricky, go with Jason back to your room." Connor's command was immediately obeyed. "Owen, get some towels." Owen stood gaping at the scene. "Now!" I'd never heard Connor so angry. Owen took off to the pool hut. Vini had vanished.

Bonnie was dripping and shaking. Her hair was plastered to her head, her mascara was streaking down her cheeks, and the thin fabric of her costume stuck to her legs. Her shoes had sunk to the bottom of the pool. Connor took the two large towels from Owen and wrapped them around Bonnie. He instructed her to go upstairs, telling her he would be up shortly to get her some dry clothes. Connor's concern for her welfare added fuel to my anger. In my opinion, Bonnie deserved what she got.

"Everyone go inside. The show's over," Connor told the onlookers.

Owen led the group back to the living room. "Start the music. We've got a party going on." He was doing his best to relieve the tension.

Connor ignored me and headed toward the house.

"How very nice of you to help Bonnie," I called out. "You better not keep her waiting."

He turned abruptly. The look on his face made me nervous. "I can't have her going home like that. I thought you, of all people, would have a little compassion."

"Compassion! I'm supposed to have compassion for someone who's trying to steal my boyfriend right in front of me?"

"Do you really think she stands a chance?"

"Why didn't you ask her to leave? It's just like the last time."

"I did." He ran his hand through his hair and lowered his voice. "Micaela, I can't do this anymore. I love you, but I can't be with someone who doesn't trust me." He turned and walked into the house, leaving me standing alone and feeling miserable and scared.

When I tried to open my car door, my hand shook so badly I could barely get the key in the lock. Sitting behind the wheel, I placed my head against it and wept. I didn't feel the jealousy anymore, just an intense anxiety and fear of losing Connor. I glanced at the house. A shadow passed across an upstairs window. The drapes moved aside, and I saw Connor staring down at me. My gaze fell to my wrist, where my angel and dolphin dangled, as if taunting me. I started the car and waited, hoping Connor would come down and get me. He didn't. He had vanished from the window and maybe my life.

CHAPTER 25

Connor was gone. His boat was not docked at the marina, and everyone I spoke with had neither seen nor heard from him in nearly a month. An operator informed me his mobile number had been changed, but it was unlisted. My heart felt like it had been ripped from my body and thrown in the ocean for fish food. I struggled with schoolwork; my grades were slipping and my health was going in the same direction. This time, it was worse than when Dad had issued his edict. Now it was Connor's decision. I'd pushed him away with my jealousy and lack of trust. Guilt consumed me. Every night, I begged whatever power had saved me from drowning in the storm to bring him back and give me a second chance. It seemed no one was listening. Whenever the phone rang, I'd cross my fingers, close my eyes, and say a silent prayer before answering. It was never Connor. I'd sit on my bed, holding my bracelet as if it was a rosary and concentrate on sending out positive, loving messages. Nothing worked. I remembered our first kiss, the afternoons making love on the boat, how he'd shared his deepest feelings and told me he loved me. It couldn't possibly be over.

Thanksgiving came and went and still no Connor. I decided to call the McKenzies. It was my last resort. I'd put it off in the hope that Connor would return for the holiday. I'd convinced myself that I didn't want to upset Ricky, who might already be overcome with worry and anxiety. The truth was, I didn't want him to know I might be responsible for his brother's absence. I feared hearing he knew exactly where Connor was, and had been given strict instructions not to tell me. My imagination conjured up numerous unpleasant scenarios.

Mr. McKenzie answered. He had no idea of his son's whereabouts and seemed impatient with my questions. Ricky had gone with his mother to California. I was no further ahead.

Dad and Vini were convinced Connor would come back. "Just give it a little time; he'll come around," Dad said. I was sick of hearing how time could fix everything. It wasn't like I had tons of it left, and Dad had been the one to remind me of that fact. His intentions were good, but he, of all people, should know that time has its own agenda.

Vini tried reassuring me. "I know the guy," she said. "He just wants a little space for a while. He'll be back, and you two will be doing the wild thing like a pair of lovesick rabbits."

"What if he doesn't want to come back? What if this is permanent?"

Vini didn't respond. For the first time, she didn't have a plan to fix it. She was taking on her own guilt. She was sure Connor had left because he was angry she'd thrown Bonnie in his pool in front of all their friends. I kept insisting she was wrong. He wouldn't just vanish because of something like that. I told her it was my jealousy and lack of trust he'd had enough of. I'd thought about it a lot. I now understood jealousy was like a disease, eating through the fabric of reason and creating an illusion of self-righteousness. I had become my own victim.

Vini thought my revelation a bit dramatic and told me to stop beating myself up, although she was one to talk. She kept repeating,

"Connor loves you. He's just being a jerk right now. Jason can tell you he's done it before. It's his way of getting his head together. He always comes back."

That information didn't comfort me. "So he runs away when something gets tough?" I thought it, so I said it. It made me realize how little I really knew Connor.

"I guess. Sometimes he does, but it seems to help him think," Vini said. "You go all silent and stuck-up when you're hurt or angry."

"I suppose, but stuck-up is a bit of an exaggeration."

"You get my point, right? We all have a way of dealing with our shit."

In an effort to cheer me up, Vini bought a strawberry shortcake, and we shared it at my kitchen table. This time, she got it right. I loved strawberry shortcake with heaps of whipped cream.

She told me about her friends, who was dating whom, which girl got caught smoking in the washroom, and who cheated on their exams—all people I didn't know and information that didn't interest me, but Vini loved gossip, and it sidetracked me momentarily.

That evening, I sat on my bed, trying to study. I had trouble concentrating. It was a hopeless task. I had an exam on music theory in one week, which made studying even more difficult, as I hated the theory part. My grades reflected my lack of enthusiasm, but I knew how disappointed Dad would be if I didn't at least pass, so I persisted. Winter break was coming up, and I wasn't looking forward to one month by myself. School gave me something to focus on. Vini only had one week left before she would be with her family over Christmas. I dreaded Christmas without Connor.

The phone rang. I didn't run to get it. Within moments, Dad knocked on my bedroom door.

"It's your friend Owen. Do you want to speak to him?"

I couldn't imagine why Owen would be calling but hoped it had something to do with Connor—something good.

"I think I know where he is." Owen's revelation was like handing a bacon double-cheeseburger to someone who's lived on rice and water for a month.

"Where is he? How did you find him?" My excitement was difficult to control. Owen was the last person I'd have guessed who'd know where Connor might be. He wouldn't divulge any information on the phone.

"How about you meet me at Carley's Burgers on the strip tomorrow after school. You can bring Vini. She'll be like a cat looking for catnip if we don't include her."

I thought it was a funny analogy. We both knew how Vini liked to be informed. I agreed. Whatever Owen wanted to tell me had to be too important to share on the phone.

Carley's was packed with teenagers buying food their parents probably wouldn't approve of. We were lucky to locate a table. I waited for Owen to disclose his findings.

He removed a small brown envelope from his jacket pocket and held it in front of me. "Before I give this to you, you have to promise me you won't jump to conclusions." He turned to Vini, sitting beside him. "And you keep your mouth shut."

I was becoming suspicious on top of my excitement.

"What the heck do you think I'm going to say?" Vini said, while emptying the contents of a ketchup packet on her fries.

"Just keep any comments to yourself, and you know what I'm referring to."

"Okay, okay!" Vini stuffed three fries in her mouth.

My curiosity skyrocketed.

Owen handed me the envelope but didn't let go. "Promise!" he repeated.

"I promise," I said. "But why would I jump to conclusions?"

Owen didn't answer. He simply let go of the envelope.

I experienced an instant exhilaration. "Owen you're amazing. I love you." It felt like I'd just won the lottery.

"Sorry, sweetie, I'm taken, but hold that thought."

I ripped the seal and pulled out three Polaroid pictures. The first one was Connor docking a boat. I could see part of my name on the side, confirming it was his. My heart beat double-time. The second was Connor standing on the deck. It was far away, but there was no mistaking the hair. The third picture made me gasp. It was definitely Connor. He was standing with his arm draped around the shoulders of a woman in a green bikini. Blazing red hair peeked out from under a ball cap. She was wearing sunglasses, but I knew who it looked like. An older man was taking their picture.

Vini grabbed the snapshot, took one look, and practically gagged on her fries. "What the hell is Connor thinking? See? I told you." She nudged Owen's arm. "I figured she was up to something when Jason's friend said Bonnie hadn't been at school for nearly a month."

"I told you to keep your mouth shut." Owen took the picture from her before she got ketchup all over it.

"You don't have to be rude." Vini wiped the condiment off her chin. "Sorry, it just slipped out, and anyway, I just call it like I see it. No Connor—no Bonnie; two and two and all that."

"I know what you two think, but it could be just a coincidence," Owen said.

"Come on, Owen! That's too much of a coincidence, if you ask me."

"Nobody asked you, Vini. You're upsetting Micaela." Owen reached for my hand.

Tears were forming, and I couldn't stop them. "I guess I was right all along. Maybe my jealousy had some basis in truth. Maybe Connor fooled me."

"Then he fooled all of us," Vini replied.

I tried to recall if I'd seen Bonnie around school. I'd been so focused on my misery and getting through the day I hadn't paid much attention.

Vini wouldn't let it go. "I wasn't going to mention Bonnie's absence, at least not yet." She turned to Owen. "You're the one who showed Micki the picture. Don't blame me for making her cry."

"You're right. Maybe I should have held that one back, but it's the one with the information on the back."

"You could have copied it to a piece of paper." Vini shoved more fries in her mouth.

"Stop it, you two. I'm glad you showed it to me. I needed to see it." I let go of Owen's hand and wiped my eyes with a napkin.

"I told you not to jump to conclusions," Owen reminded me. "It could be a tourist for all you know."

If conclusion-jumping was a sporting event, I would win a gold medal. I was sure it was Bonnie. "I just can't believe Connor deceived me. He's a better actor than I am."

Vini shook her head. "Nope ... nada! Cancel that thought. I've known Connor most of my life, and he's not a liar or a con artist. Something isn't right here. My money says that sleaze followed him, and she's up to something." She took a bite of her cheeseburger.

Despite how crazy it seemed and Vini's support of Connor, I couldn't help my imagination forming a picture of him and Bonnie, watching sunsets and laughing at how stupid I was.

Owen placed the picture in front of me and pointed to the woman we thought was Bonnie. "Take a closer look. I'm not an authority on women's physiques, but those don't look like Bonnie's legs ... more like tree trunks. The hair's the same and the frontal equipment is similar, but those aren't Bonnie's legs."

Vini and I both looked at the picture. I wasn't sure. Vini added a comment. "You might be right, but the camera could have created some kind of distortion."

"Will you stop it, Vini? You're not making Micaela feel any better. Who knows? Bonnie could have the flu."

"Maybe she has a killer virus." Vini looked pleased at that ridiculous possibility.

"Or maybe she's on holiday with her parents," Owen added.

"If that's true, I hope it's in Alaska and she freezes to death."

I shot Vini my 'don't-be-stupid' look. "Who took these pictures?" I had been so excited I'd forgotten to ask.

Owen explained he'd hired a private detective, the kind women hired to find out if their husbands were cheating.

"Oh!" I was too overwhelmed to say more. I looked at the writing on the back. It listed the name and address of a marina at Sanibel Island.

Owen noticed me reading it. "The guy hung around for a few days, and he's pretty sure Connor is docked at that marina on a regular basis, taking out tours."

I looked at the picture of Connor alone on the boat. I missed him terribly.

"You won't know the truth until you talk with him, and I'm guessing you're going this weekend. Do you want Jason and me to come with you?"

"What about me?" Vini asked.

"You're kidding, right?" Owen shot her a look that suggested Vini was out of her mind.

Vini rolled her eyes. She understood the implication and finished off her fries.

Owen was correct. I *was* going this weekend, but it was something I had to do alone. I wanted Connor to look in my eyes and tell me he didn't love me anymore. If Bonnie was with him, then so be it. I still needed him to say the words. I thanked Owen and offered to pay for the detective. I had no idea how much they charged, but I couldn't let him take on that responsibility because of me.

He shrugged. "No big deal. I'm not sure now whether I did the right thing."

"You did."

Vini started packing up her garbage. She had only eaten half the cheeseburger, which was unlike her. She reached for her purse and stood. "When you see him, and on the off chance that really is

Bonnie, tell him he's an ass." She tossed her garbage in the bin. "I'll take the bus home." She seemed upset.

"I thought you wanted to go to the arcade," Owen said.

"Don't feel like it now." She turned and left.

"She's certainly got her panties in a knot." Owen added two containers of cream to his coffee and stirred it. "There's no possible way she should go with you. Good God, could you imagine what she'd do if Bonnie was there. I know she thinks the world of Connor—we all do—but I suspect she's angry at him."

I wasn't angry yet, just confused and hurt. I gathered up the pictures and placed them back in the envelope. "Thanks again for doing this."

"Don't thank me yet. By the way, make sure Connor knows it was me and not you who found him. He might be pissed."

"I thought I knew him, but I guess you never really know a person."

"That's the truth," Owen said. "Jason is still trying to figure me out. We all have our secrets and demons ... some more than others." Owen took a sip of his coffee. I knew by the change in his expression and his downward glance that he was recalling his own childhood.

"What if he won't talk to me?"

"He will, sweetie. He's not a complete ass. Jason wouldn't be his friend if he was."

"I guess I'll find out."

"Call us when you get back, and please drive safely."

I left Owen to finish his coffee. I had to make plans for the weekend. Whatever I found out, I hoped I had the courage to face it.

CHAPTER 26

Convincing Dad I would be fine was a monumental task. "Parents worry. It's their job," he'd said. "It doesn't matter how old you are." I wasn't able to change his concern, but he couldn't sway me from my mission. I had two days to locate Connor and find out the truth. Dad agreed to lend me money with a promise I would pay him back when I had money of my own.

I left just as the sun welcomed the day. What I hadn't counted on was the weather. I was halfway across the causeway to the Keys when a dense fog wrapped around my car, and a light drizzle of rain required my full focus. I hoped it wasn't an omen. By the time I arrived at Sanibel Island and found a room, half the morning was gone. December was peak season, and the proprietor of the bed-and-breakfast told me I was fortunate. He had one room left. My luck had changed, canceling out the negative feeling created by the fog.

There were at least twelve marinas in the area. Without the information Owen had provided, it would have taken most of the weekend to locate the exact one. All I had to do was figure out how I would approach Connor. My nerves tingled, and anxiety clenched my muscles into knots. I'd practiced my speech to the point I felt confident in my delivery. When faced with actually using it, my confidence sprouted wings and flew off.

After a quick shower, trying not to get my hair wet, I applied makeup, making sure it looked perfect. I dressed in what I thought was a sexy outfit—a black T-shirt with a butterfly on the front that Vini got me for my birthday, which I wore off one shoulder with my black leggings. The T-shirt was short enough to expose some of my midriff. I chose large gold hoop earrings. I thought I looked very Madonna. Not my usual day look, but I wanted an edge on Bonnie, if she was actually with him. I pulled my hair to one side, tucking it behind my ear, letting the curls fall on my bare shoulder. I secured it with a clip with three purple butterflies attached. Vini would approve.

As I made my way to the pier, the stares and whistles I received confirmed my look was successful, although I felt a little uncomfortable with what I was projecting. The fog had lifted. It was a perfect day. Sandpipers scurried along the shoreline, and a few gulls squawked overhead. Several pelicans were perched on channel markers, like statues. I remembered Connor's fascination with birds. *He must love it here*, I thought.

I found the marina but not his boat. I checked the name on the back of the picture. It was the right one. There were several empty slips. I determined he must be out with a tour, but I had no idea how long he would be. I'd simply have to wait.

It was already past one o'clock, and it could be hours before he returned, so I grabbed a coffee and Danish at an outdoor restaurant across from the marina and kept my vision glued to the dock. At two o'clock there was still no sign of him, and I was getting fidgety. I started thinking about all the what-ifs.

What if the detective had made a mistake? What if Connor had decided to leave? What if, when I did see him, he was with Bonnie? There was an endless stream of what-ifs. I was only driving myself crazy.

I wasn't sure it was the heat from the afternoon sun or my apprehension that created beads of perspiration on the back of my neck. I passed another hour looking at tourists, playing a game in my head. *Where are they from? What do they do? Are they married?* I liked making up stories that matched their appearance. I stared at them. They stared back at me. The game soon became boring. I needed to move, so I headed for the dock.

I was admiring a large cruise boat when I spotted the *Micaela*. My heart beat so hard I thought I saw the butterfly on my shirt move. I sensed a distinct tingle, and the Danish felt like a boulder in my stomach. A wave of nausea sent a clear message that fear was taking over. I wasn't sure if I should just walk up to him and say hi or wait until the people left. I decided my best option was to wait; I hid behind the cruise boat until I was sure he was alone. I took several deep breaths to calm my racing heart and recited an affirmation in my mind. I repeated, *You can do this*, until my fear and nausea eased. I was a lot more nervous than when I was waiting in the office for Connor at the Blue Lagoon.

I peeked out from behind the bow of the boat. Connor was shaking hands with several people as they disembarked. Two senior ladies passed a camera to a young man, and both stood on either side of Connor while having their picture taken. I noticed his arms draped around their shoulders. The photo of him with the redhead popped into my mind. Maybe Owen was right, and Vini and I had jumped to conclusions. Maybe Connor was just being friendly. Maybe Vini and I were idiots!

I waited until everyone left and Connor was cleaning the deck. One last deep breath, and I approached. He didn't look up until I was beside the boat. No startled expression or even a hint of surprise on his face. He said nothing. We just stood staring at each other. I was afraid to speak. It didn't take a degree in psychology to figure out his first response.

"What are you doing here?" The tone of his voice registered annoyance. He continued putting paper cups and various pieces of litter in a garbage bag, as if my presence meant nothing.

"I came to talk to you, if that's okay." I sounded like a child who had just been disciplined, seeking reassurance of her parents' love. If this was going to work, I'd have to change that.

"Dressed like that! I'm sure half the men on the island are following you."

My choice of clothing wasn't having the desired effect. I instantly regretted it. "What do you care how I'm dressed?" It seemed childish, but I was annoyed and disappointed.

"Come on, Micaela! Stop it! Just say what you came to say and leave."

I wasn't angry before, but now I was. He'd left without a word after leading me to believe I was special to him, and now he was treating me as if I meant nothing. My anger dispelled any fear of falling. I grabbed the side of the boat railing and jumped safely to the deck.

"What the hell do you think you're doing?"

I glared at him. "I said I came to talk to you, and I'm not going to have a conversation standing on the pier while you try to ignore me." This time I sounded more confident.

"Okay, you made your point. What is it? And by the way, how did you find me?"

"I want to know why you left without at least talking to me." Then I told him what Owen had done.

"What the hell!" He ran his fingers through his hair. "Tell him to mind his own business." He tied the garbage bag and threw it on the dock. "You have five minutes. I have to get ready for another tour."

I used my authoritative voice. "Connor, what is going on? Where is the guy who convinced me to go out with him, told me I was his earth angel, and made love to me? I deserve some kind of an answer. Was it all a lie?"

I thought I saw sadness pass across his features. "It wasn't a lie. Things can change. I don't know what you want to hear."

I wanted to ask about Bonnie but decided it might agitate him more. "Just tell me you don't love me anymore, if that's how you feel." My heart lurched. I held my breath, waiting for words I hoped would not tear my world apart.

"I haven't got time for this, Micaela. I'm sorry you came all this way. You should have just left it alone."

"How could I just leave it alone? I love you, and I thought you loved me. I'm sorry I didn't trust you. I'm trying to understand why I get so jealous. I don't want to be like that. I'm sorry if I hurt you. Please forgive me." It felt like begging, and it probably was.

"You have nothing to be sorry for. You think you know me, but you don't. Maybe you shouldn't trust me. Just go! Please?"

He turned his back and walked below to his room, closing the door behind him. I was tempted to follow and scream every insult I knew, with the intention of hurting him, even though I had just apologized. I was crushed. He still hadn't told me what he was feeling and why he'd changed. Instead, I climbed back on to the dock and ran to my room at the bed-and-breakfast.

Any hope of finding out the truth was gone, and so was my determination. I had to find a way to move on. I just wasn't sure how to do it.

CHAPTER 27

It was nothing short of a miracle that I managed to arrive home safely. Connor's words kept stabbing at my heart, creating a curtain of tears that blurred my vision the entire drive. Dad was watching some sporting event when I came through the door. I didn't stop to say hello. I went straight to my room, threw myself on the bed, and wept. There was an endless supply of tears. I heard Dad enter and felt him sit beside me, waiting patiently until my sobs turned to hiccups—an indication I was winding down and ready to talk. I rolled over on my back and stared into Dad's kind, sympathetic eyes. He listened to my rambling, incoherent explanation, which I'm sure made no sense at all, leaned over, kissed my forehead, and patted my hand.

"All things work out eventually, Micaela, even though they may seem hopeless. It will be as right as rain in no time." I did not share Dad's optimistic approach. To me, it was the end of the world. To Dad, just another life lesson. He went back to watching television and left me with my cyclone of thoughts. How was I going to forget

Connor? Every word he said flooded my mind, and I was drowning in a sea of self-pity.

When I finally fell asleep, I dreamed of Connor and Bonnie taunting me with their laughter. Connor kept repeating, "You should never have trusted me. You were a fool." Bonnie pressed her bikini-clad body against him. "I told you he was mine," she purred as she glared at me like a lioness protecting her cub.

My face was wet with tears and my T-shirt soaked in sweat when the morning sun streaked across my face, pulling me back into reality—a reality not much different from my dream. I had forgotten to close my blinds and got up to shut them, intending to spend the rest of the day in bed. My attention was drawn to my bracelet. It had become a part of me. I couldn't bear looking at it. Rage scratched and clawed its way to the surface. I released the clasp and heaved it at my dresser, where it landed beside my memory box, next to the picture of Mom. It struck me as symbolic. Connor would eventually take his place in the recesses of my mind and, like Mom, was gone from my life.

I returned to the security of my cocoon of blankets and counted backward from one hundred, trying to stifle the hurt and anger waging a war in my gut. I fell asleep before reaching fifty. I woke after lunch, my stomach churning and rumbling. I hadn't eaten in twenty-four hours. Willing my body into the kitchen, I passed Dad sitting in his recliner, concentrating on his Sunday crossword.

"There's some leftover chicken casserole, if you feel like heating it up," he said without even glancing in my direction. "What's a five-letter word for procrastination ending in R?"

The casserole sounded too much like work, so I reached for a jar of peanut butter in the cupboard, spread it on two pieces of bread, and slapped them together.

As I headed back to my room with my sandwich and a glass of milk, I called out, "Defer." Dad grunted and called out, "thanks". My heart might be withered and collapsing in on itself, but my brain still functioned. I was halfway down the hall when the phone rang.

"That's probably your friend Vini. She's called three times. You might want to answer it. She says she has something important to tell you."

"Could you please answer it and tell her I'll call her tomorrow?"

"She says she's going to keep calling. Talk to her, Micaela. I don't want her calling all day."

Reluctantly, I answered.

"Hey, girlfriend! Did you find Connor?"

"Dad said you have something to tell me." I avoided answering her question.

"You don't sound so good. Something happen?"

"Just tell me what it is." I hated being short with her, but I wasn't ready to talk.

"Okay. You know Bonnie's friend Joanne?"

"Yeah, so …" I was curious where this was leading.

"Well, I was getting my hair cut at that fancy salon downtown. You know, the one I've been dying to try. It's not that great, by the way."

"Will you please get to the point?"

"I will if you'd stop interrupting me."

I was losing my patience. "Okay, keep going."

"So … Joanne was getting her hair done too, and we got to talking, which is strange because she's one of Bonnie's posse. Anyway, I asked her how Bonnie was, like I care, but I wanted info. Guess what?"

"What?"

"Bonnie tried to kill herself."

There it was, the dramatic cliff-hanger to her story. "That's horrible. Are you sure?"

"Why would Joanne tell me something like that if it wasn't true? Bonnie's parents put her in a psychiatric hospital in Miami, and she's been there over a month, ever since the Halloween party. So she couldn't be the woman in the picture." Vini flipped gears. "Did you find Connor and talk to him?"

I was quiet.

"You did talk to him, right?"

"Sort of."

"What does 'sort of' mean?"

"He told me to leave and acted strangely, as if I meant nothing to him."

"I don't believe it."

"Believe it—it's over. I'd prefer not to talk about it." I returned to the subject of Bonnie. "What would make her want to kill herself? That's so awful."

"Yeah, I guess. It's no secret I hate the girl's guts, but you're right. No one should try and off themselves. You don't suppose it had anything to do with Connor?"

Knowing Bonnie wasn't with him was a relief. I tried to feel compassion, but Vini's question disturbed me. Could Connor's disappearance be related to Bonnie? This thought confused me more. None of it made sense. I didn't comment.

"You still there?" Vini noted my quiet contemplation.

"I'm tired. We can talk tomorrow. Thanks for telling me about Bonnie, even though it's pretty horrible."

She said good night, and I returned to my room. I tried erasing everything from my mind before I had a complete meltdown, but it was impossible. If Bonnie wasn't with Connor, then who was the woman in the picture?

School was the last place I wanted to be, so I stayed home and watched soap operas all day, which was a stupid idea, since the plots were about broken relationships and heartbreak. When Dad came home and saw the mess of dishes in the sink and me still in my pajamas, he had something to say. He reminded me he wasn't paying my tuition so I could indulge my broken heart. I had to stop feeling sorry for myself and get on with my life. He called it *tough love*. Dad was right, but I wasn't sure just how to do it. Even my dream of becoming a broadway actress had faded. Without Connor, it all seemed pointless.

I had just gotten into bed when I heard the door buzzer. It was too late for Vini to drop by. Dad had a friend from work who often came over, brought a case of beer, and watched the football game with him. I figured that's who it was. Dad's knock on my door startled me. "Micaela, you might want to get dressed and come out here. There's someone who wants to talk to you." It obviously wasn't Dad's friend.

I looked at the clock on my dresser. Vini could be a pain sometimes. *What on earth would make her take the bus and come over?* I thought.

I grabbed my robe from the back of the door. I didn't think it necessary to get dressed for her.

As I approached the living room, I could hear talking. It wasn't Vini; it was a male voice, and it was familiar. A shock wave of astonishment tore through my body. I stood, almost frozen, staring at Connor sitting on the sofa beside Dad. He stood. I felt a kaleidoscope of emotions. First happy, then bewildered, and then angry. I wasn't sure how to respond. Dad excused himself and went to his room.

"Why are you here?" It was déjà vu in reverse. I vacillated between asking him to leave and running into his arms. The first option closed the door on any possibility of reconciliation, which I secretly hoped for but tried not to expect. The second might expose me to more rejection. I resolved to put my emotions on neutral.

"I'm not sure where to begin." The anger and annoyance were gone from his voice. In its place, I detected a sadness with just a hint of humility. "I'll understand if you want me to leave. I was cruel to you, and I can't even begin to tell you how sorry I am."

This was a complete turn-around, and I wasn't sure I could trust it. "You're confusing me, Connor."

"I get that. Do you want me to leave?"

What I wanted was to run into his arms and kiss him, but my brain stopped me.

"I *do* love you, Micaela. More than you possibly know. I left because of how much I love you. I don't expect you to understand. I have a lot to tell you if you're willing to hear me out."

I struggled with my desire to get answers and my residual anger. Connor interpreted my silence as an indication of refusal and walked toward the door.

"I am truly sorry I hurt you. I hope, in time, you can forgive me."

My resolution to remain neutral dissolved, and I grabbed his arm as he passed me. There was no denying his sincerity. I could see it in his eyes. Forgiveness was not something I was ready to give at this point, but I was willing to listen.

CHAPTER 28

Now

An early morning snowfall dusted the roofs and trees, providing a festive spirit for Christmas shopping. Jess convinced me to accompany her and the twins on their annual Santa visit to the mall. It had been a refreshing distraction from the gloomy mood that clung like burrs to my nervous system.

Tina insisted the mall Santa wasn't real because the real Santa was in the North Pole, looking after reindeer and helping the elves make toys. Her sister decided to test that theory. As soon as it was her turn to sit on Santa's lap, Nora reached up and pulled his beard, which snapped back, leaving the poor man stunned and embarrassed. Jess apologized and lectured Nora on acceptable behavior, while Tina giggled hysterically. I couldn't help but laugh, and I needed to laugh.

For a few hours, my depression receded into the background. We listened to children's Christmas songs on the drive home. Jess didn't inherit my gift, but Tina's voice held promise. After exchanging hugs, kisses, and numerous I-love-yous, we said goodbye, and I was faced with the rest of the day alone with my thoughts.

Dinner was leftover tuna casserole. I willed myself to eat. My head gave me strict instructions to put food in my body, but my stomach resisted. I managed a few bites, gave up, and threw it out. I took an apple from the basket on my kitchen table as a healthy alternative and sat watching the setting sun through the branches of naked trees in my backyard. Bands of red and orange painted the evening sky as the last remaining glow signaled the oncoming night.

I watched as Morty, my neighbor's cat, jumped over the fence, pranced up to the sliding glass doors, and waited for his usual handout. I ignored him. My attention drifted to the shopping list I'd posted on the fridge over three weeks ago. I'd been excited, anticipating Vini's visit, much like the twins on Christmas Eve. I'd included all her most-liked snacks, even a chocolate cake.

Vini's phone call that evening not only brought disappointment but an overwhelming sadness. She wouldn't be coming. Her mom had a massive heart attack and died on the way to the hospital. I remembered Lydia DeMille, her warmth, her sweet smile and quirky sense of humor like her daughter's. The last time I'd seen her was at Jason's graduation ceremony. She'd been so proud of her son.

I cried with Vini. Her pain resonated through the phone and melded with my own.

I hoped she and Jason understood why I hadn't gone to the funeral. Not in Clearwater. I wanted to support my friend, but returning, especially in my weakened condition, would have been too overwhelming. Instead, I sent flowers and a card. Vini understood, but Jess couldn't figure out why I didn't "pull it together" and be with my friend when she needed me. Telling her my condition had deteriorated, which was an exaggeration, would increase both her concern and her lectures on keeping my oncologist appointment. I hated adding to her worry, but I couldn't explain my fear of returning to the place where the darkness had originated. I couldn't even explain it to myself.

I felt guilty for not going. Letting Jess believe I was worse than I actually was just added to it. Guilt and remorse could be its own kind of cancer.

Morty still waited for the cat treats. I admired his persistence and gave in. Without even a meow of thanks, he sauntered off, leaving me feeling alone and vulnerable. The sensation that something awful was going to happen still clung to me. It only made my depressed state worse. I attributed it to exhaustion and losing my job.

It had been difficult hiding my condition from my students and fellow staff members. Getting through each day depended on several coffees and my usual energy drink. The constant spike of adrenaline and its accompanying crash made it impossible to feel normal. It affected my nervous system. My patience was virtually nonexistent.

There had been two complaints from my students. I lost my temper with two young women who kept texting during my lecture, probably to each other. My rules on cell phone usage during class time did not coincide with school policy. I had no idea they even had a policy allowing cell phones in the classroom. I thought it was ridiculous, but taking a stand made no difference. The school administrator requested I take a leave of absence. It was clearly not a suggestion. He appreciated my enthusiasm for teaching, but my performance over the past few months was in question. When I finally explained my situation, his admonishment turned to compassion. He was convinced my taking time off was necessary and expected, and he sounded relieved. My cancer had obviously justified his original decision. My perspective was different. I didn't want to stop teaching. It was my last and only connection to my love of theater. Even Jess thought I should take time off, but I stubbornly insisted I would be fine. Dad used to tell me I was as stubborn as a Missouri mule when I wanted something. There was nothing I could do but accept the decision.

The administrator wished me the best and asked me to keep the school informed of how I was doing. Fat chance! I had no desire to see or speak with him again. I wasn't sure I wanted my job back. It was entirely possible the decision to return would be taken out of my hands anyway, if the cancer took my life. Even though I knew deep down that leaving was the right thing to do, I wanted it to be on my terms. I felt the world was abandoning me.

Now that I was home, the days dragged, and it was becoming more difficult to stifle memories of Connor. My dreams were filled with him, each one becoming more intense. There was something lurking in the shadows, making me uneasy. Each dream was beginning to feel like a pathway to some inevitable conclusion, and I couldn't find a detour. I thought of taking sleeping pills, but they only made my brain fuzzy and depleted more of my energy. I needed something to keep me busy. I had once loved writing poetry and children's songs. There was no reason why I couldn't do it again. Maybe I might record a collection. The idea had merit, and I could feel a hint of exhilaration I'd thought was long gone.

Perhaps out of boredom or keeping my promise to Jess, I went to the oncologist. What I really wanted to know was whether the natural regime I was following, although not religiously, was working. It meant more tests. This morning I received the results.

It was the clichéd good news/bad news scenario. I chose the bad news first. The tumor still resided in my bladder, and it had grown. The good news was the cancer cells hadn't sent out an army to infiltrate my other organs. There was still hope. To the doctor, it meant the chemotherapy treatment should be started immediately. To me, it meant I would remain on my regime but be more diligent. His demeanor, when I turned down the treatment, was like a priest issuing last rites. He said the odds of success were about 35 percent if I started the treatment right away, and he made it sound positive. He suggested I give it more thought and discuss it with family members, as if I didn't have a mind of my own. I didn't feel the odds were great enough to risk the chemical backlash.

Jess would not be happy with my decision, so I decided to lie. I was doing a lot of that lately with her. Aunt Florence insisted all liars went to hell. She quoted scripture like I quoted passages from hit musicals. My mom told me I should weigh my decision to be truthful against the damage it might create for someone. I preferred her reasoning. Fire and brimstone was a risk I was willing to take for self-preservation.

I called Vini and told her the truth. She understood. Hearing her voice was comforting, but it didn't dispel the sense of dread I'd been feeling all day.

I thought of Tina and Nora. What if something had happened to them? I canceled that thought. It didn't feel right, and Jess would have called and told me. It was something else. I never thought of myself as psychic. It was Vini with the sixth sense, not me. I was noted for my overactive imagination.

I turned on the television, hoping to find an interesting program that would distract me. Nothing interested me. Switching off the lights, I headed for the shower. It didn't have the emotion-numbing result it usually did. Sleep was impossible while my nervous system tingled with apprehension. A relaxing tea was my next option.

I was halfway down the stairs when my cell phone rang. I'd left it on the kitchen table. I ran down the hall, almost slipping on the ceramic tile. Breathless, I retrieved the phone without noticing the caller identification. A woman asked to speak with Micaela Webster. I knew as soon as I responded that something awful had happened. My pulse accelerated. Her words will forever be imprinted in my mind.

"I'm sorry to have to inform you, but your father passed away an hour ago. He was fine this morning, but he took a turn after lunch. I'm so sorry for your loss." She said nothing more.

I closed off the call and stood staring into the darkness. The ominous sensation that plagued me was gone. It had become an actualization. My dad had died, and I didn't get to say goodbye.

"Dad, why did you have to leave now? I love you so much!" I yelled, hoping somehow my words would penetrate the veil that separated us. He was still my daddy. The man who made me laugh, tucked me in at night, and searched for monsters under my bed when I was little; the man who held me when I needed hugs and listened to my stories; the man who put up with all my teenage angst and never judged me when I made mistakes. Tears brought no relief from the pain that engulfed me. I wouldn't see my wonderful, loving father anymore. Something Aunt Florence told me long ago, when I thought my world had been shattered and my heart was torn to pieces, ran through my mind like skywriting.

"God never gives us more than we can handle." I'd concluded then that God was a cruel dictator, testing my endurance, and not even he knew the extent of my strength until the results were in. I must have failed the first time, so I was getting another shot at it. Dad had a more practical viewpoint.

"Life doesn't come with guarantees, Micaela. It's basically a crap shoot. When the dice don't come up your way, you accept it, deal with it, and then, maybe if you're willing to try, you throw them again."

"You were wrong, Dad. There is one guarantee. We all die!" I said it on the off chance he could hear me and then collapsed on the floor and wept until the darkness took me.

CHAPTER 29

Dad never wanted a funeral. "Just cremate me and flush me down the toilet," he'd said.

My response had been, "You're joking, right?"

"Just the part about the toilet," he'd replied.

Years later, he agreed I could give him a proper send-off, but I was to make sure there was no religious "hoopla," as he called it. I had strict instructions to avoid all the trappings of a conventional funeral. He said he'd haunt me if I succumbed to family pressure or an overzealous funeral director. The idea of seeing Dad again held some allure, but I agreed to his desires—no church, no priest, not even a wake. He'd changed his mind about cremation after watching a stupid horror movie where someone was burned alive in a coffin. It didn't matter how often I told him it was ridiculous, he said he wanted to take his chances with the worms.

Jess and I sat in the funeral director's office, going over particulars. Everything was fine until he insisted on a three-day showing period. He proceeded to inform me it was my duty to my father to allow people to pay their respects. It annoyed me, so I vented.

"My dad is the one who requires respect, and that's not what he wanted. Please don't presume to know what my duty is."

He recoiled as if I'd placed a venomous snake in front of his face.

Jess actually supported my outburst. "Way to go, Mom. Grandpa would be proud." She knew her grandfather.

Vini would be arriving in less than an hour. She insisted on coming as soon as I called her to tell her dad had passed. I was grateful, but her quick decision triggered another wave of guilt.

Jess drove me home and asked if she could come by later. She was excited to see her Aunt Vini but not nearly as excited as I was.

Vini rearranged her schedule at the last minute to fly to Toronto. It was more than I had done for her. I warned her my appearance had changed drastically. I knew what she looked like. She was the queen of selfies.

The sound of the cab pulling up announced her arrival. I pinched and rubbed my cheeks, hoping to add color to my pasty complexion. As soon as she saw me, she jumped from the cab and ran into my arms. Tears flowed. The cab honked. Vini paid him, collected her luggage, and followed me into the house.

"You look great, Micki. I was expecting a shriveled carcass, the way you made it sound. Love your hair. Very chic."

"I think you're just being kind."

"Will you shut up. I tell it how it is, girl. You know that." Vini patted her stomach. "I've put on some beef. It's that damn premenopausal crap. You started yet?"

"I haven't had a period in months. I guess it's because of the cancer."

"Well, that's a perk."

We both laughed, but I didn't think it was such a great perk, considering the reason.

I showed Vini to the guest room. She looked amazing, even better than her last selfie. She used less makeup and straightened her long curly hair. It was shoulder-length and swished back and forth when she moved her head. Her lashes were still full, and I still envied her. The flamboyant clothes had been replaced with a black designer suit. An ivory silk blouse, unbuttoned to show a hint of cleavage, along with two gold chain necklaces, completed her professional look. She was barely a year younger than me, but she didn't look a day over thirty, even with the extra weight. The years had been kinder to her. But she didn't have cancer.

"Have you had dinner?" I asked.

"Ate on the plane." Vini flew first class now. "I might have a glass of wine. It's damn good to see you, but sad it has to be under these circumstances."

I hugged her. "Ditto." I left her to unpack.

I was pouring two glasses of the red wine she brought when Jess arrived with take-out chicken dinners. Vini joined us in the kitchen, wearing a red jogging outfit with purple fuzzy slippers. That was the Vini I remembered. Jess thought she was the most inspirational woman she'd ever met. She compared her to Oprah. I thought it was a little over the top, but Vini loved it. She was on her second glass of wine when she spotted the cake tin on the counter.

"It's chocolate. You want a piece? I warn you—it's not fresh, and it's store-bought."

"You kidding! Of course I want a piece. Maybe two, if it's good." Some things never changed.

After Jess left, Vini and I called it a night. We both had too much wine, and I'd probably regret it in the morning. I dreaded the next day but was grateful to have my friend with me.

Vini had made coffee when I came downstairs in the morning. She was already dressed in the same black suit, but this time she had on a gray blouse tastefully buttoned to the collar.

"Sleep well?" I asked, pouring coffee into a mug.

"Like a friggin' baby."

"You want breakfast?"

"No thanks. I'm not much on eating first thing in the morning."

"Good! I don't feel like cooking." That made Vini laugh. We both knew my culinary skills were sadly lacking.

I watched as she put three heaping tablespoons of sugar in her coffee. I cringed and made a face.

"What? I happen to like sugar." No surprise there. "Took me long enough to find the stuff in your cupboards." She actually drank it. "Jason sends his regards," she said between gulps.

"How is he? And how's Owen?"

Vini put down her coffee cup. "Jason's good. He's getting a lot of work, and his design company is growing so fast he had to hire an assistant."

"That's awesome." I wondered why she hadn't mentioned Owen. I sipped my coffee. "I feel badly I let thirty years go by without even calling them. They were such good friends. Something always stopped me."

"Life takes us in different directions." She glanced out the window. I sensed a distinct mood change.

It suddenly occurred to me that Owen and Jason might have broken up. By today standards, thirty years was a long time in any relationship, and they had been together for over two years when I knew them.

"I didn't know you had a cat. What a cutie. He looks like a mini-lion."

Morty sat in his usual spot, waiting for treats. I could swear that cat had radar. He always knew when I was in the kitchen. "It's the neighbor's cat. His name is Morty. He just likes me because I give him treats."

"Can I give him some?" Vini had already opened the sliding door and let him in by the time I'd found the fish treats. She knelt on the floor while Morty rubbed against her knees. She stroked his back, and he crawled into her lap. By the sound of his purring, Morty was happy—even happier when she gave him the snacks. She loved cats. I decided to forgo asking Vini about Owen until later. I had to get dressed and prepare for the awful day ahead.

We arrived at the funeral home at the same time as Jess and Jack. Jack hugged Vini. She accepted it. I wasn't as gracious.

The room had been set up with folding chairs, and four huge baskets of flowers sat in tiers on either side of Dad's casket. I couldn't believe my amazing dad was lying in the coffin. I'd insisted on it being closed, another thing that annoyed the funeral director. Various pictures representing Dad's life were arranged around a spray of lilies. I loved the picture of Dad, Mom, and me, with my dog, Chippy, on the front porch of our house. Mom and Dad's wedding picture was beside it.

What little family we had sat on one side of the room. I knew they wouldn't be pleased with my decision to forgo a religious church funeral. Ignoring their stares and whispers, I took a seat up front on the other side. Aunt Florence was too sick to travel, but her son, Paul, and his sister, Rosalie, had come with their spouses. Paul was six years older than I was, and I'd only met him once. Rosalie and I had shared a bedroom the first year I lived with Aunt Florence. She never liked me. Dad told me to ignore her petty comments. He figured it was just jealousy, but I was never sure why she would be jealous. She was a lot prettier. I was relieved when she moved out the year after I moved in.

My fear was that she knew my secret. I prayed she wouldn't mention it. Aunt Florence, Rosalie, Vini, and Dad were the only ones who knew. After Rosalie left, I never saw her again. Aunt Florence was always praying for my soul. She said she wanted to ensure my entrance into heaven. I decided to stop visiting her after I moved out. I didn't need reminders of what I had done. I thought how hard it must have been for Dad to watch me suffer and not be able to do anything. He never spoke of it, and I loved him more for it.

Two of Dad's cousins sat by themselves at the back. They barely spoke English, and my Ukrainian was limited to the names of foods and some swear words Rosalie had taught me. They approached me and said something I didn't understand. I nodded, hoping my gesture corresponded with what they'd said.

The celebrant, Jess, chose incorporated anecdotes from Dad's life. It was tasteful and compassionate.

I preferred driving my car to the cemetery rather than be in the limousine provided by the Funeral Home. Vini and Jess came with me, while Jack followed in his car.

At the grave site, the celebrant read passages from the Bible that Dad liked. He believed in God but not formal religion. "Too dogmatic for me," he'd say.

Vini and I stood quietly, staring down at Dad's casket. I saw her wipe away tears and suspected she was recalling her mother's funeral. Most of the family began leaving. I was grateful Rosalie had left with them. She never spoke with me once, and that was okay with me. I had kept an eye on her when I saw her speaking with Jess and held my breath, expecting the worst. After seeing no drastic reaction from Jess, I breathed a sigh of relief. I asked Jess what they had talked about. She said Rosalie went on and on about her kids and how great they were—totally boring. Jess added that she thought Rosalie was too full of herself, and she didn't like her. For that, I was thankful.

Jack stood a respectful distance away from the grave site. I wanted more time with Dad, and Jess stood beside me, holding my hand.

The wind had picked up, sending leaves twirling and dancing around our ankles. The sudden chill indicated winter wasn't far off. Jess gave me a kiss on the cheek, and we walked back to join Jack at his car. Vini came with us. Jess hugged her goodbye and asked her to please keep in touch. Before leaving, Jack approached me and kissed me on the forehead. This time, I let him. He repeated how sorry he was.

"Art was a great guy," he said. I found this an interesting evaluation, considering he rarely spent time with Dad. "Jess and I stopped by the seniors' home and picked up the boxes of your dad's things," he informed me. "I put them on the dining room table."

I thanked him. It made me sad to think that my wonderful, loving father's life had been reduced to a few cardboard boxes. The tears I held back all day began to flow.

"Are you going to be okay to drive home?" Jack sounded genuinely concerned.

"I'm good. You and Jess can go." I stood watching Jack's car disappear and waved goodbye to Jess. Vini and I returned to the grave site.

"How you holdin' up, kiddo?" Vini asked.

"I'm okay now that everyone has gone. I was terrified Rosalie would say something to Jess."

"I stuck close enough to them, just in case an intervention was required. All she talked about was how her daughter graduated from Princeton with honors. I think she bored Jess out of her mind."

"Thank you, Vini, for being with me. It means a lot."

"That's what friends are for."

"But I didn't—" She wouldn't let me finish.

"Don't go there." She knew I was thinking of her mom's funeral. "Jason and I were aware that coming to Clearwater would be difficult for you. We had each other."

A formation of geese flew over, honking as they passed.

"I think your dad just got a tribute." Vini glanced at the headstone where my mom's name was beside Dad's. "Katrina is a lovely name. I don't recall you ever telling me. She was always just *my mom*."

"She was as beautiful as her name. I wished I'd looked more like her." An image formed in my mind of Mom running to Dad and embracing him. They looked just as they did in their wedding picture. "Do you believe in an afterlife?"

"Of course. There's got to be something to look forward to after all the crazy stuff you have to go through on this planet."

A twinge of sadness poked at my heart as Connor's face replaced the image of my parents. All of them gone from my life. Wherever Connor was, I wondered if he ever thought of me. I shivered, partly from the cold and partly because of a feeling the vision of Connor evoked.

"I miss him, Vini, even after all these years."

I didn't have to tell her who I meant. "I know." She saw me shivering. "You ready to go? You must be freezing."

I took one last look at Dad's coffin and blew a kiss upward.

Vini waited until I composed myself. "I've got an idea. That is, if you're up to it." Vini always had ideas.

"What?"

"Enough of all this sadness. Why don't we drive downtown, do a little shopping, and have an early dinner at the CN Tower? I've never been there. I'll bet your dad would approve."

I could hear Dad's voice clearly in my mind. *"Go, Micaela. Have a good time."*

"Sure. Why not?" I think I surprised Vini with my answer.

She reached in her purse and pulled out her Visa card. "We're going to do some serious damage with this."

I laughed. Dad's voice was still in my head. *"That's my girl!"*

CHAPTER 30

Then

Connor loved me, and I loved him. Anything he had to tell me wasn't going to change that fact, but it might affect whether we continued to have a relationship. Sometimes there are things that are too difficult to overcome and forgive, regardless of how much you love one another. If we were going to get past this, I needed to understand why he left so abruptly and deliberately hurt me. Just loving each other was no longer enough. I'd endured too much pain.

Connor sat on the couch, and I chose Dad's recliner across from him. It was less of a distraction that way. His tan didn't hide the dark circles under his eyes, and it looked like he'd slept in his clothes, but it didn't make him any less attractive.

"First of all," he began, "I want you to know it wasn't because of your jealousy of Bonnie that I left. I understand why you felt that way. Bonnie came on pretty strong. If the situation had been reversed, I would have felt the same, maybe even more."

"Then why did you tell me you'd had enough?"

"At the time, I overreacted to your lack of trust, and trust is a huge issue for me." He ran his hand through his hair. Strands fell across his forehead, and he pushed them back. "I realize I was reacting to my own guilt. Your lack of trust wasn't misplaced."

"Guilt about what?" I was nervous of his answer but continued to listen, trying my best not to show how agitated I was becoming.

"I felt guilty about lying to you. You had every right not to trust me."

My heart beat a staccato rhythm. The memory of my dream resurfaced. I fought the wave of jealousy and anger. I had to keep reminding myself that no one was perfect. I certainly wasn't.

Connor went quiet, as if thinking about his next words.

"Please just tell me." I wanted to get this over with so I could process whatever he declared and find a way to handle it.

"Okay. First, I have to tell you what happened the night of the Halloween party." He paused again and took a deep breath. "When I went back upstairs, Bonnie was in the bathroom. I saw you in your car, and I was about to run down and stop you, but Bonnie came into my room in a towel. She dropped the towel."

Connor saw the look on my face. I was about to tell him not to say any more, but he quickly cut me off.

"Nothing happened, if that's what you're thinking. She tried, and I kept pushing her away, but she wouldn't stop. She said she was going to accuse me of raping her and tell you the truth."

"What truth?"

"I'll tell you, but let me finish. She came at me, trying to claw my face. I grabbed her arm. She lost her balance, slipped and fell, and hit her head on my dresser. She was lying still, and there was blood on the carpet. I thought she was dead. I panicked."

"My God! That's horrible." This wasn't what I'd expected to hear.

"It gets worse. I didn't call an ambulance. I wrapped her in a blanket and got her to the laundry room without anyone seeing me.

207

The party was still going, and it was pretty noisy. I drove the jeep around the side of the house, and when I went to get her, Jason came out of the kitchen. I'd forgotten to close the door. He felt her pulse and told me she wasn't dead."

"You mean Jason's known about this all along?"

"I made him swear on our friendship that he'd keep his mouth shut. We agreed to say she fell in the shower and hit her head. The fact she was naked made it plausible. Pretty flimsy, but if she died, Jason said there would be an investigation with possible third-degree murder charges."

"What on earth were you two thinking?"

"We weren't."

"So what did you do?"

"I drove her to Emergency. What could I do? It was pretty damned awkward, but I think they bought the shower story."

"She lived, right?"

"Yeah. It was a concussion. I stayed at the hospital until Bonnie's parents arrived. I'd calmed down by then and told her mother the truth. She knows what Bonnie's like, and she knew about her obsession with me. I had to tell her; if I didn't, Bonnie would have. Clarisse, Bonnie's mother, is a pretty okay lady. She agreed to tell the doctor that Bonnie was unstable and not to believe anything she said. I had to make sure, so I went back to the hospital the next day to talk to Bonnie."

"What happened after that? Vini told me Bonnie tried to commit suicide."

"She did."

"But how? Why?"

"She was pregnant."

I gasped.

"It wasn't mine if that's what you're thinking. I never touched her—at least not after I left university. She told her parents it was mine, but Clarisse suspected she was lying. She knows her daughter. Her dad's another story. I think he believed her, but Clarisse wears the pants in that family, so he backed off when she told him to. Bonnie claims it happened the night we had dinner with our parents."

"But how?" I remembered the day we took Ricky to the show and bumped into Joanne and her friend. I could feel apprehension gnawing at my gut, and I clenched my fists, digging my nails into my palms in an attempt to control a negative reaction.

Connor offered his explanation. "You and I weren't seeing each other because of your dad. I lied to you when I told you I had nothing to do with her."

"Connor, how could you?" I dug my nails into my palms even harder and blinked several times to hold back my tears.

"I knew this would upset you. I'm so sorry. Do you want me to finish, or should I just go?"

"I'm confused. Just finish what you have to say."

"Well, Bonnie wanted a ride to Joanne's, but when we got there, Joanne wasn't home, so she asked me to drop her off at Kelly's, the girl who was with Joanne when we were at the movies. I didn't think much of it, but when you got upset at Bonnie's even being at the dinner, I just avoided telling you."

"So why do her parents think it could have been you?" I was still confused.

"Bonnie told her parents we were at the beach and had made out. I guess she was gone long enough to make it believable, and they knew she'd left with me. The real truth is, Bonnie did get pregnant once before."

"Why would you feel badly about that?" I was desperately trying to stay composed, but I had a sinking feeling what the answer was going to be.

"Because it was mine."

It required all my acting skills to remain calm. I wanted to jump up and hit him.

He pushed his hair back again. I was beginning to understand that was a nervous gesture. "She was fifteen. I was just starting university and seeing someone pretty steady."

"Alicia, right?" I was still desperately trying to remain calm.

"Vini told you?"

I nodded.

"It was kind of an on-again/off-again thing. We fought a lot, usually about my choice of friends. I knew Bonnie from high school. She was a cheerleader in her first year, and I was the football quarterback in my senior year. She kept following me around. I asked her out, but I had no idea she was fifteen at that time. She told me she was seventeen, just about to turn eighteen, and had been put back a year in primary school. She hung out with older girls, so I just assumed she was the same age. I never told my parents about her. I guess in hindsight, I should have, since my mother knew how old Bonnie was. I thought Bonnie was past tense when I started university, but she kept turning up at the same parties I went to. Alicia was pissed. She was sure Bonnie was obsessed, even to the point of being crazy."

"Why would you even consider getting involved with someone like Bonnie?"

"That's a really good question … I don't have a good answer. I thought Alicia was just jealous. She kept insisting I had my head up my ass, and maybe I did. I didn't pay much attention to Bonnie until after Alicia and I broke up for the hundredth time. My parents were away for the weekend, and Ricky was with his grandmother in California. I called Bonnie and asked her over. Don't ask me why. It was just one of those stupid things. I'm not trying to make excuses. There is no excuse. We got drunk and went skinny-dipping in my pool, and one thing led to another."

"So you lied to me when you said she didn't mean anything and that you just dated."

"Yes, sort of. I thought I loved her when I was a teenager, but I got over it quickly. She never accepted it. She didn't mean anything, at least as far as a relationship was concerned." Connor cleared his throat and asked for a drink of water.

I was beginning to understand why he felt guilty.

He took the water, finished it in one gulp, and then continued, "Alicia and I had just gotten back together when Bonnie called me to say she was pregnant. I stupidly told my father; I figured because he was a doctor, he would know what to do. He knew her age since our moms were friends, and I got the lecture of my life, and Bonnie was intimidated into silence. If her dad found out, she'd be grounded for the rest of her life. My father had a pregnancy test done, and yeah, she was pregnant and underage. That's a jail sentence, Micaela."

It was all sounding like one of the soap operas I watched. I could hardly make it real. I wasn't sure whether I wanted to hear any more, but I remained silent.

"My father arranged for an abortion. Bonnie told Alicia we were sleeping together on a regular basis but not about being pregnant or the abortion. I guess Alicia had enough, and we broke up. This time it was permanent. She transferred to another university. It was hell living with my parents, so I just gave up, quit school, and bought my boat. Time passed, and it was like it never happened, but I didn't get much smarter. I felt sorry for Bonnie for what she'd gone through and invited her to Jason's party the night I met you."

"That still doesn't quite explain why she tried to kill herself."

"I'm getting to that. I can't be totally sure, but Bonnie has issues. She lost her younger brother in a boating accident when she was six years old. They'd been fooling around, and Rusty fell overboard and hit his head on a rock. Her dad blamed her, and she blamed herself. It screwed her up."

I suddenly felt some compassion for Bonnie; considering how I felt about her, that was a generous feeling.

"Could be why she couldn't accept loss." Connor cleared his throat again. "I went to see Bonnie in the hospital. She told me she was pregnant again. We argued, but I think she finally accepted I wasn't going to take the fall for it. I explained there was such a thing as a paternity test, and she wouldn't get away with accusing me. She finally broke and told me it was Joanne's boyfriend, Marcus."

"Wow, that girl has no morals at all."

"Apparently, she hooked up with him when she and Kelly went to a bar that night. She was terrified Joanne would find out. I agreed to keep her secret if she backed off and left me alone. Her mother called the next day to tell me Bonnie had been released from the hospital, but before going to bed that night, she checked on her and found Bonnie with a plastic bag over her head. There was half a bottle of sleeping pills on the floor. Damn good thing Clarisse checked on her, or Bonnie would have died. They took her to some psychiatric hospital in Miami."

"So you blame yourself?"

"Partly. I was disappointed in myself and couldn't face you. I had to get away. I thought you deserved better. You have your dreams. I figured you would get over me."

"You figured wrong."

"That's how I felt at the time."

"And now?"

"I'm hoping you'll forgive me. I lied to you, and I hurt you. How could you possibly trust me?"

"You made a mistake." I felt better for knowing the truth, but I would have to work on the forgiveness part. "What made you want to tell me now?"

"When I saw you Saturday, I knew how difficult it was going to be to forget you. You looked pretty damn appealing in that outfit."

I secretly congratulated myself. My choice of attire had worked.

"When you jumped into the boat and confronted me, I think I fell more in love with you, but the guilt drove me nuts. I couldn't sleep, so I went for a walk. I thought about how selfish I'd been in not telling you the truth and having you believe it was your fault. It hurt me to think how confused and disappointed you were. I kept thinking about it. I knew I had to face you. I'm so sorry."

"I'm sorry too."

"You have nothing to be sorry for. I should have respected our relationship and told you the truth from the beginning and let you make up your own mind."

"I have." I sat beside him and rested my head on his shoulder. "I can't be without you. My dreams mean nothing without you to share them with me. Please promise to never go away again."

"I promise." He pulled me to him and kissed me.

I remembered the snapshot. "Oh ... who was the redhead in the picture?"

"What picture?"

I told him the detective had taken a few shots of him on his boat, and we'd seen a woman who looked a lot like Bonnie.

"I don't know whether to thank Owen or bust his ass. But if he hadn't done that, you would never have found me, and I wouldn't be here now."

"Then I guess you'll have to thank him. Well? Who was it? And I'm not jealous, just curious."

"If it's who I think it is, it was Bonnie's mom. Her parents come down to the Keys pretty regularly, and they spotted me. I couldn't avoid them. They came on the boat and asked how I was, and I asked them about Bonnie. I might be an idiot, but I do care."

"I understand that."

"They told me Bonnie is keeping the baby. I decided to tell them about getting Bonnie pregnant when she was fifteen and how terrified I was of going to jail. I needed to get it off my chest. Clarisse was pretty good about it, except she wasn't thrilled that I'd lied to her, and she felt she should have been with her daughter when she had the abortion. She asked if my mother knew. I think she was relieved when I told her my father didn't share that information with her, as those two have been friends since high school and pretty much share everything. Bonnie's dad wasn't too pleased, but there isn't much he can do about it now. Did you think it was Bonnie in the picture?"

I hated to admit it. "Yeah. Both Vini and I did, but I don't think Owen did."

"Clarisse would be flattered. She's over fifty." Connor turned my face to his. "So are we good?"

"We're good." We kissed again and swore to each other that nothing would ever separate us again. Dad had been correct; things were as right as rain.

CHAPTER 31

Downtown Clearwater was filled with last-minute shoppers scurrying like mice from store to store. Connor and I joined the frenzy. Store windows with stenciled snowflakes on frosted glass and sparkling tinsel added to the festive spirit but didn't quite complete it. I missed real snow falling like hundreds of white flower petals, melting as they kissed my cheek. We stopped to listen to carolers standing amid palm trees against a background of tourists baking on the beach. What appeared perfectly natural to Connor seemed strange and out of place to me. A nostalgic longing for snowball fights with Dad and decorating our tree while Mom made hot chocolate after an afternoon of tobogganing compelled me to share my memories.

"You're lucky to have those memories. My mother hired a tree decorator, our dinner was catered, and Ricky was hidden away with a nanny so my parents wouldn't be embarrassed by what they called his 'affliction' when guests came over. We got tons of presents but nothing we wanted. Always something my parents figured was practical."

There was no mistaking the resentment in Connor's voice.

"That's sad." The more I heard about Connor's parents, the more I appreciated mine.

"Yeah, it is." Connor drew me into his arms and kissed my forehead. "How about we get some hot chocolate and make believe it's snowing." He bent down, swished his hand across the pavement as if scooping something, pretended to roll it between his palms, and threw it at me. "There! You've been hit by a snowball."

"You're crazy, Connor McKenzie." I played along and mimicked throwing one back at him. He ducked. I laughed.

"Yup, I'm crazy. Crazy about you." I got another kiss.

The waitress at the restaurant brought us hot chocolate complete with whipped cream, which she must have found odd, considering Clearwater was experiencing an unusually warm winter.

Connor was emphatic that I should not buy him a present, knowing I didn't have money of my own. I pretended not to listen and hummed "Jingle Bells" while staring out the window.

"I mean it, Micaela."

I continued humming

"You can stop any time."

I persisted.

"Now who's the crazy one?"

I kept humming.

"Okay, I concede. Another poem would be nice, but I don't think you can top the one you did for my birthday."

He had my attention. "As long as you don't let Vini read it."

"Ouch! You got me. Sorry about that, but I loved it so much, and since she's your friend, I wanted to share it. Won't happen again. Promise." He leaned across the table and wiped whipped cream off my chin. "Speaking of Vini, I haven't heard from her since Halloween. Is she pissed at me?"

"Maybe a little but probably more with me."

"Why you?"

"Because I wouldn't tell her why you left."

"Thanks! I appreciate that."

"It's not my place. It's your private information. How's Ricky?" I wanted to switch the subject. The day was too perfect to spoil with bad memories.

"Not so good."

"What's wrong?" I sensed it was going to get spoiled anyway.

"He's not talking and is very distant." Connor sighed and ran his hand through his hair. "I guess there is no easy way to say it. My parents are divorcing."

I'd never known anyone whose parents were divorced. "I'm sorry. That's so terrible." There was nothing else I could think of to say.

"No need to be sorry. It was inevitable. To tell you the truth, I'm glad. Their constant fighting upset him."

"What's going to happen to him?"

"Right now he's with Grams in California. My mother has a new boyfriend and is moving to Colorado, and my father is never home. They won't let him stay with me. My father thinks I'm too irresponsible. That's a joke, coming from him." He ran his hand through his hair again. "I have a favor to ask, if you don't mind."

"What?" I didn't know what I would be agreeing to, but if there was anything I could do to help, I would, and I knew Connor wouldn't request something unreasonable.

"My mother is bringing Ricky here tomorrow to spend Christmas with my father while she deals with selling the house. Could you spend some time with him? It might cheer him up."

I got one of those aha moments. "I have an idea."

"You sound more like Vini, minus the swearing. What's your idea?"

"How about you and Ricky spend Christmas Eve with Dad and me and Christmas Day with your dad? That is, if he doesn't mind."

"I don't imagine he'll care, but I'll check. Ricky would love that. What about your dad?"

"He won't mind. He's the more-the-merrier type on holidays. He does all the cooking. Just thought I'd throw that in as a selling feature so you won't get scared off."

Connor smiled. "Good to know."

"Do you like Ukrainian food?"

"Never had it."

"You'll like it. Tons of carbs. So you'll come?"

"I don't see any reason why not. You just made two guys very happy."

"All in a day's work."

The rest of the afternoon was spent finding gifts for our friends. We grabbed a take-out pizza, headed back to the boat, and made love until we were exhausted. The day had been pretty close to perfect. Connor had an evening cruise, and I'd promised Dad we could choose a tree and I'd let him beat me at a couple of games of Scrabble. Tomorrow was Christmas Eve, and I was determined to make it special for Connor and Ricky.

CHAPTER 32

The morning had been spent preparing food. The scent of garlic filled the air, and the kitchen table was taken over with bowls of mashed potatoes, chopped onion, grated cheese, and other various ingredients ready to be blended. Dad put me in charge of making the borscht. I grated the beets well and chopped the dill successfully and was congratulating myself when I cut my finger while slicing an onion.

"Get a Band-Aid. You're bleeding on the onions."

"It's mixed with beets, Dad. Who's going to know?"

He shook his head. "Why don't you let me finish up here?"

I gladly handed him the knife and took off to the store to find treats and comic books for the stocking I'd bought Ricky.

By the time they arrived, delicious aromas permeated the apartment and I was just finishing setting the dining table with Mom's Christmas china. Ricky ran straight for me, grabbed me around the waist, and kissed me on the mouth; more like a chicken peck, but it startled me.

"Whoa, big guy! You're messing with my girl." Connor tried pulling Ricky off me.

"Happy! I love Micaela."

"She needs to breathe. How about you let her go and let me have my turn." Connor kissed me, and it wasn't a chicken peck. He shook Dad's hand. "Your daughter has quite the effect on the McKenzie brothers."

"I can see that."

Connor introduced Ricky. It didn't go well. He remembered Dad's hospital visit. "You made Micaela cry," he said.

Dad looked puzzled. "I did?"

"You wouldn't let Connor or me see Micaela."

Connor stepped in quickly. "It's all better now guy. Micaela isn't sad anymore, and we can see her whenever we want. We're here now, right? And remember you saw her at the Halloween party?"

Ricky burst out laughing. "Vini threw Bonnie in the pool."

Dad looked even more puzzled, and Connor rolled his eyes. "Oops, guess I shouldn't have gone there."

It was my turn to step in. "How about you help me decorate the tree." I handed Ricky an ornament.

Dad offered Connor a beer.

"This is creepy." Ricky dangled a glittery web with a silver spider in the middle from his finger. "Why would a spider's web be on a Christmas tree?"

"Good question, son," Dad said. "Do you want to hear a story?"

Ricky's eyes lit up. Dad sat in his recliner, with Ricky sitting on the floor beside him. He began sharing the Ukrainian legend of a woman whose husband dies, leaving her very poor, so poor she had nothing to decorate her Christmas tree.

"That's very poor," Ricky commented.

"Yes, it is," Dad said. "Her children were very sad. She hung nuts and fruits outside her door and prayed that it would make her children happy at Christmas."

"That's silly," Ricky said. "What if the squirrels ate it?"

"No squirrels where she lived."

I was amazed at Dad's patience with Ricky's constant interruptions.

Dad cleared his throat. "On Christmas Eve, the mother prayed so hard that all the spiders in the land heard her and came in the middle of the night and decorated her tree with webs. When the sun came up in the morning, the webs glistened and glittered and made the tree look beautiful. The children were very happy." Dad added, "The end," just in case Ricky didn't realize the story was finished.

The grin on Ricky's face was priceless. Dad had won him over.

"Maybe the woman could have made popcorn strings instead," Ricky said.

I could tell Dad didn't want to even attempt a response.

"I think these are a lot prettier than popcorn," I said, hanging a web on the tree.

Ricky did the same. Connor was the tallest, so he had the honor of placing the star on the top—a task that had always been mine, but I gladly relinquished it to him.

After all the decorations were on the tree, Dad turned to Ricky. "How about you and I find the brightest star in the sky."

This was a ritual Dad and I did every year. I loved that Ricky now took my place. He looked at Connor for permission and was given a go-ahead nod.

"What's that all about?" Connor asked

"The brightest star tells the world that Jesus is born," I explained. "What Dad really believes is that it's Mom watching over us."

"Is that your belief?" Connor asked while helping me put the food on the table.

"It's nice, and it makes Dad happy. It's been a custom since I was able to walk."

The balcony door slid open. "We found it, Micaela. Your mom is looking at us."

"See? I told you."

"I think it's a beautiful belief." Connor kissed me on the cheek. "I'll be your shining star when it's my turn to leave."

"Don't say that. What if I go first? Anyway, you are already my shining star."

"You're an angel, and I'm a shining star. Looks like we're a great match."

"Is it time to eat?" Ricky was already seated at the table.

We joined him.

"It looks amazing, Mr. Lewiski." Connor waited to see if we said grace.

"Call me Art." Dad recited the usual Christmas prayer and made a traditional Ukrainian toast.

"What does that mean?" Ricky inquired.

"It means ... may all your burdens be lightened, and may you forgive all those who bring you harm."

"Okay, so *now* can we eat?" Ricky asked.

Dad passed him the pierogis and explained what it was. I smiled at Connor, and he smiled back.

If second helpings were any indication, they were now fans of Ukrainian food. While Connor and I cleaned up the dishes, Ricky helped Dad light the candles on the tree. When we were finished, each of us got comfortable in the living room. Connor and I curled up together at the end of the couch; Ricky was on the floor, which seemed to be his preference; and Dad in his recliner.

"How about Ricky gets the first present?" Dad said, handing him a note.

Ricky looked mystified and read it out loud. "Look behind the closet door."

We didn't have a fireplace to hang his stocking, but I wanted it to be a surprise; the hook on the back of the closet was the only option I could think of.

He ran and opened it. "*Holy smokaroonies!*" He'd seen the Batman and Robin comics peeking out from the top of the stocking.

"How did you know he's a huge Batman fan?" Connor snagged one and flipped through it.

"Lucky guess."

"Look at these, Connor?" Ricky found the baseball cards and ripped open the plastic packaging. "Thanks, Micaela. I love them."

"Cool," Connor said and then whispered in my ear. "That's pretty special. Thank you."

"Ricky's pretty special."

I gave Dad his present. He loved his wallet even though we both knew it was his money that had paid for it. I included a letter, telling him he was the best dad in the world and how much I appreciated everything he did for me. He swiped at his eyes, but the tears flowed anyway. I got up and retrieved Connor's card and present from behind the tree and handed them to him.

"What's this? I told you not to get me anything."

"Listening isn't one of Micaela's strong points, and she's stubborn, like her mother."

He opened the card first.

"I swear, Connor McKenzie, if you read that out loud, I'll sink your boat."

"Trust me. She'd do it," Dad said.

He read it silently and turned to wink at me; then he placed it in his pocket. It was X-rated. He unwrapped the present while giving me the evil eye. Jason had informed me that Connor needed a new compass and helped me choose one. I'd written a note and placed it inside the box: *May every direction you take lead you to me.* Connor was speechless. He was so taken with his compass that he almost forgot Ricky's present. I nudged his arm and pointed to his backpack.

"Oh yeah!" He retrieved the brightly colored package and gave it to Ricky, who was still engrossed in his comic books.

Ricky tore at the wrapping and ripped the top off the box, and when he saw what was inside, he jumped up and down like a small child. It was a baseball cap identical to the one he'd lost in the storm.

"Look at the band," Connor said.

Ricky looked and let out a hoot, jumped up, and lunged at Connor, giving him a huge hug. "It's super-cool."

Unable to contain his curiosity, Dad asked to see it. Ricky handed it to him. "How the heck did you get Michael Jordan's autograph?" Dad sounded impressed.

"It's always about who you know," Connor said. "Actually, it was our friend Owen. He has some interesting colleagues and called in a favor."

"It seems we have lots to thank Owen for." I was already indebted to him for helping me find Connor.

"He's an all-round great guy. He and Jason are probably enjoying their Christmas Eve cocktails at the pool bar in Cancun." Connor went back to playing with his compass.

I'd forgotten the present Owen had given Jason. I pictured them enjoying silly drinks with umbrellas and pineapples. Owen would definitely have a martini as a chaser.

"Where's Micaela's present?" Ricky asked.

Connor passed me a folded piece of paper. "If you read this out loud, you'll be on my boat when it sinks."

Ricky thought that was funny.

A picture of a chalet nestled among snow-covered mountains with a horse-drawn sleigh was stuck to the front of the paper. I looked at Connor.

"Don't judge. It's from an old Christmas card of my parents', but it says what I wanted."

I opened the paper and silently read, "This entitles the beautiful, amazing, adorable Micaela Lewiski to three fun-filled days in Stowe, Vermont to ring in the new year with her charming, lovable, and sometimes stupid boyfriend. Guaranteed snowball fights, great sex, sleigh rides, great sex, and hot chocolate by a blazing fire and more great sex. Nonrefundable. I cleared it with your dad. Say yes!"

"Which part did you clear?" I teased.

"The snowball fights."

I looked at Dad. He handed me another envelope. "Go, Micaela. Have fun. Get yourself some ski clothes or whatever you'll need. This should cover it."

"If I go, that means you'll be alone for New Year's Eve."

"It's just another day. I have to get used to not having you around. Might as well start now."

I thanked Dad and told Connor I would go. He almost glowed he was so happy.

"Where are you guys goin'?" Ricky looked up from his comic book.

"To a place where there's lots of snow," Connor replied.

"Can I come?" he asked.

"Not this time, guy, but when you come again in March, I promise we'll do something special."

Ricky seemed satisfied.

Saying goodbye was difficult. Connor had to pry Ricky off me. Lots of thank-yous and promises to see each other again. Connor gave me a discreet kiss in front of Dad and Ricky.

"I can't even begin to tell you how much this meant to both of us," he said. "You truly are my angel. Thank you for a beautiful memory, and I can't wait to make more."

After they left, Dad and I sat in the dark, watching the candles flicker on the tree.

"Thanks, Dad, for this evening. You made it special."

"I like him," Dad said matter-of-factly. "I know your mom would too."

"I like him too, Dad."

Neither of us spoke. We sat in silence, remembering Mom, until Dad blew out the candles and went to bed. As I closed the living room drapes, I looked out. A star flickered in the night sky. Mom approved.

CHAPTER 33

The chalet exceeded my expectations. It could have been the inspiration for Connor's Christmas card. Tucked in the foothills of Mount Mansfield, with a background of soaring white peaks against a robin's-egg-blue sky, it looked like a painting. Giant fir trees, their branches heavily laden with snow; dormers with frost-stained window panes; and rows of shimmering icicles clinging to the roof's edge added to its charm.

As promised, we cavorted like children, trying to make the perfect snow angels and bombarding each other with snowballs. We made love in front of a roaring fire and went skiing—I needed more practice, but Connor excelled. We made love in the Jacuzzi—awkward but no practice required, although I insisted on an encore—and the evening sleigh ride with horses named Dancer and Prancer was beyond romantic. We ordered room service and made love until we lay, spent and exhausted, in each other's arms. Every moment held a magical quality, and to say I was happy was an understatement. The greatest gift a person can give is their love, and loving Connor made every day brighter. I almost forgot I'd be leaving him behind, trading the magic for my dream of being a Broadway actress. I wanted both.

We lay quietly under the warmth of the down comforter, my head in the crook of his arm, my leg draped over his hip. We listened to icicles, warmed by the midmorning sun, dripping from the dormers, lulling us into a peaceful stupor. Connor ran his finger across my cheek and tucked stray curls behind my ear.

"You are so beautiful. I can't find the words to tell you how happy you make me. I wish I could take this moment and put it in a box. I'd open it every night after you're gone."

"Please don't make it sound so final. I know we won't see each other very often, but we'll find a way to be together." I was trying to sound positive, but even as I said it, I felt a heavy depression pushing up into my heart.

"I envy your dedication to your dream. Taking people on tours every day gets monotonous, and there's no future in it."

"I thought that was something you wanted."

"Thinking you want something and truly wanting it in your gut is different. I haven't given up on being a doctor. It's just one of those maybe-someday things."

"But if you keep putting it off, the years will go by, and eventually it becomes 'If only I had,' and then it might be too late."

"Not only is she beautiful, she's wise too," Connor said as he rolled on top of me, kissed my nose, and then extracted himself from the blankets and headed for the bathroom. "Okay, wise one, I'm taking a shower. Want to join me?"

"Only if you promise to wash my back."

"You got a deal!"

By the time we entered the dining room, breakfast had turned to lunch. Connor stopped to read a poster taped on the wall. It was an announcement for a New Year's Eve dance to be held in the Great Room.

"How would you like to 'trip the light fantastic' this evening?"

I'd lost track of the fact it was New Year's Eve. "If you're asking me if I'd like to go dancing, I thought we were going to take the gondola to the top of the mountain and watch the fireworks."

"We still can. But it might be nice to go—unless you're intimidated by my dance skills." Connor did a two-step and pivoted on one foot.

"Impressive! Have you looked around? We're the youngest couple here. It might be older music. You sure you can handle that?"

"If you're referring to my dancing or social skills, I've been known to 'cut a rug,' and I think I'm fairly personable."

I laughed. "With all those old sayings, you'll fit in just fine." I hooked my arm though his. "Mr. McKenzie, I'd be honored to strut my stuff with you."

We were a hit, at least Connor was. All the ladies wanted to dance with him, which left their husbands to dance with me. I didn't mind sharing him, but I did mind being held a little too tightly, especially by men I didn't know. An elderly man groped my back, his hand drifting to the base of my spine. I extricated myself from his grip and motioned for Connor to save me. He tapped the rather bold man on the shoulder and took his place.

A fox-trot turned into a jive, and Connor whirled, twirled, and dipped me, which cleared the dance floor to make room for some pretty spectacular moves. We ended the dance with Connor grabbing my waist and sliding me between his legs, drawing me up, and pulling my body into his. It felt awkward, but the clapping and hooting indicated the onlookers were impressed, and so was I.

"Connor McKenzie, you are a fabulous dancer. Where did you learn to dance like that?"

"Ballroom dancing when I was twelve. My mother thought it would be useful—for what, I don't know—but if you tell anyone, I'll ..."

"You'll what?"

"I'll put you over my knee."

I pretended I was thinking. "Hmm! Who can I tell first?"

Connor laughed and drew me into his embrace as a slow song brought couples back to the dance floor. His hand trailed along my spine and rested at my lower back. I could feel the heat of his body through my taffeta cocktail dress.

He leaned closer and whispered in my ear. "How about we go back to the room and change? You still want to see the fireworks?" The look in his eyes told me his intentions went beyond just changing.

"Maybe you can practice putting me over your knee," I teased.

"Now you've really done it." He took hold of my hand and directed me to the exit. Connor's intentions did not go unnoticed.

I heard a woman comment as we passed, "That's one way of celebrating the New Year. Oh, to be young again."

"Do you really want to go out on such a cold night and watch a bunch of fireworks? Wouldn't you rather stay warm and toasty next to me?" Connor's finger circled my breast.

I pushed him away, jumped from the bed, grabbed a pillow, and threw it at him.

"You're a sex maniac. Haven't you had enough?"

Connor put his hands in the air in a submissive gesture. "I plead guilty to the first accusation, and I can never get enough of you." He reached for the pillow and swatted my butt.

I fell backward on the bed. Before I could get up, he pounced on top of me, pinned my arms down, and pressed his mouth to mine. Then, just as quickly, he released me, stood, grasped the sheet, and wrapped it around his waist.

"What? You suddenly became modest?" I reached for my robe at the end of the bed.

"It's a little difficult to talk seriously with my equipment exposed."

"Doesn't bother me. What do you want to talk seriously about?"

Connor sat beside me on the bed and took my hand. "I meant it when I said I can't get enough of you in my life, but I can't ask you to stay and give up on your dream. There's nothing in theater in Florida. What if I come to New York?"

I turned to face him. "You'd do that for me?" The idea had crossed my mind, but it seemed too big an imposition and absurd to entertain the thought for more than a moment.

"I'd follow you to the end of the world. Sounds crazy, but it's true. I don't want to lose you to some pretty-boy actor or for you to forget me when you become a famous star. Ricky is in California, and with you gone, nothing much matters."

"Connor, that's not going to happen. You're not going to lose me. Yes, I love the theater, but you're being presumptuous about my becoming famous. Pretty-boy actors, as you call them, don't turn me on, and you are anything but forgettable. To be honest, I have been afraid you'd forget me. Are you sure you could give up your charter business and live in a big city? We can see each other on holidays."

Connor was right—I couldn't and wouldn't give up my dream. And, as much as I tried to sound optimistic, holidays didn't seem enough. His moving to New York sounded too good to be true. I had to be convinced.

"I'm sure. It will be an adjustment, but yes, I'm absolutely sure. There's a lot of stuff I have to straighten out first, but if you'll have me, I think I can make it happen."

"Have you! Are you joking?"

I threw my arms around his neck. I'd fantasized our being together, sharing a cozy loft apartment—me, a struggling actress with a part-time job as a waitress; Connor, studying to be doctor. It seemed like an impossible dream, but Mom used to tell me anything was possible if I just believed it with all my heart.

He released my arms and held both my hands. "Now that I'm on a roll, let's move to step number two. That was step one."

He let go of my hands, held the sheet tightly around his waist, and hopped to the wing chair where he had thrown his pants. He removed a small blue box from the pocket. In the process of hopping back, his foot caught the bottom of the sheet, and he fell to the floor. He knee-walked, dragging the sheet behind him, to where I sat watching; it looked like a scene from a comedy. I couldn't help it; I burst out laughing.

"This isn't how I planned it, but the moment presented itself. I was going to do it at midnight after the fireworks. Do you think you could stop laughing? My pride is at stake here."

I pinched by thigh hard enough to cause a pain that would sidetrack me from my fit of giggles, also to test reality. It hurt. I stopped laughing, and I knew I couldn't be dreaming. Connor was on his knees, holding the box. He flipped it open. My breathing ceased, and I pinched myself again.

"Micaela Lewiski, will you do me the honor of becoming my wife?"

I couldn't take my eyes off the beautiful pearl ring surrounded by a cluster of small diamonds. I was still holding my breath.

I released it. "Oh my God!"

"I'm not sure if that's a yes."

"Yes! Yes! It's a yes."

He took my hand and slid the ring on my finger.

"That went a whole lot better than I expected. I thought I might get another women's lib speech."

"I'm not against marriage. I'd like to believe I can have both. I'm not naive. I know it will be difficult."

"You're right. It's not going to be easy at first, but there is something that might make a difference. When my father's dad died, my Grandpa Bill, he left money in trust for Ricky and me, but there's a catch. My father says I will only get it if I go back to university."

"How much?" I didn't want to sound mercenary, but I was curious.

"Somewhere around half a million … $250,000 for each of us."

I almost choked. "You're kidding."

"Nope, not kidding. By the look in your eyes, I'm glad I asked you before I told you about the trust."

I knew he was teasing, but I felt the need to clarify. "That's not funny. I was thinking how it would make the impossible possible, and it would more than pay for your tuition."

"Let's take it a step at a time. I haven't made up my mind about university just yet. I was thinking of hiring a lawyer to fight my father on releasing the trust. I haven't entirely dismissed the idea of getting my degree, but I want to become a doctor on my own terms, not just to get the money."

"But it's your money, not your dad's."

"Precisely, but like I said, one step at a time."

I held my ring up to the light, watching the little diamonds twinkle like tiny stars. "It's so beautiful. How did you know I like pearls?"

"I saw you eyeing pearl rings when we went Christmas shopping."

"I wasn't hinting. My mom had a pearl ring, and they remind me of her."

"I know you weren't. It suits you. I want you to know I've given this a lot of thought. When I was in the Keys, I did everything to forget you, but no matter how hard I tried, you were the first thing I thought about when I woke up and the last thing I thought about before I went to sleep. You even invaded my dreams. At Christmas, when I saw you with Ricky, I knew for sure you were the woman I wanted to grow old with and to be the mother of my children. Your faith in our love—and in me, even though I treated you badly—convinced me of what I knew from the moment I met you. We were destined to be together." Connor looked into my eyes that were swimming in tears. "I'd better quit my speech before I have you bawling. You still want to go outside?"

"I'd like to. I love fireworks."

"Your wish is my command." He struggled to rid himself of the sheet and walked to the bathroom while I admired my beautiful ring. He turned. "Oh, and if anyone asks how I proposed, would you mind altering the story a bit?"

The view from the top of the mountain had a magical quality. A crescent moon peeked out periodically from behind a blanket of dove-gray clouds as they passed, bathing the valley in a shroud of opaque light. The snow crunched like sugar crystals under our feet as we climbed to the spot where benches were placed for those who simply wanted to enjoy the vista spread out before them. I was glad we were alone and that no one else had taken advantage of the midnight gondola ride.

We sat listening to the silence that hung in the frigid air. Connor pulled a blanket from his backpack that the chalet had provided to stave off the chill. He'd purchased a bottle of champagne and borrowed two wine glasses and a corkscrew. He removed the foil from the bottle cap and inserted the corkscrew, twisting it until it was ready to pop. He checked his watch. We counted down to midnight. He popped the cork, and it shot like a bullet into the dark void below us. He filled our glasses, and we kissed. I was shivering, and my teeth began to chatter, making it impossible to continue kissing. I cuddled into him, pulling the blanket around my shoulders. The silence was broken by colorful bursts of light, like giant asterisks exploding, one after another, blazing the sky in greens, magenta, scarlet, and golden light. Connor made a toast.

"To a future filled with just enough challenges to make life interesting. And no matter what happens, we always have each other."

I thought it was an interesting toast and clinked his glass as I watched pinpoints of jade, silver, and gold reflect across his eyes.

"Always and forever," I said as the cold bubbles tickled my nose. I thought of Dad bringing in the New Year by himself, and I made a wish. I hoped someday he would find a woman just like Mom and be as happy as I was with Connor. Strains of "Auld Lang Syne" floated up from the valley. Connor finished his champagne. I didn't like it but finished it anyway. We cuddled together until the finale of multicolored explosions popped in succession. As cold as I was, I didn't want this moment to end, but the promise of lying in front of a warm fire changed my mind.

On the way back down the mountain, Connor kissed me again. "Thank you for accepting my proposal. For as long as I live, I will honor our love." He pointed to a cluster of stars that appeared as the clouds whisked past. One in particular shone brighter than the rest. "I think your mom approves."

"I know!" What I didn't know was what the future held for us, but I understood Connor's toast. No matter what life threw at us, as long as we had each other, no problem was insurmountable.

CHAPTER 34

Time does not play favorites. Lovers aren't granted special privileges any more than saints or kings, but it's made more precious in the knowing. I couldn't recall where I'd read the phrase, but I understood its meaning. The time Connor and I spent together was made more bearable by the knowledge that we had the rest of our lives to be together, but it would be months before Connor could settle his affairs and join me.

We decided to wait until next summer, when we could all be together again, to be married. Connor finally agreed to apply to the New York School of Medicine. It had to be New York; anywhere else meant we would be separated and have to postpone our wedding, something neither of us wanted.

His decision was made without my having to pressure him. I have to admit I did try influencing him. Any time I spoke of our future, I would say things like, "When you become a doctor ..." or "When you graduate ..." I called it positive reinforcement. If Connor wasn't accepted at NYU, it would be disappointing, but he said he would make adjustments and try for a degree in social services, guaranteeing him entrance. We argued about it. I didn't want him sacrificing his dream any more than I wanted to sacrifice mine. It was a standoff.

I hadn't told Dad about our engagement. I chose to wait until we had more concrete plans. He had very strong ideas about the survival rate of young marriages, and I knew we would butt heads. He had been married at twenty-one to an eighteen-year-old Ukrainian girl. She'd left him for a man who owned a string of clothing stores and offered a more comfortable life than Dad could provide—goodbye, Brooklyn; hello, Manhattan. I'm glad she did, or Dad wouldn't have met Mom, married, had me, and moved to Toronto. His perception was distorted by his own unfortunate experience (or fortunate experience, depending on how you looked at it).

I'd take my ring off before I got home. I didn't want a lecture. Dad's stand was somewhere between stupid mistake and irresponsible decision. It was something we would have to ease into. Vini, on the other hand, went ballistic. She wanted to plan the wedding and decided she'd be my maid of honor. I hadn't asked, but it was one of those self-evident conclusions. She was adamant about what she'd be wearing. No fluffy pastel-pink or powder-blue chiffon dresses with satin bows. She gave me the choice of deep purple or hot pink, and it had to be slinky with no poofy crinolines. Green was not an option, as it gave her skin a yellow tone. She decided that Jason would be the best man, and Ricky and Owen would be ushers. Another self-evident conclusion. She wanted to go dress shopping immediately, and I had to pull in the reins. She loved my ring and informed me that she'd read somewhere that pearls symbolized purity, honor, and loyalty, and the wearer would be brought wealth. I wasn't sure how true that was, but I smiled, thinking about the wealth part. I had decided not to share Connor's good fortune. It was his private information. Owen decided we should celebrate anywhere he could get a good martini, and Jason said he knew Connor and I were destined for each other and liked the idea of celebrating, with or without the martini. It bothered me that my friends knew before my dad did, but I was too happy to risk an argument with him.

Saturday nights and Sunday mornings were the only times I got to spend with Connor. Dad was now accustomed to my overnights, but he missed our breakfasts together. My determination to take my grades from mediocre to excellent and rehearsals for the school production of *West Side Story* kept me busy. I could hardly believe I landed the lead role. Despite the fact that the girl I was competing with for the part was, in my estimation, a much better actress, I'd been a shoo-in because I knew all the songs and had mastered a Puerto Rican accent. At least, that's what I guessed was the reason.

Dad and Connor took me out for dinner to celebrate. I don't know where my head was, but I forgot to take off my ring. Dad noticed. I kept quiet and let Connor manufacture a suitable explanation.

"It's a promise ring," he told Dad.

"What are you promising?"

"It's a promise to be faithful while Micaela's launching her career in New York, and who knows? Maybe someday, when we're older, it will have a wedding ring beside it."

Dad just grunted, "Good luck with that." He felt about long-distance relationships the way he felt about young marriages.

Later, I thanked Connor for his discretion. I still hadn't shared with dad the fact that Connor had applied to NYU, as I suspected he would become suspicious as to our intentions. I planned on telling him—just not yet.

"It wasn't a total lie," he said. "The only thing I altered was the maybe-when-we're-older part. Don't worry, Micaela. We'll cross that bridge when we come to it."

"Let's hope the bridge doesn't collapse when we get there."

"I think once your dad is comfortable with the fact that we know what we're doing, he'll come around."

"I hope so."

The months flew by. Ricky wasn't able to come for March break, as he had the flu, and his grandmother didn't feel it was wise for him to travel. Connor handled Ricky's disappointment by calling him several times and promising he could spend the summer on the boat with him, but Connor would have to convince their father. He didn't tell him about our engagement. We wanted to do it together.

It was close to the end of the semester, and we still hadn't heard anything from the Admissions Department of the university, which put a damper on my birthday celebration. We decided to combine it with Jason's birthday, our one-year anniversary, and our engagement. This time, Vini brought a date, the guy who'd replaced Connor at the Blue Lagoon.

They say opposites attract—Jason and Owen, a perfect example—but instead of being opposites, Adrian and Vini were carbon copies of each other. They both had the same chocolate-colored skin; thick, wavy, long black hair; and—more surprising—long black lashes. They even dressed similarly. She wore a purple tank top with a denim skirt. He paired his tank top with jeans. Owen wouldn't stop making wisecrack remarks.

"If he starts singing 'Girls Just Want to Have Fun,' I'll kill myself," he said after three martinis.

Jason punched his arm. "If Vin hears you, she'll do it for you."

It was hard to believe a year had passed, and I was leaving for New York in three months. If Connor didn't hear something soon, we'd have to implement plan B. It was not nearly as nice as Plan A. Connor had reluctantly filled in applications to Johns Hopkins in Baltimore and Columbia, which at least was in New York. His SAT scores were high enough, but he thought his chances were slim. This was one of those challenges we'd have to overcome. It was like taking a road trip without a map … you knew there would be detours and roadblocks along the way, but you eventually would arrive at your destination, and it would be worth it. It would just take longer than expected.

I aced my finals and started my last semester with above-average grades. Still no word from the university. I tried not thinking about it and kept busy with rehearsals. As the play got closer, those all-too-familiar butterflies formed in my gut. I decided I needed a break. Ricky was allowed to spend the summer with Connor, as his father was moving to a condo in Tampa and would be out of the country on business for most of the summer. Connor doubted it had anything to do with his father's profession.

Ricky was flying in on July 3, the day before Independence Day. I'd have a two-day holiday. One official, one not so official. I wanted to surprise Ricky, and Connor agreed to take me to the airport to greet him. He was scheduled to arrive at one in the afternoon. I told Connor I'd be at the boat around eleven but decided to extend the day by arriving earlier and surprising him.

I got to the marina just at sunrise. A fog had settled over the ocean as a result of an overnight rainstorm. The heat of the morning sun created wisps of clouds that moved across the dock like ghosts encircling the boats. Fishermen checking their lines nodded as I approached. Foster Dickson, or "Old Man Dickie," as the locals referred to him, was releasing his boat lines from the mooring as I passed.

"Hey, pretty lady! You lookin' for Connor? Don't think he's up yet. He's not much of an early bird. Aren't you supposed to be on your way to school or somethin'?"

"Playing hooky, and he's expecting me." I didn't add *but not this early.*

"Lucky guy." He smirked while easing his boat from the slip. "You two have a good day, and don't do anythin' I would do." His laugh was more of a cackle.

What a letch, I thought as I pulled the *Micaela* closer to the dock. I was always a little paranoid about falling in the water. My proficiency at getting in the boat without assistance was improving, except I still chose to jump. I almost slipped on the wet deck and grabbed the railing just in time to keep from falling. I steadied myself and looked around to see if anyone had been watching. My dignity was intact. As quietly as I could, I opened the cabin door and moved down the steps, avoiding the squeaky one. Connor was still sleeping. The only visible part of him was his hair. I tiptoed to the bed, removed my shorts, T-shirt, and underwear, and carefully slithered across the blanket to lie beside him. He made a snorting noise and turned to face me but didn't wake up. Connor slept like the dead. Holding my breath, I slipped my hand under the blanket, inching slowly down until I found my target. Connor opened his eyes and smiled.

"That's the way every man should greet the day."

"You bum! You knew I was here all along, didn't you?"

"The way you landed on the deck, I think you probably woke up half of Clearwater." Pushing the blanket aside, he rolled on top of me. "How do you feel about omitting the foreplay and going straight for the real action?"

I raised my hips to meet his and pulled his mouth to mine. "Good to go, Captain."

Our stomachs churned and growled in sync. Connor laughed. "I'd like to think we could live on love alone, but it probably doesn't provide all the nutrients required to maintain a healthy body. How about I whip up some eggs and bacon, or would you rather go out?"

"I'll take the eggs here." I didn't feel like going back out into the world just yet.

Before Connor was able to plant his feet on the floor, a man's voice called out from the dock.

"Coming aboard! Get your ass out of the sack."

Connor looked startled. "Shit, it's my father. He never comes here." Grabbing his jeans, he slid them on, minus his underwear.

"Do you want me to stay in the cabin?" I'd never met Connor's dad. The opportunity never presented itself, and I felt this might be somewhat awkward for a first meeting.

"Not unless you feel more comfortable. My father isn't the huggy-bear type, and he'll figure you're some girl I picked up in a bar. He's got that kind of mentality."

I raised an eyebrow.

"I don't pick up girls in bars, so quit with the look. Maybe it would be better if you stayed here."

"Get your ass out here or I'll come in and haul you out." Connor's dad was already on the deck.

"He looks professional, but he talks like a truck driver." He put on his T-shirt and headed for the deck. "I'm coming!" he yelled.

He left, shutting the cabin door, but it wasn't soundproof.

"Hey, Dad! What brings you here?" It was the first time I'd heard Connor refer to his father as dad. I knew him well enough to hear the annoyance in his voice and the effort he was making to sound civil.

"Two things: a letter from NYU. It's postmarked two months ago. It went to our old house instead of being rerouted to my new address. I was away at a symposium in Nevada, so I didn't get the opportunity to check the mail. You should have come by the house and checked, so don't blame me for the delay."

"Two months is a pretty long symposium. Hope she was worth it."

I sensed Connor had overstepped a boundary.

"Watch your mouth, son. I didn't have to come down here to give it to you. But I figured might as well because the second thing is, I'd like you to come with me to pick up your brother."

"He's expecting *me* to pick him up." I could hear the disappointment in Connor's tone.

"I haven't seen Ricky since Christmas. I don't want him to forget what his old man looks like."

Connor didn't respond.

"You got an issue with some father-and-son time?"

"No, sir." Resignation seemed to be Connor's only option.

My excitement at surprising Ricky and spending the rest of the day with them sank like an anchor in my chest.

"Aren't you going to open the envelope?" his father asked.

"I'd rather do it alone, if you don't mind."

"Why? Are you afraid you didn't get accepted, and I'll be pissed? Don't worry about letting me down. It wouldn't be the first time. There are other universities. I hope you didn't apply to just one. You've got a lot at stake here, son."

"Yeah, I know." I knew Connor was referring to me, but his dad wouldn't have a clue.

"Believe me, Connor, I know how much is in that trust, and it's nothing to turn your back on. So if you want the money, you won't let one rejection hold you back. Get dressed, and I'll meet you at the Clearwater Cafe … say, about twenty minutes."

The anchor of disappointment embedded itself deeper into my chest. I heard footsteps retreating, and Connor mumbled something that sounded like *asshole*. When he returned to the cabin, the air was riddled with tension.

"I suppose you heard all that. He's not going to win the Father of the Year award. I'm sorry, but I'm stuck."

"It's okay. If you don't mind, can I wait here?"

"I have no idea how long we're going to be, but I'll try to ditch him; I'll tell him Ricky and I have plans to go to a baseball game. Hopefully, he won't want to tag along. Of course you can stay here, but won't you be bored?"

"I'll get something to eat at the coffee shop and go to the bookstore. For a change, I'll read something for pleasure." I stared at the envelope still in Connor's hand. I felt like a contestant in a game show, waiting to find out what was behind door number one. "I guess you want to open it by yourself."

"I just told him that because I didn't want to share the moment with him. It belongs to us, no matter the outcome." He sat beside me on the bed. I was already dressed, anticipating leaving. He ripped open the envelope. "You ready?" He pulled the letter out but waited to read it.

I placed my hand on his arm. "If you don't get accepted, it's not the end of the world. We'll work out something. Maybe we'll just have to wait longer. We have the rest of our lives."

"You'd make a good baseball player."

I looked at him quizzically.

"You cover all the bases," he said, kissing the end of my nose. "Here goes."

We read it together. Normally, I wasn't a squealer, but what came out sounded pretty close. Jumping off the bed, I did my version of a happy dance, knocking over Connor's new light. He picked me up and twirled me around, and we collapsed on the bed.

"How about a celebration quickie?"

I pushed him back. "You have about ten minutes to shave, get dressed, and meet your dad and tell him the good news." Connor's hand slid under my T-shirt. "Stop! You're tempting me."

"Okay, but I'm taking a rain check. Not sure when I'll be able to cash it in. Now that my parents are divorced, and my mother is traveling with her boyfriend, my father's never around, so I have Ricky most of the summer. Grams needs a break."

"Knowing you, I'm sure you'll find a way."

He squeezed my breast. "Count on it, babe."

"Always and forever, remember?"

"Always and forever, my beautiful angel."

CHAPTER 35

Almost an hour passed before I found a book that interested me, purchased a lemonade and cheese sandwich to take out, and maneuvered myself back on to the boat. The fog had lifted, and the blazing sun was drying up puddles on the deck. I located the bench cushions, found a New York Yankees ball cap, and grabbed my sunscreen, slathering all exposed body parts. I sat at the end of the bench, my back against the cabin wall, bent my knees, and propped my book against them. A crate I found in the galley closet served as a table for my drink and sandwich. It felt good to do nothing but indulge my love of reading. I made a promise to myself—absolutely no thinking. All thought was vanquished. The book, a suspense thriller, had me totally engrossed. I was just getting to the part where the female archaeologist discovers an ancient tomb containing a significant religious artifact, and her nemesis, who just happened to be a very handsome art dealer, kidnaps her, when I sensed a presence near me. Glancing up, I saw my own nemesis staring down at me. She was wearing shiny orange hot pants and a candy-floss pink tank top, obviously without a bra.

"I suspected you'd be here. Where's Connor?" were the first words out of Bonnie's mouth.

I did my best to act nonchalant, as if seeing her meant nothing to me.

"He's at the airport, picking up Ricky. I don't know when he's coming back. Would you care to wait, or should I just tell him you stopped by?" I almost choked on the sweetness in my voice. There was no reason for jealousy to rear its ugly head. I would never doubt Connor again. My curiosity at Bonnie's sudden appearance outweighed my annoyance.

She handled getting in the boat like a pro, confirming my belief that her fall into Connor's arms on his birthday had been calculated, and she wasn't as drunk as she'd let on. She took a seat on the bench across from me.

"I'll wait. You're probably just saying that, hoping to get rid of me."

"Can I get you something to drink? Connor has some cola and beer in the fridge." I was astounding myself with the politeness.

"I'll take a beer."

"Glass or bottle?"

"Bottle is fine."

We sounded like two friends sharing an afternoon. Bonnie had been in my company for about ten minutes and still hadn't made possessive references to Connor. Maybe she'd changed, but it was doubtful. I handed her the beer and an opener and waited. The shock still hadn't worn off, and I wasn't sure how to initiate the conversation.

She opened with, "I guess now that Connor's parents are divorced, Ricky's been shipped off to his grandmother's." She caught my surprised look. "I may have been out of the loop for a while, but our moms are friends, and my mom filled me in." She opened the beer and took a sip.

She had no way of knowing Connor told me her secret, but thanks to Joanne, most of Clearwater Beach and St. Petersburg knew why she'd been sent to a hospital in Miami. Small talk seemed ridiculous, so I decided, *To hell with it; no beating around the bush.* I pulled a Vini—direct and to the point. "I understand you decided to keep your baby."

Bonnie looked like I'd slapped her. "That's none of your goddamn business." The real Bonnie was emerging.

"Sorry." I wasn't the least bit sorry, and I was enjoying her agitation. *I must have a dark side.*

"Did Connor tell you I was pregnant?"

I said nothing, just sipped my now-warm lemonade.

"He did, didn't he? Figures! Well, for your information, I'm looking for him to let him know we had a daughter, and I'm living at home while I finish school. For some reason, his mobile number doesn't work." Her smug tone stripped away any compassion I was feeling. "My mom's taking care of Riley—that's her name. It's Connor's middle name. Every firstborn in the McKenzie family has that name, but I guess you already know that."

My buttons had been pushed. "Enough of all this crap. You're delusional. Connor told me you screwed your best friend's boyfriend and decided to pin it on him."

Bonnie's eyes looked as if she could send fireballs from them.

I kept going but tried to make my voice sound more compassionate. "You don't have to worry. We'll keep your dirty secret, but Joanne will learn the truth sooner or later. Life's funny that way, Bonnie. Have you ever heard of a paternity test?" She started to speak; I cut her off. "Connor already told you he'd request one. How foolish will you look when it turns out he's not the father? Do you really want to put yourself and your family through the humiliation? Think about it. Connor also told me he got you pregnant when you were a minor, so you can save yourself the trouble of thinking you're going to expose him and hurt me. What you didn't count on was his dad arranging for an out-of-state abortion."

I could tell by her expression I was hitting a nerve. The fire in her eyes abated, and she looked like she was going to cry.

"I'm sorry, Bonnie, that you went through that, but what you need to understand is this: Connor isn't some dumb teenager anymore, and for years he's carried the burden of guilt, almost destroying his own future. If you love him, like you say you do, then wouldn't you want him to be happy? He's got a future now. He's going back to university."

It was as if she missed half my speech, perhaps even all of it, lost in her paranoid delusion. "Did he also tell you that he tried to kill me?"

"Will you stop with all the drama queen crap? It was an accident, and you know it. You brought it on yourself."

"He tried to rape me."

"No, Bonnie. That was a story you were going to tell people when he rejected your attempt to seduce him." I tried appealing to her feelings for Connor again. "If you believe you love him and care anything at all, why do you keep hurting him with all your lies?"

This time, tears welled up in her eyes, smearing her mascara when she blinked. "All I ever wanted was for us to be together. Then you came along and spoiled everything."

"Believe what you want, but the truth is you spoiled it for yourself. No one can be manipulated into loving you. Sex isn't love. It's the by-product. I guess you could call it love's perk. If you hadn't forced it, maybe he might have grown to love you in time. Using Connor to ease the loss of your brother and the guilt you felt at how he died was self-defeating." I thought I'd throw in some pseudo-psychology to get her to open up and face the truth.

She gasped. "Connor told you about my brother? He shouldn't have done that."

"Maybe not, but even though I never had a brother, I lost my mom, and I know the heartbreak of losing a loved one." I tried compassion. It looked like it was working.

"It was my fault." She was sobbing. Black streams of mascara tracked down her cheeks.

"Bonnie, you were just a kid. Accidents happen, even terrible ones. Living with the thought you were responsible for your brother's death had to be horrible. Think of Riley. Focus on her. Don't you want her to grow up to be a strong, independent woman who honors and respects you? Someday, she will ask who her father is. Are you going to feed her lies? The truth will eventually come out. It always does. Wouldn't it be better to face it now? You might lose Joanne as a friend, but it's better than living a lie and risking your daughter's anger." My speech had come from a genuine desire to help her. I was surprised.

"Joanne's not my friend. That bitch told a bunch of people I tried to kill myself. I'll bet she told Vini, and she told you. There's another one who can't keep her goddamn mouth shut."

I didn't admit she was right about Vini. "I'm glad you weren't successful, or Riley would have died with you. In time, everyone will forget. I haven't heard it mentioned in months. The hot topic now is Carter Dodd." Vini had told me Bonnie had been dating Carter on and off when she wasn't stalking Connor. "He stole a car and crashed into a truck. He's okay, but the police found cocaine and some sort of other drugs, and his trial is coming up soon."

This information distracted her. "What an idiot. I'm glad I dumped him." She stopped crying and finished her beer.

"Do you still insist Connor is Riley's father? Because if you do, it will turn out badly." I hoped something I said got through her thick skull and messed-up emotions, as Connor's demanding a paternity test and the possible backlash it would create might complicate our plans, so I hoped something I said intimidated her.

She didn't answer. She seemed to be thinking, if such a thing was possible. There wasn't much more I could say to convince her. I changed the subject.

"By the way, what's your problem with Vini, other than the pool incident?" Bonnie's nose was a testimonial to the two breaks she'd received, but she'd never believe she deserved them. "Why have you treated her so badly? And don't deny it. Vini doesn't lie. She may be a lot of things, but a liar isn't one of them."

"She's a colored person. Everyone knows they're lazy and useless."

If I thought I was shocked at seeing Bonnie, it wasn't half as shocking as her pronouncement. I didn't live in a vacuum, and it was a time of unrest, so I knew racism existed. I'd seen protests and uprisings on television, but this was my first collision with a racist.

"What are you talking about? How could you be so prejudiced? That's a stupid, ignorant thing to say. You're a colored person too! You're white with brown dots and flaming red hair. What if I told you that researchers discovered red-haired, freckled people were inherently crazy and prone to violent tempers?"

She touched her freckled cheeks as if suddenly they were offensive.

"Where did you learn such a ridiculous idea?" I was still incredulous.

"Don't you watch television or read newspapers? My dad told me black people don't belong in a white world. Neither do Jews or gays."

"Sorry, but your dad is wrong, and he's an idiot. Vini is sweet, kind, smart, generous, and beautiful. I'll bet that's why you don't like her. You're jealous!"

"Of her? You've got to be kidding."

"Not kidding! You also described my two other friends, who have more integrity in their little fingers than you have in your whole body, if you have any at all."

"Guess there's no accounting for taste."

"That's the kind of thinking that creates the violence and unrest in our world. Do you want Riley to grow up believing such trash?"

I sat beside her, placing my hand on hers in an attempt to be compassionate because I really believed it started with the kids. "Please, Bonnie, raise your little girl to love all people, and get your life together. Someday, a good man will want to be her father."

She pulled her hand back as if I had some rare disease but not before noticing my ring. "Did Connor give that to you?"

"Yes. We're planning on getting married next summer."

"Well, I guess you're the lucky one." She wiped her cheeks, which only smeared the mascara across her face; then she stood. "Tell Connor I wish him the best."

She climbed from the boat to the dock and walked toward the street, yelling over her shoulder, "Thanks for the beer. Have a nice life." There was very little sincerity in her voice.

I stood watching her, wondering if any of my speech had even dented her disturbed mind. It was not how I expected my day to turn out, but I felt a huge satisfying relief. I'd faced off with Bonnie. Vini would be proud of me. *I* was proud of me. I did another happy dance, and this time, I didn't knock anything over.

"I hope that's a new form of exercise. You look funny, dancing without music." The voice was Connor's.

I turned to face the dock. The McKenzie brothers were approaching—Connor smiling and Ricky laughing. Their dad was nowhere to be seen.

"I'm practicing for the show." I continued, adding some real dance moves, hoping it looked realistic.

"Those are some pretty funky moves. You'll have to teach me," Connor teased.

Ricky looked different—older. His curls were gone. His hair was shorter, with waves in front, slicked back with hair product. He was wearing skintight jeans with a loose denim shirt, open almost to his waist, exposing two gold chains around his neck. The cuffs were rolled up to his elbow. In six months, he'd transformed from a boy to a young man. I barely recognized him. His grin was the same, except his teeth were tracked with braces.

"Hey, Micaela! Long time, no see." I got a hug, but it lacked the exuberance it once had.

"You look amazing," I said. "I like your new haircut." It was true, but I missed the curls I'd grown to love.

"I'm a California dude now."

I looked at Connor, who shrugged. "I can see that."

Connor noticed the empty beer bottle. "Looks like you had company. Let me guess ... Bonnie?"

"How did you know? It could have been Jason or Owen. Maybe not Owen since he hates beer."

"We saw her at the bus stop when we pulled into the parking lot. It was an easy guess."

"She looked like shit," Ricky said.

"Cool the swearing, buddy."

"Why? You and Vini swear."

"Don't go by what we do. You don't swear! Got it? How about you unpack while Micaela and I go shopping for some food. We don't want you starving to death."

Connor handed him his suitcase. The other Ricky would have insisted on coming with us; the new version opened his backpack, took out a CD player, and popped in some ear buds.

"See ya!" he said as he disappeared into the galley.

As soon as we were near the parking lot, I asked Connor, "Did you really want to go shopping or just talk privately?"

"Both. I have very little food left that Ricky likes, and yeah, I want to know what happened with Bonnie."

"No biggie. She just dropped by to tell you she's going back to school and living with her mom. Oh, and she had a little girl." I didn't divulge the child's name, or Connor would become suspicious to Bonnie's real intention.

"I guess that's good. You sure that's all you talked about? She looked pretty rough."

"She cried when she told me she was sorry for involving you. Cheap mascara."

"She actually said she was sorry?"

"Not in so many words, but I got the gist."

Before Connor started the jeep, he paused as if a thought found its way into his mind. "Why do I sense you're not telling me the entire truth? That was far too easy. I've got a waiting-for-the-other-shoe-to-drop feeling." He looked at me with his serious face.

"No other shoe. I applied the Lewiski psychology, and it worked." At least, I hoped it worked.

Connor shook his head and turned the ignition. "You better not be acting right now. I don't want Bonnie hanging around and causing trouble."

"If you must know, I reminded her of the paternity test, and she kind of caved."

"What does *kind of* mean?"

"She started crying. She wished us a nice life."

"I guess that means you believe what I told you about her."

"Never doubted."

"Beautiful, talented, wise, and clever. Think I'll keep you."

"You're stuck with me."

He took my hand and kissed it. Life was good.

CHAPTER 36

The weeks flew by. Rehearsals and exams had to be primary, but I made one exception. The Saturday before my performance in *West Side Story* was the Van Halen concert. Connor had forgotten about his birthday present and had purchased tickets to a Chicago Bulls basketball game, which sent Ricky through the roof with excitement. I had no idea how we were going to manage both in the same day, considering the game was in Gainesville, nearly two hours from Tampa, but Connor assured me it was possible—he'd drive like a bat out of hell. *That* certainly wasn't happening. He said he was teasing, although I got the impression the bat might be fibbing. There was no way we were going to disappoint Ricky, who still idolized Michael Jordan, in spite of his new California persona. We also didn't want to let our friends down and not show up for the concert, so I agreed to maybe just a little speeding. It was tight, but we managed to enjoy the game, get Ricky back to the boat, and meet Jason, Owen, and Vini in front of the concert hall with ten minutes to spare—and no speeding ticket.

Rock concerts were, to me, like taking a cold shower—unpleasant but definitely stimulating. Connor played air guitar and mimed along to the songs he knew, while I tried to discern the lyrics. The thump, thump, thump of the bass resonated throughout the auditorium. It ricocheted off the walls, creating vibrations that pulsated through my feet and sent shock waves of throbbing rhythm up my spine with such intensity that I thought my brain was going to explode. Every so often, I'd glance down across the aisles where Vini, Jason, and Owen sat. Vini was bouncing around, waving her arms in the air and lost in rock-and-roll heaven. Jason stood and got Connor's attention, and the two of them pretended to duplicate Eddie Van Halen's guitar riffs. Owen, like me, looked as if he was enduring it for the man he loved. He looked at me, pointing to his ears. It took me a second to figure out his pantomime, but I got it—earplugs! Now why hadn't I thought of that?

After the concert, we met outside, and Vini was still bopping around and going on about how sexy David Lee Roth was. Our taste in men differed radically.

"If I wasn't already in a committed relationship, I'd let him into my bed," she said, still experiencing the residual energy created by the mass of crazed fans.

"Does Adrian know he's in a committed relationship with you?" Jason asked.

We all knew Vini's tendency to exaggerate. His accusation earned him a sisterly poke in the ribs.

"For your information, smart-ass, Adrian and I will be renting an apartment here in Tampa. I'm finishing my course next week, and beginning in September, I will manage a salon, and Adrian will be working at a bar. I forgot the name of it, but he's also taking courses in accounting during the day. So stuff that where the sun don't shine." You couldn't miss the smugness in Vini's voice.

"That's fantastic!" I hugged my friend. "When did all this happen?"

"If you and Connor could come up for air once in a while and weren't so damned busy, you'd have known."

Vini was right. We didn't see each other or talk on the phone as much as we used to. I made a pact with myself to rectify it and asked Connor if he minded driving Vini home so we could have some girl time. We said good night to Jason and Owen, who looked relieved they didn't have to drive all the way back to St. Pete. Owen knew an all-night bar he wanted to check out with Jason. He blew me a kiss and promised he wouldn't let Jason drink too much. He, on the other hand, intended to get plastered.

Vini and I huddled together in the back seat of the jeep. She shared every detail of her new romance, even the more intimate ones. I caught a glimpse of Connor looking at us in the rearview mirror. His raised eyebrows and crooked smile indicated he heard the juicy parts of our conversation. I smiled back. Vini was definitely in love, despite her lusting after David Lee Roth.

Connor came to both my performances. On the first night, he sat with Ricky and Dad. I was on an emotional roller coaster. Anxiety reached its pinnacle, then turned and became nervous jitters, and then suddenly I reached the peak again, and exhilaration took me right through the drop as the curtain closed on our third standing ovation. All three of my men met me backstage, each with flowers and hugs. Dad's eyes were glassed over, and his voice was husky with emotion.

"That was worth every penny of your tuition," he said.

"I liked it when Micaela sang 'I Feel Pretty,'" Ricky announced.

Dad cleared his throat. "Great job on the accent. I wish your mom could have seen it."

"When you were singing that 'Somewhere' song," Ricky said, "and Tony was dying in Maria's arms, Connor cried."

"No, I didn't," Connor replied emphatically. "I had something in my eye." Pulling me into an embrace, he looked into my eyes, as if examining them. "Were you really crying? Your voice even trembled. It was pretty powerful."

"Yes, those were real tears. I pictured you." The memory of pretending Connor was dying in my arms still lingered like a fog over my heart, and I leaned into him.

Later, after we'd driven Ricky to his dad's condo, Connor cashed in his rain check. We finally had a night to ourselves as Mr. McKenzie had requested an evening with Ricky. We made love like it was the first time—hungry for each other's touch, with a sense of urgency, and as if it was the last time, with a poignant need to be locked tightly in an embrace, our bodies fused for eternity.

The second performance was jinxed as soon as my leading man, Wes Langly, was replaced with his understudy. Wes irresponsibly went skateboarding that morning, and while trying to hurdle a ramp, he fell and broke his leg and cracked his stupid skull. During the performance, his understudy panicked, forgot some of his lines, and tripped over his own feet in a major dance scene. It wasn't a total fiasco, but it left me disappointed. I was glad Connor had experienced the first performance. Jason and Owen hardly noticed the faux pas and said it was as good as the movie. Owen added that it reminded him of Romeo and Juliet, only in a current New York setting. Vini loved it and, like always, wanted to celebrate. Owen seconded the motion. Again, I opted out of the cast party, preferring to be with the people I loved. In one week, I'd be leaving, and every moment counted. I also was starving, so we headed for the only all-night restaurant in Clearwater.

Time is a thief. It steals every second, minute, and hour, hoarding each day and month with no intention of giving them back. It left in its wake a series of fleeting memories, stored in a vault within the recesses of my mind, and I wanted to make more of them.

Connor was able to join us and asked how my performance went. I told him he'd seen the better one.

I glanced around the table at the four people who'd come to mean so much to me. I wondered where time would take us. I'd miss Owen's glib demeanor and oddball sense of humor, Jason's constant bantering with his sister, and Vini—dear Vini—whose outspoken candor and vibrant personality had changed my life. If it hadn't been for her boldly approaching me, I would never have met Connor, a debt of gratitude it would take a lifetime to repay. Connor and I would be together again after Christmas, but the time between my leaving and then would be torment.

While I devoured a burger, Vini savored a hot fudge sundae. Jason ordered his usual beer, and Owen had a double martini. Connor and Jason reminisced about some crazy stuff they'd done as kids. Owen and I listened, and Vini laughed hysterically when they recounted one of their antics that included her. Owen lifted his glass in a toast and gestured to me.

"Here's to you, kiddo. You know what those guys are doing, don't you?"

I shook my head.

"They're trying not to think about you flying off to Neverland in one week, and all of us going our separate ways."

Vini heard him, put down her chocolate-covered spoon, and sat quietly. Tears flooded her eyes, and she wiped them away before doing any serious damage to her eye makeup. I couldn't recall ever seeing her cry. As bold and open as she was, there was a sensitive, private side she never exposed. I reached for her hand, held it, and squeezed, hoping to convey the affection I felt for her.

"I'll be back next year for the wedding. The time will fly by with your new job and Adrian. We can call once in a while." I tried to reassure her, but I felt the same sadness. We all knew this day was coming, but it didn't make it easier.

"It won't be the same." The tears escaped. "Growing up sucks."

"Can't say I agree with you." Owen tossed back the rest of his martini. "My childhood was a screaming hell, and I like this adult gig." He motioned for the waiter and provided a quick change of subject by asking Connor a question. "When do you start university?"

"Won't be until next September, unfortunately. I have unfinished business here, but as soon as I get it settled, I'll be joining Micaela in New York, hopefully before Christmas."

Jason contributed his own attempt at cheering Vini up. "Hey, sis! Maybe you can help Owen and me find a new apartment."

He was successful. The somber atmosphere had lightened, and Vini perked up.

"How come you're moving?" She went back to scraping the remains of chocolate from the side of the dish.

"We've decided to move closer to Tampa. I've given up on the California thing," Jason explained.

"But what about your dream of being a set designer?" I asked. Following one's dream was huge in my book.

"Hear him out," Owen interjected.

"Well, I like designing, but it doesn't have to be sets in Hollywood. I just thought, 'cause I'm black and gay, it would be easier there, but Owen convinced me it wouldn't matter where we go; bigots are everywhere. We have friends in Tampa, and Owen's right. Here, I might be the big fish in a small pond. I'm opening my own design company, and Owen will manage it."

Owen accepted his third martini and lifted his glass again. "Hear, hear, to that."

Vini was thrilled. At least she wasn't going to lose her brother too. Connor congratulated Jason on his decision.

"I've got an idea!" We all stopped and looked at Vini. She always had an idea. "How about we celebrate, and make it a going-away party for Micaela too."

"Sounds good to me." Owen finished his third martini, and Jason leaned into him and whispered in his ear. I guessed it had something to do with how much alcohol Owen was consuming and a directive not to order any more.

"So what do you think?" Vini's mood had certainly changed. "Maybe the Blue Lagoon for old times' sake." She licked her spoon.

"I don't think Micaela would want to go there," Connor said.

"Why not?" I looked at him. "It's interesting, the music is good, and Adrian works there." I knew exactly why she chose the Blue Lagoon.

"I'm giving my notice on Saturday, so I might not be able to get it off," Jason said.

Vini wasn't going to let that be a problem. "We'll go on Friday night, when it's not as busy, and you can sneak some time away. What's the worst thing that can happen? That Joe fires you?" She laughed, and Jason shrugged. "Okay, then, it's a date." Vini had spoken, and it was settled.

I hated disappointing Connor, but I was too exhausted to spend the night on the boat and wanted to curl up in my own bed. I'd promised Dad we'd spend Sunday morning breakfast together, like we used to. I avoided telling Connor I didn't feel well and that the last few mornings I'd woken up feeling like I'd been hit by a truck. He didn't need to know, or he'd worry about me. I put it down to exams and the play. Getting sick right now wasn't in my game plan. I'd also missed my period, but that too could be because of all the stress of the past two months. At least, I hoped it was.

CHAPTER 37

Now

Dinner with Vini at the CN Tower was an extravagant indulgence. She'd already put a lot on her Visa card at three major clothing stores, and it would take a serious hit after paying the bill for dinner. I surprised myself by eating more than I had in a week. It was too expensive and delicious to waste.

"Looks like your appetite has returned," Vini said. "You packed that away pretty good. How about something yummy for dessert?"

I passed, but Vini, of course, ordered a triple-fudge brownie drowning in chocolate syrup, with mounds of whipped cream and chocolate shavings.

"I thought you were complaining about getting fat?"

"I'm watching my weight ... watching it increase." She patted her stomach. "I do pretty well during the week, but this is a special occasion." She thought about what she'd said and clarified it. "Not exactly special. I didn't it mean quite that way because of your dad … that's sad, but being with you is special."

"You know what they say about women who crave chocolate?"

"No! What do the infamous *they* say?"

"It's a substitute for sex."

"Well, *they* are wrong. Goes to show you—you can't trust anything *they* say." Vini called the waiter over and ordered the decadent dessert. I ordered a coffee.

"Guess that new guy you told me you were dating worked out."

"Hardly! He was a huge disappointment. One of those 'Wham! Bam! Thank you, ma'am' types. I'm seeing a guy I met at the gym. He's not too bright but dynamite in the sack."

"Vini, you're incorrigible. What about love?"

"Been there. Done that. Threw away the T-shirt!"

"And …"

"He died."

If Vini meant to shock me, she succeeded. "I'm so sorry. I didn't know."

"Yes, you did!"

"You never told me. I'm sure I'd remember something so devastating."

"It's not important. It was a long time ago." Vini glanced out the window at the Toronto skyline as it passed slowly in front of us. "This is pretty cool. Now I can say I've been to a revolving restaurant." It was evident the subject of her lost love was closed.

I couldn't recall a man in Vini's life—someone she'd loved, someone who had died. An uneasy sensation clawed at my nerves, and I suddenly felt nauseated and wanted to leave. I waited patiently for Vini to finish her dessert while I sipped my coffee. Nothing more was said.

We hailed a cab to take us where I'd parked my car and drove home in silence. I was immersed in guilt for not remembering something so important to Vini, and she seemed lost in her memories, staring blankly out the window.

The overpowering smell of flowers greeted us when we walked through my front door.

"Smells like a friggin' flower shop in here." Vini kicked off her shoes and headed for the living room sofa. "You have any of that wine left?"

"Just enough for a glass each."

Vini looked at her watch. "It's still early. You up to a nightcap?"

"I think I can manage it." I'd already used up my energy reserves, but it was my last evening with Vini, and I wasn't sure when I'd see her again.

The wine bottle still sat on the dining room table where I'd left it. Everywhere I looked, there were flower baskets, along with the three large boxes of Dad's belongings on the table. I couldn't bear the thought of going through them. I'd wait until the weekend when Jess was able to help.

Vini was curled up at the end of the sofa, scrolling through her phone, when I returned with the wine. I curled up in the opposite corner. "I think I'll take the flowers to the nursing home tomorrow."

"I thought you liked flowers." Vini put her phone on the coffee table.

"I do. Just not those. I'd prefer not to be reminded of what they represent."

"If I remember correctly, your favorite flowers are lilacs and white roses. You were wearing lilac perfume the night ..." Vini glanced down at her skirt. "Oh, stupid me. I got chocolate syrup on my good skirt. You wouldn't have a cold cloth?"

I went to the kitchen to find something to wipe her skirt. Her reference to my love of lilacs had tripped a memory. I returned to the living room and handed her the damp cloth.

"By the way, it wasn't perfume. It was body spray. Connor gave it to me on my birthday. I used it on my hair."

The recollection of Connor nuzzling my neck and sniffing my hair made me freeze. We'd been dancing—the song was "One More Night" by Phil Collins. The lyrics played back clearly in my head.

I could feel Connor's hands stroking my back as if it was actually happening. It consumed my senses. Then … nothing. The dark void returned, as it always did.

"Are you all right? You look like you've seen a ghost."

"I'm good. Probably just the aftermath of a difficult and emotional week." I sipped at the wine, hoping to steady my nerves.

"So! Look at us," Vini said. "Two post-middle-aged women. Where the hell did the time go? The future just creeps up on us. Remember how we made jokes about being old ladies together?"

"Not so sure it's creeping; more like long jumps." I didn't remind her my longevity was in question.

I asked her about Owen, hoping it wouldn't be sad news. Vini took a deep breath, and I braced myself. I couldn't imagine that he and Jason had broken up. They were inseparable.

"Owen died in a plane crash."

"No! When? My God!" Owen's face was imprinted on my mind. My heart stuttered; my breathing came in short bursts.

"It was a private plane. A friend of his. He died too. They were flying back from his sister's wedding in Washington. They hit some bad weather, and that's pretty much all I know. Jason told me the night before Owen left that he'd called and said he'd had a nightmare about the plane crashing. He was scared shitless, but it didn't stop him."

I was barely listening. I could hear Owen's voice; see him sitting with me in the office of the Blue Lagoon, sharing his sad story about his parents; the night we met at Jason's party; dancing with me at the Halloween party; and dozens of other memories. I never realized how much I missed him until this moment. "When did it happen?"

"It was just after you had the baby."

I was stunned and didn't even react to her reference to my lost child. "I can't even begin to comprehend this. What's the matter with me? Maybe the cancer has affected my brain. I feel terrible. I can't remember someone you loved dying, and now Owen. Oh my God! Poor Jason!"

"He's fine now. Rough in the beginning. He even tried to commit suicide. Good thing he sucked at it. He's with someone else now. Ken's a sweetie. They met at a grief counseling session. Ken lost his partner as well, to cancer. They've been together nearly twenty-four years."

"Why can't I remember?" The frustration was eating at my nerves.

"To be fair, I didn't tell you about Owen."

"Why would you not tell me? I loved him too. I can't believe you wouldn't tell me. Why Vini? How could you do that?"

"Think back. You were pretty messed up. You'd just given up your son and were seeing a psychiatrist, and you'd started drinking heavily. On top of that, you were about to audition for your first big Broadway part in *West Side Story*. Jason and I thought it would mess you up even more. Then time went by, and we rarely saw or even heard from you. I'm sorry."

"What you're saying is, I am too weak and thoughtless."

"That's a bit extreme, and it was just so long ago."

"Well, what do you mean, exactly?" I was angry.

"Remember, I call it how it is. So ... yes, you were a little self-absorbed. You went through a lot, but you weren't the only one who lost someone. I get why you gave up the baby, but you never called me the entire time you were pregnant, and when I tried to see you in New York, you didn't want to have anything to do with me. Maybe I just didn't want to tell you. I was hurt, and I guess I thought you wouldn't care."

"Not easy to be sympathetic when you have no idea what happened. As far as not calling you, I just didn't want any reminders of Connor. I was hurting and confused. For that, I am sorry, but like you said, it was a long time ago."

"If you'd bothered to call Jason or me, then you would have known."

It was hard not to miss the contempt in Vini's tone, and it startled me. I had heard it before when we were teenagers, but it was another one of those things I'd forgotten.

"I had my reasons, and you know that."

"I get it, but I don't think Jason does. He knows he's a huge reminder of Connor, but he hasn't been able to wrap his head around why you won't face reality."

"Do you really understand?"

"I do. I guess we each deal with loss in a different way."

My head felt like it was in a compression chamber. "If you're talking about Connor's deserting me when I was pregnant, after everything he said to me, and asking me to marry him, and having to give up our son, then yes, you're right. My way was to put it behind me and get on with my life. I chose not to dwell on it. When Connor didn't return my letters or calls, I was devastated. His number was no longer in service. I couldn't get hold of Ricky, and I was scared. ... No, not just scared ... terrified. If it hadn't been for Aunt Florence, I don't know what I would have done. She's the one who sent me to a therapist when I started having the black-outs, but it only made it worse. The drinking came later. It was my way of numbing myself. It was stupid, and it cost me parts I wanted desperately, so I stopped. You make it sound like I was an alcoholic. My heart bleeds for Jason's loss, and I wish I could turn back time, but I can't."

"Okay, I'm sorry. And for the record, Connor didn't desert you."

"How can you say that?" Anger had a vise grip on my throat. "Then where is he?"

I saw her mouth twitch, which meant she was hiding something. Vini's facial expressions always gave her away. Her attention returned to dabbing at the stain on her skirt. My guess was that the stain never existed in the first place. It was simply a diversion.

"If you know something, for God's sake tell me."

She didn't respond. She reached for her wine and sipped it.

"You know, don't you? Vini, talk to me? You've been keeping something from me all these years, haven't you?" Shock increased my anger.

"Sweetie, let's not do this." Vini finished her wine and placed the glass on the coffee table. As she reached for her phone, I grabbed her wrist.

"Don't *sweetie* me. Damn it, Vini! I'm not some weak, neurotic, pathetic woman who will fall apart—at least, not anymore. You're hiding something, and you've got to tell me."

She wrenched her arm free. "You've had a long day, Micaela, and I have an early flight in the morning. I'm calling it a night." She headed for the stairs.

This didn't register as real. I felt I had fallen off a cliff into a raging sea, badly broken but still alive. I wanted to climb back up and find it had all been a bad dream. "Why are you doing this to me?"

"I'm not doing anything. You're doing it to yourself. Good night."

She retreated, leaving me feeling betrayed and confused. The safe little world I had constructed over the years was crumbling, and I didn't feel so safe anymore.

Sleep was impossible. The argument with Vini stirred up thoughts and feelings that wouldn't leave me alone. Shutting down the memory center of my brain for the past thirty years had been easy, considering I'd gone from numbing memories with alcohol and one-night stands with men I barely knew to being a wife, mom, and teacher and filling my days with meaningless tasks. In time, I'd succeeded in building my wall. Now, it was forming cracks and allowing visions to seep through, testing the endurance of my emotions. Maybe it was true. Maybe I was weak and pathetic. But nothing justified Vini's keeping something so vitally important from me.

Dreams of Connor kept coming. They were like a road map to some obscure destination I didn't want to visit. There was something I was missing. Had dark forces in my brain sabotaged my recollection? Did I know where Connor was? Did Bonnie actually resurface? Was I lied to the entire time for some reason that eluded me? It just didn't seem possible.

I always knew, at some level, that being with Vini might force memories to surface—memories that hurt too much. There was always that niggling discomfort. How would I ever forgive her if she knew where Connor went and why? How could she say he didn't desert me? Even as I thought about it, I sensed an uneasy agitation in my gut. Not telling me about Owen was just as unforgivable. And trying to justify it by claiming I was unstable was, in my estimation, more cruel than not telling me. Vini's comments were more like heat-seeking missiles aimed directly at my wall.

For the first time in many years, I felt an urge for something stronger than herbal tea. Jack had forgotten to take a bottle of scotch that was somewhere in the kitchen pantry. I'd kept it. Why? I didn't know. I'd forgotten about it until now. I decided the hell with the cancer and my resolution to be more health-conscious. Cancer had a mind of its own anyway. Losing Dad and the possibility of Vini's betrayal seemed good enough justification for indulging my craving.

I sat at the dining room table, staring at Dad's boxes, overwhelmed by the powerful scent of lilies and orchids. Rather than reminding me of the scent of a tropical island, it called up the long-forgotten memory of Mom's funeral. It struck me; I had just become an orphan.

I swirled the alcohol in my glass, watching the light from the chandelier reflect like tiny diamonds in the crystal. I didn't want to try to remember anything … just drift on a current of passivity, letting it take me along its path until it emptied into a sea of emotion so vast I would drown and be lost forever. I swallowed the scotch in one gulp, letting it burn its way into my stomach, sending warm tendrils of fortification through my nervous system. I continued to stare at the boxes. I poured another drink. I wouldn't wait for Jess. I could face it alone and continue on my path to oblivion until my mind ceased to function.

I opened the largest box first. Dad's books were on the top: *A Tale of Two Cities, Moby Dick, The Adventures of Huckleberry Finn,* and *Crime and Punishment*—all classics that kids nowadays wouldn't be familiar with. Dad loved reading. His shaving kit, glasses, and watch were next. I finished my drink and poured another glass of fortification. His old, well-worn navy-blue sweater—the one he'd been wearing the last time I visited him—was folded on top of his other clothes and shoes. It had to be over forty years old. The elbows were worn, and snags of yarn protruded in areas, but that wouldn't have concerned Dad. My collection of Dad memories usually included that sweater.

A familiar tightness formed in my chest as my hand brushed across the sleeve. I held it close and hugged it, trying to recapture Dad's essence. A faint smell of Old Spice Lime aftershave, his signature scent, still lingered on the fabric. Closing my eyes, I pictured Dad and me sitting at our dining room table in St. Pete, playing Scrabble. He'd been wearing that sweater, and even then, it looked worn and old. I could visualize him as he placed letters on the board.

"Dad, there is no such word as *dinkel.* You're cheating!" I'd said.

"Sorry, you're wrong." His comment echoed from the past. "It's a masculine noun in German, referring to the male organ in mammals. In other words, penis! And don't look so shocked."

"Okay, then!" I countered with the Ukrainian word *pizda,* using Dad's I and tripling my score. Now Dad looked shocked.

"Where on earth did you hear that?"

"When we visited Aunt Florence the summer I was thirteen. She yelled it at the woman who lived across the street. I looked it up."

"That's strange, coming from such a Bible-thumper like your aunt. If I'd said it, she'd have hung the rosary beads around my neck and made me recite ten Hail Marys." Dad laughed so hard I was afraid he'd give himself a hernia.

The image dissolved. I kissed the sweater and placed it back in the box. I took a deep breath and another sip of my drink ... then another sip ... and opened the second box. Three framed pictures of Mom and two of me were tucked in with more of Dad's clothes. I pulled them out and propped them on the table. I removed a picture of Jack, me, and Jess when she was three, and put it aside. Another picture was of my high school graduation. I stared into the eyes of my seventeen-year-old self. All my hopes and dreams stared back at me. I was going to take on the world.

"What happened to you? How did you get here, Micaela Anne Lewiski?" I spoke the words to the optimistic young woman I used to be.

I finished my third drink and was beginning to feel light-headed and welcomed it. Something shiny caught my eye at the bottom of the box, peeking out from under Dad's jacket ... another box, a black velvet container with three brightly colored butterflies etched in the top. Waves of recognition flooded my mind. Dad had kept my memory box. I'd left it behind the day I'd flown to New York. My resolve to keep fortifying my wall was obliterated by the nostalgic longing for the past, probably intensified by the alcohol. I placed the box in front of me and tentatively opened the lid. Two Playbills were on the top—*The Sound of Music* and *West Side Story*. I smiled remembering how good I'd felt and how strongly I loved the theater. My dog Chippy's heart collar and Mom's pearl necklace lay on top of something shiny and gold. My breath caught, and my heart skipped. Looking up at me were my tiny angel and dolphin. It was as if they were saying, "Remember us? Where have you been for so long? Why did you forsake us?"

I lifted the bracelet and kissed each one and then returned it to its rightful place on my wrist. They danced together, happy to be home. The day Connor had given it to me played like a movie in my mind's eye. I simply let it pass. It didn't produce the pain it would have prior to the alcohol.

I found at least two dozen photographs. My thoughts drifted back to the moment each was taken. I kissed the picture of Owen with his wine glass in one hand and a martini in the other, while Jason made bunny ears over his head.

"Owen, wherever you are, thank you for being my friend and all you did to help me. I wasn't a very good friend to you." My tears flowed. Owen deserved them.

There were several of Jason and Owen together. There was one I took of them kissing. I'd hidden it from Dad. He would never have understood, even though I learned later that his stand on gays was, "To each his own." I flipped through my Vini photos. Vini in her Cindy Lauper costume; Vini in a purple bikini, posing like a model on the beach; Vini with her mom, standing outside their house in St. Pete—I put that one to one side, thinking she might want it—and then the four of them together, with Connor, the tallest, standing in the middle. There he was. Up until this moment, he'd inhabited my dreams—his image, vague, distorted by time—but the picture brought him to life as he was then. The quirky smile, the thick mane of brown hair with the piece that constantly fell across his forehead, and the expressive amber eyes that crinkled at the corners when he smiled. I flipped the picture over to see when it was taken. *June '89* was printed in ink...two months before Connor left me.

My brain was fuzzy, as if filling slowly with candy floss. Memories were sticking but overlapping and confusing me. I wondered if time had been kind to him. Did he look like his father, with thinning hair, combing it to one side in an attempt to look youthful, or did he have a distinguished, ageless look and kept that gorgeous hair? I would never know. Another picture of Connor and Ricky, taken before Ricky went all California cool, made me smile. I wondered where Ricky had ended up. I hoped he was happy. Perhaps he was with Connor somewhere. I'd never said goodbye to him. The last time I'd seen him was the night before my going-away party, and it was also the last photo taken of him and Connor with my camera. We had gone out for dinner and told him our big news. I didn't have to ask him if he was happy. He'd jumped up, knocked over his chair, and yelled, "Hey, everyone! I'm getting a new sister."

Connor and I didn't look old enough to be Ricky's parents, but two people came to our table and congratulated us on my pregnancy. Very embarrassing and awkward, having to explain what he really meant. I smiled at the irony of the situation. At the time, I'd suspected I was pregnant but didn't find out for sure until two weeks after arriving in New York. By then, Connor was nowhere to be found, and I was left to deal with it on my own.

The rest of the pictures were all of Connor. One of him standing on the deck of the *Micaela*, his hair tousled by the wind, and a funny one of him and Ricky at the basketball game, making silly faces. I had forgotten the one Connor took of me on the beach while I took a picture of him. The photo Vini took when I was walking across the stage at the Blue Lagoon with Jason made me smile, and then, the one of Connor I especially liked and put in a frame—him standing by the rail of his boat, the glow of the sunset creating an aura around him.

I spoke to his image as if he were standing in front of me. "How could you have stopped loving me? What happened to always and forever? Why did you ask me to marry you and tell me you were coming to New York? You seemed so sincere. Was I really that gullible and needy that I fell for it, or did something happen to make you change your mind? I never got to tell you I was pregnant."

I felt tears pushing their way into existence but fought them back. "We had a son. I gave him up, Connor. I didn't want to, but I had to. I couldn't raise a child on my own, and Aunt Florence made me do it. I tried contacting you. The marina told me your boat had been sold. Why would you want to disappear again?"

A spark ignited in my brain. "Vini told you I was pregnant, didn't she? You couldn't handle it, just like with Bonnie."

The anguish and confusion I had been feeling when Vini and I had argued returned. It became a deep, seething anger—for Connor and for Vini. I was tempted to charge upstairs and confront her. It made perfect sense. That's what she was hiding. Instead, I finished my drink. My stomach churned. Vini's comment, *He didn't desert you*, now held new meaning. No, of course not; he left deliberately. He wouldn't have thought it was desertion. I stared again at his face, and all my thoughts scattered like mice. No … that couldn't be true. Connor was a deeply caring, loving man. He loved me. Something was pushing up through the mess of emotions and quagmire of debris left by my muddled thoughts. Flashes of images … Vini, her face smeared in blood, crying and screaming; a torn and twisted body, the face barely recognizable, staring up at me blankly; Owen, his shirt and face covered in something black; blood streaming from his forehead; and Connor, carrying Jason.

A lightning bolt of pain seared my brain, and the images evaporated, leaving a nagging dread in their wake. I grasped the end of the table to stop the spinning. *"Micaela, breathe. Focus on me."* The words rippled in the air, but they weren't mine. Connor's voice resonated around me—through me. Instinctively, I turned to look behind me, knocking the velvet container and sending it crashing to the floor, spilling the remaining contents. A small blue jeweler's box lay at my feet. I knew what was inside. As I bent to retrieve it, waves of nausea closed the door to any conscious thought. I stumbled into the living room, knowing I would never be able to navigate the stairs to my room. I wanted to pass out and give in to the swirling ebb of darkness consuming my mind. I collapsed on the couch and wept until I escaped into the black abyss.

CHAPTER 38

Then

Each pivotal moment in our lives—a first tooth, a first step, a first word—signifies forward movement in our development. Then there is a first love. Every other moment gets swallowed up by the magnitude of its existence, and we are suspended in a bubble, floating through time. Reality is shaped by our desire. Who we are and what we become all centers around our driving need to express the depth of that love and feel its reciprocation.

Those were the words I wrote in my journal, and I believed them with all my heart. Connor had become the core of my universe, and everything else was secondary. He was my addiction, the drug of my soul. Each day felt brand new—the sun brighter, the sky bluer, and the smell of flowers more intoxicating.

I continued to write:

> Real love is what's left over after the initial wanting passes, when lust is satiated, and the desire and anticipation of its expression burns away, settling quietly in the soul, strengthened by harmonic cadence with its recipient. All else is self-serving and only masquerades as love.

There were five more empty pages. The irony was not lost on me. There were five more days until I closed this chapter of my life and started a new one. I flipped back to my beginning entries, a week before leaving Toronto. I read the words describing my excitement at being accepted at college and moving to Florida. The intensity and passion of my dream shouted from every sentence. It wasn't nullified by loving Connor, but without him, it all seemed like empty ambition. At the time I wrote it, I had not given much thought to what my personal life would look like. I'd assumed the gratification of realizing my dream would supersede all other needs. I was wrong! Six months ago, I dreaded leaving. My fear of losing Connor and saying goodbye to my friends dampened my enthusiasm but not my appetite for success. Knowing Connor would be joining me in December and that we would be married in a year made my future brighter than I'd ever imagined in any of my fantasies.

Everything seemed to be falling into place except for one problem. I still hadn't gotten my period, and it was now two weeks late. I was normally quite regular, but I wasn't ready to panic. With the play, exams, and preparations for my move to New York, I'd flooded my body with enough stress hormones to disrupt my cycle. My hope was that it wouldn't announce itself before Friday. It was our last chance to be together and make love before I left on Sunday. I didn't want it spoiled. Saturday, Connor had excursions, I had to finish packing, and I'd promised my last evening to dad. Connor was driving me to the airport. Except for what I'd need for the next five days, I started packing. My journal went into my carry-on. I'd complete it on the plane. Dad poked his head in my room while I was pulling clothes from my closet.

"Micaela, I'd like to talk with you. I've made some tea."

I joined him in the kitchen.

"So ... looks like this is it. My little girl is heading out into the world. You ready for it?"

"As ready as I can be."

"I sold your car this morning ... got four hundred dollars for it." He passed me an envelope. "It should help a bit."

I passed it back. "It's your money."

He passed it again to me. "Just say thank you."

I accepted it. "Okay, thank you."

"Are you all right? You look a little pale."

"I'm fine." I sipped my tea. "Just stress catching up with me and the realization I'm leaving people I love behind."

"Not totally." Dad explained he'd accepted a teaching position at the University of Toronto. "Maybe you might visit from time to time. That is, if you're not too busy. I can fly to New York and stay with your aunt and see you in plays. It sure would be nice if you could come home for Thanksgiving."

I smiled. Dad still thought of Toronto as home.

"I found a two-bedroom apartment near the university."

"It's a date." I finished my tea and got up to put the cup in the sink, but Dad stopped me.

"Not so fast. There's something else I have to say. If you think I'm stupid enough to believe you and Connor aren't planning something, then you have rocks for brains."

I tried pretending that I had no idea of what Dad was suggesting. "What do you mean?"

"I'm sure his choosing New York University isn't just a coincidence. Pretty convenient, if you ask me. I suspect you two are moving in together.

This surprised me.

"Don't look so startled. I overheard you talking on the phone about Connor applying to NYU. Promise ring be damned. I'm not *that* gullible. Just tell me you're not getting married right away."

"Yes, on your first assumption, and no, not until next year." I held my breath waiting for a lecture.

"No eloping or any of that nonsense. I want to be able to walk my girl down the aisle."

"Does that mean you're not against the idea?" I felt suddenly hopeful.

Dad took my hand and kissed my knuckles. "I don't think you want one of my speeches. The way I figure it, you can't fight the inevitable. You and Connor will find your own way. It wouldn't make any difference what I thought anyway. You've got that stubborn streak. Why are you crying?"

"I'm happy. I felt awful not telling you." I explained our plans and told Dad about Connor's trust fund.

"Seems like you two have it all figured out. Your mom would sure be excited to plan a wedding. Sure wish she was here."

"Me too. Vini is all hyped up and wants to plan it … and speaking of Vini …" I looked at the clock. "I promised her I'd meet her downtown, and now that I have to take public transit, I'd better get a move on."

"How 'bout I drive you?"

I accepted his offer. For the first time in months, I felt completely relaxed with Dad. His acceptance surprised me, and I was right—people could change.

Vini wanted to meet at Carley's Burgers, but the thought of greasy food made me gag. We settled on the restaurant across from the marina. The *Micaela* wasn't in her slip, which meant Connor was working a tour. He'd arranged a late dinner with Ricky to share our news, so I had a few hours to kill. I ordered a tuna sandwich, and Vini ordered her usual cheeseburger. It didn't seem to matter what restaurant we chose; Vini always had a cheeseburger and fries.

After several minutes of listening to Vini recount a movie she'd seen on the weekend and how stupid it was, I told her that Dad figured out Connor and I were planning on living together and getting married, and he'd accepted it.

"Well, now that's out of way, I guess you feel better. Are you coming back for graduation ceremonies?"

"Don't think so. Dad is moving back to Toronto the end of August, and I don't have the funds to make the trip. I can't ask him to pay for it after all he's done for me."

"I don't think it really matters. It's just a stupid ritual anyway." She reached for the ketchup bottle and proceeded to drown her fries. "I start my new job in two weeks. Then I'm looking for an apartment for Adrian and me. He's giving his notice at work this weekend. I get horny just thinking about him. My mom will have a shit fit when she finds out. She's not into this sexual revolution stuff. To quote her, 'It's the ruination of the sanctity of marriage.' Whole lot of good marriage did her. Maybe if she'd lived with my father for a while, she would have found out what an asshole he was before being saddled with two kids. When you think about it, what difference does a piece of paper make? Either a guy is committed to the relationship, or he isn't. I don't care about the marriage thing, and I'm not sure I even want children."

"Our mothers would have gotten along well." I recalled the speech Mom gave me when I was thirteen and started menstruating. She passed along a phrase her mother had told her: "Why should he buy the cow when he can get the milk for free?" It took me a year to figure out what she meant.

Vini had already finished her burger and was working on her fries when I noticed several people leaving the marina and a new batch heading down the dock. That would be Connor's second group. One more to go. I barely touched my sandwich. My stomach felt a bit queasy.

"I'm spending the night at Adrian's place on Friday after the party," Vini said. "It's my first sleepover. I get tingly just thinking about it." She showed me her arm. There were definitely goosebumps. "The shitty part is, I got my period today. I sure hope I'm finished with the damn thing by then." She slathered more ketchup on her fries and shoved one in her mouth. "Doesn't matter. There's a lot of stuff you can do anyway. Adrian loves blow jobs."

"Vini! I'm going to pretend I didn't hear that."

"Oh, don't be such a prude. I'll bet Connor likes it too. You should be finished with your period by now, so you and Connor will be good to go."

"I haven't started yet."

"You're always finished about two weeks before I get mine." She stopped stuffing fries into her mouth and stared at me. "You're not pregnant are you?"

"It's just been two weeks. It's no big deal."

"What do you mean, no big deal? That's too long. Is there even a possibility? You guys always use a condom, right?"

I was quiet.

"You're kidding!"

"There was one time we didn't. I told Connor it was okay because I wasn't ovulating. I keep track. It was just that one time."

"One time is all it takes. For someone who's so smart, that was pretty dumb."

"Do you think you could pass on the judgment call? I already know it was irresponsible, and I'm having trouble coping with the possibility. Right now, I'm not sure."

"Well, get sure. This is pretty serious."

"That's stating the obvious." I tried swallowing a bite of the sandwich, but it felt like it was stuck in my throat.

"You're pregnant! You just bit my head off, and you look as if you're going to cry—sure signs!"

I couldn't deny thinking about it, and Vini was adding to my concern. "Vini, I'm scared."

She reached for my hand. "I know. The first thing we're going to do is go to the pharmacy and buy one of those home pregnancy test kits."

"Now?"

"Yes, now. Finish your lunch. We can go to my place, and Connor can pick you up there."

Sitting in Vini's bathroom, waiting for the test strip to provide a result was, to me, like those minutes before death when your life is supposed to flash through your mind. All my plans and dreams could be obliterated in one final moment. I closed my eyes and prayed, hoping this was all a waste of time; that I would be granted my dreams and not have them stolen from me because of one thoughtless decision. I opened my eyes. The strip indicated a negative. Relief swept through every cell of my body, and I said a silent thank-you. Vini sat on the edge of the tub, across from me, reading the directions.

"It says here the morning pee is the most accurate. Also, a negative result is not conclusive in the early weeks. There's also something about a false positive. I think you need to try again in about a week." She placed the instructions back in the box and handed it to me. "I would also suggest you find a doctor as soon as you get to New York."

I handed the box back to her. "I can't take it with me and risk Connor or Dad seeing it. Throw it out."

"Are you going to tell Connor?"

"No! Not unless I find out for sure. There's no point in having him worry about something that's not definite."

"Suit yourself."

"Please don't tell Jason or mention this to your mom."

"Who do you think I am? The local gossip queen?"

I shot her a look that signified the possibility of her owning that title.

"Okay, maybe a little, but my lips are sealed." She pretended to run a zipper across her mouth. "Promise me you'll call as soon as you know. I kind of like the idea of being an aunt."

I gently swatted her knee. "That's not the least bit funny."

"Didn't intend it to be. Cheer up; it will all work out."

"You sound like my dad."

"Wanna see what I'm wearing Friday night? It's a designer knock-off, and it's so incredibly sexy."

I welcomed the change of subject.

Vini was modeling a plum-colored cocktail mini-dress with a deep V neckline when the doorbell rang. She was right; it was incredibly sexy.

Connor and Ricky waited in the jeep until Vini and I hugged goodbye.

"See ya Friday night, girl. We are going to look hot, hot, hot." She waved at Connor, and he waved back.

I slipped into the passenger seat, and Connor leaned over and kissed me. Ricky sat in the back seat. He had his ear buds in and his transistor radio on his lap, and he was bopping around like a fish on the end of a hook. He didn't even look up.

"You okay?" Connor asked. "You look tired."

"Didn't sleep well last night, but I'm fine."

"How was your day?"

"Just ordinary, nothing special." I completely forgot to tell him about what dad had said.

"Let's see if we can rectify that."

I cleared my mind of worry and leaned over and kissed him. "Connor McKenzie, you're my something special."

"How about you keep telling me that for the rest of my life?"

"You have a deal."

CHAPTER 39

I decided nothing was going to spoil my last evening with Connor and my friends, not even the possibility I was pregnant. There was no point dwelling on something I had no control over. The pregnancy test indicated a negative, and judging by the ache in my lower back, which always accompanied the onset of my period, I had nothing to worry about, except its making an appearance sometime this evening.

Connor requested I wear the red dress I'd worn the night of our first kiss. Other than the black taffeta cocktail dress I'd worn to the New Year's party, it was the only evening dress I owned, so it was an easy decision. I couldn't buy a new one anyway, unlike Vini, who would prefer to go a month without chocolate than wear the same dress twice. How she was able to afford it, I never asked. Her mom worked two jobs. Probably one of them was to support her daughter's fashion addiction.

Dad had to work late to tie up loose ends at his office and was training someone to fill his position, so he wouldn't be home when Connor picked me up. We'd arranged for the three of us to have breakfast together in the morning before Connor drove me to the airport.

I hadn't told Dad where the party was. By Florida law, I was still under drinking age. I let him assume the party was at Connor's parents' house—a huge omission but a necessary one.

As soon as I saw Connor approach the front door of the apartment building, my heart did one of those fluttery things. He wasn't a shirt-and-tie kind of guy, always preferring a more casual look, but he'd exchanged his jean jacket for a black blazer with the sleeves rolled up just below his elbows. He wore it open, exposing a white crew-neck T-shirt and slim-fit black jeans. The dark aviator sunglasses reminded me of Tom Cruise in *Top Gun*, a movie Connor must have seen at least four times. No jewelry like the guys at school wore, just his watch with the wide black-leather band.

I borrowed one of Vini's expressions. "You look wicked hot."

"You look pretty hot yourself." He bent down to kiss me.

"Watch the makeup! It took a few hours to achieve this look."

"I doubt that."

"You have lipstick on your lips."

He rubbed his mouth with the back of his hand. "I've been marked by an angel. I'm one lucky guy."

"Show me how lucky you are later," I teased.

He raised his eyebrows. "Well, that's a promise I'll fulfill."

The nightclub was packed. Strobe lights danced across the ceiling and walls as couples undulated to the throbbing beat of the music. We nudged and pushed through them to join Jason and Owen at one of the side booths.

Owen stood and kissed my cheek. "You look stunning, as usual."

Jason looked different. He wore a red silky dress shirt, open at the collar to show off a number of gold chains. On his wrist was the bracelet his sister had given him, and a rather large ruby ring was on his middle finger. It was a huge contrast to the Jason I'd known all year, and I wondered if this was the real Jason or just a statement he wanted to make at the moment. He was starting to grow a mustache, and the hint of a beard circled his jawline.

All I could say was, "Interesting look." I didn't totally dislike it, but it would take some getting used to if it was permanent.

Vini, who snuck up behind me and poked me on the back to announce her presence, heard my comment and added her own. "He's trying to look like Bob Marley, but if you ask me, I think it looks stupid."

"I didn't hear anyone asking you, Vin," Jason said.

Owen added his own comment. "I like the look, but I have to say, it tickles."

"Don't think anyone needs to know that." Jason looked embarrassed.

"I didn't say where. You guys have dirty minds."

"Speak for yourself, Owen," Vini said. "Enough of this crap. Let's get this party going."

The waiter brought our drinks. Vini and I had a cola. She wasn't happy, but Jason reminded her he didn't want to have any trouble, especially now he'd given his notice. He wanted to leave with a clean record.

"Where's Adrian?" I asked.

"Getting ready to do the karaoke thing. We've got a surprise in store for you."

I was suddenly apprehensive. Vini's surprises made me nervous.

The strobe lights stopped and a spotlight was focused on Adrian at the microphone. The crowd gathered in front of the stage in anticipation of the first singer. Adrian flipped through his cards and then stopped and looked directly at Connor and me. My nervousness meter was escalating. I looked at Connor, and he shrugged. I suspected he knew what the surprise was.

Adrian opened with, "Ladies and gentlemen!" This seemed humorous, in light of the fact that some of the gentlemen could be ladies, who were far removed from my impression of what a lady represented.

The crowd cheered and hooted. "I have an announcement to make," he continued. "Someone most of you know from his time working here has asked a very lovely lady to marry him. And guess what? She said yes. Let's hear it for Connor and Micaela."

Vini was the first to let out an ear-piercing whistle, and several other patrons followed suit. If this was Vini's surprise, so far, I could handle it.

"Will you stand up." Vini made it sound like a command.

Connor took my hand, and we both stood while the hooting and whistling got louder. His arm circled my waist and pulled me close. He pressed his lips against mine, letting his tongue explore the inside of my mouth as his body pressed against me. His hand slid across my hip to the base of my spine—which created more hooting and obscene comments. I went with it and clutched his butt muscles, knowing it would create an even greater reaction from the crowd.

I heard a woman at the next table say something, at least I thought it was a woman; I couldn't be sure. "My God, I've always wanted a piece of that. I'd like to trade places with her."

Connor smiled his incredible smile. "Guess we gave them a show."

"I guess we did."

Adrian settled the crowd and, before we could sit down, motioned us to come to the stage. I looked at Vini. She pretended not to notice. Adrian glanced at Vini, his obvious source of information, and continued announcing.

"I've been informed that Micaela has an incredible voice, and so … it gives me great pleasure to announce that Connor and Micaela will be singing the Michael Jackson song 'I Just Can't Stop Loving You.'"

Connor whispered in my ear. "Remember your comment about us singing a duet? Well, here's your chance." He took my hand and dragged me reluctantly to the stage.

As I followed the prompter, I understood why Connor had chosen this song. When he sang the lyrics—"I need you; God I need you; I love you so much"—his arm came around me, and he looked directly into my eyes. I sang, "I can't live without you," while staring into his.

Adrian took the microphone when we were finished. "Wasn't that fantastic?" The whistles and catcalls made it difficult to hear him. He waited for them to diminish. "Let's see if any one of you can top that." He announced the next singer.

As Connor and I returned to the booth, we were stopped by several people who offered their congratulations. We passed the woman/man—I still wasn't sure but decided to go with woman—who had made the comment about Connor earlier.

I stared directly into her eyes as she ogled Connor's butt. "Don't even think about it," I snapped.

"Darlin', there's no harm in lookin'. Don't be such an uptight bitch." She turned to a man holding a drink and whispered something in his ear.

Vini thought her idea of having Connor and me do a duet was cool and wouldn't stop telling us. She looked at Connor. "How 'bout you and Jase sing a duet like you used to?"

"Sorry, Vini. I only sing in the shower and to Micaela now."

We listened to a number of brave candidates sing various pop songs. Vini hadn't taken her eyes off Adrian the entire time. When the karaoke part of the evening wrapped up, he joined us at our booth. She looked like a puppy greeting its owner. Jason shot him a look that, if I didn't miss my guess, held a hint of annoyance. Maybe older brothers were like fathers. Connor and Adrian talked about what it was like working at the club, and I got the distinct impression Adrian didn't have much tolerance for alternative lifestyles, which made me wonder why he'd even taken the job. I suspected by Owen's glare at Adrian that he sensed it too. He snuggled into Jason, making a statement of his own. I had a better understanding of the odd look I saw on Jason's face. We both had figured out Adrian's opinion of gay people. Vini was oblivious.

"Dance with me, babe?" Vini pulled on Adrian's arm.

285

"Guess that's my cue." He followed her to the dance floor. Vini was all over him, sending out very distinct vibes. Their bodies wrapped together, entwining like snakes in a mating ritual.

"Adrian's got his hands full with Vini," Owen said, watching the scene in front of him.

"Not so sure about that," Jason said. "She barely knows the guy. I've seen him with some of the women who come in here. We call them gawkers, as they just come for the experience of being in a gay bar. He's a definite player. She won't listen to anything I say. She's got those rose-colored glasses on right now, but I swear if he hurts her, I'll kill him."

"She's going to have to find out the hard way, Jason. Just be there if she gets hurt." Connor's words were drowned out by the change in music. It was "Two Hearts" by Phil Collins. Connor asked me to dance. He took my hand and twirled me onto the dance floor. Again, people moved to give us room.

He sang the opening line. "Two hearts beating in just one mind, beating together 'til the end of time." I secretly thanked his mom for giving him dance lessons as a kid. He pulled me closer as the song ended. "One More Night," another Phil Collins song, was announced by the deejay. Apparently, he had a fondness for the British pop star.

We stood swaying back and forth, and Connor whispered in my ear as I placed my head against his chest. "Micaela, I love you more than you know. I can't wait until December when we can spend the rest of our lives together."

I looked up and smiled. "Me too."

"Your hair smells amazing." Both his arms encircled me.

"Lilacs. It's the body spray you gave me."

He kissed the top of my nose. "You are my angel."

A deep hollow sound, like a thunder clap, lasting a second, not long enough to register its existence, shook the room. The floor heaved, and I felt my body wrenched from Conner as if a giant shock wave reverberated through me. Reaching, grasping, flailing to make contact with him, I was suddenly thrown like a projectile across a space, landing against a booth. The shrill, deafening sound of an alarm erupted and then was cut short by another louder boom.

All light was gone. Pieces of wood, like shrapnel, shot through the air, impaling whatever got in its way. Shards of exploding glass rained down from above. Crawling under a nearby table, I curled into a fetal position with my arms around my head. My brain ceased functioning; all my survival instincts kicked in. Smoke billowed around me; the rich oaky smell crept into my nose, burning its way to my lungs. Flames belched from somewhere near me, sending dozens of burning embers shooting in different directions.

Someone yelled, "A bomb! It's a bomb!"

Screams reverberated in my ears from everywhere around me. People pushed and shoved their way past me in a frenzied rush. Seconds turned into minutes; time had no meaning. Suddenly, my brain sent me a message. *Connor! Where is Connor?* I screamed his name over and over.

CHAPTER 40

Frantic desperation seized my vocal cords. I tried finding my voice again, but nothing came out. My brain kept telling me not to panic, but my fear refused to listen. Deep breathing accomplished nothing more than sending smoke-filled air into my lungs, causing me to choke.

My eyes scanned the darkness. Shadows and shapes formed as the flickering light from the nearby fire illuminated the area in front of me. Fragments of tables and chairs and unrecognizable debris were scattered where I sat frozen, fighting to overcome my terror. A quiet—grim in its contrast to the screaming of minutes before—created an eerie stillness. I had to find Connor. *He has to be alive. He must be alive!*

I tried crawling out from under the table but felt a large obstruction blocking me. Reaching out to push it away, I touched something soft and malleable. I quickly pulled my hand back as my mind acknowledged the feel of flesh and fabric. With difficulty, I was able to maneuver my torso so my legs were in front of me. One of my shoes was missing. I kicked off the other one. Pulling my knees to my chest, I shoved as hard as I could to extricate the body from where it lay wedged against the table. Swallowing back my revulsion, I pushed three times until I felt it move enough to free me. I instructed my mind not to think about it and inched forward on my butt. Ducking my head under the table top and pushing upward, I managed to stand, averting my gaze from what lay at my feet. Grasping the edge of the table for balance, I stepped carefully over the body.

A blast of heat scorched my bare skin. My eyes stung, and I blinked several times to keep them from drying out. Screaming again for Connor, my voice cracked, and I gagged on the smoke, now getting thicker and hotter. Every moment of silence filled me with dread and terror. I inched forward, feeling my way through the rubble, praying I wouldn't encounter another grizzly sight. A sharp knifelike pain seared through the bottom of my foot. I bent to investigate and gasped as I pulled a shard of glass from my heel. I heard someone calling my name. Frantically, I searched the darkness. I heard it again. Connor's voice instantly alleviated my fear. Tears of relief streamed down my hot cheeks.

"Connor, I'm here."

"I can see you. Can you see me?" he yelled.

"No."

"Don't move. I'm going to try to come to you."

I waited what seemed an eternity, but I still couldn't see him, and my fear returned.

"I won't get to you in time," he called out. "You're going to have to come to me before the side of the building collapses and catches fire. Follow my instructions carefully."

I instantly panicked. "I can't." My heart raced. I clung to the hope he would get to me and make everything all right.

"Yes, you can. The stage has collapsed, and the floor has split open. I'm too heavy to cross it. I can't risk it collapsing even more. I want you to move slowly to the back wall."

I tried taking deep breaths to calm myself, but the smoke-filled air burned my throat. I had no choice. I backed up until I felt the wall. I could feel the heat of it even before I touched it.

"Okay, now move to your left and toward my voice."

Slowly, I stepped over tables, broken chairs, and what I knew were bodies, testing each step for broken dishes and glass. I saw what Connor was talking about. A huge crack had formed in the floor where the stage had come down. A sound, like splitting wood, made me freeze. Fear paralyzed me.

"Micaela, keep moving."

Holding my breath, I cautiously and slowly moved to my left, continuously testing each step. The heat was gaining intensity, and my skin prickled. I tried to ignore it and focus on Connor's voice, urging me forward. A large object that felt like wood was in my way. In an effort to avoid it, I lost my balance and again stepped on broken glass, sending a shooting pain up my leg. Connor heard me yelp.

"Are you okay? What happened?"

"Stepped on glass, but I'm okay."

Each step was agonizing. A dim light from somewhere behind and above where the stage had once been cast a glow across my path. Bodies soaked in blood were splayed like rag dolls; some draped over each other—faces rigid in shock, eyes staring blankly—made me shudder. I looked away. I fought back nausea. In the light I could see the deejay booth hanging sideways, precariously balanced against the side of the stage. A body hung from the smashed glass of the box. I heaved, and bile burned my already parched throat. Suddenly, I was able to see Connor. He was standing across from me. We were separated by a gaping hole that had formed between where the stage had fallen and what remained of the dance floor. It appeared to be about four feet wide. I had difficulty judging it. I looked at Connor's face. Blood trickled from a cut in his forehead, but he was there. He was alive! I stared at the hole.

"I can't jump across."

"Yes, you can, but I can't. I told you the floor might collapse under my weight if I try. You will be fine. You can do it. It's not that far. If you can jump into the boat, you can do this. Piece of cake."

I didn't share his optimism. There had to be another way.

The air was getting hotter, the smoke thicker. Every breath felt like a hot poker being jammed down my throat. "I won't make it. I can't do it."

"You have to. There's no choice, and you've got to do it now."

He stepped closer to the hole and held out his arm. I reached for his hand and could almost touch it.

A crashing sound behind me—glass exploding, sparks filling the air like hundreds of fireflies—motivated me. A spark singed my shoulder. I brushed it off, ignoring the pain. I began to tremble.

"Micaela, focus on me. Take my hand."

I tried and failed. I couldn't breathe. I tasted the smoke, and my nostrils were inflamed.

"Look at me, Micaela!" I looked into his eyes. "Now, try again. Grab my hand."

"I can't."

"Yes, you can, goddamn it. If you stay there, the whole side of the building will cave and catch fire, and we'll both be burned alive. I won't let you die."

The authority in his voice made me respond instantly. Leaning forward, I stretched my arm out to him as far as possible. All thinking was suspended. I connected with his wrist and held it. He slid his arm along mine and held it so tight it hurt.

"Keep looking at me. Just do it."

A snapping sound, and the floor shook.

"Now! Jump now!"

I lunged forward, and Connor's other arm quickly reached out and grabbed me. My shoulder felt as if it had come free from its socket. I was safe. I clung to him. Another huge bang.

"We have to move." He pulled me back and away from the gap just as the rest of the stage sank deeper into the floor, and the deejay booth hurtled down and smashed in front of us—body and all.

I shuddered. My shoulder hurt and my feet throbbed, but I assured Connor I was okay. He was coughing almost to the point of gagging. He held me as we stumbled toward where the steps to the stage once were. The back hall was just in front of us, and he pulled me forward. I stumbled across something. I shouldn't have looked. An arm lay at my feet. I saw the huge collection of bracelets and the large turquoise ring on a finger. The woman who'd made the comment about Connor's butt lay twisted and broken; her eyes were open and large pieces of glass stuck out of her head.

"Oh God!" I gagged and pressed my hand against my mouth to keep from vomiting.

I clung to Connor as we moved down the back corridor. Another body blocked our path. I recognized the curly black hair and the black silk shirt with the gold medallion against the chest. The face was unrecognizable ... half of it was missing, but I knew it was Adrian. I grabbed Connor.

"Vini, Jason ... Owen ... Oh my God, Connor! We have to find them."

"Don't think. Just keep moving. We'll find them. Don't let go of me," Connor instructed. "Think about what it will be like when you get to New York and how great it's going to be when we are finally together and when we get married."

Connor coughed again. The effort to speak was getting harder. He took his jacket and wrapped it around my head so I could cover my mouth and keep sparks from singeing my hair. The smell of burned flesh was overwhelming. He guided me slowly, each step a struggle. An involuntary quiver shook my body as I felt the brush of a leg across my ankles or tripped over an outstretched hand. Connor finally gathered me in his arms and carried me along the back hallway, past the office and toward the red exit sign. The smoke wasn't as thick, and our breathing became easier. I nestled my head into his chest and felt his heart hammering against his rib cage.

A muffled sound came from somewhere near us. Connor stopped by the men's washroom. He called out, "Anyone in there?"

A voice responded. "Is that you, Connor?"

Connor knew immediately who it was. "It's Jason."

He put me down and tried opening the door. It moved slightly, but something blocked it. He attempted to force it open with his shoulder. With the first thrust, we heard a scraping noise across the tile. One more shove, and it moved enough for us to get through.

I followed closely behind Connor as he slipped through the narrow opening. Jason lay on the floor amid broken tiles and mirrored glass, his legs pinned under a large beam. Half the back wall was missing, and smoke swirled in clouds, creeping along what was left of the ceiling.

Jason looked up. "It's sure good to see you guys. Are Owen and Vin okay? Are they with you?" He knew the answer by the look on Connor's face.

"They're more than likely safe. First thing is getting you out of here." Connor looked around, assessing the situation. "I'm going to move the beam. Can you use your elbows to shimmy out?"

Flames hissed and curled like snakes slithering across the underside of the beams above Jason. The cracking sound of tiles behind him sent a look of fear across his face.

"It's no use. The place is going to go any second. You two go. Leave me."

"I'm not leaving you," Connor said as he tried pulling up on the beam.

"Don't try to be a hero. Get out of here." Tears tracked down his soot-covered cheeks. "Tell Owen I'm sorry. Tell him I love him, and tell Vin to be strong for Mom. God, I hope they made it."

His sobs broke my heart.

"You can tell them yourself." Connor turned to me as more smoke wafted into the room, and the flames danced across the ceiling. "Micaela, you have to go."

"I'll help you."

"No! You'll go."

"But"—I grabbed his arm—"not without you." More smoke filled the hallway, burning my eyes.

"I have to help him. I can't just leave him. I have to try. Please understand. I'll be with you shortly. Just follow the red exit sign. There's a door on your right to the back stairs."

"What if it's locked?"

He pushed my hair from my face. "It won't be. You're going to be fine, babe."

"Promise me you'll be okay."

It would kill Connor to have to make a choice. I knew that. He pulled me into his arms and kissed me. I tasted the salt on my lips … from tears, mine and his. I clung to him. He pulled away and held my shoulders and stared into my eyes.

"I love you. Body and soul … forever and always. You're my angel. Now move before this whole place goes up in flames."

He released me and disappeared into the smoke. I moved quickly, fighting sobs that wracked my body. I followed the exit sign until I located the steel bar on the door below it. I pushed it, ran down the stairs, and opened the back door. I gulped for air through my sobs and stumbled into the night. I breathed in deeply, letting the cool air fill my lungs. Someone shouted; arms pulled me, and two firemen wrapped me in a blanket. I shrugged it off.

"My boyfriend is still in there. He's trying to get his friend out. He's trapped in the washroom. Help! Please help!" The fireman just stood there. "Please … you've got to help them. The building is going to collapse. Isn't that your job?" I screamed it at him.

"Ed, people are still in the building. Get a couple of guys. Move it!"

Lights flashing, fireman pulling hoses and blasting streams of water, policemen pushing onlookers back—it all blended into the chaos around me. Sirens blaring, sounds of crying and mournful sobbing, and high-pitched wailing blended together, creating a cacophony of sound. Tarped forms lay in rows on the pavement. Medics loaded bloody bodies on to stretchers and placed them in ambulances. I couldn't move. My eyes were glued to the back door. My pulse raced. Seconds felt like hours. Where was Connor?

"Please, God, help them!" I yelled. Someone was beside me, touching my arm. I flinched.

"Where's Jason? Where's Connor?" The words were garbled, but I could make them out. The trembling voice belonged to Vini.

"Adrian … I can't find him. Has anyone seen a black man wearing a black shirt and black jeans?" she yelled at no one in particular. Frantic and desperate, she searched the crowd. No one responded.

I looked at her face. Her left eye was swollen shut, pieces of glass stuck to her cheek, and red streaks were running down her face. She was whimpering uncontrollably. I saw blood oozing from a gash in her shoulder where her dress was torn, and I smelled smoke in her hair.

"They're in there … Jason's trapped … Connor's helping him." My words came in fragments.

"Oh my God. No!" Owen was beside us. His hand reached for mine. I couldn't speak, so I squeezed his, as if by doing so, I could pass on my faith and belief that they would be fine. Owen released my hand and placed one arm around me and the other around Vini. We each stared at the door, waiting. "They'll make it," he said.

Suddenly, the door flew open. Smoke belched from the darkness. A fireman raced to a waiting ambulance with Jason over his shoulder. Another fireman held Connor as he hobbled beside him. There was blood on his hands and legs and ash on his face. Owen ran to Jason as the fireman passed him to a medic. I breathed a sigh of relief and said a silent prayer of gratitude. I ran toward Connor, staring constantly at the blackened face of the man I loved more than anything in the world. He saw me, grinned, and made an A-Okay sign with his fingers.

An explosion reverberated through the night. A man yelled, "Get back!" and fiercely tugged me backward and held me firmly.

In that one moment, the entire back of the building collapsed in a torrent of flames. Connor and the fireman were gone. I stared at the place where Connor had just stood. Only burning timber and clouds of smoke and embers swirling in the air remained.

A scream—mine! "No ... no ... Connor ... no!"

I wrenched free from the arms that held me and ran toward the flames. The heat seared my skin and burned my eyes. I was grabbed again. Kicking violently, I tried shoving away from the hands of the man who held me.

"Connor ... I love you ... Please ... I have to get to him." My screams choked me. My head burst with pain. Then I felt myself fall. A mass of emotional chaos shook my body, and I drifted into oblivion.

CHAPTER 41

Now

A sudden violent jolt woke me. Screams echoed through my brain, trailing off into the distant recesses of my mind. The wall that once separated my conscious awareness from the shadows of my past was gone. I was free-floating in the debris. My eyes wouldn't open. A long, dark, narrow tunnel formed behind my eyelids, and lightning bolts flashed intermittently as a tidal wave of anxiety flooded my body. My breathing came in short bursts while my heart hammered against my rib cage. I gasped for air. I sensed a presence near me, a hand reaching out and stroking my head. The tunnel vanished, my vision cleared, my eyes opened—and Vini's face, illuminated by the streetlight outside my house, appeared like an apparition from the surrounding darkness.

"It's okay, sweetie. You're okay." Her voice was soft and comforting. Her hand felt cool against my clammy skin. "You must have had a nightmare. I heard you screaming."

I felt the dampness of my cotton nightshirt against my chest and tasted salt on my lips—I'd been crying. Vini was kneeling on the carpet beside the couch, still gently stroking my head, as I'd done so many times for Jess when she was a child, waking from a bad dream. I took three deep breaths and looked into her kind, beautiful eyes. I tried speaking, but nothing came out.

"I'm going to turn on a light, so shut your eyes." She reached for the lamp on the side table and switched it on.

I blinked several times, adjusting to the brightness. I found my voice.

"I remember! I remember it all. It was so real, like it just happened. I could smell the smoke, feel the heat of the flames, and I saw Connor standing in the doorway, smiling at me." My voice cracked as a sob burst from deep inside me, and a wave of profound sadness resonated from my gut, sending shards of pain, like a thousand pieces of broken glass, ripping through my heart. The rhythm of my breathing changed.

"You're starting to hyperventilate. Breathe with me."

She inhaled slowly and then exhaled through her mouth. We did it in tandem until my breathing returned to normal. Vini noticed I was shivering and took the afghan from the armchair and handed it to me while I tried sitting up. Wrapping it around my shoulders, I curled into the corner of the sofa. Vini sat at the other end, just as she had done earlier. We sat quietly until my heart calmed, and I was able to speak. I remembered our quarrel.

"Oh, Vini! I'm incredibly sorry for all the things I said. You were right; Conner didn't leave me, at least not on purpose. How could I have thought he'd abandon me? All these years I pretended he was out there somewhere. I even pretended he'd just been a dream and never existed at all. I sensed something bad must have happened, but I didn't want to face it. How did you manage not to say anything all that time?"

"Do you remember when you were taken to the hospital?"

I shook my head.

"Well, anyway, the next morning Owen and I found your room. You didn't even acknowledge us; you just stared into space. Your dad was there, and he spoke with Owen. He explained you were in a deep state of shock and heavily sedated. Before we left, you yelled out, "Can anybody tell me why Connor left me?" I thought it was a pretty strange thing to say, so I tried to explain what happened, which I later learned was a huge error. You screamed at me. Told me I was lying, and I was never to speak to you again. You were an entirely different person."

"I'm so sorry. I don't remember that at all."

"I called your dad to see how you were and if you got off to New York okay. He told me the doctors suspected PTSD."

"What's that?"

"Post-traumatic stress disorder. I asked my doctor about it. It's like a part of the brain just cuts itself off from reality. Symptoms include flashbacks, dreams, and often nightmares and severe anxiety. You can have uncontrollable thoughts about the event that created the trauma and even make up scenarios that are more comfortable to accept."

Vini's explanation was making sense, but it was a lot to take in. "Dad never told me."

"He couldn't without risking more trauma. The doctor told him that you needed psychiatric help, but you had already left. Your dad didn't know what to do, but he called your aunt and informed her. The pregnancy might have made it worse. You know, I suspected you were pregnant the day we did the pregnancy test in my bathroom, but I didn't know for sure until a year later, after you had given up your baby."

"So my aunt knew about this too." It amazed me that both of them had never spoken of it. Now I understood why Aunt Florence insisted I see a psychologist.

"Owen looked up information about PTSD on his computer at work. He told me that any reference to the event could send you into a deep psychosis, and you could remain in that state for the rest of your life. You know the guy thought the world of you. He carried a picture of you in his wallet."

That information sent more tears streaming down my face.

"Jason understood we were triggers," Vini said, "but after Owen died, he was upset you didn't contact him. I shouldn't have said what I did earlier. Jason was out of his mind with grief at the time and wasn't thinking rationally." Vini noticed the bracelet on my wrist. "You found that in your dad's boxes?"

"Yes, and all my pictures, and my ring. Maybe that's why I had the nightmare and can remember now."

"It probably prompted it. Have you had other dreams?"

"Yes."

"When did they start?"

"Just after my cancer diagnosis."

"Bingo! Owen also mentioned that another stressful event could increase the level of the nightmares and either send you over the edge or unblock your memory."

"Thank goodness it was the latter, but I wish it would have been something else and not the cancer."

"You're made of tough stuff."

"Not so tough. I spent thirty years doing everything I could not to face reality. I messed up my life and hurt others in the process."

"For God's sake! You didn't mess up your life. You have Jess and your granddaughters. You were a big movie star and made a gazillion dollars. Okay, so you married an egotistical asshole; no one is perfect. You didn't hurt anyone. It was the PTSD, and you couldn't control that."

"You lost someone you loved too." The image of Adrian lying dead at my feet flashed through my mind, and I shivered. "I saw him, Vini. I know what happened."

Vini interrupted me. "Don't tell me. I don't want to know the details. I just hope it was quick."

"I think it was."

We both sat in silence, as if honoring our lost loves.

"I have a confession to make." Vini broke the silence. "Adrian and I weren't really moving in together. I lied." I started to speak but Vini kept talking. "I hate liars. God knows, I see enough of them in my work, but I was jealous of you and Connor. Adrian was moving to Tampa. I was just following him. That's why I took the job in the salon. I can't tell you how much I hated that shitty job." She paused and took a breath. "I loved that guy big time. Haven't loved anyone like that since ... and probably never will." I saw tears escaping her eyes. She wiped them away quickly.

"Thank you for never telling anyone about my son," I said. "You kept your promise, and I love you for it."

"You didn't need any more stress, and there was no reason to bring up the subject. It was a done deal."

"I thought at Dad's funeral that Rosalie would tell Jess."

"Good thing she didn't, but *you* need to tell her."

"How can I tell her she has a brother? She'll want to find him."

"Is that such a bad idea? I have another confession ... Sorry, but this might come as a shock ... I found him."

"How is that possible?"

"Easy. I just kept looking on websites where adopted people post requests for information on their birth parents. It took a while, but after three years of searching, I got lucky and found a picture of a young man resembling Connor. I did some background checking—the perks of my position—and found his adoption certificate. The date coincided with the time you gave him up. I didn't have to look too far for confirmation. Once you see him, you'll see why. He could be Connor's twin rather than his son." Vini looked at me. "Are you okay?"

My hands were shaking and my body quivering. "I'm okay. Just a little shaken. This is a lot to digest."

"I probably shouldn't have told you. You've barely processed the shock of your nightmare."

"No, it's fine. It's good that you have." I wrapped the afghan tighter around my shoulders and tucked my feet under it. "What's his name? Where does he live? He probably hates me. What kind of mother gives up her child?"

"Now you're being stupid. You were nineteen, with no income and an incredible career ahead of you. You couldn't support yourself, let alone a child. He'll understand. Here's another shocker, if you can take it, but it's a good one. He's Dylan West."

"I don't know that name."

"You really have been out of touch. I'll bet Jess knows who he is. He's a famous singer/songwriter. He won a Grammy three years ago. I could hardly believe it was him. Guess the apple doesn't fall far from the tree."

"I'd like to find him."

"Okay. If that's what you want, I'll put the wheels in motion."

"What if he doesn't want to see me?"

"He put the request on that site, so he must want to find out who his birth parents are. He'll be blown away when he finds out who his mother is."

"I doubt that. I'm a has-been."

She changed the subject. "I guess you never knew who placed the bombs in the club. It was in all the local papers at the time, although it might not have made it to the New York papers. Now, it would be all over the internet. It was a religious cult—crazies who were against homosexuality. They planted another one in a bar in Tampa. The cops finally got them, but it took a long time. That's what inspired me to become a prosecutor, but it seems that for every crazy fanatic I put away, ten more take their place. It doesn't help alleviate my guilt, though."

"Why would you feel guilty?" It never occurred to me Vini would feel responsible.

"It was my idea that we go to the Blue Lagoon that night. I figured Owen and Jason would be more comfortable, but if the truth be known, my real reason was a selfish one. I wanted to see Adrian."

I reached across the couch and took her hand. "Please don't feel guilty. I thought it was a pretty cool place. I could have objected, but I didn't."

"Connor saved Jason. There's not a day goes by that he doesn't think about it. Connor gave his life for him."

"He saved me too. I would never have made it out of there if it wasn't for him. If only Connor hadn't stopped to look at me."

"Life is full of if-onlys. We turn right rather than left, and we get into a car accident. Someone forgets a cell phone and goes back into the house, and there's a gas explosion. A guy forgets important papers and goes back into a building, just as an airplane crashes into it. It seems like a series of random events, but maybe it's destiny. Who knows? You can't beat yourself up about the if-onlys. You just have to move on."

"Are you listening to yourself?"

"I guess I have my own share of if-onlys."

Vini sensed my anxiety returning and changed the subject. "Guess who I ran into at Target when I was visiting Jason?" She didn't wait for me to guess. "Bonnie, of all people."

The image of Bonnie walking down the pier and wishing me a good life came into my mind. Other than her presence in my dreams, I hadn't thought about her since that day.

"She's huge and has more wrinkles than an English bulldog."

The comparison made me laugh. Vini had the weirdest expressions.

"I knew you'd laugh."

I realized I was still holding her hand, and I squeezed it. "You always could make me laugh. Did she talk to you?"

"Yeah! She didn't seem too bothered by talking to little old black me. Can you believe it?"

"People can change, Vini." It pleased me to hear Bonnie might have altered some of her opinions.

"You know what felt really good?"

"What?"

"Picture this … I was wearing a hot-pink sundress that looks amazing on me, and I just had one of those professional makeovers. I looked pretty hot, if I do say so myself."

I had a good idea where Vini was going with this. "And? What did Bonnie look like?" I didn't care, but I knew Vini did and wanted me to ask.

"This is the good part." She smiled, and I detected a certain smugness. "Now keep picturing it. She was wearing ripped denim shorts, way too tight and short. Her ass hung out, and the top of her thighs rippled with cellulite. You picturing it?"

"I guess." It wasn't a pretty picture.

"And get this … She was even wearing a tight tank top. You know how she was … just got to show off the boobs. But it didn't quite cover the roll of fat hanging over her shorts."

It was apparent to me that time hadn't changed Vini's opinion of Bonnie. I was more curious how Bonnie's life had turned out, rather than her physical appearance. "Did you ask how she was doing?"

"Didn't have to. She volunteered it."

"And?"

"She's been divorced twice, which doesn't surprise me. What guy in his right mind would stay with her? She's currently living with some guy in Pensacola. She was in Clearwater, visiting her mom. She's got two kids—a son and a daughter."

I remembered Riley and hoped she'd turned out different from her mom. I'd only told Vini that Bonnie had gotten pregnant by her best friend's boyfriend but never said the child's name or anything about Connor's involvement. "Did she talk about her daughter?"

"A bit. I can't remember her name, but she told me that she married some insurance salesman and lives in Ohio. Oh … and she's expecting a baby. Bonnie, a grandmother—seems weird. It sure makes you realize how fast time goes by."

I'd never know if what I'd said to Bonnie that day on Connor's boat had made a difference. I just hoped it had.

"She wanted to know if I was married and had kids. Told her I had no interest in a husband and kids. I loved my job as an attorney in New York too much, and I was super-busy making a shitload of money."

"You didn't!"

"Yup, I did, and it felt damned good. I had to get that in. You should have seen the look on her face."

"Did she ask about me?"

"She knew you had been an actress. You'd have to live in Outer Mongolia not to know that. I filled her in on Jess and the girls and said you still looked amazing."

"That's not true."

"Yes, it is. Thing is, she blames you for Connor's death."

"Me? Why?"

"You know her. She thinks if Connor had chosen her instead of you, he'd still be alive today."

"She might have a point."

"That's crap, and you know it. Believe me, I straightened her out on that."

I yawned.

"Obviously, I walked away scoring all kinds of points."

I yawned again.

Vini noted that I was beginning to get tired. "Do you think you're going to be okay now? We both need to get some sleep."

"I feel different ... lighter. I can remember Connor now and feel the love, rather than pushing it away. I'm not afraid anymore. Thank you."

"Good, 'cause I have to get up in three hours and get to the airport. Don't bother getting up. I'll be pissed if you do. We'll see each other soon. I have some time between Christmas and New Year's. Maybe, if you want, I can fly up."

"I'd love that." I stifled another yawn. Suddenly, I had an urge to go to Florida. "Vini ... I want to go back. I want to see Jason and find Ricky."

"Are you sure you're up to it?"

"Never surer."

After turning out the light, I started toward the stairs with Vini following me. I stopped by the dining room and gave her the portrait of her and her mom. She thanked me and kissed the photo. Her glance fell on the half-filled scotch bottle and the empty glass.

"I see you found some liquid gold." Her voice held a hint of concern.

"It was just this one time. It was Jack's. He forgot it when he left. I'm not drinking again. Promise. I don't need to. And by the state of my brain, I wished I hadn't last night."

"Better not be."

Vini hugged me and I returned it. "I love you, Vini."

"I love you too, Micki."

I did sleep, and for the first time in months, I didn't dream.

Vini had left by the time I got up. I booked my flight to Florida and called Jess. I told her my intention. She questioned by decision.

"I have to do it. I'll explain when I get back. I love you, Jess."

"I love you too, Mom."

CHAPTER 42

Was I ready to face my past? The memory of Connor's death left me between a state of shock and a blessed sense of emotional release. I spent the entire flight to Florida dealing with my trepidation, but if I was going to move forward in my life, whatever amount I had left, I had to come to terms with the thirty years I'd lost and the people I'd lost with them.

The Tampa skyline had grown. Where once the city was defined by a few buildings off in the distance, now it was like a group of silver dominoes lined up against the bright blue sky. The Gulf of Mexico spread out around me as I drove across the West Courtney Campbell Causeway, headed into Clearwater. Condominiums and hotels dotted the horizon. When I reached the corner of Causeway Boulevard and Gulf Boulevard, I remembered it was where I'd made my first major driving error. Dad's voice played in my head.

"Micaela! Pay attention to the signs! Use your turn signals, and change lanes before you get to the intersection."

I smiled at the memory. "Thanks, Dad, for your incredible patience. I almost had us killed." I said the words to the empty seat beside me, as if he was still sitting there.

Clearwater also had made huge advances over the past thirty years. The movie theater, the clothing store Vini loved, and the ice cream shop were gone; restaurants and outdoor cafes now lined the walkway. The quaint mom-and-pop motels that once skirted the shoreline were replaced by luxury high-rise condominiums that obscured the ocean view. The sleepy little town was gone. Developers reigned, and tourism flourished. I preferred the Clearwater of the past. I recognized nothing, which, for the most part, was probably a good thing—less pull on the heartstrings. It was like opening a time capsule and discovering the once-cherished contents had rotted away.

I rented a condo on the beach at Indian Shores across from the Intracoastal Waterway, where Connor had docked the boat the day of the storm. It hadn't been deliberate. A friend of Vini's was kind enough to offer it to me, and even though I knew my emotional endurance would be tested, I accepted. It was at a reduced price that fit my budget.

I parked my rented car in front of the building and stared across the street. Ben's Ice Cream had morphed into a pub with an outdoor restaurant. I pictured Connor, Ricky, and me, our ghostlike images walking hand in hand. I blinked several times in an attempt to stave off tears. The ghosts evaporated.

The area hadn't succumbed to the mass development, as I once thought it would. I still recognized houses and motels, although the years had not been kind to some of them.

Exhausted from traveling, I left my suitcases by the bedroom door, opened the window, and collapsed on the bed. I was lulled into a deep sleep by the repetitive swish of the waves as they kissed the shore. It was a sound I loved and hadn't heard in thirty years.

I woke to moonlight streaking across the room. I unpacked, showered, changed into sweatpants and a hoodie, and walked across the street to the restaurant. The air was cool, and the sky was a mass of stars. I glanced upward, staring at the myriad galaxies against a black canvas. It always filled me with a sense of wonder.

I ordered a clubhouse sandwich and iced tea and found a place on the beach to sit and eat. I searched for the brightest stars. I felt a connection to their energy; my soul infused with a sense of awe at the spectacle. I closed my eyes and allowed memories to flood my mind. They came like the waves in rhythmic succession—Connor on his boat, the wind whipping strands of hair across his face; chasing me on the beach and twirling me around when he caught me; wrapped in each other's embrace while watching the sun set over the ocean. Each recollection was accompanied by audio—Connor's laugh and the rich tone of his singing voice. My senses had their own memory. I could feel his arms around me, his lips against mine, and the way he touched me when we made love. All the good memories pushed the bad ones aside. Young love held an irresistible magic that wove a powerful spell, convincing you it would last forever. For the first time, I wondered if our love could have survived my career, his struggle to establish a successful practice, and raising a child. I'd never know. We didn't get our happily-ever-after. It wasn't our destiny. There actually was something valuable in the time capsule—our love. It would remain constant, untouched by the fickle winds of change.

A young couple, about the ages Connor and I were when we walked the beach at night, strolled along the shoreline, their bodies linked together, focused only on each other.

As they passed, I couldn't resist commenting to them, "Treasure this moment. You don't know how many of them you'll have."

They looked at me strangely, kissed, and moved on.

I remained staring at the night sky until all the memories faded; then I returned to the condo. Checking the time, I decided it was still early enough to call Jason. His address and phone number were in my purse. I willed myself to make the call. I was nervous of how he would respond. Before I lost my nerve, I keyed the number on my cell. A strange voice answered. I assumed it was his new partner, Ken.

I identified myself.

"Lovely to hear from you." He had a distinct British accent. "Jason's told me all about you. All good things, of course. He's expecting your call. Hold a moment, won't you?"

I waited. This call would be difficult for both us.

Finally, he answered. "Vin told me you would be calling. She said you had a breakthrough. You remember Connor died."

He didn't ask how I was or even sound the least bit interested. There was a difference in the tone of his voice—a kind of detached monotone. I wasn't sure what I was expecting, but the Jason I remembered had been very personable and caring, like his sister. This was not the same man. Time had taken its toll on him as well. The matter-of-fact way he stated this was unnerving.

He paused, as if thinking about his next words. "I'm glad for you. It must have been dreadful to live with the anxiety for so long and not understand the reason why. I can't forget. Wish I could."

I started to tell him how sorry I was about Owen, but he cut me off.

"Ken and I have to be at an art exhibit in twenty minutes. Can you come by for lunch tomorrow? Vin gave you my address, right?"

"Yes, she did." I accepted his invitation.

Jason's condo was stunning. I'd heard decorators use this term in describing artfully placed antiques in a room filled with beautiful paintings, displayed by accent lighting, with colors that take your breath away. It was a suitable word.

Italian marble floors went on forever, with luxurious handmade vintage rugs, which might have been from Milan, Morocco, or India, defining the sitting areas. A massive octagonal hand-painted wood coffee table, which I recognized as Moroccan, was surrounded by three large white sofas, laden down with throw pillows in various colors and designs. Two huge Moroccan leather pouf hassocks sat in front of the window that stretched the entire length of the room. Massive cushions stacked on top of each other picked up the colors of the throw pillows. It didn't look overstated against a background of white walls and ten-foot ceilings. The panoramic view of the ocean was even more amazing from such a high vantage point. The condo lived up to its name—it was grand.

There was no evidence of any Christmas decorations. It was a few days away, and I recalled that Jason loved the season. He and Owen would celebrate both Hanukkah and Christmas. Perhaps that too had changed.

Ken had greeted me at the door and escorted me into a kitchen that made mine look tiny in comparison. He offered me a glass of red wine while I waited. Jason was finishing up some calls in his office.

Ken was the complete opposite of Owen—a lot shorter, bald, and Asian. He had been raised and educated in London, England. While preparing a typical Moroccan dish of couscous topped with lamb and vegetables, he explained that Jason had visited Morocco six years ago and had been taken with Marrakesh. He'd purchased rugs, accessories, and furnishings and had them sent to Florida. Jason, obviously, had done extremely well with his design business. I thought about Bonnie and the things she said to me about Jason and Vini. If only she could see this—brother and sister both successful. A huge leap from their humble beginnings. A certain satisfaction accompanied the thought.

A whirring sound made me turn. Jason was entering the kitchen in an electric wheelchair. Now I understood why the rooms were so massive and spacious. Vini hadn't prepared me. I tried not to appear shocked.

"Vin didn't tell you, did she?"

"No, she didn't." There was no point in pretending I wasn't startled.

"She should have."

"Jason, I'm—"

"Don't say sorry. It wasn't your fault. How about we eat on the terrace."

He turned the chair and followed Ken outside, where a table had been set for two. Ken excused himself, saying he had errands to run. I expected he wanted to give us some privacy.

There was an awkward silence while we sat contemplating how to open the conversation. Jason reached for a decanter of red wine, poured himself a glass, and asked if I wanted more.

I declined.

His features had changed. He no longer resembled his sister. His face was thinner and deep creases lined his mouth and etched his eyes. His black curls were silver and worn tied back with a ribbon. The beard he was growing when I'd seen him last was gone, but the mustache remained, only it too was silver. While his sister appeared much younger than her forty-nine years, he looked ten years older than his fifty-three. The suffering had left its mark. His eyes, which once reminded me of my dog Chippy—a warm brown— now betrayed that warmth. There was also a cool detachment in his demeanor.

I wondered what he was thinking about me.

He extended his sympathies about my father and my cancer diagnosis. They were simply words; I detected no genuine empathy. Our exchange seemed shallow. I felt at a loss for words, but I took a leap and told him how sorry I was about Owen. His eyes glassed over, the first indication of any emotion.

"Ken's a super person, but Owen was the love of my life." He reminisced about some of the funny things Owen did and admitted he had a drinking problem, which I'd already surmised. The subject changed to Connor, and the previous detached attitude returned.

"So … you remember."

"Yes." My turn for detachment.

"I've never stopped feeling guilty." He sipped his wine and stared out toward the ocean. "He should have just left with you."

"He did what he felt was right. He never could have left you. I know you would have done the same if the situation had been reversed. There is no reason to blame yourself. If anyone is to blame, it's the firemen, for not acting quickly. And the one with Connor should never have let him stop when he did."

"They were too close. Wouldn't have mattered. Owen saw the whole thing. He kept telling me how lucky I was. I didn't feel lucky. I lost my best friend and my legs."

"Vini lost Adrian," I added in an attempt to divert his self-pity.

"That wasn't much of a loss. The guy was a womanizer. He was seeing another girl the same time he was leading my sister on." He sipped his wine and stared out at the ocean, avoiding looking at me. "There is something else I regret. I only told Owen. When I was on my way to the washroom, I saw Adrian with Nicki, one of our servers, making out in the corridor behind the stage. He was just about to discover that Nicki was actually Nicholas when I grabbed him. I caught him off guard, so I got the first two punches in. Nicki took off. I have no idea whether she made it out of there or not."

He went quiet for a moment and took another sip of wine. He looked back at me, and I thought I saw a flicker of sadness cross his features. I waited until he felt like continuing.

"I broke Adrian's nose. It appears the DeMille children are good at that sort of thing. He fell, and I kicked him in the ribs ... several times. He didn't move. I left him there and went into the bathroom. That's when the first bomb exploded. I didn't even get to pee. Adrian didn't stand a chance of getting out. He was too close to where it went off. I have to live with that too. But there's no sense dwelling on it."

"Under no circumstances ever tell Vini that. Let her cherish her memories."

"Vini would never speak with me again if she knew, so I would appreciate it remaining between you and me. I have no intention of shattering her fantasy. It's done. There's no sense dredging it up. It's no longer important. It's only me who needs to carry the guilt. Let's not talk anymore about it. Let's just enjoy this wonderful lunch."

As we ate lunch, we talked about his career. He still dabbled with his guitar; he said it was his way of relaxing. He didn't seem interested in my life or the fact I might not have much left.

We'd run out of things to say when Ken returned and asked if we wanted something more. I was grateful for the interruption. I thanked Ken for the lunch and explained I had to leave. There was something I needed to do. I told Jason I wanted to contact Ricky. He asked me to wait, left for a few moments, and met me at the door holding a black notebook. He requested a pen and paper, which Ken promptly provided, and he proceeded to write something.

"I haven't spoken to or seen Ricky in nearly eighteen years. He wanted help renovating and decorating his house. That was the last time I saw him. This is his number. Could be he's changed it."

He handed me the paper. I thanked him.

"Good luck. It was nice seeing you. Take care of yourself, and keep in touch."

I kissed his cheek and promised I would but got little reaction.

I spent the rest of the day driving around St. Pete Beach, looking for familiar landmarks. I found the location of our apartment building, but it had been torn down to make way for a massive hotel. A new wing had been added to the school, and the parking lot had been enlarged, encompassing the area where Vini and I first met and shared many lunch hours. Nothing worked to keep my mind from drifting back to Jason and how distant and cold he had become. I hoped seeing Ricky wasn't as disappointing.

CHAPTER 43

The cell number Jason provided for Ricky was still active. It went straight to his voice mail.

You've reached Richard McKenzie. If you'd like to leave a message ... go for it! Chances are good I'll get back to you before I kick the bucket ... just kidding!

I detected the same childlike quality in his amusing greeting. I used Micaela Lewiski to identity myself since that was what he knew me by. No sooner had I closed out my message than my cell rang. It was Ricky.

"My God, Micaela! Is it really you?"

"It's me. I'm truly sorry I let so many years go by. I hope you can forgive me."

"This is amazing. I'd given up. Where are you?"

His positive reaction was more than I expected, and it dispelled the residual disappointment I'd experienced with Jason. "I'm in Indian Shores."

"Cool! I'm in Belleair Beach, near where I used to live. Can you come over now?"

I was still in my nightwear and looked like something the cat dragged in, but I accepted and told him I'd be about an hour. He provided his address and said he was looking forward to seeing me. His enthusiasm dispelled my fear that he too might have changed drastically.

I took time with my makeup and hair and chose a blue-and-green floral sundress. I placed my bracelet on my wrist. I'd promised I'd never take it off. He didn't have to know it had sat at the bottom of my memory box for thirty years.

I thought it odd that Ricky lived in such close proximity to his previous home. Driving slowly down the street, I looked at each house, trying to locate it. I'd almost given up by the time I spotted it. The two-story stucco, with four large windows across the bottom floor and six on the top, hadn't changed much. The palm trees that once obstructed the view from the road were gone. I had been impressed when I first saw the house, but time now altered my perception. It was not nearly as grand as the homes of people I'd met in California.

I parked the car by the curb and stared as phantom images playing out scenes in front of me ... Connor holding my car door while insisting on a date; Connor's jeep in the driveway; Connor looking down at me from his bedroom window. I pulled away from the curb. I had to stop tormenting myself.

Ricky's home was similar in design, but the landscaping was prettier. Bougainvillea trees in full bloom, a profusion of white, purple and red blossoms, draped across a portico. Rows of pink hibiscus bushes lined the walkway that led to a bronze door inlaid with glass panels and decorated with ornate patterns. It opened before I could ring the door chimes.

Change was inevitable, but I would never have recognized Ricky if I passed him on the street. There was only a hint of the boy I remembered in his features. The man who stood in front of me was slightly taller, and his hair was thinning and what was left was streaked in gray. A shaggy, unkempt beard, peppered irregularly with gray, and wire-rimmed glasses perched on his nose masked the cute, adorable boy he once was. A Los Angeles Lakers basketball jersey clung to exaggerated chest muscles, and his sweatpants hugged his thighs. I guessed that Ricky worked out. He appeared to be taking in the changes in me as well. Neither of us referenced how different we looked.

After we got past the initial shock, he pulled me into an embrace.

"I still can't believe you're actually here. Come in. Can I get you a drink?"

"No, thank you." I assumed he meant an alcoholic drink.

He led the way into a living room—smaller and a lot cozier than Jason's. A Christmas tree with an eclectic assortment of decorations stood in the corner. He motioned to a tan leather sofa overlooking a terrace similar to his parents.

"Do you mind if I make myself a drink?" he asked.

"Not at all." It was only just past lunch hour, but who was I to judge? There had been days when my breakfast had consisted of vodka and orange juice, and I rationalized it by thinking I was getting my daily intake of vitamin C.

"Excuse me for a moment. I just need to change. I was working out."

My assumption was correct.

Glancing around the room, I saw a long, narrow credenza against a side wall that displayed an assortment of pictures. Ricky had a family. There was no reason why he shouldn't. My gaze went to the largest of the grouping. An attractive brunette with a brilliant smile, her hand pressed against Ricky's chest, was beside a young girl. I guessed her to be about sixteen. She looked like her dad. Beside Ricky, another brunette, who looked a few years older, reminded me of Ricky's mother. Various pictures of the girls at different stages of their lives were dispersed among the collection. A photograph of Connor and Ricky caught my attention. I picked it up. Ricky returned, wearing a crisp, light-blue cotton dress shirt and black jeans, holding a small glass of something with ice cubes that clinked when he walked.

"That picture was taken a month before he died," he said. He picked up the family portrait. "This is my wife, Janette, and this is Margot." He pointed to the girl beside his wife. "She's seventeen, and my other daughter is twenty-two."

I returned the picture of Connor and Ricky to its resting place. "What's her name?"

Ricky hesitated and threw back his cocktail in one shot. "Her name is Micaela."

"You named your daughter after me! Why?"

"Does it upset you?"

"No, but I don't understand."

"You treated me like a normal kid. You meant a lot to me. I had a huge crush on you, and I have very special memories." He cited a few, some I'd forgotten.

"Thank you. Your family is beautiful."

"Micaela is studying journalism at Tampa University. She's with her mother and sister in San Diego, visiting my wife's parents."

I returned to the sofa. Ricky took the club chair by the Christmas tree.

"Guess you're wondering why I live down the street from my old house."

I admitted to being curious.

"It was up for sale. I like the neighborhood, so I bought it. Simple as that. Bought it eighteen years ago. Jason did a lot of the reno work, and Janette added her input with all the interior decorating stuff. She's pretty good at it."

I told him it looked lovely and asked him about his grandmother and parents.

"Grams died of heart failure when I was nineteen, so I went to live with my mom and stepdad in Colorado for a while. They still live there. My dad wasn't interested in having me live with him. I got in the way of his lifestyle. He drank himself to death. I went to college, but it didn't work out, except that's where I met Janette."

"I'm sorry about your grandmother and your father."

"Don't be. Grams had a long life, and Dad was a shithead."

"So tell me about your life. It looks as if you did very well."

"When I was twenty-five, I came into a friggin' fortune. I had my own trust, plus I got Connor's, and Grams left me a great deal of money. Dad pissed away his, so there was nothing from him. I made a few good investments, and I have more money than I can spend in two lifetimes—not bragging; it's just a fact. So what about you? Last thing I heard was you got married, left the movie business and moved back to Toronto."

I filled him in on Jack, Jess, and my granddaughters. He looked sad when I told him I was divorced. His concern was for Jess. I explained she was a resilient kid and showed him recent pictures of Jess and the girls on my phone.

"You, a grandmother! It feels like just yesterday you were all starry-eyed about my brother. I don't mean to trespass on your privacy, but why didn't you contact me? I thought you got so famous you forgot me."

I explained about the post-traumatic stress disorder and that I'd just recently remembered Connor's death. Ricky asked me dozens of questions that weren't easy to answer. I told him my dad passed away.

"I'm sorry. He was a good guy. I'll never forget the Christmas I spent with you and your dad. I can never look at a star without thinking of you both." He reached over to the Christmas tree and removed an ornament. It was a silver spider in a silver web.

I laughed. "Where did you get it?"

"Online, of course." He placed it back on the tree. "There's something I'd like to show you. It's my 'Connor room.'"

I followed Ricky down a hallway, past an atrium filled with exotic plants that led to another shorter hallway. Ricky stood by a closed door.

"I hope you can handle this. I don't want to be responsible for hurting you."

I told him I'd be fine but had no idea if that was true. He opened the door.

Everywhere I looked, there were pictures of Connor. One wall displayed his bird pictures, beautifully matted and framed. Shelves were loaded down with mementos, bits and pieces of a life cut short—his football jersey and trophies, his baseball glove, his old scuffed baseball shoes, and even his keys on the chain with the little rabbit's foot I'd given him. It was a silly gift, but he really wanted it. Dozens of pictures formed a collage above the shelf. Some I recognized because I'd taken them. Others were of his childhood. Jason and Vini were in several, and I was in a lot.

"You okay?" Ricky kept glancing at me as if expecting some sort of breakdown.

I was controlling my feelings rather than letting them control me. I preferred to acknowledge the love we shared, not the pain it created.

"Yes, more than okay. Thank you for sharing this with me."

Ricky set a photo album on a small desk, which he informed me had been Connor's in grade school and most of high school. I sat on a rustic ladder-back chair and ran my hand across the surface of the desk. I felt every scratch and indentation, one in particular. I could make out "CM & BW" carved inside a heart. It looked as if someone had tried to sand it off.

"Connor did that when he was about eighteen. He tried sanding it out, but it was too deep."

"Is BW who I think it is?"

"Yeah … Bonnie Walker. She was a piece of work."

I still felt the pang of jealousy. I'd always hated that he'd been sexually active with her before me. I opened the album, and my dolphin and angel clinked against the edge of the desk.

"You still have it."

"Told you I'd wear it forever. I'll probably be buried with it." I wasn't sure why I'd added that, but I liked the idea. The grin on Ricky's face was worth the little white lie.

The album was entirely me. Every picture Connor had ever taken, even the two badly water-stained ones that had been on the wall of his cabin during the storm, were taped on the pages. Some of the pictures I didn't remember. He must have taken them when I wasn't looking, as I was facing away from the camera. The cards I made him were tucked into the flap at the back.

"Connor put the pictures in the album. I put in the ones on the last few pages."

They were from fan magazines when I was Michelle. The contrast with my younger self was startling. I missed the girl full of dreams and ambition, in love and happy. I closed the album. That chapter of my life was over.

"Do you have another hour or so?" Ricky asked. "There's something else I want to show you."

"I'm free, but there's something I need to talk to you about."

"Sounds serious." Ricky shut the door of his shrine, and we returned to the living room.

There was no easy way to tell him, so I blurted it out. "You have a nephew."

He looked like I'd poured ice cubes over his head. "How? What?" He struggled with a response.

"When I left for New York, I was pregnant, but I wasn't sure, so I didn't tell Connor. I was living with my aunt at the time, and she was extremely religious. Abortion wasn't even a consideration. I was confused and lost any will of my own. You could have told me to hang myself from the rafters, and I would have done it. I was more zombie than human."

"You were in shock. Do you know where he is? Have you tried to find him?"

"That's the part I'm ashamed of. I never wanted to. I had my marriage and Jess, and I didn't want any reminders of Connor or what I'd done. Vini located him." I explained how she'd found him and discovered his identity but that it was two years ago.

"Wow! I have a nephew. What's his name?"

"I named him Dylan Connor when he was born, and his adopted parents kept it. His last name became West."

"You've got to be kidding!" Ricky practically fell out of the chair. "*The* Dylan West, the singer and songwriter?"

"Yes, according to Vini."

"That's so cool."

"I've never heard of him."

"Have you been living under a rock all these years?" Ricky thought about what he'd said and apologized. "He was in a band called the Misfits in his teens; then he went out on his own. He sang 'It Should Have Been Me.' It was the theme song for a movie, and he won a Grammy." Ricky sang a few bars. It was a compelling song, but I didn't recognize it. "I'll bet your daughter would know who he is." Ricky still looked at me as if I'd taken stupid pills.

"I never paid much attention to what Jess listened to. Our musical taste is quite different."

"You've got to contact him, and it's not because he's a famous singer. He's part of Connor. I'll bet he'll be blown away when he finds out who his mother is."

"I doubt that. I'm old news. His generation wouldn't have a clue who I am."

"Don't be so sure. *The Streets Have Eyes* is running on Netflix."

This amazed me. "Vini's going to set up a meeting between us. Let's just drop the subject. I just thought you should know."

"Damned straight. Thanks. This has been one hell of an afternoon." He started walking into the kitchen. "I have to find my keys. We have to drive to the surprise." I heard him say "Dylan West is my nephew" three times, as if trying to absorb the magnitude of the new reality.

Ricky drove a red Ferrari, which, he was quick to point out, had nothing to do with a midlife crisis. He'd owned three of them since he was twenty-five, when he got his money and his license. Watching him drive was an experience I thought I'd never witness. He'd come a long way from the goofy kid I remembered. Not just his appearance but his confidence and the way he spoke was light-years from the childlike young man who'd won my heart. There was no way of suspecting he was afflicted with autism.

Once we passed Clearwater Beach and were halfway to St. Pete Beach, I assumed our destination. I wasn't sure, but my guess was that Ricky had purchased a boat and named it after me too, and like his shrine, he kept it at the Clearwater Marina as a tribute to Connor.

My assumption regarding our destination was correct.

The marina had made a few changes, but it was still recognizable. We parked in the same spot that was once Connor's. Ricky turned and looked at me, and for a brief moment, I saw Connor in his place.

"Remember when I had you put on a blindfold? Don't have one, so could you please close your eyes real tight and keep them closed till I tell you to open them?"

This confirmed my suspicion. I indulged his request.

When I opened my eyes, I was shocked. It wasn't a new, more modern *Micaela*. It was the original, just as I remembered. I felt as if I'd slipped through a time warp. "It can't possibly be seaworthy."

"It's taken a lot of work—new engine and mechanical parts—but she's watertight." Ricky helped me into the boat.

"I can't believe you'd want to keep her."

"Why? I've got good memories of Connor on this little tug. Some people keep old running shoes; I keep an old boat. My dad sold it after Connor died. Took me a while, but I found the guy who bought it and offered him twice what he paid. I sometimes spend weekends just cruising along the shoreline. Not sure I'd want to take her out any farther. The girls prefer my Sundance Cruiser. They call this an antique and wouldn't want to be seen on her."

Pointing to the paint-chipped cupboards, he told me he didn't want to change anything in the galley. I noticed the Formica counter still had the scorch mark from one of my cooking attempts. "However"—he opened the door to the sleeping cabin—"this I did change."

The warped wood paneling had been replaced with teak cupboards from floor to ceiling and had a built-in entertainment center. Where Connor's bed once was, a white canvas sofa now wrapped halfway around the room. A navy-blue carpet with matching navy and white throw pillows provided a nautical feel. Pot lights replaced the wall sconces and table lamp. The tiny window had white canvas drapes rather than the old brown linen ones Connor had used.

"I had to finish it. The mildew was taking over."

"I like it." I positioned myself on the sofa in approximately the same area I'd once sat on Connor's bed. Ricky sat in the corner with his feet up on a white canvas ottoman.

"Can I tell you something in private? It's going to sound like I've lost my marbles," Ricky said.

"You're looking at a woman who might have lost a few herself over the years."

Ricky laughed. It was the same sound I'd loved. "After Connor's funeral, I stayed on the boat a couple of nights. He paused, as if reassessing whether he wanted to share any further information. "I saw him, Micaela … I saw him."

I was hesitant to ask but did anyway. "What do you mean, you saw him?"

"I saw Connor standing over there." He pointed to where the entertainment center was. "It wasn't a dream. I thought it was at first, so I slapped myself hard. He still stood there, smiling at me. I wasn't freaked out. Later, I found this psychic in Miami. She was the real deal. She described him perfectly, and how he died, and lots of stuff she couldn't possibly know. She told me people with autism are more sensitive. I've tried sitting here dozens of times since, but that was the only time I saw him. I still talk to him because I'm sure he can hear me. She said Connor was trying to reach you, but you were lost. That's how she put it."

I wasn't sure how to react. A part of me wanted to believe Ricky, but another part had difficulty accepting it. The part that wanted to believe hinted at a possibility that maybe Connor was trying to reach me, and that's why I was having all the dreams. I struck that thought from my mind.

"Thank you for sharing that," I said. "It means a lot."

On the drive back to Belleair Beach, Ricky talked incessantly about his girls. I shared anecdotes about Jess, Nora, and Tina. It took my mind off Ricky's encounter. We came to a cemetery. Ricky turned in. If I wanted closure, this would be it.

I walked with him down a path lined with cypress trees until we came to a clearing. A gray marble stone beside a magnolia bush was Connor's final testimonial to his life. I read the inscription.

> CONNOR RILEY MCKENZIE
> 1966–1989
> TAKEN FROM US TOO SOON
> HIS LIGHT WILL SHINE BRIGHTLY

"I added the last part," Ricky said as he took my hand.

Knowing the way he died, I was curious, and asked Ricky what was in the coffin.

"Each of us put something in to honor him. I put my baseball cap, Dad put in Connor's bat, and Mom put in his old record collection. Grams wrote something, but we don't know what it was. Vini and Owen put a really nice picture of his boat. Jason was still in the hospital at the time, but he had Owen take the compass you gave Connor from the boat and put it in. Owen found the note you had written when you gave it to him. It was on the front window of the boat. He put that in with it."

Vini hadn't mentioned anything about it, but I understood she couldn't without risking my having a breakdown. I was grateful Jason thought of it and there was something from me included. A morbid thought entered my mind. Instead of pushing it away, I asked if any part of Connor had been located and placed in the coffin. I knew as soon as I asked that I didn't want the answer.

"His skull."

My legs turned to rubber, and my knees buckled. Ricky grabbed me around the waist to keep me from falling.

"I shouldn't have told you that. I'm sorry."

All my defenses crumbled, and the world around me blurred. Sobs ripped through my chest and my muscles trembled and quivered in an effort to expel the grief. Tears flowed in torrents down my cheeks. My breath came in gasps. Ricky held me tighter, and, without speaking, he waited, allowing me to experience the last remaining remnants of my anguish. Finally, my sobs turned to hiccups, the quivering subsided, and my breathing became quieter and more regular. "I want to go home."

Ricky couldn't know what home I meant. I didn't mean Toronto. All I wanted was to be with Connor, Dad and Mom. I loved my daughter and granddaughters, but home had a different meaning to me now.

CHAPTER 44

A whirlwind of thoughts swept through my mind. Each time I tried to grab on to one, it was snatched away and pulled into the twirling mass of images. My curiosity had been satisfied, but my overstimulated emotions requested a timeout, and my brain, inundated with impressions, wanted peace. I needed to return home. This time, I did mean Toronto. I didn't want to die.

The walls were gone. The darkness that once swallowed me whole was filled with light, and I was beginning to feel a new, more profound freedom. I wanted to get on with my life in a different way.

I stood on the beach, looking out at the ocean. The sun, a yellow ball of fire, was falling quickly to meet the sea. Rich scarlet and brilliant orange stretched across the sky, blazing a trail through purple-tinged clouds. Then it dipped below the horizon, leaving a hint of radiant light in a now luminescent sky. The wind picked up as the night absorbed the day. Like a warm embrace, it caressed my cheeks as I looked up. The first star appeared—a shiny silvery orb, blinking on and off like the star on Dad's Christmas tree. Others followed in clusters, casting a hazy glow against the inky sky.

Christmas Eve was in three days. I thought of it as a turning point, a time imbued with love. I looked forward to being with Jess and the girls. It could be my last Christmas, but an ounce of optimism dissolved the heavy oppressiveness I'd been feeling. Light had broken through the darkness. The shadows that demanded to be seen faded, as do all shadows in the evening light. I no longer feared the cancer or its outcome.

A strange stillness encompassed me. The wind ceased; the waves became quiet as they met the sand, and the air was infused with tiny electrical impulses, prickling my skin. All thought was obliterated. I became conscious only of a silence so intense it felt as if I was floating in the vacuum of space. I sensed a presence near me and turned.

He stood behind me. He smiled. He looked just as I remembered him when he picked me up on that horrible night. In my mind, I heard his voice.

I'll be there in the whisper of the wind in your ear, the gentle touch of a warm breeze against your cheek, and a song that reminds you of me. I love you, Micaela. When you see a twinkling star, it's me, smiling at you. Always and forever.

The vision dissolved. I looked up. A streak of silver light crossed the night sky. A star blinked.

EPILOGUE

The touch of a warm hand roused me from sleep. I was dreaming—a sunset cast a pink glow against an azure sky; a gentle breeze tossed my curls; and he was there, beside me. A cloak of serenity enveloped me as I gazed into his face. His hand reached for mine. I went to grasp it, and then he was gone. I awoke to my daughter's eyes staring down at me.

"Hi, Mom. Sorry for waking you."

Still in a groggy stupor, I could do no more than attempt a smile and try to enclose my fingers around her hand.

"Can I get you anything?"

I tried sitting up but required Jess's assistance. I pointed to my sweater draped across the back of a chair. She helped me put it on.

"How are you feeling today?"

I found my voice, but it sounded weak and strained. "Not so good. I'm tired. Very tired." I took a deep breath, and the whoosh of a ventilator accompanied it.

Jess pulled the chair closer to the bed. A nurse entered the room, bringing a vase of flowers, but she couldn't find a place to put them, as I already had dozens of baskets and vases. This one was two dozen white roses. Jess placed them on the windowsill and read the card.

To my wonderful, talented mother: Get better soon. You still have a lot of music in you. Love, Dylan. I didn't recall ever telling him how much I loved white roses.

Jess sat in the chair and pulled an envelope from her purse.

"I have something for you, Mom. It's from Aunt Vini. It just came from the lawyer's office. Nobody writes letters anymore. She always used to email, and sometimes she actually used the com-link, but this time she chose to write a letter to you. It was sent by air post. She knew it would be difficult for you to talk on the phone, and you never bothered to get a com-link. I can read it to you." Jess took her glasses from her purse and began to read.

Hey, girlfriend!

I'm writing this while I still can. Doc says I have about one more month before the tumor turns my brain into mush. You'd think, after all these years, they would have discovered a cure for the stupid thing. I'm not sad, so don't you be.

Jess stopped reading as she noticed tears in my eyes. She took a tissue from the side table and gently wiped them away. Fragments of memory, like puzzle pieces, came together. Vini had died two months after I contracted the pneumonia.

"Do you want me to keep reading?"

I nodded. She continued.

I sure hope there's chocolate cake where I'm going. We did it, girl. We grew old together. Hard to believe in three months I'll be eighty-two. I guess you, Jess, and Dylan will have to celebrate without me. Do you remember the day we met? I thought

330

you were so pretty. I had to meet you. I knew we would be friends. My sixth sense, right! Those thirty years were damned hard. I came close to telling you about Connor many times, but Jason stopped me. I miss him so much. I'm still pissed at Ken for giving him AIDS. Isn't it ironic that I'm the one dying of cancer? I don't feel like going through what you did, taking all that natural stuff—too much work, and I'm too damn tired, and there's no way I'm taking chemo. Agree with you on that one. I've had a long run, as you used to say about your time in the theater, and I'm ready to pack it in. I'm glad you beat it and got to enjoy your beautiful family.

Jess tells me you're going to be a great-grandmother again in the spring. Nora's a breeding machine. Aren't four kids enough? I listened to Tina's recording last night. Wow, Micki, she sounds just like you. I loved the duet she did with Dylan. You must be so proud of them both. Dylan can put his Grammy beside yours. Your song "The Best of Me" is your greatest work. You still got it, kiddo. I think my nurses are getting sick of hearing it. I impressed the hell out of my night nurse when I told her you were my best friend.

Jess sent me pictures of Dylan. Too bad his marriage didn't turn out, but he sure looks good for an old guy. Still got that hair. Guess you know what Connor would have looked like if he'd lived. For a girl who didn't have much family when I met you, you sure have a tribe now. Thank you for sharing yours with me. Never did find the right guy after Adrian, at least not one who could make my skin tingle and my heart flip-flop. I think my being a Supreme Count Judge scared the shit out of them.

I may not have solved the problems of the world, but I put away a few bad guys. Tell Jess I'm proud of her for passing her bar exams. I laughed when she com-linked me and told me Jack was on wife number three. That guy never quits. It's amazing he can still get it up. (Sorry, I know how you dislike my vulgarity.)

I'm happy your life worked out. You were different when you returned from Florida. We sure did have a lot of great times. Gotta sign off. My nurse is here with my pain meds. Thank you again for all the wonderful years. Hurry up and get better, and for God's sake, don't think you have to come to my funeral. Something weird just popped into my head. Remember my toast on Connor's birthday? I don't think I could ever forget that day. Slamming Bonnie felt so good. Anyway, the toast went something like this, if I remember it correctly: "No matter where our journey takes us, may we find our way back to each other."

I have no idea why I made that up, but it sure feels right now. Guess it won't be much longer. See you on the other side. We'll have a party, with or without cake. BFFs forever.

Love,
Vini

Jess sat quietly holding the letter. I saw the tears on her cheeks. The only sound was the constant hiss of the ventilator and an ambulance approaching the hospital. I slipped into a space unoccupied by reality.

"Mom … Mom …" Jess's voice pulled me back. I saw the fear in her eyes.

"I'm okay," I whispered.

She bent over and kissed my forehead. "I'll leave this here in case you feel up to reading it later." She put the letter beside my water jug on the tray.

"Oh, I almost forgot. Ricky called, and he's flying in on the weekend. He says he's not going to let a little heart attack stop him."

I tried speaking. Jess bent closer to hear me, "Did you remember to bring my jewelry box?" I took another deep breath.

She took it from a bag and laid it on my lap. She watched as I removed my ring from the box and placed it on my finger. I handed her my bracelet, indicating I needed her help to clasp it on my wrist.

"What a beautiful ring, and the charm bracelet is adorable." She fastened the clasp, and the angel and dolphin brushed against my wrist in greeting. "Connor gave them to you, didn't he?"

I smiled and nodded. It made me happy the day I shared all my memories of Connor with her and Dylan. He and his uncle Ricky became very close. We had spent so many vacations with Ricky, Janette, and his girls. The years had been filled with love.

"Can I get you anything before I go?" Jess placed my jewelry box on the bedside cabinet.

I shook my head. "Tired ... very tired. I just want to rest."

"Go back to sleep." She kissed my forehead again. "I'll see you tomorrow. I love you, Mom."

As I slipped into the twilight between sleep and reality, a song played in my head. I recalled how I'd felt the first time I'd heard it, years ago. I sang it many times, hoping Connor might hear me. The beautiful words resonated through my mind.

You're where I belong ... I belong with you ... you're part of my heart ... there's nothing I can do.

As the lyrics trailed off, my body began to slip away. A tranquility beyond conscious thought took me to a state of euphoria. Connor was with me. He stood in a light brighter than anything I'd ever seen. He reached for my hand. His voice was clear, and he was smiling.

Vini's planned a party. Your dad and mom are waiting. Jason and Owen can't wait to see you. And you are going to love this—your dog Chippy is excited too. You are so beautiful.

I touched my hair and felt the curls on my shoulder. I reached out and took his hand. I saw the light behind him. I saw Mom and Dad and heard Chippy barking. Vini was jumping up and down, and Jason and Owen were waving.

We've been waiting.

We were finally together. Always and forever. I was truly home.

ACKNOWLEDGMENTS

A huge thank-you to Marni Bachuk for plowing through my first draft and offering advice and encouragement. Loved the times in your kitchen. Your gorgeous painting was even better than expected. Your kindness and friendship mean a lot.

The story would never have been written had it not been for all the wonderful talks with Micaela Tyson. I miss them. Thank you for inspiring me and allowing me the use of your beautiful name. Also, for taking the time from your busy life to read the story.

Thank you to Jenn Dekker, my book buddy, for her patience in reading my rough draft and challenging me to make my opening chapters better. I am grateful you are in my life.

Without Derek Gebhart, I would have floundered with all the technical stuff. Thank you for your help and contributing your creative input for the cover design. It was perfect.

If it weren't for Brad Heyerdahl, I would never have considered writing. I will never forget our days working together and how we shared our love of the written word. My vocabulary is always better around you.

And a special thank-you to the unseen forces that got me through all those moments when I was tempted to give up.

Cover design by Derek Gebhart and painted by Marni Bachuk.

9 781532 069246